Shadows in Heaven

NADINE DORRIES grew up in a working-class family in Liverpool. She spent part of her childhood living on a farm with her grandmother, and attended school in a small remote village in the west of Ireland. She trained as a nurse, then followed with a successful career in which she established and then sold her own business. She has been the MP for Mid-Bedfordshire since 2005 and has three daughters.

Also by Nadine Dorries

The Lovely Lane Series
The Angels of Lovely Lane
The Children of Lovely Lane
The Mothers of Lovely Lane
Christmas Angels

The Four Streets Trilogy
The Four Streets
Hide Her Name
The Ballymara Road

Standalone Novels
Ruby Flynn

Short Stories
Run to Him
A Girl Called Eilinora

Nadine Dorries

Shadows in Heaven

HEAD of ZEUS

First published in the UK in 2018 by Head of Zeus Ltd

975312468

A catalogue record for this book is available from
the British Library.

ISBN (HB): 9781786697493
ISBN (XTPB): 9781786697509
ISBN (E): 9781786697486

Typeset by Adrian McLaughlin

Printed and bound in Great Britain by
CPI Group (UK) Ltd, Croydon CR0 4YY

Head of Zeus Ltd
First Floor East
5–8 Hardwick Street
London EC1R 4RG

WWW.HEADOFZEUS.COM

To Rosie de Courcy –
my editor, my friend,
my angel

Chapter 1

1940

Tarabeg village, on the west coast of Ireland

'I don't want to be here. Seamus made me come.' Nola Malone had sat as still as she could while having her Sunday-best frock repaired by Ellen Carey in the tailor's shop. But she kept glancing over her shoulder and out of the window, tea slopping from cup into saucer, waiting to catch sight of her husband and son as they rode down from the farm up on Tarabeg Hill in the horse and cart. She'd fixed her eyes on Ellen's foot, expertly depressing the pedal on the Singer sewing machine, until it became almost too much for her to bear and she had to speak out.

'Oh, don't I know that,' Ellen replied as she grabbed the wheel of the machine, stopped the needle, took it back half a turn, flicked up the foot and removed the fabric. She snapped the thread with her teeth. 'I've put a new hem on this frock. You can farm and cook, Nola, and you make the best butter in all Mayo, but you cannot sew, and that's for sure.'

She placed her hands in her lap and sighed. 'Look, I know

you don't want to be here – when was the last time a busy woman like you sat with me while I worked? Seamus has told me why, Nola. It has to be done. The lovebirds cannot meet anywhere else. That girl's father would take a gun to him, and her too, if he knew they were together.'

Nola blinked back the tears of self-pity that had sprung to her eyes. All thoughts appeared to be for young Sarah McGuffey from the fishermen's cottages, the girl Michael had fallen in love with. The daughter of Kevin McGuffey, a man who had already done well from the war, using his boat to smuggle goods around the coast to the North more often than he used it for fishing. A man famed for his bad temper, his love of money and drink, and someone most people avoided where possible. 'But what about me? His mother.' Her voice faltered.

Both women were fully aware that this could be the last time Nola ever saw her youngest son. She would have loved nothing more than to spend this, the last hour Michael had in Tarabeg before he left to fight in the war, in the farmhouse together. Checking his bag, counting his socks, feeding his belly. Fussing. It was what she did best. But her husband, Seamus, had persuaded her otherwise not two hours since.

She had been keeping herself busy enough. Making oatcakes for Michael's journey to stop from thinking how empty the house would be once he left, how hollow her heart would feel. She'd been in the middle of stoking up the fire to warm Michael's coat as he took his final wash down in the scullery when Seamus had unexpectedly walked into her kitchen and laid down the law.

'Leave the lad alone,' he said firmly. 'He wants this time for himself, with Sarah. I'll be bringing him down the hill to the village on the cart, say your goodbyes then. I'll stay out in the field until the time comes, so they can have the place to themselves.'

Nola bristled. 'Say goodbye to my son in the middle of the village? Along with everyone else? Does a mother have no privacy to shed her tears? Am I to cry them in front of the likes of the O'Donnells and every gossip we know? My boy is not away to America to send home the dollars. He's going to war, Seamus. He might die.' She hissed these last words, even though Michael could not have heard her with all the noise he was making in the scullery – a large man going about his ablutions in a small space.

Seamus had removed his cap and was studying the brim as though he had never seen it before. 'Nola, there will be no send-off in the village. You know how it is. Ireland is neutral, for a good reason. The people don't want us to be fighting for the British.'

Nola waved the poker in her hand in the air. 'No one to see him off? My son is putting his life at risk, and not an ounce of gratitude in any one of them.' She threw the poker back into the fireplace with force and it clattered against the blackened stone chimney.

Seamus was relieved. He had regretted speaking the moment she'd turned from the fire to face him, the tip of the poker burning as red as her round apple cheeks. He looked about him awkwardly and inclined his head towards the open farmhouse door to check if Pete Shevlin, the farmhand, was waiting for him.

Sarah would be there soon. He had seen the first of the fishing boats leaving as he rode down from the top field, dragging the prickly yellow whin in bundles behind the horse to hedge off the bull with a stubborn taste for freedom. Sarah would be there in minutes. It was time for Seamus to take charge. To separate his wife from the last of her brood.

She didn't yet know it, but she was going to need her husband to support her when the moment of truth hit her, to comfort her and absorb her tears. Even though they had six other children who'd already left for foreign shores, and even though tears had been shed at their leaving, this parting would be the worst.

Michael might never return to Tarabeg. This might have been his last night in his own bed. The last breakfast she would serve him. She might never again complain about the water on the floor after he'd finished his wash. Michael wouldn't be sending home happy letters stuffed with dollars like the others, or a hat at Christmas from Macy's like the six in New York had bought and sent home together, in a huge hat box that half of the village had gathered in the post office to watch her open. A hat Nola would never wear. She had no notion yet how Michael's leaving would rip her heart in two, but Seamus did, and this, this sudden removal of Nola from the house, was a part of his plan to save her, if only from a fraction of the pain of parting.

'Come on, the horse is ready and Ellen Carey's expecting you. I saw there was a rip in your dress at Mass on Sunday and Ellen has it. I took it down yesterday.'

Nola spluttered in disbelief. 'You did what?'

Seamus continued undeterred. Nola would not have her way, not today. For her own sake. 'Pete isn't due to collect Daedio from Paddy's bar until four. Let's go.' He had removed all her avenues of protest and he was doing something he was simply not used to doing. He was crossing a line, taking charge inside his own house.

As they made their way down the hill, the horse harnessed to the cart, and Nola stoic, resentful and silent, they came upon Sarah, her eyes alight, her skirt bunched up in her hands so as not to trip her, and her golden-red hair flying in the breeze behind her. Seamus lifted his hat in greeting. 'I'll be back for him in an hour, Sarah. You don't have long.' His heart pained for her. Just sixteen and already she'd experienced far more heartache than any girl of her age should.

'I've left food on the table,' said Nola. 'Make sure he eats, would you, Sarah? There's oatcakes and buttermilk on the side of the fire on the griddle, keeping warm.' She grabbed her husband's arm. 'Seamus, stop! Stop the horse, would ye.'

But Seamus hadn't stopped the horse. He hadn't even slowed it. He kept the cart moving and by the time Nola had finished her sentence, Sarah was behind them, waving down to them, disappearing into the distance. He cracked the reins and the horse trotted smartly down the hill.

Nola turned abruptly to face him. 'What did you do that for, you fat maggot.' She slapped him on his back with her bag, but not too hard. 'I had things to tell her, instructions... God in heaven, you will be sending that lad away starving hungry.'

Seamus didn't reply. He whistled to the horse and flicked the reins and they trotted on to Ellen Carey's and the dress that didn't need mending.

'Promise me you'll wait for me until it's all over and I'm back,' Michael begged Sarah as he held her in his arms in the final minutes before he left.

The stars had aligned, the weather was fair, the tide was in, the fishermen out. It had all come together to give them this precious hour alone. But it was a risk, as Sarah's mother was painfully aware. 'God be with you, Sarah. And be careful, will you,' she'd admonished. 'They are only loading the nets yet. If he catches sight of you from the shore...'

They rarely referred to Sarah's father by name; it was always 'he' or 'him'. But Angela McGuffey's words had fallen on deaf ears and she'd been left standing at the door, watching her daughter scramble up the escarpment from the beach to the road, the blaze of her golden-red hair seeming to hang in the air behind her long after she'd gone.

Now, all passion spent, Sarah lay on her back, her head in the crook of Michael's arm. She turned onto her side to face him. 'After what you've just done to me, I have to wait all this time for you to come back home! I can't believe you are actually going, Michael Malone.'

It would forever be her secret that this seduction had been her plan all along. She thought that if she let him make love to her, tempted him into her arms, he would be unable to leave her. Surely that would make him change his mind. He would want more than just the once; he would stay in Tarabeg.

'Will this not make you so sad to leave me, you cannot possibly go?' she said theatrically but also with real feeling, her eyes shining with emotion.

The past hour had gone exactly as she'd hoped. He had kissed her in the way he had during all of their clandestine meetings, but this time she'd pulled him closer in, for more. She had held his face in her hands and looked deep into his eyes as her own sent him a thousand messages of seduction. She felt no fear and, apart from the tremble in her hands which threatened to betray her, none of the nervousness that she had worried would be her undoing when the time came. With the boldness and skill of a woman ten years her senior, she had guided his hands over her virginal body. They had sought out her breasts together and, pulling them free, she had arched her body as her hair tumbled down her back, guiding his mouth as she eased his unresisting head down. She'd been in charge right up until a moan had escaped her lips and taken her unawares, not in her plan, and the control passed from her lips to the tips of his fingers. The sensation that flowed through her made her weak at the knees and she was truly lost, her plan abandoned. He had kissed her until her head spun and she felt faint. She was beyond reason and oblivious to danger. Once he had undone the final buttons on her blouse, her hands tore at his own shirt, all shyness forgotten, all sermons from the pulpit unheard, all thoughts of tomorrow vanquished.

'Sarah, I have to go, I'm signed up and it's a war.'

Her face fell. She had failed. 'You don't have to, Michael, that's just it. Ireland is neutral. You don't have to be doing nothing.'

Michael groaned and placed the flat of his palm on his forehead. 'God in heaven, Sarah, I do. For one thing, I knows I will see some of the world and learn about something other than picking potatoes and stacking turf ricks. There are other places to live and I want to make a fortune one day. I can't learn how to do that, here on a farm. If I stay here, we will both have to work to save to travel to America or Liverpool. This way, I get the money quicker and sure, how long can the war last?'

Michael had propped himself up on his elbow and was stroking her breast. His finger, encircling her nipple, strayed to the bruise on her shoulder. He pulled back in horror. 'What in God's name is that?' he asked, then gently placed his hand over the large yellowing patch of skin.

She raised herself onto her knees and hurriedly yanked her blouse back up over her shoulder and began to fasten the buttons. ''Tis nothing. I fell on the rocks on the shore. I'm always doing it, so I am.'

Her eyes left his, the air left the room, and for a brief moment Michael had no idea how to respond. He had heard the rumours of how moody Sarah's father was. Kevin McGuffey's temper was legendary in a village where no home held secrets. But this? He lifted her chin with his finger and forced her to look at him. 'As soon as I'm back, things are going to change. Do you understand that, Sarah?'

Sarah was on the verge of tears, her mind racing. What could she do now to keep him? What else was there left that she could use to persuade him? She had given him herself, her all. She had nothing else. 'Michael, don't go. Do you not love me now, after what we just did together? Has it not changed anything at all? Won't you stay now?' Her eyes were wide and pleading, her lips trembling.

Michael pulled her towards him and groaned. He was weakening. There was nothing he wanted more than to stay with Sarah, to marry her tomorrow. To take her away from the home that was more often than not the talk of the village. 'I will be back before ye know I'm gone, Sarah, I promise. I swear, as God is true, I'll be straight home to you as soon as it's all over and I will drag you to that church if I have to. It can't be another year at the very most.'

Sarah half laughed at the prospect of being dragged to the church and collapsed on top of him. 'It could be even less. It might be only weeks. God, I will pray so every day. Are ye proposing to me now after this, or what?' She was teasing, half teasing. Wanting to believe his words but seeking his confirmation that he meant them. She was stunned by his response.

He sat up on the mattress, the look on his face earnest and intent, his black curls falling over his eyes as he brushed them back and lifted her up by her shoulders. 'Yes, Sarah, I am. Just wait until this is all over and I am back. Promise you will wait for me? Be my wife, please, will you? Wait for me?'

Sarah nodded furiously, unable to answer, her throat thick with emotion as the tears ran down her face and she struggled to speak. 'I... I do love you, Michael. I wouldn't have let you do that if I didn't. I've never done it before...'

'Shush, I know that.' He grabbed her to him and smothered her face as he kissed away her tears. He moved his lips to her eyes, her nose, her cheeks, and as his passion rekindled, and with it the knowledge that there was now very little time left to them, that she was not his wife and he had no right, his own tears began to mingle with hers. Their breathing quickened as they stroked each other's faces, hands, hair and held each other so tightly, committing each second to memory – the taste, the feel, the smell, each kiss.

They both heard the wheels of the cart outside the house.

'I have to go,' Michael said softly.

Sarah pushed down the skirt she'd hurriedly pulled up during their lovemaking, having had neither the courage nor the time to remove it, and wiped her eyes. 'I can't bear it,' she whispered as she tucked in her blouse. 'I'm not as strong as I thought I was. I can't do it.' She was trembling, her complexion white, her eyes full of fear.

'Don't you worry, my love,' he whispered back, placing his arms around her and hugging her into his chest, her tears soaking though his vest. 'I'll be home before the year is out.

9

And I promise you this too: you will be the next Mrs Malone, because I love you. I'm going to dress you in fine clothes and shoes and no one is ever going to lay a finger on you again. Do you understand? You will be safe with me.'

They both jumped at the sound of Pete's polite and gentle knock on the door. Sarah began to shake uncontrollably. She bit her lip, fighting every instinct to cling to him, to lose all self-respect. *Hold on. Hold on.* The words raced through her mind as she closed her eyes, holding on for dear life. 'I cannot do this, I cannot,' she whimpered.

Michael knew this was his only chance. He had to run now, he had to run and do something, grab at any opportunity, to make a better life for them both. Another moment of hesitation and he would falter, and that would be it. They would live their entire life there on the farm, scraping by, hand to mouth.

'Wait for me, Sarah. Just one year at the very, very most. Count the days. As soon as I am back, 'twill all be different. God in heaven, I promise. Don't go marrying anyone else when I'm gone, do you hear me? If you need to get away from home for any reason, come here, to my mammy and daddy. They will help you.'

Sarah couldn't speak. She couldn't see. Her nose ran with her tears and she wiped her face with the back of her hands, too afraid to say anything. And then, turning from her abruptly, he was gone.

As the cart pulled into the village, Nola, listening for the familiar sound of the horse's hooves, raced out of Ellen Carey's shop to hug her son goodbye.

Just at that moment, Sarah, having ran in the opposite

direction, to the shore, reached her own cottage. She stopped outside to catch her breath, then almost fell through the door, tears still pouring down her face, as she called to Angela. 'Mammy, I'm back.'

She froze to the spot at the sight of her father standing before her, his belt in his hand. His gun, glinting in the light from the door, lay menacingly on the table, and her mother was sitting on the floor in the corner, her back against the wall. Instantly, Sarah understood. She knew that position. It was where they both shuffled to with their feet to edge away from his lashings, instinctively knowing that the wall would save half of their body from the blows raining down on them.

Angela was rocking, holding her shawl to her head, blood seeping through it.

How had he known? That was the first thought to flash through Sarah's mind. No one knew about her and Michael. No one. She'd made sure she wasn't seen as she crossed the boreens rather than take the main road from the shore to the bottom of the boreen that ran up Tarabeg Hill to the farm. No one had seen her apart from the tinkers, the Maughans, who were camped on the side of the hill, away from the Malones' land but close enough to help themselves to their crops and orchards. No one spoke to the Maughans, so it couldn't have been them.

'Where the feck have you been?' McGuffey snarled.

Sarah paled and felt faint with fear. The brass of his belt buckle caught the light from the fire and winked at her. She felt her bladder weakening and her head spinning, and then she heard the whip of the belt as it cut through the air. Before it made contact with her face, the familiar wave of darkness saved her as she hit the floor.

Chapter 2

Five years later: 1945

Rosie O'Hara's shoes, still wet from the walk to school that morning, squelched as she finished damping down the fire and made her way across the scrubbed wooden floor to the classroom windows. She reached across to fold the bottle-green shutters. Peering down the street, she caught sight of young Theady O'Donnell heading home, dragging his feet as he went. He was walking alone, so he must have been the only child in detention in the boys' room. Rosie pulled the ribbon that held her long, shiny auburn hair tighter and tucked the strands that had escaped during the day behind her ears. It was late June and the freckles that dappled her nose and cheeks looked almost painted on against her pale skin. Her grey eyes reflected the grey sky and as her insides churned with hunger, she sighed.

She had remained late to wipe clean the slates and polish the girls' desks; she'd worked quietly as she went, to avoid attracting the attention of Mr O'Dowd, the school principal. A loud and cheerful man with a thick thatch of badly cut dark hair, he was also the teacher in the boys' room. He was wont to pop into her classroom at the slightest excuse, to see what she was doing, and had a habit of talking to her about things she knew nothing of – football and fishing. If he paid less attention to both, she thought, he might have found the time to marry. He spent most of the day sitting in the chair behind his desk, smoking his pipe, and when school was finished, he headed straight over the road to Paddy Devlin's bar.

Mr O'Dowd also ran the local football team, which played out on the flattest field in the village every Saturday morning. Rosie, often cold and suffering from painful chilblains in her toes, could never understand the attraction. She shivered in sympathy for the poor muddy boys, made to wash in the freezing Taramore river before they returned home.

It was rare for Rosie to keep any of her girls in detention and she often felt sorry for the boys Mr O'Dowd kept behind, especially those who had to walk back home to the hill farms. ''Tis different altogether with the boys,' Mr O'Dowd would say to her. 'Someone has to stay on detention at least once a week, whether they need it or not. 'Tis a warning to the others. Best form of discipline, in my book. I hardly ever need the stick, and don't I have the best-behaved class in all of Ireland to show for it.'

Rosie never answered Mr O'Dowd back. Shy by nature, she felt diminished by his overly gregarious nature. He was liked and respected by every single parent, and for timid, withdrawn Rosie, being in his presence highlighted everything she was not. She strove for respect but mostly what she earned was pity.

Theady was the child who lived closest to the school. He was also one of the few who possessed a pair of sturdy shoes, being the only O'Donnell child left at home who had not emigrated to America. Rosie had noticed a difference in him of late. Once the most pleasant boy in Tarabeg, he had in a matter of months become one of the most sullen. She had commented to her only real friend in the village, Teresa Gallagher, that a great change had come over him.

'His mother, Philomena, is the scold of the village, with a tongue sharper than any knife,' Teresa had said. 'He's been the same since the last brother ran from her house on the day he had the fare saved to take him to Cobh for the boat to New York. It must be awful for him, being the only child left with that woman, and him being too young to escape. His da spends most of his day anywhere but in the house. She missed Mass twice last week, can you imagine?' As Father Jerry's housekeeper at the presbytery, Teresa seemed to find this far more significant than Theady's unhappiness.

'He is a sensitive boy, his heart must be breaking for his brothers,' said Rosie, almost to herself. She knew Theady loved to please. It was easy enough with her, but seemingly a near impossibility at home with his mother. He was always the first to arrive at the school in the morning, long before Mr O'Dowd appeared, and he would always ask Rosie, 'Shall I take the basket to fetch the kindling, Miss O'Hara, to get the fire going for you?'

'You do that, Theady,' she would say, and straightaway he would head off up the hill to collect bits of wood and anything else that would catch for long enough to sustain a flame and start the fire in the schoolroom. He was never quite so keen to leave Rosie once they had got the fire going and it was time to line up in the cinder yard when she rang the bell.

The school comprised just two classrooms, one for girls,

the other for boys. Mr O'Dowd, originally from Dublin, had taught there for many years. He did not divide up the grant that they were paid from fairly or in the manner that he was supposed to, but kept the lion's share for himself, which meant that Rosie, who had arrived six years ago from Connemara, received a pittance. Without the kindness of Teresa Gallagher she would have struggled to survive.

Mr O'Dowd was also profligate with the kindling Theady brought back, and Rosie struggled to keep enough back to ensure they never had a truly cold day in the girls' room. He used more of the turf that the families were required to provide for the benefit of the school, too, leaving her with less for the girls.

For all that, Rosie knew that he was such a great man of the community, such a well-regarded figure and a friend of all, that no one would believe her, a girl from Connemara, if she complained about him, an educated man from Dublin. And she was doubtful if they would see anything wrong in a spinster teacher being paid such a pitiful salary. Shamed, she would be sent away from Tarabeg. And for reasons that were very close to her heart, that was the last thing Rosie wanted to happen. For now that the war was over, she was sure that Michael Malone must be coming home, and Rosie wanted to be there and waiting when that day arrived. She was older now, more of a woman than a girl. This time, she would not allow her shyness to repel him. Even if it killed her, she would win his affection back.

Rosie wriggled her toes, cold and still damp in her cheaply made shoes. Her heart sank as she took in the heavy mist on the hills and the rain bouncing off the cinder playground. She would be wet for the second time today when she left for home. The rain had been relentless. 'Even in summer,' she whispered.

Her breath had misted up the pane of glass and she rubbed it with her sleeve as from the corner of her eye she caught sight of Teresa Gallagher. She was pulling up the reins of her horse with force.

'Whoa! Whoa!' Teresa shouted. With the agility of a woman half her age, she got down from the trap before the wheels had fully stopped, turned in through the gate and hurried up the path towards Rosie. She had news to tell, that much was obvious.

Teresa was a purveyor of news. As housekeeper at the presbytery, she got to hear everything – it all came to her door. This news, however, was so important that all pleasantries were dispensed with as she marched into the empty classroom. Her silver hair was always fixed in a small tight bun at the nape of her neck and she wore the same style of dress as she had for the past forty years: long and black, with a change of collar, always made by Ellen Carey. Narrow, wire-framed spectacles perched on the end of her nose and she never set foot outdoors unless she was wearing a hat. Today was no exception and her oilskin bonnet was tied tightly under her chin.

'Well, you will never believe it, Michael Malone is on his way home,' she said as she shook out her oilskin cape. It cracked as she did so and the raindrops covered Rosie's feet in a light shower. But Rosie hadn't noticed; her heart had stopped beating right there and then. 'He's sent a telegram and Mrs Doyle has to take it from the post office to Seamus as soon as they all stop drinking the tea. Keeva is in a right flap, she thought it was another death in the village, she was all for running up to tell Father Jerry if I hadn't been there and heard it all myself. Mrs Doyle was put out indeed. "Your job is as my assistant, miss. You don't run the post office," she said to Keeva. Anyway, I thought I would stop to tell you before I'm off to see my sister, thought you might like to know the news.'

Rosie felt her heart restart. It beat in her chest with the force of a trapped bird. Her mouth dried, the palms of her hands moistened and she struggled to reply. An awkward silence filled the space between them as Teresa, a stranger to self-doubt, wondered if she had made the right call. Rosie had never discussed Michael Malone, or taken the bait that Teresa had thrown down for her a million times, so it was all guesswork on Teresa's part. However, she was sure that Rosie was sweet on Michael and had been since almost the day she'd arrived in Tarabeg. 'Even a blind man can see that,' she had once said to Father Jerry. 'Sure, wasn't he once sweet on her too? I cannot get a word out of her, no matter how hard I try. I'm never wrong though.' Now, in the confines of the schoolroom, she studied Rosie's face for any indication of her affection for Michael. She was disappointed.

As calmly as if she were discussing the weather, Rosie replied in a voice she barely recognised. 'That's good news. His family, they will be relieved that he wasn't one of the soldiers who never came back then.'

'Oh, they'll be thankful he's alive all right, praise be to God for that. But they will know the way people are feeling about those who fought with the British, they will have heard all about that. He will be back off away out of here the minute he turns up and he finds out what's what. Nola won't let him jump from a frying pan into a fire, so she won't.' Teresa tutted and shook her head in irritation. 'They're even talking about passing a law, so I hear, to stop soldiers like Michael from getting proper work and benefits when they come home. They are going to be calling it the starvation law, can you imagine? Call them deserters, so they do, because they fought with the English army. He'll not be forgiven in a hurry. Doesn't Father Jerry know all about it. He spends his life, so he does, trying to get them not to listen to Kevin McGuffey and his wicked words of hate towards the English. There are enough lads from the villages round here who haven't made it back, who died in a field to keep the Germans out. He's a bog maggot that man McGuffey is.'

Rosie picked up the white duster and began wiping the blackboard in earnest, keeping her back to Teresa and her hands busy. Her face was inscrutable, but she took no chances as Teresa continued.

'Will they listen to Father Jerry though? No, not a word. They would rather follow the gospel according to McGuffey, one filled with hate, and walk along a path that leads straight to Galway jail. My sister, and as you know we were both very well educated, she says that the people around here have no idea, no idea at all what it would have been like had Hitler marched over the hill and into Tarabeg.'

Teresa stopped talking and studied Rosie's swaying back. She was disappointed. Rosie was composed, she was giving nothing away. 'Anyhow, I'm off to my sister's. Will Father Jerry and I be seeing you later for your tea?'

Rosie turned, slowly laid the chalky rag down on her desk, and nodded. She wanted to decline, to hide away and secretly digest this news. But there would be more, she was sure, in the hours between now and teatime and, despite herself, she wanted to know, to know it all.

*

Mr O'Dowd had already departed, as was his routine, leaving Rosie to lock up while he headed to the tobacconist for his daily craic and supply for his pipe before making his way to Paddy's bar. As Rosie turned the key in the huge green-painted wooden door, ready to begin her walk home, she saw the postmistress, Mrs Doyle, coming out of the post office. She was clutching the telegram in one hand and the heavy gold crucifix that hung from her neck in the other. Her breasts, free from the restraint of a folded pair of arms, ricocheted about like rocks in socks.

Mrs Doyle had barely supressed a yelp of delight when the telex machine had erupted into life of its own accord and began tapping away behind the counter. 'Keeva, would ye look at that, we have a telex coming through. Put the kettle on, would ye.'

Keeva Power had only just finished clearing away the mugs from the last round of tea. Tea was always required when two or more women appeared in the post office at once, and most definitely when one of them was Teresa Gallagher, the only woman to know more than Mrs Doyle. 'What, again?' she muttered. 'It's barely cold from the last flamin' lot.' She grudgingly loaded up used cups onto the wooden tray and hurried over to the range next to the fire to slide the kettle across.

She was keen herself to see who it was who was trying to make contact with them. Her mother would be all ears too, for she was convinced that with a little ingenuity the telex could be used to bring messages from the dead. Keeva would be sure to fill her in when she got home that evening. The two of them lived together on a farm two miles outside the village.

Her father had died and her sisters and brothers were all scattered across America, so Keeva and her mother survived on the dollars sent and on Keeva's wage from the post office. The dollars were intermittent, but the wage was weekly and therefore essential.

Keeva's shoulder length hair was wild and red and her eyes were as green as the first spring shoots of the wild angelica that grew along the banks of Tarabeg's Taramore river. She was thin from spending the entire day on her feet, walking an hour to work and another hour back in the evening, and never resting until she hit her straw mattress at night, but she loved her job. The post office was the hub of the village, the place where all news arrived, and being a part of it relieved the repetitive routine of her life.

The telex had caused quite a stir the day it was installed and had not ceased to amaze since. The women of the village still sometimes gathered round it, gazing, waiting, bending their ears to the background hum as they stared in wonder at the occasional involuntary half jump of a key as it threatened to beat out a message.

Finding Seamus Malone on this wet afternoon was not a difficult task for Mrs Doyle, who knew he would be up at the farm on Tarabeg Hill if he wasn't in the village. Along with the post office, the main street comprised only the tailor's shop owned by the Careys, the tobacconist's, a hardware shop, the new baker's, the public house, the schoolhouse, Paddy and Josie Devlin's butcher's shop, with its own second bar at the back, and, finally, the old barracks and Garda post, the church and the school.

'Where are you off to with that?' Ellen Carey shouted to her from the door of the tailor's shop. Mere seconds before, she'd been sitting by the large-paned window, pedalling away at her Singer sewing machine as her eyes scanned the village. It was a draughty spot, and furthest from the fire, but it afforded Ellen the best view, and that she would never relinquish. She had spotted the mustard-coloured envelope in Mrs Doyle's hand before she was ten paces from the post-office door.

Without breaking her stride, Mrs Doyle gasped, 'Oh, I can't stop, Ellen, I've left Keeva looking after the post office and if I'm too long, she'll have given all the money away in wrong change. 'Tis for Seamus. I have to see is he in Paddy's. Oh look, would you, his horse is there! I've caught him, praise be to God.'

Her still-black hair was drawn into a loose chignon on the nape of her neck, in the local style, and bobbed up and down to the rhythm of her breasts. Her long black skirt and white blouse had been dry when she left the post office only moments earlier, but the rain hit the black serge of her outer skirt with the force of the wind behind it, penetrating the linen slip beneath and seeping through to her stick-thin thighs. Her shawl, draped across her shoulders, was in danger of slipping off as she lowered her head and ran, trying to keep her face dry.

'If it's for Seamus, it must be news of Michael,' said Ellen. 'Wait for me.' She stepped back into the tailor's, grabbed her own shawl from the back of the chair, turned the 'Open' sign to 'Closed' and, slamming the door to the sound of the jangling bell, threw the shawl over her head and shoulders and headed off down the street after Mrs Doyle.

'How are ye, Miss O'Hara?' she shouted to Rosie, not stopping to wait for a reply. 'Mrs Doyle has a telegram, so she does. For Seamus,' she called over her shoulder by way of an explanation for her bad manners.

As Rosie watched Ellen's back disappear around the corner, the thunder of the fast-running peaty river resounded in her ears. It came crashing down from the mountains over flinty boulders and smooth, centuries-worn pebbles, drowning out the intrusive rhythm of her own pulse, which had been beating a tattoo ever since Teresa had imparted her news. The rain poured, the river roared and the scattered cottages of the village were thatch-soaked and wretched and looked as miserable as a jilted lover. She had never wanted to be anywhere as much as she wanted to follow Ellen Carey and run into the Devlins' bar and know the exact contents of the telegram, dictated by Michael. Her mouth dried and she swallowed hard as her hands scrunched up the fabric of her thin coat. A telegram from Michael!

She breathed in and out, slowly. *Keep calm. Keep calm.* It was the hardest thing. Five years had passed, but she could give nothing away. She continued slowly down the main street, heading home. *Keep calm.*

She had reached the butcher's shop, and, looking up, saw Josie Devlin behind the counter, and John O'Donnell, Theady's father, along with Bridget McAndrew. They were all, each one of them, watching her. She smiled nervously, unclenched her hands and pulled her frayed coat across her chest against the wind and the rain. She dropped her gaze to her feet and without waiting to see had anyone smiled back, continued her journey. If she had looked up instead of down, she would have noticed that Josie had indeed smiled kindly, John had touched the rim of his cap out of respect for her role as the teacher of his son, and Bridget McAndrew, who knew the secrets of most hearts in Tarabeg without needing to be told, had sent her a look of deepest pity. Rosie would have been glad to have missed that.

The Devlins' shop and home was divided into two, with two entrances. The meat counter in the front opened onto the main street, presenting a respectable frontage, whereas the bar at the rear was reached through a side door. A wooden shed in the back yard served as the slaughterhouse and contained a fridge which hid the salmon that were illegally poached from the Taramore river as well as the holy herrings during Lent. The running of the butcher's shop and the bar was also divided up: Josie served customers at the front, while Paddy was either in the slaughterhouse or at the bar. From there he would dispense Guinness and, when the barrel ran out, whiskey and porter; when that ran dry, a mysterious milk churn full of poteen would appear, distilled from Malone potatoes and hidden away in Paddy's yard until it was needed.

Those who wanted to avoid incurring the wrath of the wife or attracting the attention of Teresa Gallagher bypassed the public house and kept their custom for Paddy's bar. Respectable men had no notion to be seen stepping off the main street and in through the doors of the public house in the middle of the afternoon; and so, in a village where gossip was currency, they slipped through the side door of Paddy's instead. Among their number was Father Jerry himself, Brendan O'Kelly, the clerk and magistrate for the area, and Mr O'Dowd. Respectable men supped with the fearful, the hen-pecked and anyone else who chose to partake of the cheapest drinks in town. There were also those who ducked in from the butcher's, through the dividing curtain, to down a quick glass of whiskey, for medicinal reasons, while Josie wrapped up the pig's trotters in the front.

Paddy was in the process of filling a half pot of Guinness from a wooden barrel for Seamus Malone. Father Jerry was sitting next to him, stuffing a dudeen with tobacco. Teresa did not allow smoking in the presbytery. "'Tis an unholy act altogether,' she would protest every time he tried, and so, to keep the peace, he kept his pipe for the back of Paddy's. Porick McAndrew, Bridget's husband, was sitting by the fire, well away from his wife. While he nipped around the back for whatever Paddy had on offer, Bridget herself always sat on one of the wooden chairs in the butcher's shop, drank tea and talked to Josie. Brendan O'Kelly was at the table in the window, reading the *Irish Times*, having patiently waited until three in the afternoon for the mail van to arrive. He studied the crossword and chewed his pencil as he worked his way through half a pint of Guinness. The bar was silent apart from the rain hitting the windows and the slow drip, drip onto the wooden floorboards from the coat stand where Seamus had just hung his oilskin cape. A puddle began to form below it.

'I'll join you in a quick one, Seamus,' said Paddy. 'Will you be wanting a top-up, Porick?'

Porick looked woefully into his glass. 'I would like that, Paddy, sure I would, but you know, she would know I had, given that she has the sight. I can keep nothing from her and you would hear her all the way back if I did.'

Paddy smiled. Nothing was missed by Bridget. The village apothecary, she spoke to the spirits and healed people with the potions she made in her cottage up on the hill. 'You shouldn't be such a lazy fecker, Porick,' he said.

Porick's face took on an expression of deep hurt. 'Paddy, do you have no sympathy for the cut of my back? Gone, it is, and it won't ever be coming back – the doctor says that and he knows more about it than the witch I am married to.' He shook his head self-pityingly. 'You have no notion of the pain I am in. Besides, I still cut the turf and do odd jobs on the farm.' He stood up slowly to leave, making a show of his aches and pains.

Paddy made no response, just flicked back the tap and placed Seamus's Guinness to the side to settle. Porick was the laziest man in the village and Bridget the hardest-working woman. Everyone agreed that there had never been such a mismatched couple.

'Has Teresa left already?' Seamus asked as he walked over to the fire to dry off. 'I suppose she must have if you are here yerself, Father.' He half raised his sodden cap to Father Jerry, then shook it onto the flames of the turf fire, which spat back at him in protest. Paddy never opened the bar of an afternoon until Teresa was clear of the village, sent away from the presbytery by Father Jerry on special errands or to visit her sister.

'Aye, she left not minutes since,' said Paddy. 'She's a desperate driver, that one.' He had watched her turning the corner from the main street, both inside wheels leaving the ground as she drove her horse and trap out of Tarabeg, then stopping suddenly at the school. 'There will be no one on the roads this afternoon and that's for sure. She drives every sober man indoors before lunch until they know she's back at home and the coast is clear. I cannot imagine what possessed you, Father, to give her the use of your horse and cart.'

'Really?' said Seamus with a smile and a wink towards Father Jerry. 'Well, the fact that Father is often the first through the door as soon as she's away down the road ought to give you a clue, ought it not?'

Father Jerry pulled hard on his pipe and grinned. ''Tis the horse I feel sorry for,' he said.

Seamus chuckled. ''Tis you, Father, I'll feel sorry for if she ever finds out you are over here in the afternoon. She'll be down here giving out to you, all right, and Josie won't be up for stopping her. Thick as thieves, the women in this village are.'

They all looked out of the window, across the road to the seven acres of wasteland that spanned the Taramore river. Where the land bordered the main street stood the Church of the Sacred Heart, peering down at them, and the presbytery, where Father Jerry lived, along with his housekeeper, Teresa. Officially, Teresa kept records of the village births, marriages and deaths; unofficially, she also recorded all that mattered in between. She was often to be seen standing in front of the tall dark windows that blinked in the sunlight, missing nothing that occurred in the quiet village.

Just as Paddy carried the two pots of Guinness towards the fire, Seamus opened his eyes wide. 'Feck,' he said.

'What?' Paddy turned his head to follow Seamus's gaze out the window. ''Tis only Guinness.'

But he received his answer soon enough as, with little ceremony, the door was flung wide. The rain hurtled in first, and then came Mrs Doyle, the only woman in the village apart from Josie who could set foot near the bar without being talked about.

'Oh Holy Mother of God, you are here,' she gasped to Seamus.

Ellen Carey shuffled in behind her and slammed the door shut. It was acceptable to enter the bar with Mrs Doyle. If another minute had passed, her cloak of respectability would have disappeared. She pulled her shawl across her chest, folded her arms and pushed her shoulders back; if her short, thin hair hadn't been soaked to the scalp and plastered to her face in wet strands, she would have looked important.

'Hello, Paddy, Seamus.' Mrs Doyle directed her pointed chin and beady black eyes straight at the earthenware pot that Paddy was placing in front of Seamus.

Seamus jumped to his feet and pulled out a wooden chair from the bar's only table. It stood in front of the fire and was covered in a bright green gingham cloth – a homely touch added by Josie. 'Here, woman, would ye sit down,' he said. 'Ellen, here, you too. Paddy, pour a pot for Mrs Doyle, before she takes bad, and Ellen too, would you now.'

Mrs Doyle flopped down into the chair he held out for her.

'What have ye there?' he asked. 'Here, drink this. God in heaven, ye'll be doing yerself no good, running like that at your age.'

Mrs Doyle's eyes flashed with indignation – her age was the best-kept secret in Tarabeg – but Seamus failed to notice.

Josie bustled through the curtain. She had seen the tail end of Ellen's shawl as she flew past the butcher's shop window. 'Is it a telegram?' she asked, looking at the mustard-coloured envelope in Mrs Doyle's hand. Telegrams no longer inspired the dread they had only weeks earlier. The war had been over more than a month since. Enough young men had died; there would be no more now. 'Only John O'Donnell is in the shop and he wants me to check, before he's away home. He doesn't want to be missing the news now and having to wait until tomorrow like everyone else up the boreens. And besides, if Philomena finds out a telegram arrived when he was here and he can't tell her what was in it, she'll be giving out to him something wicked.'

Seamus placed the pot of Guinness in Mrs Doyle's hand. Her gaze met his and she winked as the draught slipped over her toothless gums as fast as it would those of any man. Her shawl fell from her dark hair and landed on her shoulders, and her eyes closed in ecstasy.

Mesmerised, Paddy, Josie and Seamus watched her noisily gulp down almost the entire contents of the pot.

'Jesus, she'll be needing a second,' muttered Seamus to Paddy, unheard by Mrs Doyle, who, as she finished, slammed the empty pot down on the table with one hand and proffered the ransom telegram to Seamus.

She sucked the residue of the Guinness from her gums. ''Tis for you, Seamus,' she wheezed, as though there had been any doubt, and, turning to Josie added, 'Tell John he can be on his way now. 'Tis from Michael. He's coming home.'

For the briefest moment, no one said a word. Seamus, yet to open the telegram, stared at her open-mouthed until Josie broke the silence and bustled back through into the butcher's shop.

''Tis from Michael,' they heard her say.

Seamus flinched as John O'Donnell's response floated back through the curtain.

'Sure, is he dead? The fecking bastard should be, fighting with the English. A traitor, he is, after what the English did to us.'

'Stop, would ye,' they heard Josie reply. 'Surely to God, the war is over, the fighting is over, the worry, 'tis all over, and if you carry on like that in my shop, John, as sure as God is true, 'twill be over for you too.'

They all heard a loud slap. Seamus hoped it was contact between John's face and the flat of Josie's hand, though Paddy knew it would have been the rashers John came in for every Thursday afternoon hitting the counter.

Josie warmed to her theme. 'The Germans lost, we can all

have a bit of peace at last, Jesus, Holy Father, can we? At last, please, would you, John? Just shut the feck up and keep all yer bellyaching for Philomena. Don't be bringing it in here into my shop, to me.'

They heard the crash of the wooden till drawer and the sound of change hitting the counter.

In the bar, Seamus said nothing, just raised his eyebrows at Paddy.

Paddy, embarrassed, adjusted his cap and then thrust his hands deep into the pockets of his coarse brown butcher's apron. 'Go on then,' he said to Seamus, inclining his head towards the telegram, even though it seemed a little pointless now that Mrs Doyle had announced the news it contained. He brought out a small boning knife and handed it to him.

A muscle in Seamus's cheek flickered as he eased the knife into the edges of the envelope. He was well aware that his every action would be described and amplified within every home in the village inside of the hour.

To Paddy, it felt like he was taking an age. He picked up a cloth and began to wipe the tap on the Guinness barrel to fill the time. The door opened and they all turned to see who it was had arrived at such an important moment.

'Ah, what have we here?' boomed the voice of Mr O'Dowd as he shut the door behind him.

'A telegram,' said Paddy, and they all turned their attention back to Seamus, who had laid the telegram on the table and with the flat of his hands was smoothing out the paper as though gluing it to the gingham fabric.

Impatient, Paddy threw his dirty dish cloth into the sink. 'Well, what has he to say?' he asked.

Father Jerry rose from his chair and moved to stand beside

Seamus. Mr O'Dowd, so tall and broad that his head almost reached the ceiling, walked over and stood at Seamus's other side. They read the telegram over his shoulders. Brendan pushed his pencil behind his ear and turned his chair away from the window to face the room and observe the moment.

'He's away home,' Seamus said. 'He was finally demobbed along with the lads from Galway and Cork, the ones in his regiment. They will be back home before the week is out, he says. They've been in Liverpool and will be catching the boat to Dublin and then the train to Galway. He doesn't say what day or time exactly, but then that would be our Michael, would it not. He'll surprise the life out of us all and turn up when we least expect him.'

'Thanks be to God.' Father Jerry blessed himself, and the others followed suit.

Seamus smiled broadly. 'He's alive. I don't care when the hell he comes home. He can do whatever he wants.'

Josie walked back into the bar. She entered the room like a small tornado, the force of her personality taking up more space than her physical form required, and being the well-fed wife of the butcher, that in itself was considerable. Her face was damp around the hairline and still flushed from the heated exchange. 'John O'Donnell has gone off with my voice ringing in his ears,' she told them, even though they had all heard her shouting. In a silent act of defiance, the rashers safely in his coat pocket, he'd slammed the door and set the bell ringing out in painful objection. 'Sure 'twas a bad reaction, that was, and 'twill be all over the village soon enough. You know what people are like, Seamus. Some will have an opinion we won't care for.'

'Aye, so it is,' said Ellen, who had remained silent until then.

'As soon as he gets home, he'll tell his shrew of a wife, and then there'll be no stopping it. The news will have reached Newport by dark. Philomena is as quick to spread the gossip as she is the slurry.' She turned to Seamus. 'Do you think Michael will be having any notion at all of how bad it is here? He'll be finding it hard to get work if he comes home, will he not? There's to be a law, they say, to punish those who fought with the British.'

Paddy spat on the sawdust-covered floor. ''Tis disgusting itself how many around here wanted the Germans to win. Some say that even if the Germans were filling the roads on the way to Mayo, they would still rather that than support the British.'

Josie, a woman who never usually sat down, pulled out a chair next to Mrs Doyle and sank into it. 'Well, welcome news it is. I had given up on him altogether, the war has been over for that long. Wait until our Tig hears. He'll be that pleased his best friend is coming back, sick with worry the lad had been. I'll have to stop him running up the hill to the farm to wait for him.'

No one, from a place of kindness, corrected her by pointing out that Tig, who had one leg markedly shorter than the other, a pigeon chest and poor lungs, never ran anywhere. Even in Tarabeg, a mother could dream.

Paddy smiled at his wife. Her bark was very much worse than her bite. As round as Mrs Doyle was thin, she had bright, twinkling, blue eyes and, despite her grumbling, was of a kindly nature. He watched as she took a handkerchief from her pocket, dabbed at her forehead, then wiped the moisture from her eyes and John O'Donnell from her mind.

Josie Devlin rarely drank, but that afternoon she took two pots. No one could remember the last time she'd done that, but she was making a point, one that Mrs Doyle would carry back to the post office, Ellen to the tailor's and both of them to Mass. Michael Malone was alive and well and his return home was to be greeted with much cheer. And besides, he was a good lad. He'd been a true friend to Tig, standing up for him when he was bullied, always sure to include him when there was a dance or a social. Tig had missed him rotten these last five years, Josie was well aware of that. The boys had been friends since they were born, as were Josie and Paddy with Seamus and Nola. Now was the time for her to help her friends in the best way she could. As stalwarts of the village community and purveyors of the most essential provisions – rashers, trotters, sausages and Guinness – the Devlins' opinion carried some weight. Seamus knew exactly what Josie was doing and was grateful.

'Well, sure, Michael hasn't been the only one to fight for the British,' said Ellen. 'There's been plenty more.'

'Yes, but Michael was the first and he is the only one from around here to return home alive,' said Mrs Doyle, who had delivered telegrams which held the worst news any parent could receive.

'Who will be telling Michael about Sarah, Seamus?' asked Josie, whose voice had dropped an octave. 'Kevin McGuffey has sworn that if Michael goes anywhere near the cottage, he will shoot him. You will have to warn him. Surely to God, the boy will have survived the Germans only to come home and be put in the ground by a monster like McGuffey.'

'Now then, we won't be having talk like that.' Father Jerry frowned. Keeping a check on the violent nature of Sarah's father was a challenge he struggled to meet.

'Well, if he does even harbour such a notion, 'twill be

McGuffey that suffers,' said Seamus. 'He has not a friend from one side of the country to the other, and what the feck is he talking about – the man is never sober enough to take a straight aim. Michael and Sarah, they were sweethearts, after all. Pledged to each other, they were. The only person who didn't know that was McGuffey, and doesn't that tell you all you need to know.'

'And Rosie O'Hara,' said Mrs Doyle, boldly, but no one heard, as was often the case when Rosie's name was mentioned.

Ellen Carey pulled herself up to her full five feet three inches and spoke. 'Seamus, Sarah McGuffey, she is to be married to Jay Maughan, and soon.' Her eyes darted about the room and rested upon Father Jerry. 'There, I've told him.'

She hoped no one would ask her how she knew. Jay Maughan had dropped a bolt of fabric around the back of the shop and asked her to make her two dresses for Shona, his grandmother. She'd made the last one for her over five years ago. Ellen told no one. Business was bad enough without a curse from Shona to make it worse. She had never spoken to Shona, none of the villagers had. It was Jay who did the talking and he'd been very keen to talk to Ellen, when, after dark, he had called around the back to collect the dresses.

Seamus had heard nothing of this. He was speechless with the shock of it and could only look aghast at Father Jerry, seeking confirmation.

Father Jerry removed his dudeen and laid it against his chest in a clenched fist. The air felt heavy, the fire spat. ''Twill not be happening in my church. The tinkers, they have their own priest. 'Tis a sin McGuffey is committing, marrying her off to a man she can't abide. And a cruelty, too, I would say, when the man is a tinker like Jay Maughan. Not to speak of his sinful grandmother, Shona, cursing and calling on the Devil as she does.' He looked down apologetically at the sawdust floor. 'I'm afraid 'tis true, Seamus. She will be married, I would think, even before Michael is home.'

'Is... is there nothing you can do, Father?' Seamus stammered the words. His son was coming home, but if he returned to find his Sarah married, it would be worse to him than the pain of any wound inflicted by the Germans. His gut tightened at the horror of it. The girl Michael had written about in every single letter home for the past five years was to be married, and to Jay Maughan of all people. Right under their very noses.

'I cannot come between a man and his own wishes for his family,' Father Jerry replied.

All present knew this to be the truth. Kevin McGuffey was a madman and Father Jerry was as scared of him as everyone else in the village.

Paddy voiced what they were all thinking. 'He's a wicked one, that McGuffey. He's spent too much time in his own company out at sea, fishing. He has a temper on him worse than any bull in any field, so he does.'

Brendan was standing by the fire, warming his backside and pulling on his pipe. 'Paddy, is Bee working tonight?'

They all turned to look at him. This was usual: when Brendan spoke, everyone listened. Bee Cosgrove was Sarah's aunt and worked evenings at the bar to relieve Josie.

'She is.'

'Well, I'll have a word with her then. Such news will be best coming from family, do you not agree, Seamus? Angela and Sarah should know what the rumours are, what McGuffey and Maughan have been putting about, in case there is any alternative action to be taken.' Brendan looked over to Father Jerry. 'Now I'm not sure it isn't all talk from the big man, but Sarah has a right to know, and I can't imagine she does, wouldn't you be saying, Father?'

Father Jerry frowned, met Brendan's eye, put his pipe back in his mouth and said nothing.

Brendan was well aware that the father would never condone any mortal being undermining the way a man ran his family business, regardless of his personal opinion. The fact that the father had remained silent in the face of his question told him all he needed to know. 'Right, well, leave it to me then,' he said. 'I'll have a quiet word in Bee's ear and see what can be done.'

Seamus banged his pot on the table and retrieved his cape. 'I have to leave you good people now. I'm away home to tell Nola, Pete and Daedio the news.'

As he made for the door, Paddy walked with him. 'Don't be worrying about any wedding, Seamus. I haven't seen sight nor sound of the Maughans in weeks. No, 'tis all gossip and don't you be worrying about any of it. Not at all, do you hear me?'

Seamus raised his cap in farewell, fastened his oilskin cape at the throat and went out to untie his horse from the post. A group of farmhands were coming around the corner on their way to Paddy's, and Keeva was ahead of them, already running up the path to the bar. Grabbing hold of the door jamb, afraid of going inside the bar, she shouted from the door, 'Mrs Doyle, the post office is full of people wanting to know what was in the telex. Am I to tell them?'

Seamus couldn't hear Mrs Doyle's reply. The farmhands, all of whom he'd known all of his life, raised their caps to him and shouted their greetings. He shouted back, ''Tis a bad afternoon, you'll be needing a stiff whiskey to get your blood running again,' but as he did so he couldn't help wondering if it had been one of them who'd told Kevin McGuffey about Sarah being with Michael on his last day. Had one of them seen her from the fields where they were working? Had they known about Michael and Sarah? It was that which had started the trouble. He felt a weight in his heart when he thought of it, recalling what Bridget had told him, how Sarah and her mother had suffered at the hands of McGuffey.

He began hitching the horse to the cart. He could hear the murmur of the farmhands' voices as they entered the bar and it seemed the news of Michael's homecoming had reached them already. They must have passed John O'Donnell on the way – he was almost as big a gossip as his wife. Seamus stopped to listen a moment.

'There won't be any trouble, Paddy, keep your hair on.'

'There's no need to be worrying about Michael. He won't be here for long enough, so he won't.'

'Sarah's father will shoot him dead before he takes his boots off, you know the temper on McGuffey.'

'If Jay Maughan doesn't get there first! He and Sarah will be married as soon as McGuffey gets back from his smuggling trip to the North. The deal has been done, sure. Anyway, Michael will have forgotten her name already.'

So it was true, Seamus thought. McGuffey had promised Sarah to Jay Maughan. It seemed that everyone knew – everyone except those who needed to know. He heard Josie firing back her angry response, giving the farmhands as fierce a tongue-lashing as she had John O'Donnell. He sighed as he heaved himself into the cart. Josie would have her work cut out for her if that was how everyone was to carry on when they heard the news of Michael's return.

He pulled the oilskin tight over his knees and shoulders, flicked the reins and directed the horse towards the boreen that would take him up Tarabeg Hill and home. As he turned onto the track, he glanced along the coast road. There was no distant glimpse of the ocean today, thanks to the rain, but he did catch sight of Bee Cosgrove, Sarah's aunt, further along the road. She was making her way towards the village, ready for her shift at Paddy's. He decided not to wait for her; she would find out soon enough, and he was keen to take the news to Nola.

As the wheels of the cart trundled from one deep rut and puddle to the next, he kept his eyes focused on the pricked-up ears of the horse in front of him. With a heavy heart he prayed that Michael would come home to Tarabeg Hill first, home to the farm and not to the McGuffeys'. He might have dodged German bullets in a field, but when McGuffy returned, there might be only one bullet heading towards him, at close range. Nola's heart might be broken after all.

Chapter 3

Shona Maughan lived in a caravan with her grandson Jay and, from time to time, a stolen child. They roamed the backroads and villages of Mayo and beyond, camping where they could, rarely welcome to stay very long. With her wild long white hair, no one knew how old she was and even the storyteller, at the Tarabeg harvests, fairs and dances, could not recall a time or even a story that Shona had not been a part of. She was the force of darkness in Tarabeg and every villager was terrified of being crossed by her. Every villager except Bridget McAndrew, Tarabeg's seer, a woman who lived by her visons of the future and her conversations with the dead, and Michael's grandfather, Daedio.

Daedio had crossed Shona many years since and had safely made old bones, but he knew the scheming witch had something in store for him. He'd half expected she would take her revenge when his favourite grandson went off to war, and for five long years he'd feared that Michael might not return. Shona would use her powers to wound where it had the most impact – this Daedio was certain of. And hurting the family he loved would hurt him more. The worry had taken the use of his legs away from him shortly after Michael had left for the war. But he had Annie, his dead wife and former closest friend of Bridget McAndrew, to keep them safe.

'Something is occurring, Daedio,' Bridget confided in him when she called up to the farm for butter.

Nola, Daedio's daughter-in-law, was the best butter-maker in the village. No one called round just to buy butter. Everyone stopped, took tea and sat on Daedio's truckle bed in front of the fire to bring him up to date with the village gossip.

'I have plenty, Bridget,' Nola said as she took the dish to fill from Bridget.

'I have not the time to be making butter as well as potions,' said Bridget. 'I'm happy to pay for it, Nola.' She made herself comfortable on the end of Daedio's bed, which creaked in objection to the extra weight.

'You will do no such thing,' Nola replied as she headed out to the dairy, 'but if you have a bottle for the rheumatism for me and one to keep Daedio's appetite up, that would be grand.' She paused at the door. 'Now, don't mind me, I've to be getting on with the chores before Seamus gets home from the village. Did you see him at all Bridget? It's that wet out today, I'm behind with everything.' Nola hadn't waited for an answer and for that, Bridget was grateful. The door banged behind her as she headed for the dairy.

''Tis on the wind, Daedio. I can feel it,' Bridget whispered to Daedio. She laid a herb-stained hand on top of his, which were bent and disfigured from years of tilling the land. 'Shona, she is up to something.'

Daedio's eyes lit up. He had news of his own. 'Bridget, my dreams are strong, so they are. I wake up troubled and not knowing why.' He shuffled himself further up his bed as

Bridget nursed the cup of tea Nola had placed in her hands. He was glad she'd called; she was the only one who understood.

'That's not dreams, Daedio, 'tis Annie.' She stared into the flames of the fire. 'Coming back to let you know she's there for when you need her. 'Tis my guessing that she's trying to make you see her more often, to tell you something, but you either don't want to see it, or you can't. They have their own way to let you know, gently like, often in a dream. She is only in the next room, but the walls of that room, well, sometimes she can see through them and you can see her back. She will pass across and draw a little closer to ye if she can, and knowing Annie Malone, she will, because never was there a more determined woman. She will protect her family in death, as she did in life. She is still here, Daedio. I can see her – she's just here, now, stood by the fire. I've been looking at her, trying to make out what she's saying to me.'

A tear sprang into Daedio's eye. 'I can't see her.' His throat was thick and his voice croaked.

'I know. 'Tis harder for men, but you can feel her, can't you?'

Daedio could, he could feel her so strong. Despite the heat of the fire, the air had cooled between them. 'I can, and I feel she is trying to warn me of something because sometimes I feel uneasy, like when Nola and Seamus have had a fight and have gone to their room to blast it out and I'm left sat here – it's that feeling.' He propped himself up against the pillow. 'As for Shona Maughan, Bridget – she has no trouble getting into my dreams. She's been so often now, and she scares me. She's never forgotten, you know.'

'She's a woman who lives for revenge, Daedio. She's never going to forgive you for driving her out of the village and off the seven acres, sure she is not. She cursed you that day, and we both know it. But you have me and Annie to protect you, so stop your worrying. I can take on any mischief Shona Maughan or anyone else sends our way.'

Daedio smiled with relief as Bridget gulped down her tea.

What Bridget didn't say was that she'd called into the farm today because Annie had paid a visit to her own dreams and had pulled her to Daedio.

With her apothecary skills and gift of the sight, Bridget had worked hard up to now to keep Shona's misdeeds at bay, but of the two of them, Shona, a tinker seer, was the stronger. Bridget's greatest test was yet to come, of that she was sure, and she knew in her heart that at the root of it was the banishing of the Maughans from the land Daedio had bought, which had rendered them homeless. It had happened years ago, back even before Seamus was born, but the Maughans had long memories.

For reasons Bridget wasn't party to, Daedio had bought the land in secret, telling no one but her and Annie. The Maughans had parked their caravan there for generations, on the patch of land between the Church of the Sacred Heart and the Taramore river, in the middle of Tarabeg. The village was a peaceful place, as close to heaven as anyone could want, but the Maughans were a blight, and everyone thought so. They snatched and traded in children, just as their forbears had done since the time of the famine, and the people of Tarabeg despised them for it. So, when the village awoke one morning to find the Maughan clan evicted from their camp near the river, there was nothing but relief.

As they sat in front of the fire with Annie's presence between them, Bridget and Daedio were both thinking back to that time, remembering. The flames roared up the chimney like the chained dogs out in the old house when a fox slipped past.

'When are you going to tell Seamus about the land?' Bridget asked. 'Sure it's a sinful waste, all those acres in the middle of the village sitting there doing nothing and no one but you knowing anything about it. Are you going to die and shock the life out of the lot of them too? Seamus could do something with that land, make something of it. Times are hard enough as it is.'

Daedio's eyes twinkled in the firelight. 'Annie left me clear instructions, Bridget. 'Twill be soon. She said she will let me know when the time is right, and I think that's what she's trying to do now.'

'Aye, well, she was a wise one, Annie, there's no denying.' Bridget looked into the flames again, a rueful smile on her face. 'And I'm here for you, Daedio, should you need me.'

'You know what Annie told me, Bridget,' Daedio said, his gaze now fixed on the fire too. 'She said that St Patrick banished the snakes from all of Ireland, but that when we bought that land, we banished the Maughans from Tarabeg.'

He and Bridget clinked their mugs and smiled.

Seamus had made good progress despite the downpour and the heavy load along the boreen and up Tarabeg Hill. As the horse and cart followed the familiar route to the farmhouse nestled into the little valley just below the rocky heights of the mountain, he stared around him, thinking of his son and the two pieces of momentous news he'd just heard down at Paddy's bar. If he were Michael, there was no way he could give all this up, he thought, glancing around appreciatively at the comforting landmarks of his home. The bog holes where the fairies lived, the bridges over the streams he'd helped Daedio build with his bare hands when he was just a boy – they were a part of his history. He tilted his head as the heavy grey clouds began to lift and let his gaze linger on the lush green fields, flung against the mountainside like a bolt of unfurled emerald velvet, setting into relief the old thatched white cottage before him.

The cottage had once been the Malone family home, but they used it as the cowshed now. As he drew nearer, he saw Nola in the evening light, carrying a pail of milk back to the farmhouse. Hearing the horse and cart, she stopped, set the pail on the ground and waved to him. Her hair was wrapped up as always in a headscarf and her long apron hung from a bib, covering her dark blue pincord skirt. 'You took your time,' she shouted. 'I'll see ye back at the house.' She picked up the pail again and carried on along her path to the back door and the dairy.

Seamus made the sign of the cross and blessed himself, as he always did when he returned home and caught sight of the best woman in all of Ireland waiting for him. He was momentarily transported back to his boyhood and the countless times he had sat on the cart next to Daedio and they had waved to his own mother, Annie, carrying a similar pail, treading the same worn steps to their farmhouse, newly built and slate-roofed. Annie would shout to Daedio, scolding him for keeping the young Seamus out too long.

He gathered the reins into one hand and raised the other to wave back to Nola. Seeing a gossamer vision of his late mother waving back at him took his breath away. He knew it for what it was, a warning.

The image was dispelled when the horse got spooked and speeded up. The old nag was heading for home, focused on getting to his stable and his hay manger. 'Whoa!' shouted Seamus, but to no avail, and the cart turned the final corner on two wheels, just as it always did.

Through the open doors of the old cottage came the voice of the farmhand, Pete Shevlin, who had made the place his home, preferring to bed down in the hayloft above the cowshed, where once the whole family had slept. 'He will have you off one day,' he shouted as the cart finally slowed and the horse made its way in under the arch, into the near darkness of the windowless shed.

'He's like Mrs Doyle heading for a Guinness!' Seamus shouted as he wound in the reins. 'Only he has a little more grace and his own teeth.'

Both men laughed as Seamus dismounted the cart and removed the rope harness from the horse. Pete had prepared a manger of feed and a deep bed of straw for the old nag, and the old cottage was filled with the smell of sweet hay and cow. Pete carried on with the milking, singing the same comforting tune he sang every night, convinced that his music increased the cows' output.

Seamus composed his thoughts as he brushed the sweat from the back of the horse with a rough handful of straw, and allowed himself his first smile. Throwing down the straw, he patted the nag on his rump.

'I'm away into the house, Pete. I have news for Nola.'

He'd felt the telegram burning into his leg through his trouser pocket and once or twice had let his hand lie against it, to reassure himself it was still there. His heart was beating faster. The waiting and worrying were over, and now the one thing he wanted to see was the relief on his wife's face. He ran out of the barn and up the path, and before Pete could answer him, Seamus was gone.

Pete stared out of the door, open mouthed, the rhythm of the milking broken as he tried to remember the last time he had seen Seamus Malone run.

Nola let the hot, freshly baked, floury loaf drop from her hands onto the wooden breadboard as Seamus barged in through the door. She knew instantly that something was wrong. This was not how Seamus entered the house. Gentle in both movement and speech, he was more likely to creep in without her even knowing than arrive like this, running across the kitchen towards her. She wiped her floury hands on her well-padded sides and mopped the perspiration from her brow with the back of her sleeve. She spent the best part of her day covered in flour and smelling of butter, and always wore her short dark curly hair tucked into one of the frilled white cotton caps Ellen had made her. Her cheeks were as doughy as her bread and criss-crossed with tiny red veins that gave her a permanent rosy glow.

Seamus flicked Daedio's cap from his head as he trotted past the old man, who was dozing on his bed in front of the fire.

'Oi, you feckin' bastard,' Daedio shouted, woken from his slumbers. 'Give it me back. Do you want me to catch my death? Tell him, Nola, would ye.'

It was a nightly routine, the flicking of the cap, which was never removed, even in sleep. The baiting was done in ruthless good humour, to try and encourage the old man to find his legs and pick up the cap – a reason to move.

'I've done it to wake you up, you lazy old git,' said Seamus as he bent to retrieve the cap from the floor. His flick had been a good one tonight; powered by relief and happiness, the cap had reached all the way to the press behind Nola.

'Nola, put that knife down, I have news,' he said as he scooped up the cap and fitted it back into place on Daedio's head.

Nola dropped the knife onto the breadboard, next to the loaf. 'What is it?' she asked as she rubbed her hands down her apron and made her way around the table to the fireside, where Seamus was standing next to Daedio's bed.

Seamus ran his hand down his hip and ruffled the paper in his pocket. The tension was such that if he didn't tell Nola soon, the telegram would surely catch alight. Without any further preamble, he removed it and thrust it at Nola.

She looked up at him and frowned. 'What's this?' she said as her blood ran cold.

They had all heard the stories of telegrams arriving in homes across Ireland, informing parents that their sons had died in the war. There was little sympathy for those sons; soldiers who had donned a British uniform. The manner in which the British had behaved during the famine was still talked about as though it had only been yesterday. And the list of reasons why some of the Irish hated the British didn't stop there: there was the First World War, their devious tactics during the fight for Home Rule, the Easter Rising... The mothers of lost soldiers got few condolences.

'Is it Michael, is it, God love him? Tell me, is he dead?' Her eyes filled with tears she could not hold back. She began to tremble and took a step away from the fire, putting her hand behind her to grab at one of the wooden chairs.

'No, not at all.' Seamus placed a hand on her shoulder. 'Stop now, would ye. Far from it, Nola. Did ye ever really think our Michael wouldn't make it? He's coming home.'

Nola clasped her hand tight across her mouth. 'Home?' she said. 'Here, to the farm? To Tarabeg? Oh God in heaven, I don't know whether to be happy or sad. Is he in Liverpool? Does he not know what it's like? Seamus, tell him to stay in Liverpool, where there's work to be had repairing the bomb damage. That's were all the lads are heading to, you know as well as I do. The McGintys have three boys all upped and left for the building and the labouring. They say there's good money to be had. What in God's name is he coming back here for? There will only be trouble, surely to God.'

She was talking faster than usual, her words tumbling out of her. She looked from Seamus to Daedio, who was grinning from ear to ear, and knew she was making little sense. She slumped onto the chair she'd been holding on to and collapsed, then gently rose again, removed her knitting from under her rear and placed the half-finished Aran jumper for Seamus over her face. Now that she'd stopped talking, she was weeping sudden tears – of joy, fear and relief.

'Typical bloody woman,' muttered Daedio. 'She's been saying every day for five years, "I'm off to Mass to pray for Michael. I can't wait for the day when I lay me eyes on his face, so I can't."' Daedio spoke in a mocking high-pitched voice as he peered at Nola from under the brim of his cap. 'Mary, Mother of God, would ye look at the cut of her now.' He snorted, but he was still unable to remove the grin from his face. Michael was coming home, and regardless of all the problems he would bring with him, it was a moment of joy to savour.

Seamus, ignoring Daedio, sat on the settle next to Nola. 'There's one reason he's coming home and it's for Sarah

McGuffey – you know that, don't you? If it wasn't for Sarah, he probably would stay in Liverpool and earn some money before he came home. Stop the crying now.' He removed the knitting from in front of Nola's face and peered into her weeping eyes. 'Nola, listen, would ye, Michael is coming home to news he won't want to hear. He is too late – Sarah is to be married to Jay Maughan, and soon.'

If anything could make Nola's tears stop, that news was it. For a brief moment the only sound in the room was the crackling of the fire and a peat block slipping down more comfortably onto its bed of hot ash. Nola, almost uncomprehending of what Seamus had just said, blinked in disbelief.

'Feck, I need a drink,' said Daedio.

'We all do,' Seamus replied. 'I'll fetch the jug.'

Nola threw the knitting to one side and, pulling a handkerchief from her apron, wiped her eyes and blew her nose with some force, regaining her composure.

Seamus returned from the scullery with a jug of his own poteen. They made it in a still they kept in the old cottage. Every so often, when the wind blew in the wrong direction, the Garda from the village would sniff the unmistakeable whiff of the illegal brew and come marching up the hill. But the dogs and the view always gave them fair warning and Seamus and Pete could have the still out of the old cottage and hidden in a hayrick in the field before the Garda had picked themselves up out of whichever bog hole they'd invariably have fallen into on their way up.

Seamus half filled the mugs and handed one to Nola. ''Tis the best yet, this one, don't you think?'

Nola made no comment, distracted, her thoughts racing ahead.

As Seamus poured, he talked. 'As I see it, he has two choices, now that there will be no Sarah waiting for him. Brendan was in Paddy's when the telegram arrived and he will be telling Bee tonight what the news is and she will be telling Sarah. God alone knows what that will do. The farm will make more this year than last, so if Michael wants to stay, there is money here for him, but we would have to let Pete go.'

Daedio glanced up at Seamus. This was not such good news. Pete had been with them for many years and was as good as part of the family.

'Or he will do what they are all doing and go to Liverpool, or if he has enough money, to America, to seek his fortune. Whichever one it is, it doesn't matter, Nola. You will be seeing him soon and that's all that matters, for now. Take your drink, go on. You've had a shock.' He wrapped Nola's warm, plump fingers around the mug.

Their eyes met and spoke the messages of a couple who understood each other's thoughts.

'Aye, a nice one that he's coming home,' Nola said. 'Despite the disappointment waiting for him, at least we are still here. But, Seamus, his heart will be broken when he finds Sarah already married.' Her eyes filled with fresh tears at the thought of the pain this would cause her son.

'Stop fretting and drink.'

Nola sipped on the poteen and screwed up her eyes as it slipped down. The first sip was always the worst. She tutted impatiently. 'God help Sarah McGuffey if I ever see her. My words alone will cut her to shreds.'

'Shush,' said Seamus. 'You can't be blaming Sarah, 'twill all be down to her daddy, he will have been the one to be marrying her off. It's Jay Maughan she is marrying. McGuffey will have earned himself a fine bride price from the Maughans. Buying brides and stealing children, 'tis what the Maughans do best. 'Twill have had nothing to do with Sarah, of that I'm sure.'

Daedio snorted. He was reminded of Bridget's words and felt a cold shiver run down his spine. He opened his eyes a little wider and looked a little harder, trying to locate the ghost of Annie, but she was nowhere to be seen. The temperature remained warm; there was no unexplainable breeze in front of the fire, no stirrings in the air. She wasn't there to hear the news and his heart sank. He almost jumped out of his skin when Nola spoke.

'He should have stuck to Rosie O'Hara. If it hadn't been for Sarah, he would have made something of that and wouldn't that have been a grand thing, a Malone marrying a school-teacher? Instead, he fell for the daughter of a fisherman, and the worst one of the lot at that.'

Seamus squeezed his wife's shoulders as he leant back against the chair. Removing his cap, he ran his hand over his head and across his face and eyes as he let out a deep sigh. He felt weary and after only half a mug, the poteen and the fire were already having an effect. 'Pete will be here in a minute. Let's lift our pots to Michael.'

'To Michael and a safe journey home,' said Daedio.

Seamus and Nola downed their drinks in unison as the back door opened and Pete let a blast of cold air run down the room.

They went about their usual routine: Seamus banked up the fire, Nola placed the supper on the table and Pete washed his hands at the scullery sink. When he came back in to stand at the fire and warm his backside next to Seamus, Daedio and Seamus told him the news. Nola dished out huge ladles of lamb stew from a tureen into their bowls. For Daedio, who had only two teeth left to speak of, she chopped and mashed up the meat. The flames of the peat fire roared and chased up the chimney and the room was cosy as the night drew down and the rain picked up and beat against the door. On the long, scrubbed table sat a fresh jug of porter. Two candles burnt fiercely in hurricane lamps, one at each end, and as Nola bustled by with the bowls of stew held aloft, both flames dipped a respectful curtsey to the matriarch of the house.

'Come on, eat, would ye,' she said as she smiled up at her husband and set the bowls on the table. The imminence of Michael's return was warming her heart.

'Shall I be cutting the bread?' said Pete, noticing the loaf on the board as he moved from the fire, rubbing his hands together, his mouth almost watering at the sight and smell of the food.

While the men began to dip their bread in the gravy and tuck in to the stew, Nola sat on the side of the truckle bed to feed Daedio his mashed-up supper.

'How much did you pay for the pig feed?' Daedio asked as he turned his head to Seamus, having swallowed his first mouthful while Nola blew on the second to cool it. 'Your wife tried to kill me today,' he added as the lamb rolled over his gums.

'Oh shush,' said Nola. 'He's talking about the potion that I asked Bridget for. Sure, 'tis the only thing keeping you alive.'

Daedio looked at Seamus and Pete, his rheumy eyes brimming with mirth. 'Aye, because it won't be your cooking and that's a fact.'

And the night passed in much the same way it did most nights in the Malone house, filled with warmth and laughter.

Two hours later, Pete was the first to move, having finished his game of cards with Seamus. 'I'm away to my bed,' he said as he stood and picked up one of the hurricane lamps. 'I'll unpack the feed after I've milked in the morning.'

'Aye, I'll be up to the pigs with ye,' said Seamus as he stood and placed the cards back into the press drawer.

'When do you think Michael will be arriving?' Pete asked, and they all knew why he was asking. He was wondering for how long he had a roof over his head and a wage in his pocket.

Nola was sitting in the rocking chair in front of the fire, knitting. 'Don't you be worrying, Pete,' she said. 'We have no idea what Michael's plans will be. He may not even be staying here, once he knows Sarah is to be married to Jay Maughan. He could be on his way up the hill right now, or in a week, or a month even, if he finds work in Liverpool. Who knows.' She looked up at him as he made his way to the door. 'Goodnight now,' she said.

'Night, Nola. See ye in the morning, God willing. Are ye away to Mass?'

'I'm not. Not tomorrow. If my son comes home, I want to be here for him, so expect Father Jerry to be running up the hill and giving out to me by the afternoon. We all know 'tis the only house he gets a good bite of pie at when he arrives, so any excuse, eh? He may have Teresa, but try as she might, she can't beat my creamy chicken pie, and nor is her pastry made using my butter.'

Pete smiled. 'Lord knows how the man survives with that tea-drinking scold as a housekeeper,' he said as the door closed behind him.

Seamus moved over to sit on the settle near to his wife. At almost fifty-five years of age and having worked on the farm since he was a boy, alongside his own granddaddy, he felt as though for the first time the rain was giving him the rheumatics.

He looked down at Daedio, who was now fast asleep, replete with the best lamb stew he could be served, and he saw his future. The Malone men were renowned for making old bones. 'One day, that'll be me,' he said to Nola.

She laughed and shook her head. 'You will never have the temper or the cheek of that old maggot, that's for sure. But one thing's certain, it won't be me. My lot are lucky to ever make three-score years. 'Tis not many more years I have before God calls me, and I want to see my youngest son happy and settled before I go.'

'Don't be talking like that,' said Seamus. 'I won't be having it. Everyone who stays up here on this hill lives a long life. Why do we need to go to heaven when we have it right here? We live in heaven, sure we do.'

He stood and, straightening his back, placed his hands in his pockets. His father didn't stir on the mattress. Having been made comfortable, he was out for the night.

'Look, let's to bed,' Seamus said. 'There's nothing we can do or decide until the man himself gets here.'

Nola rose and carried the mugs to the sink. '"Man"!' she snorted. 'He was just a boy when he left here.' She turned to examine the table that she had already laid for the breakfast. The flour was in the bowl, ready to be made into bread at first light.

'Anyway,' said Seamus, 'if he is on his way, I reckon we'd best be making the most of the privacy before he does arrive.'

Nola looked up at him and the twinkle in his eye was unmistakeable. He winked at her.

'They should have christened you Shameless Malone, not Seamus,' she said as she grinned back at him.

She extinguished the candles in the sconces and picked up

the hurricane lamp from the table and set it on the windowsill. 'In case he comes home tonight,' she said. 'Who knows when he sent that telegram. It could have been a week ago. I don't have the same faith in Mrs Doyle's famous telex machine that everyone else has. Keep the jug with the rest of the porter on the table and cut some cheese to leave on the side with the bread, just in case. No lad of mine will arrive home from the war to an empty table.'

When a plate had been laid, covered in a cloth, and a new candle put in the window, Nola turned to her husband. 'Come on then, let's see how much of you is talk and how much is action.'

Seamus slapped her rotund backside, the width of his hand covering the white and floury imprints of her own, and she giggled in exactly the same way she had on their wedding night, many years before.

As the door closed, neither saw the eyes of Daedio Malone open as he turned his head towards the fire and the empty rocking chair. He heard a sigh, a breath, a smile.

'Is that you, Annie?' he whispered to his long-departed wife.

'It is, Daedio. I'm here, I'm with you,' she replied.

'Did you hear that, Annie?' he asked.

'I did that. Isn't it just the best news,' she replied. 'Our Michael is coming home.'

Daedio Malone smiled. A lone tear left the corner of his eye and travelled down his cheek.

'He is, and he's safe and well. Shona didn't curse him and he's coming home. He's been spared, God bless him. I'll wait for him awhile. I'll get him sorted and settled first. There's things to do, you know that, and then I'll be coming to join ye, Annie.'

The chair moved. 'I'll be here, but Michael, he will need you for a while yet. You must wait for Shona to go first, Daedio – you will know when it's time. You will see me then. Don't you worry, I'll come for you myself, I'll bring you across. You won't be alone,' she whispered back to him as he closed his eyes.

And the rocking of her old wooden chair matched the rhythm of his heartbeat as he melted back down through the folds of sleep.

Chapter 4

Bee Cosgrove was grateful the rain was easing. She hated arriving soaked through for her evening shift at Paddy's bar and always made an effort to look presentable. It was a job she needed, being a widow and with a child to raise, and she would always be thankful to Paddy and Josie Devlin, two of the kindest people in Tarabeg. They'd offered it to her within days of her fisherman husband Rory drowning six years ago; Ciaran had been a babe in arms and it hurt her to have to leave him with Rory's parents on the nights she worked at Paddy's, but he was used to it, and she had no choice.

As she hurried along the coast road towards the village, she spotted Seamus Malone turning his horse and cart into the boreen up to Tarabeg Hill. She raised her hand in greeting, but he didn't stop to chat, which was unusual. He would often give her news of letters from Michael for her to pass on to Sarah, but today he appeared to be in a hurry.

There had been no word from Michael for weeks and Sarah had been fretting. Just that morning she had mentioned it again. 'The war is done and I've heard nothing,' she had wailed. 'He promised me he would be back as soon as it was over.'

Kevin McGuffey was off on a smuggling trip and had been gone for days, so Bee had been in the McGuffey kitchen with Sarah and Angela, as she was every morning he was away. Even though it was June and the cottage was warm, the fire had been lit, ready for cooking and bread baking. They were sitting around the rough wooden table that McGuffey had made from timbers off a Spanish galleon that had risen from its grave and been washed up in Blacksod Bay, or so Angela had been told.

Sarah had just come back in. She'd been outside since early morning, weaving heather into the lobster pots that she sold for her living. At night she stored her day's work in the turf shed so that the fishermen could take what pots they needed when they set out at dawn. They left payment in money, potatoes, eggs, fresh warm milk or whatever else was available.

Bee was nursing her mug of tea as her sister kneaded the bread. The sun fell in through the front door and captured the three of them in a pillar of bright smoky light. Sarah, in an act of dramatic exasperation, sat on a stool and placed her forehead on her folded arms on the table and groaned. 'Why hasn't Michael been in touch? He should be here by now. Have I not waited long enough?'

Bee's heart contracted in sympathy as she looked down at the fan of her niece's hair; it changed colour according to the light, and this morning, spread out across her shoulders, it glinted on a spectrum of red to pale gold. Sarah was the closest to a daughter Bee would ever have. Ciaran was already in Mr O'Dowd's class at the school and though Bee was only just thirty, she knew there would be no more children for her.

'I'll ask Paddy and Josie when I go to work tonight, have they seen Seamus for the latest news, or heard anything,' she said.

Sarah's head shot up. 'Will you? Please, Bee,' she pleaded, her eyes bright with hope.

'I will that, 'tis easy enough. God in heaven, I ask after Michael so often, there will be some thinking I have an eye to him myself. It's the end of June, Sarah – have patience. He won't be long, your knight in shining army uniform. He will be here soon enough.'

Angela had laughed, something she only did when Kevin McGuffey was away on his fishing or smuggling trips. And as Bee often thanked God, he was away more often than he was home.

Bee heard the news of Michael's impending return before she had even reached Paddy's bar. She was greeted on the road by Keeva, who was on her way home from the post office.

'God, what a day, the excitement we've had,' she shouted as she trotted over to meet Bee. 'We had a telegram, so we did. But not with bad news, for a change.'

'Really?' said Bee, casting an anxious glance up the road towards the bar. She had spent longer than she should have with Angela and Sarah and didn't want to be late.

''Twas from Michael Malone – he's coming home.'

Keeva suddenly had Bee's attention. She turned quickly, her focus unwavering. 'Did he say when?' She was slightly too sharp in her questioning and Keeva looked mildly surprised.

'No, but Mrs Doyle reckons it won't be long, though if he finds work in Liverpool on the way, sure, it could be months. They've had the VE Day celebrations in England and they've all been demobbed.' She rolled her eyes. 'We all remember Michael, though – it could be any day.'

Bee blessed herself. Michael had survived and was out of danger. The war really was over. 'Thank God,' she said.

The church bells rang out for the Angelus Mass, as if confirming Keeva's words that they had something to rejoice about. 'Do we have time for Mass?' Bee said, looking up towards the Sacred Heart.

'Aye, I was thinking the same.' Keeva nodded. 'Someone has to pray for Michael Malone – he's going to need it. He is the only one to return alive and there are some not happy about him fighting for the English.'

'Come on, then. There's Miss O'Hara and Teresa, let's follow them in. Josie won't mind me being late if it's because I was at Mass.'

Bee needn't have worried; the church was packed. She filled her lungs with the smell of stale holy smoke as she dipped her knee and bent her head to the cross on the altar. She had no need to explain anything to Josie, given that she was sitting in the pew next to her. 'Will Paddy be all right?' she asked as she took her place.

'Sure, there's only a few in the bar yet. He'll be fine. Have you heard the news?' Josie whispered back.

'I have. Keeva told me. I met her on the road.'

'Well, good thing you came then,' said Josie. 'If anyone will be needing prayers right now, 'twill be the Malones.'

Bee wanted to ask how often people had prayed for her sister and her niece and the life they led at the hands of Kevin McGuffey, but with a blink of her eyes she banished the uncharitable thought as she blessed herself and looked about the church.

Mrs O'Doyle was sitting near the front next to Philomena O'Donnell, heads together, whispering. John O'Donnell was on the other side and the women from the village were scattered around. A hush fell and Father Jerry looked sombre as he took his place at the altar. Bee swallowed down her guilt as she met his eye. She had been to confession on Sunday. Father Jerry was the only man in Tarabeg who knew her secret. He held her gaze, his eyes mildly accusing. Bee was able to look away first as, with the rest of the congregation, she fell to her knees and buried her head in her hands. Her guilt was hidden, for now. She had her own soul to pray for, and she had been warned that she would need to pray and suffer penance every day for as long as she continued to live out her deepest sin.

By the time Bee got to the bar and hung up her shawl, the place had filled with the regulars. Captain Bob was sitting at the window table talking to Mr O'Dowd, who was shuffling a pack of cards. She was surprised to see Jay Maughan, standing with the farmhands and some of the fishermen. Paddy was sitting with Mr O'Dowd and Captain Bob and she threw him a look, but he sent back a shrug in response. She frowned, but she also understood: it was a difficult path for Paddy to tread. If he didn't let Maughan in, he would simply help himself to the drink in the yard when they were away to their beds. Maughan could not survive without drink. She was surprised, too, to see Brendan O'Kelly sitting with Paddy. She knew he called in of an afternoon to do his crossword and gather the local news, but though he was single, he was not one for carousing and was always in his own home at night. He was the first to walk over to her and ask for a drink.

'How is your sister?' he asked as she opened the tap on the barrel. 'And Sarah?'

Bee looked up and gave him a curious half smile. 'They are well enough, thank you, Brendan.'

'I don't know if you have heard what McGuffey is up to,' he said as she turned to face him.

Bee, feeling both perplexed and fearful, handed him his drink and shook her head. Any conversation in which Kevin McGuffey featured was bad news. She was desperate to save her sister from her monster of a husband and had already begun hatching a plan, so fearful was she that one day he would do something to Angela or her niece that even Bridget McAndrew couldn't fix.

'Well, the talk is that he's to be marrying Sarah to Maughan soon.' Brendan inclined his head ever so slightly in the direction of Jay Maughan and the fishermen standing around him.

Bee purposely didn't move a muscle, though her heart was thumping as if it might explode at any moment. Jay Maughan – that tinker! She didn't need to look over at him to conjure his image in her head. The olive complexion darkened from the dirt he seemingly never washed off; the tendrils of black hair that stuck out from under his frayed and oversized hat; the black fingernails. And creepiest of all, the eyes – black as night, set wide apart and always on the alert, always darting, watching, waiting.

Bee forced herself back into the moment, made herself focus on Brendan, who had dropped his voice as he continued.

'I'm so sorry to have to be the one to tell you this, Bee, and sure as anything I hope it isn't going to happen. But we all know what McGuffey is like when he gets the wind up him. If I were you, I'd be having a word with your sister to see what's to be done. I doubt you have much time to procrastinate.' He leant forward towards the barrel. 'Maybe you have family

Sarah could go and stay with? To get her away for a while. I'm doubting a tinker's life is what Angela has in mind for her only daughter.'

Bee took Brendan's money into her outstretched hand and said nothing. She did not discuss family with people she had known all of her life, never mind with a man who had not long arrived in the village. It was a survival technique. Life was hard for both her and Angela – herself tragically widowed at a young age, and Angela married to a man who'd become a monster from the day he realised he wouldn't be getting a son to make his life easier.

As Brendan took his change, his eyes met hers and held on; there was no mistaking his sincerity. 'Bee, you need to do something within hours, not days. Maughan is in no doubt that it's all arranged and happening very soon. If I were you, and sure, I'm not telling you what to do, I would go and see your sister as soon as you can.'

Bee's stomach lurched. Brendan was not from the country. He didn't dramatise things for sport, the way the locals did to alleviate their boredom. His common sense and his knowledge of the law made him a pillar of the community and a man to be listened to. Even if Bee found discussing her family difficult, her survival instinct told her to take note. If she ignored his advice, it might be at her own peril. 'I understand,' she said.

'Will you need help?' Brendan asked as he glanced over his shoulder.

'Come on, Brendan, 'tis your round at the cards next.' Mr O'Dowd was shuffling a pack of very worn playing cards.

'I'm coming now.' He turned to face Bee, who had her answer.

'No, we will manage just fine, thank you.' She quickly realised that her tone had sounded brusque, more so in the face
of his kindness. 'I mean that. Thank you.'

Both knew it would be futile to try and talk about Sarah's
rights. In Tarabeg, it was the men of the community who had
the power: the husbands, the fathers, and the priest. The men
of the village owned the property, the homes, farms, boats and
businesses; men were the employers, made the decisions and
occupied all the leadership roles. Even Brendan, concerned
though he was, being the local magistrate, knew and understood this. As a young woman of nearly twenty-one, Sarah had
no rights to speak of.

Sarah had spent the rest of the afternoon after Bee had left
them restlessly pacing up and down outside their cottage,
moving from the turf shed to the bench outside the front door
to work depending on the rain. The cottage stood on the top
of the escarpment, its gable end facing the ocean, buffeted by
the strong winds and fierce Atlantic storms. She couldn't stop
thinking about Michael, replaying their brief time together,
mulling over the sweet words they'd exchanged in the dozens
of letters that had passed between them. Angela appeared in
the doorway, just as the rain let up. 'Here, let's sit on the bench
while we have the chance before the rain starts again.' She held
out a pot that Sarah knew would be filled with hot sweet tea.
'I'll just put this last lobster pot in the turf shed,' Sarah said as
she picked up a perfectly crafted pot. Angela sank down onto
the bench and watched her daughter as she walked away, her
head held high, her shoulders straight, her golden red hair, no
longer worn in two girlish plaits, but hanging in a long pony's

tail, swinging across her straight back. Angela felt a mixture of pride and despair. Her daughter had grown from a girl to a woman whilst waiting for a man on the back of a promise and in the meantime, she had suffered the jibes from those that knew and had taunted her about Michael and the traitor he was to be fighting for the English.

Sarah returned and flopped, as she always did – Sarah never did anything with any patience, other than weave her pots – onto the bench and took the tea with a smile. 'Oh, Mammy, I drive you to distraction, do I not?' Angela smiled, placed her arm around Sarah's shoulders, pulled her in towards her, kissed the top of her head and for a moment, inhaled the familiar smell of her hair. 'No, you do not. 'Tis everyone else who does that.'

'Who?' asked Sarah, as she sat up abruptly and looked at her mother with a concerned face.

'All those that give you a hard time about Michael, that's who. I'd take the lot of them and bang their bleeding heads together so I would.' Sarah stared down into the steaming mug. What little blue sky was above them, was disappearing as fast as it had arrived. 'Oh, Mammy, it's not been that bad.' She lifted her mug and drank in order to hide her eyes from Angela's inscrutable gaze. 'Oh yes it has. If Bee had heard them, she would have ripped the tongues from their mouths. Not one has said a word to her in the pub, the little bastards kept it all for you.' 'They were only kids, Mammy, the lads around here, they have nothing else to talk about.' 'That may be, but not one of them would go and fight in a war, big babies, and they think taunting you made men of them, with all their threats about what they would be doing to Michael when he returned, Jesus, he'll squash the lot of them with his little finger when he hears, so he will.' Sarah let out a huge sigh, 'Mammy, when is Daddy back?' The clouds had done their work, the light faded as they wiped out the last blue blaze of sky. Seagulls screeched as they flew clear from a golden eagle as it headed back in to the mountainside with a large fish hanging precariously from its hooked beak. Angela sipped at her tea. 'I'm not sure.' 'Will it be before Michael comes home?' Angela turned to her daughter and her eyes filled with tears. She wanted to say something, anything that would make Sarah's face light up. Make her jump up from the bench and spin around with the exuberance that had always been hers. It had amazed both Angela and Bee, that a daughter who suffered, as Angela often did, at the hands of McGuffey, should have retained such a strong spirit within. She put her arm back around her daughter and pulled her to her once more. 'I'm hoping so. You know Sarah, I think I can feel Michael is close, can you?' Sarah nodded her head and whispered, 'I can Mammy, I can.' They both lifted their heads and looked out towards the ocean. 'Hurry up Michael, she's waiting,' said Angela and mother and daughter sat until the rain came, each in silent prayer, willing Michael home.

Five hours after her conversation with Brendan O'Kelly, Bee hurried back home. She smiled when she saw the light on inside her cottage, forever grateful that she lived up her own boreen, tucked into the side of the mountain just where it reached the shore. There were no windows at the rear of her cottage, no view, but when she opened her front door each morning, the ocean spread out before her like a painted canvas. Despite her tiptoeing around the side, the door opened before she reached it. She stepped inside and smiled up at the man waiting for her – Captain Bob from Ballycroy. He had done what he always did, left Paddy's long before she finished work and made his way to her cottage, stoked up the fire, poured her porter, lit the lamps, turned back the bed and waited.

'My little Bee,' he said as she fell into his arms.

He visited Tarabeg one night a week, and if he missed a week, she couldn't settle until he returned. He was her secret, her refuge, her sin. The man whose weekly attentions kept her sane and able to deal with the miserable lives of her sister and niece. She saved the money he gave her each week and from that put shoes on Ciaran to walk to school.

Captain Bob smelt of the warm tobacco he used in the pipe that lived in the top pocket of his jacket. As she laid her lips on his, his kiss tasted fresh, of the briny sea, and seductive, from the whiskey he had drunk at Paddy's.

His tongue parted her lips; he was as desperate as she was to hold her naked body against his in the few illicit, guilty hours they had together. Hungrily, he removed the ribbon at the back of her hair and combed his fingers through her auburn waves as they tumbled down her back.

She pulled away, breathless, and his twinkly blue eyes locked onto hers.

'What? What is it, little Bee?' he asked, a frown forming on his weather-beaten brow. 'You haven't been yourself tonight. Something's bothering you, I could tell.'

Her hand rose and pushed away one of his white, sun-bleached curls, then smoothed down his salt and pepper speck-led moustache and beard, ruffled from the intensity of their kiss. 'It's Michael,' she said. 'He's coming home, for Sarah.'

Captain Bob was one of the most popular fishermen on the west coast. He had resisted all calls to use his hooker to smuggle goods around to the North and as a result his honesty was renowned and most fishermen told him most things. He straightened up and looked down at Bee. He cast a longing glance towards the bed, but Bee's eyes flashed with concern – he would have to tell her now. He kissed her nose first.

'Bee, I heard today that McGuffey is on his way back round from the North. He's to be marrying Sarah to Maughan, maybe tomorrow. Michael may be too late.'

Captain Bob rarely arrived at the bar until after Bee had begun work, barely spoke a word to her as she went about her business, and left long before she was due to finish. On the first night, he had followed her home, but now he simply wended his way out of the village, down the coast road and on to her cottage, guided by the moon. The regulars in the pub believed he was heading back to his boat and sailing around to Ballycroy in the dark. The waters and the guiding stars were well known to the locals; in fair weather, anyone could sail across to the islands or around the coast without hazard.

'Why do you think he comes all the way here, to my bar for a drink?' Paddy had once asked.

'He's a man of substance, a man with intelligence,' Mr O'Dowd had replied. ''Tis the good company and the craic he comes here for.'

No one had ever suspected the real reason.

Bee had wanted to ask him if he had a wife, but she never did. She respected the privacy of others as much as she coveted it for herself. Besides, the rules of love had died with her Rory. She didn't want to forget their courtship, replace it with another. Captain Bob had accepted Bee as she was and she him. It was as if each meeting was both their first and their last, no questions asked of either. Nothing given, nothing taken away.

He was a good man, a quiet man, and the flipping of her heart at the sight of him each week told her she was lost to him. But only she would know. He might be generous and gentle, but Bee was no fool. He had a wife and children along the coast, of that she was sure.

She slipped his jacket from his shoulders. 'Brendan told me about Maughan. 'Tis a shocking thing McGuffey is doing, and Michael so nearly home. Sarah will be wretched, so she will.' She sighed. 'I have need of a favour from you.'

They had a little time for the two of them before she had to ask him the biggest favour she'd ever had to ask of anyone. She met his lips with her own. He pulled back, gave her one more long, searching look. 'Good, I want to help you,' he said, with no hint of caution in his voice, and that was the last he spoke for some minutes, while he undid the buttons on the front of her dress, one by one, all the while gazing at her as though he had never seen her before.

'Now?' he asked, and despite the urgency of the situation and the favour she had to ask of him, a smile lifted the corner of her lips as she saw that lust had replaced concern in his eyes. He undid the last button on her dress and it slid to the floor.

'Now,' she said.

'You have a wife, don't you?' she asked him a while later, as he lay on her mattress, admiring her while she rose to fetch him the porter he often brought and kept at her house for them to share.

He sat up and, leaning on one elbow, regarded her through eyes already anticipating her reaction to the honest answer he would give. This was a new turn in their relationship, the first time she had enquired. He would not lie to her. Honesty was the preserve of honourable men and, despite his many shortcomings, the one thing he always strove to be with Bee was honest. He had never intended to lie to her, even at the start.

'Aye, I do. And four children, much older than your Ciaran.'

Her hand never faltered as she filled his mug.

He noticed. 'Does that bother you?'

She looked up from the table and smiled. 'Bother me? No. Not at all. But it does mean I would like to ask another question. Can I?'

He smiled back and held out his hand for the mug she carried over to him. Then she settled on the side of the bed, tucking her long white linen slip beneath the bend in her knees.

'Aye, fire away.' He leant forward and pushed back the hair that had fallen across her face.

In every way, she was as different from his wife as it was possible to be. There was a new air of intimacy between them. They had made love many times, but talking, beyond what was necessary, this was new. They spent only the one night a week together and much of that was taken up with lovemaking and sleeping. Conversations had been few, but he loved that about Bee, loved that she never bombarded him with words. She understood that a sea captain's life was not built on chatter, that some adjustment was required when he returned to land. His wife and family knew nothing about his illicit stopovers before his morning returns home to Ballycroy.

Bee took a sip of her drink before she spoke. 'If you are married, why are you here in my bed?' She was curious to hear his answer. Was she fishing for compliments? The thought ran through her mind, as it did his. She possibly was. She felt shallow, embarrassed.

'Oh, Bee.' There was a hint of exasperation in his voice. 'Oh, Bee, my lovely Bee, do you miss the words of praise and admiration your Rory would have lavished on you?'

Unexpectedly, her eyes filled with tears. 'I do, aye, but that's not why I'm asking. I'm just genuinely curious because I know that if my Rory were still alive, you wouldn't be here. I would never have looked twice at you if I still had my Rory. He was everything to me, him and our boy, so there would have been no need. It works both ways, doesn't it?'

She looked up and wiped her eyes and nose with the back of her hand. She had no idea why she was crying, but he had touched a nerve. Being on her own had made her strong, tough, tougher than she ever wanted to be. It was how it had to be, to stop her from falling apart. To deal with the challenges of mothering her boy, coping as a widow. To keep the money coming in, to feed and clothe them both and to help with Angela and Sarah and Rory's parents. What the hell would have happened to them all if she hadn't turned herself into a fighter and a worker? The thought of the orphanage for Ciaran and the convent where she would have been sent to work was too terrifying. She turned to face him and her mouth fell open at his reply.

'Because, Bee, you are the strongest woman I have ever met in my life, and the saddest and the most loving, and you are the best mother I have ever known. You are all the things my wife isn't. It was your sadness about Rory that drew me to you, because if I ever go down, I would like to leave someone who would care that I had gone, and as it stands, there is no one. It is your passion, your ability to love that has ensnared me. I have no one who would even notice whether or not I returned home.'

Bee's heart went out to him. 'But your wife…?'

'My wife cares nothing. My wife would rejoice. I was a means to an end, the path out of a life she hated. She was a sorry wretch when I met her and I wanted to help, to give her a better life, but I was a fool. I thought that maybe, in return for my affection, she might also come to love me, but she has never changed since the day she walked into my house. My wife is only interested in money. She looks to my hand, not my heart.'

Bee felt her own heart tighten. He was the gentlest of men. The kindest of men. He was her secret. 'I think that's what I am doing instead,' she replied, before she had a chance to check herself. 'I think I am falling in love with you a little more each day.'

He didn't look surprised at her confession, just ran his fingers though her hair. 'And me you. But we both know…'

Pulling her hand to his mouth, he kissed the back of her fingers and slipped the tip of one between his lips. The rest didn't need to be put into words. There was no divorce for Catholics. She would be condemned to hell and back again for remarrying a man who already had a living wife, even if they were divorced. There would be some who would have a great deal to say, who would demand she live with Rory's memory for her everlasting earthly comfort. It would be just as bad for him. He was a married man and he would never survive the scandal. He was too decent and honest. And besides, McGuffey would never allow it, whether it was his business or not. If there was anything in Captain Bob's past to cause trouble with, McGuffey would track it down and do his worst.

Bee had placed her mug on the floor and she lay down on the mattress next to him. The straw crackled beneath her. 'There's nothing to be done, is there?'

She could feel his heart beating under the flat of her palm, heard his deep sigh. He was thinking. He had a way of weighing up every word before he spoke and she loved that about him. His caution, how every word could be trusted.

'I think there might be,' he said. 'There are places we could go where no one knows us.'

She lifted her face to his. 'Where? America? I wouldn't want to go that far. It would kill Rory's parents, never seeing the boy.'

'Well, Liverpool is a great seaport. There's always Liverpool. No one would know us there.'

Bee rolled over onto her back. She knew there would be no happy ending to this conversation. She had thought she could never leave Tarabeg, the place she and her Rory had been born and raised. They were woven into the tapestry of this, the most rural part of Ireland. 'There's Angela – I cannot leave her to suffer at the hands of that man. She needs me.'

Captain Bob slipped his arm around her shoulders and pulled her into him. 'One day things will change and we will both know an opportunity has arrived. Not least, Bee, because we are both wanting it. And just this here, you and me talking about it like this – we haven't only confessed our feelings to each other, God will have heard us, we've told him too, and it will move God's hand. He will help us. Something will give and, you know, I don't think it will be that long. I want my future to be with you. It has been burning into me. You, little Bee, you are my life and the only woman I think about. We have to find a way.'

Bee felt the heat of his body warming hers and wanted for them both to lie there for ever. His declaration of a future together, however tenuous, had brought unexpected pleasure. But as she reached up and stroked his beard, the image of Sarah flashed into her mind.

'Bob, God's hand has moved in a way we could not have imagined. Sarah needs us. We have to make a plan, we have to get her away from here, to somewhere, anywhere, and we have to do it soon. Michael may not be home for weeks. We have to save Sarah from Maughan and her father. And then maybe one day she and Michael can marry. But all that matters now is getting her away.'

Chapter 5

Jay Maughan left Paddy's and hurried across the road to where he and Shona had made camp for the night, up against the wall of the Sacred Heart and under the trees for shelter. It was church land, Shona refusing to camp on the adjacent wasteland that ran down to the Taramore river, the land her family had been evicted from by Daedio all those years ago. That was long before Jay was born, back when Shona's grandmother was still alive. Daedio Malone had bought the land from Lord Carter and evicted the entire Maughan family, under the cover of night, using guns and mad dogs while the officers from the Garda stood by smiling. But he had done nothing with the seven acres since, and it lay empty still, taunting Shona. The salmon-rich river that coursed through the land didn't belong to Daedio, and Jay would normally have made straight for it, taking his fill of the fish through the summer months. But his grandmother would not go near it, would not cross Daedio's land.

The light of the fire guided Jay to the camp, that and the iridescent glow of Shona's long white hair glinting through the dark.

'Was that Michael Malone's footsteps?' she asked as he took his place on the rush mat on the opposite side of the fire.

He looked over his shoulder and across to the distant amber lights of Paddy's bar. It was impossible to hear anyone's footsteps from where they were camped. But Shona was able to smell a Malone long before they came into view, a gift bestowed on her by her grandmother on her deathbed. She'd been taught to cast curses too, curses that terrified everyone from Donegal to Kerry. The gift of revenge and a long life in which to extract it. For Shona was at least as old as Daedio and she was waiting for him to die first, would not go herself before she had restored the land to Jay.

'No, 'twas not,' he said. 'But there was news – he is coming home. I thought you told me he would be sorted, in the war. That he wouldn't be coming back again once he left. You told me he would be dead. He's the only fecker from around here who has come home.'

Jay spat into the fire and Shona's eyes met his. She smiled. Her skills were undiminished. She could hear Michael Malone's footsteps; he was on his way, he was close.

'Are you questioning my powers, Jay?' She had stopped stirring the stew and held his gaze.

Jay was the first to turn away. He picked up one of the sticks of kindling he'd collected earlier and threw it onto the fire. The angry flames shot up as they devoured it.

'Don't you ever doubt my hatred for the Malones.' Shona's voice was low but loaded with meaning. Jay crossed his legs and shifted uncomfortably on the rush mat as he placed his hands over his knees. He deliberately dipped his head and the brim of his cap so that she couldn't see his eyes.

'Don't you dare doubt me.'

He couldn't see her, but he knew her expression by the tone of her voice.

'As long as I live, I will not forget the sound of my grandmother's wails. I still hear her sometimes – she brings it back to me, to remind me what it is I have to do. Three generations had lived on that land, since the time of the famine.' She spat her baccy through her black teeth and into the fire. The sound of hissing coals filled the air. 'The spells I cast for Nola and Seamus Malone to be deserted by their children have worked well,' she said with a throaty laugh. 'Every one of them except Michael has flown to America and not returned.'

'But not well enough,' said Jay, regaining his courage and lifting his gaze from the fire. 'Why hasn't it worked with Michael? Why is he back? If he had left for good like the others, Nola and Seamus would have given up on the farm. Maybe followed their kids to America. Daedio would never have kept the land if there was no one here to help them. What good would it have been to him?' He poked another stick into the fire and the sparks rose.

Shona had resumed stirring the rabbit stew in the black iron cauldron. The long curls and wisps of her white hair seemed to merge with the rising smoke and steam and it was difficult to distinguish one from the other.

'What good is it now? They have never moved from the farm. Look at it!' She pointed the dripping ladle down towards the land below them. 'It has stood empty since the day he bought it.' Her eyes narrowed, and venom curled on her grey and twisted lips. 'Daedio bought it to banish the Maughans. It didn't work and I will not leave my mortal body until we have it back.'

She thrust the ladle back into the cauldron. 'My spell, it has weakened over time. Nola was more fertile than I thought. I cast for six, not seven, and six have left her. I have Bridget McAndrew working against me. She's strong around here. I can hear her spells on the wind as soon as you reach Tarabeg. She's not as strong as me, she has no tinker blood in her, but she's always there, meddling. The responsibility to dispose of Michael, it will have to fall to you, Jay. If you want the land back, you must take care of Michael. Once the Malones are here no more, we have a legitimate claim in the magistrate's court. We were the last people to live on that land and we were there for three generations. The Carters cannot deny that, if the Malones abandon it for good and flee from Tarabeg. We just have to get rid of Michael. He needs to be scared away, to follow his brothers across the Atlantic and leave Daedio. Let grief suck the life out of Daedio, which it surely will. He's lost the use of his legs already, because he's terrified of me and what I will do. When he's gone from this earth, as sure as night follows day, Seamus and Nola will run. Seamus won't dare to cross me. I can get my way with him and Nola, and that's a fact. If they ever want to know a day's peace, they will run, but it will only be possible when they're alone. Michael, his blood runs high. Get someone else to sort him, but not you. Let a fool do our work.'

Jay held out his tin dish for the stew. The stared at each other through the smoke. Shona's eyes were black and smouldering, lit with an apparition of the Taramore river and its pebbled shore on the edge of the land where she had lived her entire childhood. He was afraid of his own grandmother and the powers he himself had seen working.

He placed a spoonful of the hot rabbit stew in his mouth and swallowed before he spoke. 'Kevin McGuffey has a grudge against Michael Malone, so he does. He wants to run anyone who fought with the British out of Ireland. Hates the British after what they did to his family in the famine. He's a man who bears a grudge – eats at him, so it does. He speaks of nothing else.'

Shona snorted derisively and poked the fire. 'What's that to do with anything?' she snarled. A scatter of sparks illuminated the old caravan behind them.

'If ye listen, I'll tell ye what it has to do with anything,' Jay shot back angrily, shovelling another spoonful of stew into his mouth. 'I've an arrangement, so I have. An arrangement with McGuffey that will sort Michael Malone for good, without relying on spells and potions.' He raised his eyes under his cap, just enough to see he'd caught Shona's interest, then carried on.

'I'm to marry his daughter,' he said proudly. 'In the next few days, so I am.' This time he did look up, wanting Shona's approval.

He did not get it. 'How did ye swing that – win her in a bet, did ye?' she muttered sarcastically.

Jay ignored her. 'I saw the McGuffey girl running back across the boreens the day Malone was away to fight with the British. It was obvious she'd been with Michael, saying her goodbyes, so I told McGuffey himself. Expected a reward. Such anger he had in his face at the notion of her being close to a traitor fighting for the British – 'twas well worth telling him. So he's offered me the girl now. For a decent price. Needs the money, so he does. And he's to get rid of Malone as part of the deal.'

He began to laugh.

Shona reached out to ladle more stew into his dish. Her

expression remained unchanged. Jay had always been a disappointment to her. A disappointment she hid well. As far as
she was concerned, the wedding couldn't come quick enough.
Her simple and mean-tempered grandson had kept her waiting and working for far too long.

'Get her bedded and with child as soon as you're wed. I need
help, and when the land becomes ours, you will need labour.
If you don't, we will have to keep taking children that are not
ours – and that's getting harder. I cannot be here for ever. I have
to go sometime.'

Jay slurped down the last of the stew. His eyes darted
between his spoon and his grandmother's face, watchful.

'The priest at Newranny will marry us straightaway. I'll
be keeping my hands clean. McGuffey has a gun and he's a
madman. Rumour has it he sent his own brother-in-law to
his death – Rory Cosgrove. Claimed there were too many
fishermen chasing too few fish in Blacksod Bay, so he made
Rory go out way off the headland in a storm. It was McGuffey's
fault he got caught in the squall and drowned and every
fisherman knows it, everyone except his widow. McGuffey is
an evil bastard, born with his heart missing, some say, and I
think they might be right. He will sort it for us.'

Shona smiled as she heaved herself up from the fire and
brushed down her skirt. 'Mad, is he? With a temper? Sounds
just the man for the job. Marry her. You have not been gifted
with the sight. I need a great-grandchild, a girl to pass my gifts
and my own sight on to before I go. Not one of the children
we have taken has had it. We could be looking for ever. We
need our own.'

Jay Maughan turned his gaze up to the Church of the Sacred
Heart and saw a light flickering in the window and he fleetingly

wondered who would be in the church so late at night. ''Twill be done tomorrow,' he said and he suddenly shivered as the wind ran through the branches and overhead an owl hooted its warning.

Rosie O'Hara had been unable to sleep. She had tossed and turned and finally decided to take a walk down to the bridge and back. Thoughts of Michael Malone were running wild in her head and she knew she would have to exhaust herself to be rid of them. Mulling over the past, searching for a reason why Michael had not spoken to her before he left for the war, had preoccupied her over the years. The sadness had not dimmed with time. She could still recall every moment of their brief times together. Long, shy glances at Mass and in the village when they'd passed each other on the main street. And then the dance in the Long Hall of Romance out at Ballycroy – just the one. He had lingered with her at the fair and they had walked home together with the rest of the young people from the village, in the company of Michael's friend, Paddy and Josie's son, Tig Devlin. The dances always took place during a full moon, so that there would be enough light to guide them home along the road. Michael had offered to walk her up to the teacher's house, and there had been a kiss – just the one. She'd been shy and she remembered his gentle sweetness, the nervous tremble of her receiving lips, the reflection of the moon in his eyes and the involuntary gasp in her breath.

Rosie was the only person in Tarabeg who did not know that the very next day Michael had met Sarah, sitting on the bench outside her father's cottage, weaving and repairing her lobster pots. He had not seen her since she was a child at school, always quiet, withdrawn, skinny and sullen, but now he was blinded by her. 'Jesus, was there ever a sight such as she?' he had whispered and that had been it. He never looked at or spoke to Rosie again, and it was just that, the sudden silence and lack of contact, that had kept Rosie wondering, hoping, waiting.

'Evening, Rosie, what are ye doing out at this hour?'

Rosie almost jumped out of her skin. Turning, she saw the moonlit shadow of Father Jerry, making his way back from Paddy's to the presbytery. 'I can't sleep, Father. Thought I would walk to the river and see if the air helped.'

'Ah, well, don't go too close to the church wall, Rosie, the Maughans are camped there.'

They both looked up towards the church; no further explanation was required.

'The lights in Paddy and Josie's are on late,' she said.

'Sure, they are. I was just passing by, taking the air myself, no need now to be telling Teresa that you saw me. She'll just be giving out to me and I know you wouldn't want that.'

Rosie smiled to herself. 'I won't be, Father, don't worry.'

'I heard that Michael Malone was due home, so I stopped to have a drink with Paddy and Josie, who are delighted at the news. Sure, Seamus and Nola are their best friends, they would be. They will all be away to their beds soon enough.'

Rosie swallowed. Her heart was racing, filled with the pleasure of hearing someone speak Michael's name out loud. 'His parents will be overjoyed to have him home,' she said.

Father Jerry scanned her face and understood. Teresa was right. Teresa always was. 'You should be back in your bed yourself, Rosie,' he said.

'Do they know when he's coming home, Father?' She felt

bold for asking the question, but not so bold that she could look him in the eye.

'No, no, we will hear about it soon enough when he is. He will be having things to do, special people he will be wanting to surprise with his return, people who have been waiting and counting down the days.' His reply was spoken with purpose and kindness and, he thought, without ambiguity. He was talking about Sarah; it was his way of trying to warn Rosie, to let her know.

But Rosie was thinking of herself. The lone owl hooted overhead as she raised her head. 'Of course they are, they will be. Thank you, Father.' She half whispered her words as she turned away, back to the teacher's house.

The owl with his amber eyes blinked, turned his head and watched her go.

A smile crossed Rosie's face as tears she had not expected filled her eyes and escaped down her cheeks while she walked. Father Jerry knew, she thought to herself. She was one of the people who had been waiting for this day, and the waiting was almost over.

Kevin McGuffey had sailed in at sunset and entered his own cottage in silence. It was too late to head to the village in search of a drink. He had planned to meet Jay Maughan at Paddy's bar, but the wind had been against him. He had only the one night and would have to make the next tide out with a promised smuggling drop. He had collected the crates from the cave where he stored his goods, loaded up the boat ready for the morning and headed up the escarpment to the cottage. With the money from the bride price Maughan was paying him, and the profit from his smuggling, he would have enough to leave Tarabeg, head north of the border and fight the English on the soil they had stolen.

It was late and he knew that both Angela and Sarah would have been asleep since dark. He objected to candles being burnt unnecessarily, except in the darkest winter months. 'What do I care?' he had muttered to himself as he came up the ridge, and it occurred to him that this might be the last time he climbed this path to the cottage. Once Maughan had married Sarah, he would not be taking Angela to the North with him. He was to become a soldier. He would abandon her here and she could survive or not.

He dropped the latch and listened for their breathing. Walking past his own bed, he pushed aside the curtain to Sarah's bed space at the end of the cottage. He stopped as the curtain fell, the only sound being the slow burn of what remained of the turf fire and the wind rattling the window panes.

Sarah stirred and opened her eyes. What light there was from the fire caught and illuminated her father's bright red hair. He had thrown his hat on the back of the door and his hair hung thick and wild about his head. For the briefest moment, she instinctively felt that something was wrong. Normally he yelled out as soon as he stepped inside, regardless of the time, night or day, but tonight he'd spoken not a word.

Then she heard him move and suddenly smelt the staleness of his breath on her face. She tried to push herself up her bed and onto her pillow, but he shoved her back with force and laid the flat of his hand on her shoulder to pin her down. She yelped in pain as he slammed his free hand over her mouth.

'Shut yer fecking face,' he hissed. 'If you wake your mother, you won't be able to scream, I'll see to that.'

Sarah went limp, tried to focus her attention elsewhere, the way she did with every beating. It helped a bit, sometimes.

He removed his hand from her mouth to test she had understood, then smiled. 'Now, is that not better?'

She didn't reply. Anything she said, any response, would serve as a reason for him to hit her. She had taken enough beatings to know that he meant it.

He pulled the bedcover away and leered at her, yanking at her nightgown, his eyes roving from her breasts to her legs.

Her hands automatically shot down to grab at his. 'What are you doing?' she rasped. This was new – he'd never looked at her body like that before. It was as if he was checking her over, as if she were a cow he wanted to sell. Or worse.

Her response was a stinging slap to her face.

He turned his head, as if listening. He was checking to see if her mother had woken. She hadn't.

'That's the last time you speak,' he hissed again. 'I'll be glad to get rid of ye from this house, ye moaning bitch. I'm marrying you off, so I am. To Jay Maughan. He's giving me a pretty penny.'

Sarah gasped, resisting the urge to scream, which would make things even worse for her. All she could do was clasp her own hand over her mouth and cover her nose, a barrier against the stinking sourness of his breath.

He moved his face closer as he whispered, 'Don't be thinking you're anything special – no one else will have him because of the witch, Shona. He's taking you because he's desperate.'

Her eyes had adjusted to the dark now; through her river of tears she could make out the smirk on his wavering face.

'Kevin, is that you?'

Resentfully, he lifted himself slowly from the bed and with

a warning in his backwards glance he moved around her curtain and into the main room.

Sarah let her breathing steady before she moved her hand. She pulled the bedcovers back up over her for protection and lay motionless, curled up in a ball, her mind racing, panicking, desperate. Jay Maughan! The prospect was too horrible. Five long years waiting for Michael and now she was to be a tinker's woman, travelling the roads in a grubby caravan with that white-haired witch for a mother-in-law. Her flesh went cold. She would not marry him. She would escape and hide somewhere to wait for Michael. She would go to Dublin, to Liverpool if she had to, to search for him. They had pledged themselves to each other – he had to be coming for her. She had already given herself to him, after all; that was their secret, a secret not even her mother or her aunt knew. There would be no one else.

Hearing her father's snores, she propped herself up the better to think. She would not sleep again in that bed – once her father had left on the morning tide, she would be gone. Where or how, she didn't know or even care, but she would not stay another night there, at the mercy of him and the miserable life he planned for her.

Distraught, her head in a jumble, she let her terrified sobs soak into her pillow. 'Michael, where are you? In God's name, where are you?'

Chapter 6

Sarah fell into a fitful sleep just as the cock crowed. She'd heard the door click shut as her father left to catch the morning tide. Male voices had resonated outside and she'd heard the footsteps of two, maybe three men crunch on the shale as they passed her window. They were not voices she recognised, but her father's clandestine activities were not for either her or her mother to enquire about, that much had been made clear. She heard the bray of a donkey and knew that would be the goods arriving. They would either be loaded on the boat or stored in the cave down on the shore that her father had claimed as his own. No one dared trespass near it.

She woke for the second time to her mother calling her name and shaking her shoulder.

'Sarah, are you well? It's not like you to sleep in.'

Sarah blinked her eyes open and saw her mother smiling down at her, completely unaware of what had happened in the night.

'It's a beautiful day, though I don't think 'twill be for long,' said Angela. 'Are you all right, Sarah? You look peaky.'

'I... I'm fine. Did Da sail?'

'He did, hours ago. Bee is coming over this morning, so come on, lazy bones, up! You need to check how many of the pots you made yesterday have gone – if the weather stays fine, you'll be busy today.' Angela moved from Sarah's bed space back into the kitchen.

Sarah sat upright and began to tremble, running over in her mind her father's horrendous news of the night before. Bee was coming... Bee would know what to do. Jay Maughan! She could not marry Jay Maughan. But how could she tell her mammy that was what her father intended for her?

The sound of the front door crashing open interrupted her thoughts, and Bee's voice filled the cottage.

'Holy Mother of God, the rain has finally stopped and the sun is out, but they say it won't be lasting for long, a storm is coming in from the sea.'

Sarah flew from her bed. Bee had arrived. Bee knew the answer to all problems. She had saved her and her mammy from her da on so many occasions, surely she would know how to save her from his latest plan.

'Sarah, all your pots have gone and someone has left a pullet in the shed in payment. Come on out, would ye, I have news,' Bee shouted.

'I'm coming, I'm coming,' Sarah shouted back as she pulled her dress down over her head and tied her hair back in a dark green ribbon that went beautifully with her hair and had been a present from Bee.

Moments later, she was in the kitchen. Bee was pouring tea and Angela was spreading Malone butter on oatcakes. She'd found the dish on her doorstep days ago and thought it must have been left by Seamus, when he'd come to buy fish from a catch.

'Sarah, come and sit down now. Fancy that – a pullet! We can have our own eggs.' Angela tapped the top of the table to indicate to Sarah where she wanted her to sit as she placed her oatcake down.

'I have news for you, Sarah, and you too, Angela,' said Bee as she lifted the kettle.

Angela looked up at Bee; her face showed no sign of a smile. 'Is it about that man of yours?' she whispered and frowned as she shot a look towards Sarah, who knew nothing about the secret life of her aunt.

'Oh, for the sake of all that is holy!' Bee slammed the kettle down on the hearth. '*That man* – you mean Captain Bob? The man who puts shoes on Ciaran's feet so that he doesn't walk to school barefoot. *That man*, who put an oilskin cape over Ciaran's shoulders so that he hasn't caught his death of cold. *That man*, who puts food in our bellies, aye, in the bellies of Rory's old mammy and daddy too, and a smile on my face and all!' Bee held her head inches from Angela's. '*That man*, who treats me a million times better than the one you have been married to for the last twenty-five years.'

Angela, the older of the two by ten years, would not be cowed by her sister. She had not wanted Sarah to know all the details of Bee's arrangement, but Bee had driven her to it.

'Bee, you know he is a married man. As sure as God is true, there will be a wife in Ballycroy, and you know it, 'tis sinful what you are doing, a wicked sin. The likes of Philomena O'Donnell will drive you out of the village when they find out. And Paddy and Josie, they would not be able to keep you on.'

Bee snorted with laughter. 'What I am doing is none of their business. What I am doing is nothing I haven't done before, Angela. And I know nothing about any wife,' she lied. Now

was not the time to discuss the deeper details of her relationship with Captain Bob. 'I don't want to know, 'tis not my
business. My name is not Philomena. Now be quiet and listen
to me, would you. Sarah, you too.'

Bee had run all the way from her own house to Angela's.
Captain Bob had disappeared at first light, setting sail from
further along the shore on the early tide, and had promised
he would be back when it was dark. He had left Bee with
very clear instructions about what to do. They had made a
plan and Bee knew, as God was her judge, she had to make it
happen. First, she had to tell Sarah that Michael was coming
home but no one knew when; and then she had to blow her
niece's world apart and tell her that she might not be able to
marry him after all.

She turned to Sarah, who looked as though the news that
her beloved aunt had a lover was the most shocking thing
she'd ever heard. The colour had drained from her face as she
stood teetering on the spot.

'Jesus, you look as though you're about to faint. Sit down,
would ye.' Bee pulled up the chair next to her. She held her
niece's hand and stroked the hair she had brushed so often
since she'd been just a baby. 'Listen, Sarah, don't think about
Captain Bob, don't let that worry you just now, we have other
things we need to talk about. And anyway, don't think badly
of him, or me for that matter, because he's about to help us.'

'I don't think badly of you, Bee.' Sarah looked up at her
aunt.

Angela had pulled up a chair on the other side of Sarah. She
and her sister were silently competing for Sarah's attention, as
had always been the way.

'I don't know what he is doing to help us, but I won't be

here to see it. Mammy...' Sarah turned to face Angela. 'I have to run away – Da's going to marry me off to Jay Maughan, and I think it will be soon, maybe even when he gets back tomorrow morning.' Her voice cracked, but she carried on. 'I haven't any time – I have to go now! Otherwise I won't be here for Michael. He told me last night, Mammy, when you were asleep, when he came back.' At that, the sobs and the tears came.

Angela threw her arm around her daughter's shoulders and pulled her into her chest. She didn't speak. She never rushed to opinion or judgement, she always listened first and thought things through. 'Sshh, sshh,' was all she said as she kissed her daughter's brow.

'You know already?' Bee sat upright in her chair, letting her hand drop from Sarah's hair.

Angela gasped. 'Bee, you know about this too?'

Sarah reached out and took her mother's hand. The three women were linked together in the briefest moment of misery and confusion, until a look of triumph crept over Bee's face.

'Well, what you both obviously don't know, and I do' – she smiled; she couldn't help herself – 'is that Michael Malone is on his way home! And yes, we do have to get you away, Sarah. But if that man is true to his word – and after five years, Michael is most definitely a man now – it won't be for long.'

Twelve hours later, Sarah stood in front of the fire, clutched the mantel shelf, her head leaning against the back of the hand, staring at the fire bugs flickering in and out of life on the soot-blackened back wall. In her other hand she held a heather basket she had woven herself, into which she'd placed the few belongings she could call her own. Her eyes were red raw from weeping and she was exhausted from all the emotion. She was leaving Tarabeg, with a strange man to a strange place, to save her from the fate of being handed over to Maughan in return for money and a life worse than anything she could imagine. Michael was finally coming home, but when he did, she wouldn't be there.

Angela had barely spoken a word other than to fuss and feed her and help her pack her bag. She was locked in her own nightmare, not wanting to worry her daughter further by sharing her own dark thoughts of what life would be like once Sarah had left. When Kevin McGuffey found his daughter missing, she would mightily pay the price. Of that she was sure.

Seeing the despair in Sarah's eyes, she walked over and placed her arms around her, easing her away from the fire, turning her around and hugging her into her. She buried her daughter's head on her shoulder and stroked the back of her hair.

'There, there. Stop crying. This is only a temporary arrangement. We will find you soon, Sarah, me or Michael. But we have to get you away from here, you know that, don't you? What else in God's name can we do to save you? I won't let it happen.'

Sarah let out a shuddering sob. 'How can it be this bad?' she asked, pulling away from her mother and looking into her eyes. 'Why did you even marry him, Mammy? You need to get away too. He's gone properly mad and it's getting worse every day. How can I leave you with him? Come with me, Mammy! Come with me.'

She wiped her eyes with the backs of her hands. They stung from having cried through most of the night and day and it almost hurt to open them. All day long, nightmarish images of what might lie ahead had jostled in her mind with the memories that had sustained her all the time Michael had been away. She was terrified of leaving her home – she'd never been further than Tarabeg in her life.

'I cannot, Sarah. Two of us on the run – if they caught us, they would lock us both away in the asylum, you know that. Your father would complain, blame me, and the Garda would track us down and the Church would punish us. This way, there is only you, and one is easier to hide.'

She stroked away the strands of her daughter's hair that had stuck to her wet cheeks and looked into her eyes as she spoke. 'Get yourself north of the border into what is English land – they cannot touch you there. Or if that's not possible, get to Dublin and then take the boat across to Liverpool. Keep your faith to yourself. If you go north, go to Mass if you can, but don't go anywhere near a convent for help on the way. Not unless you have a good story, and even then you would need money to give them. The nuns won't help anyone for nothing. And if the nuns get their hands on you this side of the border, you won't likely get away. The very least they will do is ask a priest to send for your father, and God help us both if that happens. Bee says that her Captain Bob will have a plan when he gets here and we must do what he says.'

Sarah was petrified, and she looked it. 'God, please, God, take down Da's boat.' She looked up to the roof as she sobbed the words out loud. If her father drowned at sea, all her prayers would truly be answered. 'It should have been him that drowned, not Rory.'

'Shush, 'tis a sin to say that.' Angela pulled her into her arms once more in an attempt to calm her rising panic.

At the sound of voices, both women looked towards the

door. Sarah began to tremble and a frown crossed Angela's face. 'They are early, surely not...'

Captain Bob wasn't expected at the cottage for a couple of hours yet, when their escape would be witnessed by no one. It was a full moon, which was not ideal, but everyone would be long in their beds when they slipped away. McGuffey wasn't due back from the North until the first tide. When smuggling, he kept very different hours to the fishermen.

Sarah's eyes widened with anticipation. 'Mammy,' she whispered. 'Mammy!' She grabbed her mother's hand in her own cold, damp palm, her voice filled with hope and want, and she gasped as the catch on the door lifted. 'Michael!' The word left her in a rush.

Angela turned her head to the door, but it was Bee, and Captain Bob behind her. Sarah's disappointment almost felled her.

'Inside, quick, before anyone sees us,' Bee urged Captain Bob. 'Stop gawping, you two,' she said to Sarah and Angela. 'This is Captain Bob, and he is about to save your life, Sarah, so try and look a bit more grateful, please God, would you?'

Sarah stood motionless, her skin the colour of alabaster. Her voice deserted her, so Angela spoke.

'I'm sorry, Bee. Captain Bob.' She too was almost lost for words. 'Where are our manners? It's just, you see... Things are a little difficult.' She had prayed for Bee's soul every single day as a result of the sins she knew her sister was committing with this man, and here he was, in her house. Her eyes scanned heavenwards, as if expecting the roof to fall in.

'I know,' Captain Bob said. 'Little Bee has explained.'

'*Little Bee?*' Angela looked at Bee with a puzzled expression. This was all new to her. Until yesterday, her life had plodded along just as it had for years, but now things were happening so fast, she could hardly keep up. The last person she'd heard call her sister 'little Bee' was their father, and he'd been dead for over twenty years.

'Sit down, Bob,' said Bee with a tenderness that Angela had only ever seen her display with Rory. 'Sarah, come here. God in heaven, would ye look at the state of ye.' Bee moved over to Sarah and, taking her hand, led her to the chair. 'Come here while we tell ye. Captain Bob has a plan, so he does.'

Sarah stared at the man she had never laid eyes on before. Bee looked over at Angela and gave her her most reassuring smile.

Captain Bob took in Sarah's bloodless complexion and her distress. He thought for a moment, then reached into his inside pocket, took out a flask and extended his arm towards her. 'Take it,' he said. 'It's whiskey – the best. Take a sip. It'll warm your insides and give you courage. You are in shock, and sure, who wouldn't be.'

Automatically, Sarah stretched out her hand; it was trembling violently. He took her hand in his and, steadying it, placed the flask in her fingers and closed them around the leather pouch.

Sarah did exactly as she was told, for no other reason than she felt as though she were about to collapse and she sensed that this might save her from the embarrassment and discomfort of falling off the chair. There was something about his round face, his twinkling blue eyes and the tone of his voice, loaded with pity and care, that made her understand instantly why he was the person Bee had confided in. She could trust him as Bee did. She nervously placed the flask to her lips and took a sip. Immediately she began to cough and splutter.

'There you go, that's opened the pipes,' Captain Bob said. 'Now take another for good measure, that'll be the one that does the work.'

He smiled up at her and through her misery she felt her pulse steady and her blood warm. Here was kindness and it had come to help her.

Bee motioned to Angela to take the chair she was holding out for her. 'I will make up some food, and you two listen to what he has planned. Sarah will want your blessing. Go on, be doing as I say.'

Angela studied her sister's face, but she was giving nothing away. Bee busied herself about the room, as familiar to her as her own, while Captain Bob explained his plan.

'Your Aunt Bee has asked me to sail you around to Bally-croy and get ye away from here, and to make a plan.'

Angela looked nervous.

'Now, don't be panicking,' he said to her. 'We will be away in half an hour and to catch me, someone would have to have a miracle for a wind and a bigger boat than mine, or he would have to be a fast swimmer. I'm the only boat hereabouts with a motor, and I've never met an Irish man yet who can swim, never mind catch me. There is a storm due in, which is why I am a little early.'

Sarah half smiled through her tears and began to calm in response to his reassuring words and the effect of the whiskey.

'What would your idea be?' asked Angela, her voice thready as her courage failed her.

'Well, I have the same plan for her that many a colleen from these parts has already taken. I will lend you the money for a passage to America, Sarah. We will sail to Ballycroy first, and then we'll get you straight down to Cobh for the ship to New

York. There's one leaving the day after tomorrow at noon. I have to go out to Cobh anyway and we'll sort out your papers there. You'll be alone for the crossing, but my sister will meet you off the ship in New York and she'll take you in. She will find you good work, the right sort, respectable, and then you'll pay her an amount per week to cover the cost of your passage over. You aren't the first we have done this for and you won't be the last.'

Sarah's sob of anguish filled the room. America! She would not be married to Maughan, but Michael might still come and she would be gone. She was to leave the place she had known all of her life, the place he was also from and where he would know to find her. It was as if the earth shifted beneath her and all that she had known and trusted had slipped away in a heartbeat. Wiped away by her father's evil deeds.

'But... Michael...' she said. 'What if he comes and I'm gone? What will happen then? He will think I didn't wait for him, and I have stood at this door every day for five long years.'

She began to cry. Self-pitying, desperate tears that pulled on her mother's heart and made Bee grieve. Captain Bob caught Bee's eye and raised his eyebrows.

'The thing is, Sarah,' Bee began, 'no one knows when Michael is coming. The farmhands were saying in Paddy's last night that some demobbed soldiers stop in Liverpool on their way home and never leave. The money is so good, for an Irishman who's used to earning his keep with butter or pullets, 'tis very tempting. And Michael, he might well do the same. Being a man who was off to earn money and seek adventure in the war, I'm thinking that's likely. Sarah, you would look quite ridiculous if you stayed here and he wasn't coming home to you at all. If he does love you and is coming back for you,' well, he will follow you or send for you. No one can come between two people in love. Now go! Ye have to go and not be seen.'

Bee almost shouted those last words at her, her patience worn thin in the face of her fear that there might not be enough time to get Sarah away. Her worst nightmare would be the sight of Kevin McGuffey opening the cottage door. She would never admit it, but she was also embarrassed that Sarah was voicing objections to Captain Bob's generosity. Instead of crying, she should have been thankful for his offer to loan her the money and more grateful at how prepared he was to put himself out for her.

But Sarah had no words of thanks. Drying her eyes and sniffing, she sobbed pathetically. 'Michael wouldn't do that. He would come for me first before he did anything. I know it, Bee...' Her words trailed off. She knew herself how hollow and desperate she sounded.

As she and Captain Bob stood up to leave, all four of them huddled together, almost as one.

Bee pushed oatcakes wrapped in a cloth into Sarah's basket, along with an earthenware flask of cold tea. 'Go on now. Go!' she urged. 'I've packed plenty to keep you going until tomorrow. God be with ye and as soon as you can, write and let us know where ye are, Sarah. Ye never know, the next one I put on a boat might be yer mammy.'

Sarah could see that stoic, life-hardened Bee was, for all her bluster, deeply upset. Their world was being turned upside down. 'Mammy!' she rasped, but she felt so physically sick with the trauma and upset, she could barely speak.

'Don't ye be worrying about her now,' said Bee. 'I'm taking her to my house, for as long as we can beat off your father.

I'll say she's on her sickbed with grief after you running off. I'll say she has lost the use of her legs and can't walk. I'll send for Bridget McAndrew to make her better – your father won't take Bridget on, he's as terrified of her as he is of Shona Maughan.'

Sarah grabbed both her aunt's hands. 'I will work,' she said, 'and get money. I'll be back.' And with that she turned to her mother. The desolation in Angela's eyes pierced her heart as she fell into her arms.

Angela wanted to scream out loud, wanted to shout, 'I can't live without you if you go. You are my world, my life, my only reason to wake up each day. There is no point to any of it without you – I can't go on with him. You are like a beam of bright sunlight in my dark, depressing life.' Instead, in the calmest voice, belying her inner turmoil, all she said was, 'Now you take care on that boat. Don't talk to anyone you don't know.'

Everyone laughed nervously.

'She won't be knowing anyone,' said Bee.

Angela ignored her. 'And remember, I'm here and you are my only child. If I had the means to find a way to save you from this, you know I would, don't you? But I haven't a penny or a place to take you to be safe.'

Tears poured down Sarah's face. She understood. She knew her mammy was as helpless as she was. Kevin McGuffey was a law unto himself and they were answerable to him in the eyes of everyone, including the Church, and yet he listened to no one. They were women, owned nothing, earned a pittance and were dependent on McGuffey for every morsel they ate, the roof over their heads and, it would appear, their lives.

'I will be waiting for news every single day, you know I will, don't you? So please God, put me out of my misery and write as soon as you can – address the letter to Bee, it will go to Mrs Doyle. I won't be here. I might already be looking for you.'

Angela looked into her daughter's eyes, and what she saw tore at her heart. The depth of Sarah's misery was like nothing she had seen before and the knowledge that even though she was her mother there was nothing she could do to alleviate it ripped her soul to shreds.

'Come here,' she whispered. She pulled Sarah into her arms and together they cried and rocked from side to side for as long as Bee allowed. Angela knew she had to remember how Sarah's hair smelt, how her soft frame felt in her arms as she cradled her as though she were still but a child, because as sure as the wind that blew past the open door was true, there was a very real chance they might never see each other again. They saw it happen all the time in Tarabeg, as one family after another waved off a child to a brighter new world across the Atlantic, on a cloud of promises to keep in touch. 'Remember me, won't you,' she whispered. 'Remember me.'

There was a cough and Captain Bob spoke. 'The weather looks like it's already changing,' he said apologetically. 'It's a full moon and she can be temperamental, so I think we'd better be heading off. If there's a storm at sea and it blows into the shore, we might not get away tonight. I have the motor on the back, we don't need the sails, but all the same...'

Sarah stared as though not understanding what he had said. Angela held on to her wits for her daughter's sake. She would have her entire lifetime to fall apart once Sarah had left. Following a gentle push from Bee, who could barely see through her own tears, Sarah and Captain Bob disappeared out of the door, towards the escarpment and the shore.

Bee turned to her sister. For a moment neither could speak, but they clung on to each other's hands. 'Right, pack what you need, come on. You won't be seeing this place for a while. You are going to be very sick and on your deathbed with the grief. You had better be a bloody good actress because McGuffey will be knocking on the door, demanding to know what's going on. You can stay with me for ever, you know – McGuffey never takes me on. No one would judge you. Your daughter fleeing from the tyrant he is, and you being paralysed with the shock. You will still be his wife, a wife who is sick and being looked after by her sister. Only I will know and it could be our secret. You would be free of him.'

'Aye, you're right, he's always been scared of you. He won't touch me in your house.' Angela took a deep breath, nodded slowly at her sister. 'We can tell him that Sarah ran away when she was taking a message to your house, that she just never came home. That he scared her with his threat of marrying her off to Maughan. What would we do without you, Bee?' She moved over to the press by the bed and began pushing her few belongings into a string bag, barely able to see for the tears in her eyes. 'I will happily lose the use of my legs, for what is the point of doing anything else when there is no Sarah here now.' She stopped, frozen, barely able to move for the hurt in her heart. The pain was so acute, it near paralysed her; every step was an effort. It might not be so much of a lie that she had lost the use of her legs, after all. 'God help us,' she sobbed, her voice little more than a croak. 'Bridget McAndrew has no potion to heal a broken heart, and that will be the cause of it.'

She looked about the cottage as though she had never seen it before. Her gaze fell on the one picture she had of Sarah as a little girl, standing on the press. She leant over and picked it up. 'There's nothing to live for now that Sarah has gone, Bee. Nothing.'

'Angela, I'm not leaving you – that just isn't possible. Come on now.'

Angela tucked the picture into her bag. 'You win, Bee – don't you always. I will come, but not until I've watched the boat sail around the corner. It's almost as light as day, I'll be able to see them from up on the cliff.' Her voice wobbled, but she was adamant. 'I will watch until I can watch no more, until my only daughter is just a speck on the horizon. And then I'll walk up the boreen to your house. But you must go back to your boy, Angela. Thank God for Ciaran. At least you and Rory did something right, when I did everything wrong.'

As they left the cottage and Bee went to lift the latch, she noticed something was missing. 'Angela, where is the gun?'

Angela stared vacantly at the blank nail rests on the wall and shook her head. 'I have no notion. He's off smuggling, maybe he thought he needed it with him.'

They stood with the door open as they took one last look inside. Bee felt it herself, the void, the bleakness after Sarah's departure; it was profound.

Outdoors, a cool wind was gathering force and the full moon illuminated the heavy clouds as they raced across the cliffs. A storm was blowing in from the ocean. The terns and gulls circled and screeched with foreboding as they flew inland towards the village and safety.

With a worried glance at the sky, Bee pulled her shawl down over her head and fastened it tighter under her chin. 'Come on, there's nothing here for you. They'll be safely away before that storm takes hold.'

Angela pulled at the door and turned to Bee. 'All my life is in there, everything I am and do.'

'No, it isn't.' Bee placed her hand over Angela's and slammed the door shut. 'Your life is ahead of you. Now run! You'll only just catch them before they disappear around the headland. Be quick, 'tis going to rain asses' legs, as God is my judge. I just felt the first drops on my face and 'tis already heavy.'

'Bee, I made her a promise and I will go and find her. She's my flesh and blood. We've spent every single day of her life together. I'm going to be the next one to run.'

'Holy Mother of God,' said Bee, and then she smiled. It had taken Sarah leaving to open her sister's eyes, to put a fire in her belly, to make her fight for her life and her self-esteem. She saw a new determination and she was proud. 'That's my girl,' she said as she squeezed her sister's hand. 'We have time to plan that one properly though. Hurry now, don't be long. I won't feel safe until you're at my house.'

They parted outside the cottage door. Bee crossed the boreen, turned away from the ocean and ran towards her house. Angela strode out along the path to the cliff that looked down over the ocean, her shawl pulled tightly about her in the now brisk and noisy wind. 'I can hear the motor on the boat,' she shouted back. As she waved her hand, the first drops of rain began to beat at her face.

'Here, take my arm.' Captain Bob crooked his arm and smiled at Sarah.

'Thank you,' she whispered, as she duly slipped her arm through his, then fell silent again. She had no idea what to say to the man by her side. Her life, repetitive and predictable, her future, pictured every day, had disappeared in a moment, and here she was, with a man she had known for less than an hour, heading towards a place she had never in her wildest dreams imagined. She could barely transfer a thought into words.

They had walked in silence along the empty path, Sarah aware only of every breath she took and the sound of the waves crashing against the shore. Her mind was in turmoil, fighting a desire to turn and run. She felt cold with fear and could not prevent her limbs from violently shaking. The path dropped down towards the coast, their footsteps silent in the sandy earth.

She stopped dead when she heard the sound of a horse's hooves.

'Quick, into the grass! Duck down!' Captain Bob crouched behind the whin and pulled her down beside him.

Sarah froze, then turned her head and looked back up towards the village. Was it Maughan? He often came to the coastal cottages, either peddling his wares to those who were too old or too idle and found the mile-long walk into the village too far, or delivering goods for her father to store in the cave for smuggling. But at this hour it might not be cigarettes or whiskey Maughan was transporting; he could be calling to collect his own merchandise – herself. Her flesh prickled with fear and her heart beat so fast, she could barely breathe. She could see the mast of the waiting trawler sticking up from the cove, but she'd shrunk so far into the gorse, the needle-like thorns puncturing her dress and threatening to pierce her skin, that she couldn't see who it was on the horse. Something made her want to scramble back up the ridge and find out.

Captain Bob placed his hand on her arm. 'No, don't. We can't take the risk of you being caught. We need to get down to the boat. Quick now, we don't have any time to lose. The wind's picking up and I don't like how dark the sky has turned.' His voice was gentle but insistent. 'We can be away in minutes, and we have to be, or it will be all over for us, one way or another.'

Remembering what had happened to Rory, caught in a storm that he couldn't escape, and spurred on by the sudden realisation that she needed to be on the water and away from the reach of her would-be tormentors, Sarah turned back to face the ocean and followed Captain Bob down to the water's edge. Within moments she was being helped into his boat.

As soon as Angela reached the cliff's edge, she saw the boat. Sarah was sitting on the end, looking back towards land. Angela thanked God for the full moon, which lit the ocean all the way around the headland. She began frantically to wave at her daughter. There was no response. She stretched her arm high and, ripping off her shawl, held it aloft. The wind, fiercer now, grabbed the shawl as though it were a mere rag and buffeted and beat it like a flag. A landmark for Sarah, if only she'd catch sight of it.

'I'm coming too. I'm going to follow you,' shouted Angela. 'You will see me again before ye know it. I'm coming, Sarah! I'm coming too!' She almost screamed the last words on a breath of exhalation as she tasted the sweetness of freedom. She had no idea how she would do it. Maybe Captain Bob would do the same for her. Maybe Bee would help and she could work in Dublin and save the fare to travel. She would disappear, change her name to Bee's, say she was a widow. She was flooded with a new determination to find a way. She would escape; she would join her Sarah and make a new life for them both.

*

Further up the shoreline, concealed behind the rocks where he had beached his hooker, stood Kevin McGuffey. He had made his drop of whiskey and cigarettes, but instead of heading for Scottish waters, he'd decided to return to hand his daughter over to Jay Maughan sooner than he'd planned.

Maughan had come to the house in the early hours to tell him that Michael Malone was coming back home to Tarabeg. The news had sat uneasily in his gut. He sensed Michael was a danger and a menace, and he knew Angela and Sarah were keeping something from him. He could see it in Sarah's face. They'd been keeping secrets from him for years, he knew that – and in his own home too. It had started the night he had beaten Sarah and knocked her unconscious, when Maughan had told him he'd seen her running back from the Malones' farm, back through the boreens, towards the coast and home, as though the Devil himself were hot on her heels. Since then there'd been something about her, her manner; she'd changed. There was a resistance in her body to the lashings from his belt, and a blaze of defiance in her eye; but it was more than that – there had been no tears. No crying, no begging for his forgiveness. He knew it had something to do with Michael Malone.

This morning he had made his smuggling drop as planned, but his pick-up had been late and had apologised profusely. 'The customs men are growing mightily in numbers. Men back from the war taking up the jobs,' he'd said.

'Another reason to hate the bastards then,' McGuffey replied.

The weather had turned. He had no intention of heading off into Scottish waters for a catch. He had more profitable business to attend to. He would hand Sarah over to Maughan as soon as he returned.

He unloaded his boat in silence, but the pick-up, a man from Donegal, never stopped talking. 'They say 'tis going to turn mighty bad,' he said as he found his balance and stretched out his arms to take the first box of whiskey. 'Real bad. Blowing up from the north and will hit us fast. Won't be able to tack into it, it'll be too strong for a trawler even.'

The evening sky had turned to night almost as quickly as McGuffey's mood had deteriorated. The name Malone was beating against the side of his brain and eating away at his guts. He would return to the cave at the foot of the cliff where he stored his goods, hide the money and make his way up to the cottage.

All his attention was taken up with beaching the hooker. As he saw the row of upturned boats lifting and shifting in the wind, he knew the men had abandoned the day's catch. One of the boats he'd seen setting out that morning was now upside down like a fat monk's belly, with a sandbag on the base to stop the wind from catching it.

Finally, safely landed and with his hooker secured and secluded in a nook in the shoreline, he paused for a breather and looked up at the clifftop. The clouds were racing in the wind, the cliffs intermittently vivid in the light of the full moon. In a sudden clear view to the headland above him, he saw his wife, waving and shouting. Something was very wrong. He reached into the boat, pulled back the oilskin and removed his gun. Was she waving for help? Or had she finally gone mad? He cracked open the gun and pulled his cape tighter. There was only one way to find out.

Chapter 7

'Take good care now, Michael,' Sam, the driver of the post van shouted as Michael alighted at the foot of the boreen leading to the farm.

The van had called in at almost every village between Galway and Tarabeg, and it was late by the time they reached the outskirts of Tarabeg. Even so, Sam had still to collect the mail sack, such as it was, from the back of Mrs Doyle's before he could call it a night.

As the van pulled away, Michael breathed in deeply, never so happy to be alive, filling his lungs with the smell of pasture, cows, turf, bogs, and the night-time river air. Looking to the village, he saw the lights from Paddy's spilling out onto the street, but there was no temptation – he had a promise to keep. The full moon disappeared from view and just as he began to head up the muddy boreen towards the farm the rain began. The vegetation became dense and the scratchy wool of his trousers absorbed the damp like a sponge. Even after five years away, every bog hole and turn was familiar to him. He was walking to his home when so many of the men he had fought alongside lay dead and buried on foreign soil. As he strode on, he imagined he heard the sound of their boots marching beside him. It was five long years since he had walked alone.

Rounding the bend, he stopped dead and gasped at the sight of the farmhouse standing in profile in the moonlight, encircled by the grazing meadows. The rainclouds had passed and the slate roof gleamed and the limestone wash shone white and inviting. He lingered for a moment to take a breath. For the briefest second, his heart stopped. He had thought of the house many times, but never like this, bathed in a magical silver light.

The ferns and the mountain trees were still. The only sounds were of the wildlife scurrying back to their playgrounds on the path now that he was quiet and motionless. The rain dripped from the leaves and rabbits bobbed in the grass, their eyes shining like glistening black pebbles.

He crept past the old cottage, its heather thatch casting a dark, undulating silhouette, the cows inside as quiet as he was trying to be. But the dogs chained up against the wall could sense him and began to bark. Before he could turn, he felt that he was being watched. Pete Shevlin, bleary eyed in his stained vest, stood in the doorway as the ghostly form of a cow in the byre shuffled behind him and snorted her own soft greeting.

'Oh, 'tis you, Michael. I'll be away to me bed then. Nice to see you back safe, like.'

'Aye, thanks. I'll see you in the morning, Pete.'

Pete rubbed his eyes and slid back into the darkness of the old cottage, whispering, 'Shush now, 'tis Michael home,' to the dogs.

A hurricane lamp burnt in the window of the farmhouse and Michael guessed it had been left to guide him on his last steps should he return in the night. A single curl of smoke rose from the chimney. He depressed the latch, the familiar click piercing the silent night air as the door creaked and gave way beneath his gentle push.

He let his kit bag slip from his shoulder onto the thick rush mat inside the door and bent to undo the laces on his boots. He hung his coat on the nail on the back of the door, undid the belt of his wet and muddy trousers and let them fall to the floor, where they landed with a soggy thud. The place smelt the same – it smelt of home. He dipped his fingers into the holy water that his mother kept at the foot of her plastercast of Mary and blessed himself.

The limewashed walls glowed orange from the dimming light of the fire and he sensed he was not alone in the room. As his eyes adjusted, he saw the truckle bed and his grandfather. Seeking warmth, he tiptoed to the fire, the rushes crackling beneath his feet. The sight of the food and mug on the table made his stomach rumble loudly, and his heart went out to his mammy for having left it out for him. He would stay for only minutes. Just long enough to change and eat and collect his da's horse.

Picking up the plate of food and the mug, he moved towards the fire and lowered himself onto the rush mat. He smiled, he sipped, he sighed.

The first person to wake was Daedio. 'Michael? Michael, is that you? Oh, thank the heavenly Lord and all the saints in heaven. You're home!'

In less than a minute, Seamus and Nola had joined them.

'Daddy, do you need the horse tonight?'

Seamus, his heart warmed by the whiskey he had poured in celebration at the return of his son, stood in the kitchen, which had been such a lonely place for him and Nola. At that moment, he would have given his son anything. Nola fussed and brought out the clothes she had kept regularly laundered and pushed her son into the scullery to wash and change. 'The trousers, they are almost too big,' she exclaimed. 'What did they feed you in that army?' Michael wasn't listening. His father was letting him take the horse and Sarah was minutes away.

Warmed, fed, clothed, and after hugging his mother half to death, Michael said, 'I'm sorry, but I have to go and fetch her. I'll be back before dawn though.'

'I think you'll need to marry her first, Michael, before you bring her here. But we will make her as welcome as Grandma Annie made your mammy, and indeed, before Grandma Annie there was—'

Michael was already on his way back to the door; he had no time to listen to a story. 'That's why I'm off for Sarah. I spoke to Father Jerry the day I left and I wrote to him months ago. We will be heading straight to the presbytery. He told me what to do.'

''Tis not that easy,' said Nola. 'There's the licence to be got—'

But it was too late; Michael was already out of the door.

As Nola and Seamus stood in the doorway and watched their son head off down the hill, Nola felt a weight pressing on her heart.

'Oh, Seamus, he isn't heading straight into trouble, is he? We only just have him home – will he not at least stay the night?'

'Well now, I'm with Michael on this. McGuffey, he has a fearsome reputation, but I happen to know he's away smuggling, and when he leaves the North, he always sails over to Scotland for the fish. Paddy told me that was so. He's not due back until tomorrow, they say. I'm thinking that Michael's timing is just right.' He smiled broadly and put his arm around his wife. 'The boy can do what the feck he likes after what he's been through – I'm not going to stop him. And it will be easier for Sarah, if her father is away. Don't you be worrying about no licence. Father Jerry will see him right, and I'll drop the whiskey down for him tomorrow.' He stared out into the darkness. 'This could not be easier for Michael. My prayers have been answered, every fecking one of them,' he said with a satisfied flourish as he pulled on his pipe.

Nola slapped her husband on the backside as a reprimand for swearing. 'Go and say your Hail Marys for that,' she said. 'Right now, or it's Father Jerry I'll be telling.'

As Nola stepped back indoors, Seamus kept his eye on his son while he saddled up and chatted to Pete, who was helping him. He hadn't managed to have a private word with him or even put his arm around him; Daedio and Nola had filled all the time that had been available to them. And why shouldn't they have, he thought. I'll have a word with him later, me and the boy.

Since he'd opened the telegram, he'd managed to keep his emotions in check, but now he blinked hard as a single tear escaped and ran down his leathery skin and onto his stubbled chin. He placed his pipe back in his mouth and took a long pull. 'God be with him,' he whispered.

He hadn't told Nola the stories he'd heard about McGuffey, and he hadn't told Michael that the man had promised his daughter to Jay Maughan. He felt it in his bones that Michael would be just in the nick of time. The Malones were respected in the village. Once Michael came back to Tarabeg Hill with his Sarah, no one would dare set foot on the boreen leading to their farm in malice or anger. Not if they ever wanted to be served another drink at Paddy's. As he banged and emptied his pipe against the outside wall, Seamus whispered again, 'God be with him,' and then in a louder voice and over his shoulder he shouted, 'I think there's a few rabbits out here chancing their luck, Nola. I'm off with the traps. Get the pan ready for the morning. There is nothing that boy loves more than a good rabbit stew.'

Bee felt troubled as she walked back to her cottage by herself, leaving Angela on the clifftop to wave her final goodbyes to Sarah. Angela had been right, of course: she had to get back to collect Ciaran from his grandparents', but she wished Angela was with her. Her heart sank as she saw the heavy clouds move across the moon. Within minutes, the rain began to pelt down with force. 'Oh God, no,' she cried out as the sky ruptured with a flash of lightning and the rain battered her face, penetrated her shawl and soaked her skin beneath. Her first thought was for Sarah and Captain Bob in the boat. She knew how ferocious west coast storms could be – storms that churned the sea and swallowed the mountains. At least Captain Bob had a motor; if there was a storm, he would be safe where others would not.

Even so, a dreadful feeling of unrest swept over her and she looked up to see if the sky was showing any sign of easing in any direction. She was disappointed. It had been only twenty minutes since she'd left the cliff, but the weather had taken the nastiest turn. The rain was so heavy now, she could barely see down the boreen. She decided to go straight back to her cottage. Rory's parents would not expect her in this weather. Like all fishing families, they respected the weather and adapted their plans as necessary.

She took her rosary out of her pocket. 'Keep them safe,' she whispered to the God she was losing faith in. 'Keep them safe.' Could things get any worse, she wondered. It was as if God knew something. 'The angels are crying,' she muttered into the darkness as she crashed in through the door of her cottage and hung her soaked shawl over the back of the chair near the hearth.

She threw turf on the fire and set the kettle on the cast-iron griddle above the embers to the side, ready for Angela. Forked lightning ripped the sky apart and her cottage lit up for a blinding few seconds. The doors shook and the windows rattled as the malevolent wind beat against them, threatening to pull her out and up into the maelstrom. Gales like this were strong enough to pick up sheep and even shepherds from the cliff and fling them into the ocean below, as local farmers knew to their cost.

Visibility was so poor now, and the downpour so fierce, she was quite sure that Angela would run the few yards back to her own cottage and wait for the worst of it to pass before coming to join her. She could hear the waves lashing the shore, surging onto the rocks on the headland. She of all people knew how vicious the sea could be when roused. A storm like this one had robbed her boy of his father and her of her husband. McGuffey would not set ashore in this. For now, until tomorrow at least, they were safe.

She lit a candle and made the bed. Slipping her hand into the covers, she imagined she could feel the warmth of Captain Bob's body. The bedclothes smelt of his pipe, of the sea, of them both and their lovemaking. She felt guilty, sinful, and looking to the statue of the Holy Mother above the fireplace, she blessed herself and whispered a prayer of forgiveness. 'You don't want me to be alone all of my life, do you?' she asked the figurine she could barely see in the candlelight. Another flash of lightning streaked through the room and illuminated the face of the Holy Mother, who winked and smiled down her benevolence in the brilliant flicker.

Bee lit another candle in the window. With a mug of Captain Bob's porter in her hand, she sat back in the chair in front of the roaring fire, pulled a crocheted rug over her knee, shook out her long, damp hair and rocked to and fro, waited for the storm to pass and Angela to arrive. She was quite sure that with the motor to assist them, Captain Bob and Sarah would both be safely ashore in Ballycroy by now. Although she would have preferred Angela to have been with her, safe and warm in her cottage, two sisters together, talking thorough the momentous change about to befall them, she was confident that Angela would be safe. Sarah was safe. All was well.

It would have taken Michael less than an hour on foot to the coast from the farm, but he was consumed by the desire to lay eyes on his Sarah. To hold her, and then, with Angela's blessing, to lift her onto the horse and ride like the wind to Father Jerry. The rain had become torrential in only minutes and now it lashed against his skin, as if beating him back. He was soaked through, but he neither felt it nor cared. He had only one thought on his mind, to reach his Sarah.

He was exhilarated to be home and as he neared the shore he was shouting, almost screaming, 'Sarah, I'm home! I'm back! Sarah, I'm here!' even though he knew that through the howling wind and rain she would never hear him.

The horse's hooves slipped on the shale and shingle as the rain swept away the sandy surface. He could just about see the McGuffey cottage ahead through the curtain of rain, its white limewash standing like a ghost against the inky sky, guiding him. 'Sarah, I'm coming! I'm coming!' He wanted to shout the words louder as he approached, but instead he chanted them under his breath, in time to the thud of his horse's feet. Finally he could contain himself no longer, and as the ground levelled out, he urged the horse into a gallop, racing across the last few yards.

Outside the cottage, he yanked on the reins and stopped the horse dead. Something was very wrong. The door was open and banging restlessly against the wall in the wind, and it was dark inside, with no sign of life. He tied up the horse, then took small, careful steps forward and merely whispered his calls. 'Sarah?' A sense of foreboding washed over him; it was so strong, it made his flesh tighten and his heart constrict. He had fought Germans, had dodged bullets, shellfire and shrapnel and survived them all, but now, faced with the open door to the McGuffeys' cottage, he felt fearful of walking inside.

He looked around him and thought he saw a bent figure hurrying along the cliff edge. It was a shadow, a shimmer of white, and then it was gone, as quickly as it had come, behind the sheets of rain. He began to shiver, violently. The rain streamed down his face and into his eyes; the wind started to shriek, tearing at the cliff edge, hurling stones and shale into the air. If it was Sarah, she would never hear him through the gale and with her head bent against the wind. But was it her? Or was it a ghost? He'd been brought up on stories of ghosts and fairies. His skin prickled. He could not be sure what it was. If it was Sarah, what was she doing up on the cliff path?

He walked over to the door of the cottage, caught it to stop it banging in the wind, and pushed it back. 'Sarah!' he shouted. There was no reply, as he'd expected there wouldn't be. He turned, hearing a noise behind him, to see a stack of Sarah's heather lobster pots rolling off into the wind as if they were made of the lightest tumbleweed.

'Sarah? Angela?' he shouted again.

Silence. He stepped inside and reached his hand out to the stone windowsill to his right, where every cottage in the west kept a candle and matches. The fire was burning low and gave off a dull glow; from the light of it, he could see for sure that there was no one home. A curtain was pulled back at the bottom of the cottage, revealing an empty bed.

He lit the candle and the cottage flared into being as his own shadow climbed the wall. The place smelt of life, it was warm, it smelt of Sarah, she had not long been here. He swung around wildly to the door – was that her on the cliffs? It was too dangerous, she would never walk along a cliff edge in this weather – there were stories in living memory of people being blown off in a squall.

'Sarah!' he shouted again.

He turned to leave and placed the candle back down on the windowsill. The gale that hurtled through the door instantly extinguished it once the protective cup of his hand was removed. The wick sizzled in the molten wax and a long plume of grey smoke rose. The air hissed and crackled with static as lightning shot through the sky, and in the blaze of light that followed, he saw his own features reflected back at him in the black glass of the rain-soaked window. Through the blanket of heavy rain he saw that it was definitely a woman out there. He crossed himself. 'Holy Mary Mother of God, who is it?' Then he shouldered his way out into the storm and followed the ghostly form towards the dangerous cliff edge.

His progress was hampered by slipping, slippery shale. The figure wore a shawl, but her clothes were not white, it was the lightning that had made her appear not of this world, almost transparent. She was moving quickly and to his frustration kept disappearing behind the gorse bushes and out of sight. It was not Sarah, that he knew, but she was familiar, and something was pushing him, urging him on. 'Run! Run!' roared the wind in his ears as he slid and stumbled and attempted to gain ground.

The woman neither turned nor looked about her. She had a crazed determination to her, as if she was running away from something, from someone; she was weaving wildly in all directions, careless of her destination, her arms grasping at the air before her, heading dangerously near the cliff edge. Michael's heart pounded against his ribs and the blood thundered in his ears. His flesh crawled with fear, he felt as though he was in the middle of a nightmare he could not wake from, and he began to shiver, more with terror than cold as the arms of gorse bushes reached out, grabbed hold of his trousers and pulled him down onto the soaked earth. His clothes ripped and his legs ran with warm blood from the thorns. Each time he regained his feet she looked more like a ghost than a woman. Through the sheets of rain she appeared to be floating, and then she stopped, and turned back, and it occurred to him that she was standing directly on the cliff edge, wavering, and she was screaming, at someone or something behind her.

His heart thumped as he ran for all he was worth, his chest

wall stabbing with the pain of it as he gasped for his breath. The rain slashed his face, cold and hard against the heat of his skin, and the waves roared and crashed onto the rocks below. He began to shiver again and raced on, willing himself to cover the last few yards. The sky ripped with a bolt of lightning. She had stopped running – he could see her clearly, and he knew in an instant who it was. 'Angela!' he screamed. 'Angela!'

Surprise mixed with panic in her eyes as she stumbled towards him. 'Michael, is that you?' she shouted.

He ran and threw his arms around her, swamped with relief that she was moving away from the edge. She felt frail and thin in his arms. 'What are you doing out here, in this?' he shouted.

'Michael, thank God! He's here! He's after me! Be careful… Go!' She was shouting up to him and even though she was telling him to go, she clung onto his arms.

In her upturned face he could almost see Sarah looking back up at him. But she was making no sense.

'Angela, where is Sarah? Get back, come on, what are you doing out here?' He put his arm around her shoulders and began to lead her back towards the cottage.

'No, no! Go to the cliff… shout to her… gone! I went to wave… he's come back, he saw me… he was after me. Out there! Out there!' She was pointing frantically towards the ocean. 'Go! Go!' she screamed.

Michael ran to the cliff edge and stared out and down towards the ocean, but he could barely even see the waves through the torrents of rain. The wind howled and the ocean roared in his ears, and he had not a clue what Angela was trying to say. He had to get her inside and away from all this; then at least he could find out where Sarah was.

The storm swirled around the two of them, flinging them

together and then trying to rip them apart, and it took all of his strength to keep them both upright. She clung onto his arm, but the wind ate her words. Sarah must be at her Aunt Bee's, he thought. They were close and she'd often slept there as a girl, he remembered. He cursed himself for having gone to the wrong cottage first.

He gripped Angela and pulled her into his side as he tried to guide them both towards the cottage. She was shouting, gabbling, repeatedly glancing back behind them. Michael assumed that McGuffey was out at sea and she was looking for him, frantic with worry.

They had barely gone a hundred yards when the wind dropped abruptly and at last they could hear each other speak. Angela stopped still and almost shook him by the arms. Clasping her tightly so that she wouldn't fall, he took a step back so he could see her face as he held her. 'What is it, Angela? Why are you alone? Where's Sarah?'

'She's gone, Michael. She's run away. And he's after me – he knows.'

Kevin McGuffey moved out from behind the rock he'd slipped behind as soon as he'd seen Michael making his way to the cliff edge and lookout. He wiped the rain from his eyes and looked over towards where Malone had stood. It was him, standing there as bold as brass, with his hands on his hips, looking out across the ocean. As quickly as he'd appeared, the rain hurtled between them like a wave and he was gone.

'Coward.' McGuffey spat the word out with the tobacco he'd been chewing. His dudeen had blown out of his hand and smashed onto the rocks, and some of the smaller boats had done the same, crushed into kindling as they'd hurtled down the beach. He'd pulled his own boat up into the cave for protection.

'What the feck do you want here, Malone?' he shouted up to the cliff as lightning fizzed across the sky and lit up Angela.

She had already seen him, and with the look of a scared cat, the one she always had before he hit her, she had turned and run. This was new to him – in the cottage, she had nowhere to run. An anger like he had never felt before swamped him. Envy and revenge slipped into his gut, curled like a cat and settled.

'I'll fecking show you, you English-loving bastard, Malone.' He hissed the words as he walked. His eyes were bulging, his nostrils flaring. His steps were heavy and determined as he climbed up towards Michael and Angela. The whereabouts of Sarah flashed though his mind. Why was Angela out there on this night of all nights, alone? But a more pressing thought drowned out that and everything else: Malone might have survived the war, more was the pity, but he would not survive coming anywhere near his cottage, his wife or his daughter.

He placed his fingers on the trigger of his gun and climbed the final ridge to the top of the cliff.

They were just ahead of him. He could barely make them out through the rain, so he waited for a break. When it came, they were facing away from him, Malone with his arm around Angela's shoulders, guiding her towards to the cottage.

'You fecking bastard, take your last breath,' he muttered as he lifted his gun, 'You're a dead man, Malone!'

Chapter 8

Mrs Doyle had heard the post van arrive, and as usual Sam, the driver, knocked on the back door to let her know he was taking the mail sack. Sometimes she opened the door, to hand him a glass of whiskey, sometimes she didn't. Tonight he was lucky. Her hair was in wire curlers, held in place with a headscarf, and her floral dressing gown was pulled tight across her and fastened with the belt from her gaberdine mac. Her face shone white from the Pond's Cold Cream she religiously applied every night, when she could get it. It was a novelty on the west coast – only those with relatives who could post it from abroad could benefit from its miraculous age-defying powers. She wore no stockings and her feet were bare in her leather shoes.

'Can you receive the telex on those curlers?' Sam asked her as he stepped inside.

'Not as far as I know, but they are made of metal and I do wonder,' she replied. 'I sometimes feel a buzzing on my scalp.' She put her hand up and laid it over her scarf. ''Tis going to be the foulest of nights, so it is,' she said as she motioned for him to step inside. 'Here, I've poured a glass ready, to set you on the road.'

'I've had company all the way from Galway,' Sam said as he knocked the glass back. He had news. He was letting her know he had news. He emptied the glass. If she wanted the news, she had to refill the glass.

She looked him in the eye – the news was worth a second glass. Her hand shook slightly as she splashed the amber Jameson into the tumbler. There was nothing that excited Mrs Doyle more than a good bit of fresh news.

'I had Michael Malone in the van, all the way.'

She placed the bottle down with a thump. 'Well, I never. You did not!'

'I did.'

'He's home already?'

'He is, and he was telling me he had a promise to keep to a certain young lady.' He winked.

'Sarah McGuffey?'

'Aye, and the first thing he would be doing, he said, would be dropping his bag and heading straight off to keep it – tonight.'

Mrs Doyle gasped, reached over to the press and took down a fresh glass. 'I need one myself,' she said as she refilled his and poured her own.

'I'm afraid you aren't the first to know, though,' Sam said.

This was news Mrs Doyle didn't like to hear.

'I had a heavy parcel for the McFees, so I thought I would save you the bother and drop it at the side of the road in the cut.' This was the drop-off point for heavy goods destined for the costal cottages. Anyone with donkey and cart who was heading out that way would then pick up the item and deliver it on. 'I saw McFee himself, staggering back from Paddy's, so I gave him a lift.'

Mrs Doyle sniffed. They all knew that McFee was one of McGuffey's smuggling partners.

'Anyway, he said McGuffey was due back tonight, and so I thought to meself, if Michael is going to keep his promise tonight, he might run into more than he bargained for.'

Mrs Doyle laid her glass down on the table. 'Lord in heaven, and here was me thinking I was off to my bed. Get that whiskey down you. You have one last call to make.'

Michael knew that the drop in the wind and the rain meant the storm would soon be blowing itself out. At last he had a chance to get some sense out of Angela. He'd tried to not let his frustration show, but she seemed almost hysterical and he was desperate to locate Sarah. She was gasping for her breath from the force of the gale, but she was also gesturing with her hands, pushing him, telling him to go. Go where? After what seemed like an age, her breathing steadied.

'She was waiting for you, Michael, waiting all these years,' Angela said. 'But now she's gone, run away to Ballycroy – in this!' She gestured again. 'In this!' She held on to both of his arms to steady herself. 'Her da wanted to marry her to Maughan, Michael, but she wouldn't, so she's away now. Go after her, will you! God willing, they'll have reached Ballycroy before it got so bad.'

Michael studied Angela's face, tried to comprehend what she was saying, needed a moment to take it all in. His brow was furrowed, his eyes creased, his hair dripping. Water ran down his face. The wind, in a dying gasp, ripped Angela's shawl from her head and whipped it into the air. She tried to hold it, but it was gone.

There was another thunderous crack nearby and Michael, disorientated, looked up at the sky before it dawned on him that the noise had come from below them. Not thunder but… His heart raced and his skin went cold. Not thunder but a sound he knew all too well from the war. A sound that made him want to dive for cover. Gunfire.

The despair on Angela's face was replaced by confusion. Her legs buckled, the light faded from her eyes and she slumped over, grasping at Michael's clothes as she slid to the ground.

Bewildered, Michael turned in the direction of the shot to see Kevin McGuffey, just yards away from them, cool and composed, unhurriedly lowering his gun. The faintest trace of annoyance flashed across his face as he wiped the rain from his cheeks. His eyes locked on to Michael's.

For seconds neither man flinched. Then Michael shouted, 'It's Angela! What have you done to her? What have you done?' Dropping to his knees, he lifted Angela by her shoulders and pulled her onto his lap, shouting her name. Her eyes, unseeing, still held a look of surprise as he bent his head and hugged her to him. 'She's dead – you've killed her,' he sobbed as he looked back to McGuffey. Then an even more dreadful thought crossed his mind. 'Where is Sarah? Do you have her? Where is she?'

McGuffey smiled, then threw his head back and laughed. Over the whistling of the wind and the crash of the waves below them on this foulest of nights, Michael could hear McGuffey quite plainly. It was a sound he would never forget as long as he lived. The warm blood from Angela's back ran through his fingers and onto his legs and the rain-soaked earth beneath them. With a sob in his throat and sorrow running through his veins, he scooped her up closer into his arms and rocked her backwards and forwards. He had seen enough people die from gunshots to know that there was nothing he could do to save her. Sarah's mother, murdered in his arms. And Sarah herself, God knew where.

He turned sharply at the unmistakeable sound of McGuffey reloading his gun. The man's hand wasn't even wavering as he lifted his gun to his shoulder, stared Michael in the face and grinned.

'Michael! Michael!'

Through the lull in the wind, someone was shouting his name. Swivelling on his heels, he heard the sound of a horse's hooves and to his astonishment saw Father Jerry riding his cart towards him, with his father, Pete Shevlin, Paddy and Tig in the back. Pete didn't wait for the wheels to stop before he leapt from the cart and was at Michael's side.

Every one of them saw McGuffey drop the gun to his side, the smile wiped from his face, Then he turned and disappeared back down the cliff path as they all rushed to Michael's side.

Captain Bob had kept as close to the shore as was possible, drawing on his many years of navigation expertise to make out the lie of the land, his eyes trained on the cliff face to help him avoid the treacherous rocks beneath. The shoreline was littered with ripped and broken curraghs, some returned by the ocean without their owners on board, left discarded on the beach as testaments to the dangers. In the dark night they loomed, sinister, like a row of nautical coffins against the white shale and sand, a warning to those who thought they had mastered this perilous stretch of the coast.

While Captain Bob steered skilfully around a rocky outcrop, having need to move further out to avoid a cluster of shallow boulders he knew lurked just below the surface, Sarah clung tight to the side of the boat. She could sense the danger. As they passed over the unseen wrecks of Spanish galleons and the graves of her ancestors deep below them, including her own Uncle Rory, the boat rolled, tossing them about with far more force than when they'd set off. She stared at the outboard motor, a novelty on the west coast, as it churned the water.

She had helped clean her father's boat many times, had removed barnacles and done any number of dirty jobs he'd assigned to her, but she'd never sailed in it. On the odd occasion he'd mentioned the possibility, her mother had found a reason why she could not go, and it now dawned on Sarah, with a slow, sickening realisation, that her mother didn't trust her father to keep her safe. But she had trusted her with a stranger tonight.

The rain had become heavy almost as soon as they'd cast off, but at first Captain Bob had seemed unconcerned. 'Ballycroy is only a half hour from here,' he'd said. 'We'll be around the headland before you know it. You'll be dry and safe soon enough, and on that big ship to America in no time at all.'

That was before the gale blew in and the rain began to beat against them as if driving them back. ''Tis worse than I thought,' he confided in Sarah, who since she had got into the boat had kept her eyes on the cottage, oblivious to everything but the shoreline she was leaving.

The rain whipped across her face like a slap as she turned to face Captain Bob, and it took a second to recover her breath. 'I can still see the cottage,' she said in reply. She pulled her shawl around her, though it was now offering her almost no protection as the rain soaked through the open weave of the wool.

'Aye, you can see it all the way until we get round to the other side of the head. 'Tis the landmark for many of us coming in. It helps better for me when the candles are lit, mind ye.'

She sensed rather than saw his smile. She could not manage one in return. She thought she would never smile again.

'Do you keep in touch yerself with any of the people who have left Tarabeg to sail to America?' he asked, trying to distract her with small talk in an attempt to calm her.

Sarah shook her head. Most of the people she'd gone to school with in the village had already left for New York, and she'd heard that some had headed out as far as Chicago and other cities and states. But they were just romantic-sounding names to her. It was the same with everyone: they left, they wrote and then, often, they forgot.

''Tis a shame,' Captain Bob said, 'because there will be plenty of them.'

'Have you been?' she asked.

'I have. I sailed there once – not on this, of course. I have visited my sister and she's a good woman. The girls love it there, so they do. Some of them go over and stay with her for a few weeks, before they take the veil. They choose to do it in America, though God alone knows why. A vow of chastity means the same whatever convent or country you live in, I would imagine.'

Sarah blushed and was thankful the sky was too dark for him to see. Taking the veil was not an option for her, having already given herself to Michael. Michael! Just the invocation of his name made her heart fold in pain. All her memories, the last five years spent waiting... She turned back to take a last look at the fading view of the cottage. She was sure she could sense Michael nearby. Even though Bee thought she was mad and assumed Michael had deserted her, Sarah knew he was somewhere, thinking of her, just as she was thinking of him. She opened her mouth to speak, to tell Captain Bob they'd made a mistake, but she couldn't form the words.

As if reading her thoughts, Captain Bob shouted across, 'Did you not ever consider living with Bee? There'd have been good reason once Rory had died, I'd have thought.'

A huge wave smacked up against the side of the boat and broke over the deck with a slap that made Sarah jump in alarm. The wind was wailing now and lightning split the sky. Her heart was in her throat. Conversation suddenly forgotten, Captain Bob lost his reassuring air of calm as water slopped into the boat. His brow furrowed as he looked about him and frowned. For the first time she detected in his eyes something of her own fear.

He picked up a handle from the belly of the boat and began to pump it up and down. 'We need to bail the water,' he shouted. 'Here, you do this, I cannot take my hand from the tiller, the wind is so strong.'

Sarah grabbed the handle and began to copy his actions. The ocean seemed to be lapping higher up the sides of the boat, or they were sinking lower, and the rain fell harder by the moment.

'Don't be worrying now,' he shouted, ''tis just a nasty squall. She's just passing over us, on her way inland.'

Glancing back, he saw the disbelieving look on Sarah's face. He didn't believe it himself, how could he expect her to? It had blown in so fast, faster than anything he'd experienced in all his years at sea. The stillness in the air just before had been eerie – he should have known, and now he cursed himself. But he had made a call, and even after all these years, he now noted to himself wryly, he could still call it wrong.

'So, why wouldn't you live with Bee then?' he asked again, his voice now falsely cheerful, as if trying to sound normal and unconcerned.

'I used to, when Ciaran was tiny, but my da wouldn't let me after a while, and anyway I wouldn't leave Mammy. At least when I am there, someone's watching him. But now there's only Bee. Bee is the only person I know who isn't scared of him. Brave, she is.'

'So are you, Sarah. What you're doing now, agreeing to travel to a new place, a new world, that's brave too.'

If Sarah hadn't been so terrified, she might have responded, but just as he finished speaking, the wind picked up and seemed to propel the boat in the opposite direction, thrusting it back towards the shore and away from the headland and Ballycroy. She grabbed on to a rope as Captain Bob fought hard to steer against the swell. As she bailed out yet another deluge of water with her free hand, she heard a scream and realised it was her own – she was petrified. She could barely see as she bent her head low, the rain lashing her face and stinging her eyes. She felt the boat lurch to port as he pulled hard on the tiller to steer away from the rocks. They were far too close for comfort.

'Are we well enough out here?' she shouted, but the wind was so loud, she couldn't tell if he had heard her or not.

'We just need to get round this outcrop – a few more minutes,' he shouted back.

Despite herself, Sarah began to sob with fear.

They were now sailing into what appeared to be a full-on storm, with the wind pushing against them. Captain Bob feared what conditions would be like once they rounded the headland; he doubted he'd even be able to land. If it didn't pass soon, they'd be in real trouble. He edged the boat in closer to the cliffs, away from the worst of the wind. They would have to sit it out ashore, bide their time. There was no choice. He turned the boat round and headed straight for the nearest beach. There was a cave in this little inlet that the smugglers used; they could shelter there.

'We need to wait on land awhile,' he shouted to a terrified-looking Sarah, trying his best to sound as if this were quite normal. 'Until the conditions are right.'

He jumped down into the water, heaved the boat on the crest of a wave, and ran with it up onto the beach. Moments later, he was relieved to lift Sarah over the edge and have them both place their feet on dry land.

'Don't you worry, the ship to America is a big one, it will slice through a storm like this with no bother at all, you won't even feel it.' He steered her gently up the beach. 'Look, you're soaked to the skin, let's head to the cave – see here, it's straight ahead.'

Sarah was trembling with the cold and the wet. The nightmare voyage was over and she was certain of one thing: she never wanted to be afloat again, as long as she lived. Now safely ashore, she felt newly defiant; bold, even. 'I don't want to go to America,' she said calmly.

Captain Bob took her arm, but she pulled away. The distance from her father was making her feel courageous; that and the relief at not having drowned. With Captain Bob there, she felt that McGuffey could not touch her. She almost wanted to demand that she be taken back home.

But Captain Bob wasn't listening to her. Sweat was pouring

down his face from the effort of beaching the boat and his beard was sodden with the rain. As the boat creaked and shifted in the wind, he lifted his cap, which he'd somehow managed to hold on to through the gale, and looked up towards the cliff. Once again, they had a view of the cottage. 'Now, now, what's that about?' he muttered in surprise, almost to himself.

Sarah turned around sharply and followed his gaze. To her amazement there were lights on the cliff. Burning torches.

'What will that be?' he asked.

'Something's wrong,' said Sarah, her face drawn, her thoughts focused on her mammy. 'And it can't be for a fishing boat, because there is none out, only us.'

It had taken Seamus and Paddy only minutes to appraise the situation and take control.

'Tig, light the flares,' Paddy shouted. 'They will be seen from the village.'

Father Jerry was on the ground, next to Michael. He gently prised Angela from his arms.

'Pete, go back down the path after McGuffey,' Paddy continued. 'Don't give chase, just see if you can tell which way he's gone. Remember, he's a man with a gun and a temper, so don't approach him. We'll call the Garda as soon as we can get back to Mrs Doyle's.'

Pete wanted to ask Paddy, was he mad? He had no intention of apprehending McGuffey.

Paddy was in full flow. 'When the flares go up, Brendan and Bridget McAndrew will see them and come running. Mrs Doyle will see them too and call for the doctor in Belmullet. And bring rope, Tig, for the cart, any rope that there is in the turf shed – we will have to take the poor woman back to her home.'

He had no need to ask, for Tig was already halfway to the shed and knew himself what needed to be done. The beacons were kept there, in the turf shed next to the McGuffeys' cottage, because theirs was the highest house, nearest to the ocean and the cliff edge. If a boat was in trouble, the beacons could be lit in minutes.

Michael was bent double, relieved to hand over responsibility for Angela to Father Jerry. He wiped his hands furiously on his knees and across his soaked trousers in an attempt to remove the blood. From somewhere beneath his robes, Father Jerry extricated his Bible and opened it, but within seconds he quickly banged it shut it again, pulling his cloak out to protect the precious book from the rain. He began to pray, but Michael could not make out the words of his chant against the thunder of the waves on the beach below.

Pete came running back into view, his trousers ripped from numerous slips on the shale, blood running down his legs, the wind whipping the hair around his face. Panting, he fell to his knees beside Michael and Father Jerry. 'McGuffey's gone – he ran. We saw him, though, Michael. Just in time, we were. We saw the gun – no one will be blaming you.' He nodded sorrowfully at Angela.

'There's one hell of a swell in the bay,' said Seamus, grabbing on to Paddy's arm as the wind buffeted him.

'Is she dead?' asked Paddy. 'She's looking mighty queer.'

Seamus hadn't wanted to look. If he didn't, it might not be so bad, or so he thought. One glance and he turned to Paddy, the colour leaving his face. 'I've never seen Father Jerry giving the last rites to anyone who was going to make it, have you?'

Paddy shook his head and blessed himself.

As the flare fired up from the cliff edge, they both turned to look at Angela. Father Jerry used his thumbs to close her eyelids, but they refused to remain shut and slowly opened again. The lightning, the flares and the full moon lit up the clifftop and the entire sorry scene as though it were daylight.

''Tis a good job there's no one out fishing or smuggling in that,' said Seamus as he tipped his head towards the ocean. 'They'd never make it back alive.'

Father Jerry stood and, removing his cape, laid it over Angela. His eyes met those of Michael, who was sobbing, his shoulders heaving. There was no hope, no mistake. Angela really was dead. 'Come on, Michael, let's carry her back to the cottage. She is with the angels now. Can you manage that?'

Michael rose to his feet, staggered, and then stood straight, with Angela laid across his open arms. The rain was falling more gently now, in soft vertical columns as the wind dropped. There was a stunned silence as the men removed their dripping wet caps and clasped them to their chests. They blessed themselves and began to mutter holy prayers of deliverance.

Michael gasped for his breath as Pete shouted, 'There's someone on the cliff – he's coming back!'

'God, no!' said Seamus.

'I need no gun to deal with McGuffey,' said Father Jerry.

An air of desolation, of something too awful for words settled upon them as they all stared at the dead woman.

Michael shook his head in disbelief. This woman, this good woman who the entire village knew kept the cleanest home, was the most loving mother and took the hardest beatings, a woman who spent her life in prayer, obedience to her husband and duty to her family, was dead.

A noise pierced the gloom and the noise became a name and that name was Michael's, as, mere yards away, Sarah stood, halfway up the cliff path, her hand over her eyes, shielding them from the rain.

Heads turned in dread. Michael looked towards the path and their eyes locked.

Sobbing, Sarah dropped her basket and ran towards him, calling his name, barely coherent.

'No, Sarah! No!' Michael tried to shield her from the bundle in his arms.

But it was too late, she was only feet away from him, running towards him for the reunion she'd dreamt of for so long. As she reached him, her eyes were drawn to the figure draped over his arms and wrapped in a cape. The wind lifted a corner of the fabric and revealed the bloodless face of her mother.

Bee had fallen asleep with the mug of porter in her hand. It had slopped onto her skirt, leaving a crimson stain, barely identifiable against the dark grey serge of her skirt, and now the mug lay empty and on its side. Her head lolled against the wooden back of the chair, having lost the cushion to the floor, when suddenly she woke with a start and saw Angela standing before her, dripping wet.

'God in heaven, I was just sleeping. You came then? Why didn't you put a coat on, you'll catch your death. I can't tell you what a relief that is, that I won't have to run up to fetch you in the morning. My bones are aching so bad, so they are.'

She squinted, but the dark and the porter and the fact that she was used to her sister's quietness meant she had no cause for alarm.

'Get into my bed, would you. Here, I'll make some warmth to dry your clothes by. Put them on the chair.'

Bee leant forward and reaching down into the basket at her side picked up two blocks of peat and threw them onto the fire. The fire going out and the famine returning were the biggest fears in every cottage in Mayo. She looked back to Angela, but she was no longer in front of her. The candle in the hearth spluttered and a curl of trailing grey smoke rose against the smouldering red peat.

Bee heard the bed creak at the opposite end of the room. 'It will all be different in the light, Angela, you will see. 'Tis your turn for a rest. You sleep now, you sleep.'

Chapter 9

The flares had done their work. Brendan arrived and hot on his tail was Bridget, who had little to do or say, given that Father Jerry had already pronounced Angela dead. She rolled Angela onto her side, examined the gaping hole in her back, then laid her down again gently.

'Jeez, 'tis an awful wound. There is nothing I could have done,' she said apologetically, shaking her head as she looked up at the faces surrounding her. In every eye staring back down she met an unwillingness to accept that she, a woman of medical mystery and authority, could not bring Angela back to life.

'Can't you do anything, Bridget?' asked Paddy, feeling both hopeful and foolish at the same time.

In answer, Father Jerry resumed chanting his prayer. Hadn't he just given her the last rites? Wasn't it obvious to all that she was dead? Who were they to argue with God's will?

Bridget shook her head as she rose to her feet and turned towards Brendan. 'We have a dreadful problem here. The woman has been murdered, in cold blood.'

'Aye,' said Brendan, ''tis a murder, that's for sure. The men saw it happen too, from the ridge.' Unnecessarily, he pointed towards the road. 'I've sent for the Garda, but my guessing is McGuffey will be well gone by now. The men have looked down on the beach, his boat is nowhere to be found. Disappeared into thin air, so he has.'

No sooner had the words left Brendan's mouth than Captain Bob appeared on the clifftop and began making his way towards them.

'What are you doing here?' Brendan asked.

'I saw the flares – I'm sitting out the storm until the morning,' he replied without even a hint of hesitation.

'Did you see McGuffey? You need to be careful – the man is on the run.'

'No, I didn't.' Captain Bob shook his head but didn't elaborate. 'Was he here?'

Sarah had fallen to the ground and was holding her mother's head on her lap. Her tears mingled with the rain and ran into the blood that smeared the side of Angela's face. Angela's vacant grey eyes were open, staring up at her daughter, and they told her nothing. 'What happened, what happened?' she screamed as she looked about her. Pivoting on her knees, ripping holes in her stockings, she scanned the faces of the men around her, each one reflecting an uncomfortable, guilty, hopeless pity. 'Is she really dead? Is she dead?' she cried.

No one spoke; they all simply looked towards Michael. He was the only person who could tell her. He had witnessed the full horror of Angela's death and it was to him that she'd spoken her last words. Every one of the men there was wondering what she'd said, each one of them conscious that for too long they'd stood aside and done nothing while Angela had suffered at the hands of McGuffey, living their life by the word of God, let no man put asunder...

All eyes turned to Michael. What a task he had, to tell the girl who'd been waiting for him all this time that her mother had gone.

Michael fell back down to his knees beside Sarah and threw his arms around her, pulling her sobbing face into his chest. 'She is, Sarah. She is.'

Only he heard her muffled reply. 'Thank God you came. You came back.'

The priest, reclaiming his place on the ground next to Angela, spoke. 'Let me pray with you, for you, Sarah, for you both.'

The gathered men fell silent.

As those in Tarabeg who had seen the flares made their way towards the coastal lights, Father Jerry's voice rang out from the clifftop. Other than Sarah's soft weeping, his was the only voice to be heard as a crowd formed around them.

Rosie was woken by a banging on her door. Lifting her head, she thought she was dreaming. But the banging was loud and insistent.

'I'm coming!' she shouted. Her blood ran cold – something was very wrong, of that she had no doubt.

She opened the door to Teresa, whose long silver hair was, for the first time ever, not tied up in her customary bun but splayed across her shoulders. It was the first thing Rosie noticed, and it was a sign of just how serious a situation it was.

'Come quick! The flares are up on the shore. Michael Malone is up there. Something's wrong. Mrs Doyle has already left.' Teresa had so much information to impart and quickly, her sentences were spoken in a staccato rhythm.

Rosie responded immediately. 'Let me get my coat.' She

turned and glanced up as an orange flare hit the sky. Her heart was hammering. Michael was home. Michael was up there? It was surely a sailor gone down, possibly the father of a child at the school. Without another thought, she pulled her coat over her arms and followed the people already leaving the village and heading towards the shore.

The news spread around Tarabeg faster than the flares rose in the sky. As one by one the villagers assembled, they were stunned into silence at the sight before them. Michael, aware that his every word was being listened to, held on to Sarah, afraid that if he let go, she would disintegrate before his eyes. He held one arm under hers and across her back as she knelt on the ground, and with the other he stroked her hair as they rocked together. He bent his head as he spoke.

'She was walking, running. I thought it was you – the rain, 'twas mighty fierce. She was talking to me and then your daddy came.' The words 'and then he shot her' wouldn't leave his mouth; they sat stubbornly on his tongue and he swallowed hard. He couldn't tell Sarah what had happened. Could not inflict that pain on her. He looked up beseechingly at Seamus, who came over and knelt bedside his son on the other side of Sarah. Putting his arm around her shoulders too, Seamus helped Michael support her, father and son both holding Sarah upright, and he said the words that Michael couldn't.

'It was your daddy, Sarah. It was your own daddy. He took his gun to her, and now 'tis our job to protect you. Me and Michael and Nola. We will look after you now. You won't be alone, so you won't.'

Michael's eyes met those of his wise father above Sarah's head and the message was unmistakeable. Say no more. She can't take it in. Only Michael knew the truth and only Michael ever would. Only he had seen the wickedness in McGuffey's eyes.

'She was on the cliff,' Sarah sobbed. She instantly knew why, but she would carry her own secret. In her mind, there was no doubt her mother had been trying to catch sight of her crossing the bay as she left. Wanting to catch and hold the last glimpse of her for who knew how long. But the priest and everyone listening would assume her mammy had been looking to see if her da was returning safely. No one would know that Sarah had been running away. She would tell no one, and without even asking him, she knew that neither would Captain Bob.

'Let's carry her home,' said Brendan in a voice heavy with sadness. 'The whole village will be up here in no time if we don't. Help me, would you, Seamus. Michael, you look after Sarah.'

Within minutes the procession began making its way to the McGuffey cottage. The sodden, bedraggled group made a piti-ful sight. The villagers had sacrificed their capes to lay them under and over Angela, covering and cushioning her with as much care as if she'd been alive. Pete drove the horse and cart and as the rain eased and the wind moved deep inland, they wound their way along the clifftop and down to the cottage.

Despite her best efforts, Sarah could not walk, even with Michael's arms around her. Her legs gave way as she took her first step and her trembling was so violent, Michael had to support her to stop her from falling down.

''Tis the shock,' said Captain Bob.

Rosie stepped forward through the crowd and, removing her own threadbare coat, laid it across Sarah's shoulders, pul-led the belt to the front and fastened it across her. She didn't speak, but before she returned to Teresa's side, she caught Michael's eye.

'Thank you,' he whispered as he scooped Sarah into his arms and began to walk with her behind the cart.

The priest, Paddy, and a growing cortege of villagers followed slowly along behind them.

Rosie's mind was in turmoil. She returned to Teresa's side and fell into step with her. Her eyes never left Michael; she studied every move of his hand as he stroked Sarah's back, feeling the gentle pressure running up and down her own spine in rhythm with his movements. She felt every stone of the shingle path through the thin wet soles of her shoes and the pain made her want to shout out, but that was as nothing to the pain in her heart and the rage in her head at the sight of Michael's hand caressing Sarah's back. She hadn't known. No one had told her.

She had to save face, to maintain her dignity. *Don't cry. Hold up your head. Be calm.*

'You got here quick,' said Keeva, who had joined them on the road.

Rosie almost jumped as she was dragged out of her reverie.

Keeva had always liked Rosie but found her difficult to talk to. She'd always assumed this was because she was the teacher and felt it was beneath her to make friends with a farm girl who made the tea and mopped the floor in the post office. Keeva had never encountered a shy person in her life, having grown up with everyone in her village. Where Rosie was reticent, Keeva was outspoken. 'He's killed her – she's dead, Angela McGuffey, and 'twas her own husband,' she said knowingly to Rosie. 'He shot her – would you imagine that! And only here in Tarabeg. It'll be as bad as Dublin here soon.'

Bridget dropped back from the rest of the crowd and joined

them. She'd seen Rosie place her coat around Sarah and knew what she was doing. 'Would you help us in the house, Rosie,' she said. 'I'll be laying Angela out with Teresa, we could do with some help. Sarah will be out of it and when they tell Bee, the poor woman will be beside herself and no use to anyone. Josie and the others will be up in daylight, but until then...'

a woman with no husband, no work and no income, you can pass judgment. Thank God Josie and Paddy gave her a job, but a few hours a night in the bar was never going to fill the pantry or the flour bin. And what's more, 'tis not up for discussion, with anyone. That woman deserves a break – and now, after this, more than ever.'

Teresa had no response. From the tone of Bridget's voice, the conversation was well and truly closed.

As the cortege reached the cottage, curious seagulls had swooped up from Tarabeg Bay and called out to one another with throaty cries of disbelief. The only sound louder than theirs was the relentless crashing of the waves against the rocks below. The clouds parted and dawn began to break, revealing a shoreline littered with torn nets, splintered fishing boats and ripped lobster pots, its glistening, well-washed sand strewn with seaweed, driftwood, Spanish glass and other unseen treasures of the ocean. The moon gave way to the sun and a blue sky presented its innocent, clean face. The cocks crowed and chickens ventured out, pecking and scurrying down the boreens.

Those villagers who'd been too afraid of both the ferocity of the storm and the dark, believing the land was walked by the dead on a full moon, now filed into the McGuffey cottage to pay their respects. There'd been no murder in a village like Tarabeg since the guard house was burnt down in 1920. But a community so close to the ocean suffered untimely losses all too frequently. When death had paid them a visit, everyone knew the sounds, felt the displacement, translated the whispers on the wind. They hurried from the village to the shore with heads bowed low and shawls clasped tight under chins, propelling themselves with the aid of whittled willow sticks and clutching bottles of holy water to hear who it was they had lost and how. One by one, sack cloths were hung in cottage windows to block out the light as a mark of mourning, and candles flared into life, their flames dangerously close to the sacking. As windows blackened and tinder boxes struck, the news spread from cottage to cottage. The women gathered outdoors and began keening and gathering at the church for news and Mass. Children woke and cried; dogs howled.

Paddy and Seamus had accompanied Captain Bob to Bee's cottage to tell her the news before she heard it from the village mourners. But it wasn't long before the women of Tarabeg arrived, clutching rosaries, whispering their condolences, keening and wailing.

Captain Bob waited impatiently for them to leave.

Seamus gestured him into a quiet corner as the last of the women filed out the door. 'Don't be worrying about Sarah,' he said. 'We'll take care of her. Just you look after Bee, and if you have to leave, let me know.'

Captain Bob squeezed his hand firmly in response. Though nothing had been spelled out, the tragedy had made it clear to him that the life he and Bee led was not as secret as he'd thought.

'Don't come back to work until after the funeral, you will still be paid,' Paddy said to Bee as he and Seamus departed.

With the door finally closed, Captain Bob opened his arms. 'Oh, my little Bee, this is too much for you. This is too hard, for you and for Sarah.'

For the next hour or more, Bee's crying came loud and desperate, ripping at his heart, but when it eventually reduced to a gentle sob, he could tell she'd begun to rise above her distress and think of a plan.

'I have to go to Angela,' Bee sobbed. 'She can't be with strangers – I am her sister. Take me to the cottage, will you. And Sarah, she still has to get away from here. I must speak to her and Michael. She isn't safe – that madman, he will come back for her, sure he will, and for Michael too.'

Captain Bob hugged her close. 'I doubt he's that brave. There'll be a guard outside the cottage door by now, and Mrs Doyle will have rung the Garda in Galway too. But sure, they won't catch him, Bee. He will be off on his boat – somewhere abroad, I'd be thinking. Sarah will be safe. Come now, I'll take you to see your sister, but are you sure you're ready?'

He tilted Bee's chin upwards and looked down at her. No words would prepare her, he thought; he would just have to be there to catch her. 'Right, let's go then.' He hugged her to him and wondered how many times over their life they would talk about this night. He still had a wife, but something had to change. He turned his face to the window and looked out across the ocean, all the way to America.

As they approached the cottage, they saw Michael standing outside. Bee gripped Captain Bob's arm and spoke urgently, fiercely. 'He has to marry Sarah soon, Bob, or as God is my witness, McGuffey will do something. The man is mad.' She stared out towards the clifftop and the sea beyond. 'I don't believe he's gone anywhere, sure I don't. I can smell the meanness of him. He's still here.'

Captain Bob was one step ahead of her and immediately began speaking to Michael outside the cottage. 'Michael, son, if ye are holding with your intention and plan to keep your promise towards Sarah, you need to do it soon, even in the face of this terrible act. If McGuffey does return, he will surely take matters into his own hands. You have to get the poor girl away, and both of you through to the other side of this, because if you don't, if he has his way, you will have lost her for good.'

Seamus, Paddy and Tig came out to join them as half a dozen women squeezed their way into the small cottage. They took Bee with them. A chorus of 'Sorry for your troubles' filled the air. The women began to keen and the sound of fresh grief flew from the cottage and past where the men stood. The men each held a mug of tea laced with whiskey in one hand, provided by Keeva, and a slice of boxty bread in the other, brought out to them by a woman shrouded in black and looking as old as the bay itself.

Keeva stopped for a moment as she handed Tig his drink. 'Are you well, Tig?' she asked. ''Tis all such a shock.'

Tig gave a sad smile as he took the drink and muttered his thanks. He was always the same in Keeva's company – speechless – and after she'd left, he cursed himself. Having one leg shorter than the other, and a bad chest to boot, had robbed him of the confidence the other young men of his age took for granted. He didn't notice the look of disappointment on Keeva's face as she turned away.

'Captain Bob is right, you have to get things done before McGuffey returns,' Paddy said as he shook out the dregs of the tea from his mug onto the grass. 'He will fox the Garda, for sure. McGuffey always gets his way.'

Captain Bob laid his hand on Michael's arm. 'You need to put this right before something worse than death befalls that girl, and I'm thinking that would be a life in the back of a gypsy caravan at the mercy of Jay Maughan and the witch Shona.'

'They won't let us – Father Jerry won't marry us after this... it would be the talk of the coast,' said Michael, sounding distraught.

Brendan, having been provided with food and drink, had been eager to escape the cottage full of keening women. He'd come out to join the other men and was listening thoughtfully.

The sun was bold and relentless for a fresh June morning and it sparkled off the surface of the now calm ocean. There was a moment's silence as they all looked down at a trawler sliding through the unresisting breakers. The news had spread and the trawler blew its horn as a mark of respect. The men raised their caps in acknowledgement and thanks.

'Off for the herrings,' said Captain Bob.

Brendan took a swig from his mug and flinched as it hit the back of his throat. 'I will have a word with Father Jerry, Michael. Leave him to me – he and I, we are due for a battle of principle. Sure, I'm always the loser in our arguments about morality – he has the upper hand on me there.' He raised his eyebrows. 'But I always win on the law. The father has a terrible nature for poaching – he thinks the salmon belong to God and anyone can help themselves. And what's more, he thinks I don't know.' He glanced up at Paddy, Seamus and Tig, all of whom were suddenly mighty interested in the dirt on their boots. He focused on Michael. 'Father Jerry can bury Angela, and then I suggest, if it is what you and Sarah both want, you marry straight after. I will ask Father for a hasty burial – how does tomorrow sound? I can't think anyone will object to the fact that McGuffey won't be in attendance, least of all Sarah.'

For all his pious talk about poaching, the men were reassured by Brendan's calm authority.

'Will it really be possible to have the funeral tomorrow?' asked Seamus.

Brendan didn't hesitate with his reply. 'It will. I will make it so. Once the funeral is over, take my advice and get Sarah the hell out of this remote cottage and into the safety of the village. Leave McGuffey and Maughan to the Garda and the men, to Captain Bob and meself, even, if he dares show his face. Though I'm thinking he won't. He's long gone and the Garda know it.'

'Will it not be a scandal if we are to marry so soon?' said Michael, knowing that Sarah would be afraid of local opinion.

Brendan drank from his mug and flinched again at the strength of the beverage. 'Jesus, there is more whiskey in there than there is tea.' He looked into the mug as he spoke, just as Rosie arrived with a tray to remove the empty mugs. 'Rosie, you will have me on my back, so you will. The strength of the drink.'

Rosie was neither looking at Brendan nor listening to him. Her eyes were on Michael, who hadn't even noticed she was there as he absentmindedly placed his mug on the tray.

'You're right, it would be a scandal under normal circumstances,' Brendan said. 'But for Sarah an exception will be made. Especially should someone have a mind to let everyone know that McGuffey was to marry her off to Maughan. No man in his right mind wants that life for his daughter.' Brendan winked at Michael as he spoke. 'I'll away to the gravedigger's now. I'll help them myself if I have to, while the whiskey is working. I'll have a word with Father Jerry first and get him to agree to marry you both tomorrow, so I will. Sarah can then move up to the farm, where she can be safe.'

The tray tipped up out of Rosie's hand and a clatter of tin

mugs and dudeens fell to the ground. Rosie bent to retrieve the mess and Brendan squatted down to help her. 'Will you be wanting a lift on the cart back into the village, Rosie?' he asked.

Rosie shook her head. 'No, I'm just helping Teresa in the kitchen here. We'll walk back. 'Tis Saturday,' she said by way of an explanation for her being able to stay. She was answering Brendan but glanced up at Michael, her eyes bright, her heart pounding. She wanted to scream, 'No, don't do it, it's too quick. Take time, wait...' Instead she asked, 'Would you be wanting more tea, Brendan?'

Michael made to say something to Brendan, but the words stuck in his throat and he had no answer.

Seamus put his hand on his son's arm. 'Thank you, Brendan. I think that would be a grand idea if you can get that sorted, thank you. We need to look after these two and do what's best for them both now.'

Captain Bob placed his mug on Rosie's tray and gave her a kindly smile, which made her blush. 'I think that would be best for Bee too,' he said. 'The man has never crossed the line into Bee's house, but I wouldn't put it past him if he knew Sarah was there. Her being unmarried, he has the right to take her, should he come knocking.'

'He'll be for the noose if he comes knocking here,' said Brendan.

'You'll have to catch him first,' said Captain Bob. 'We all know that the guards from Galway won't be here for long if they think he's gone, and then it'll be down to you – there's no one else here.'

They all knew that Captain Bob was right. McGuffey was afraid of no one and Sarah was in danger.

★

When the visitors had left and the cottage was quiet at last, Michael sat down next to Sarah at the top of the kitchen table, alongside Angela's head, and Bee sat on the other side. Bridget, who being the village seer sat with every corpse in the village, and Teresa had laid a bedsheet on the table and another over the top of Angela, covering half of her body. A fresh tallow candle burnt at each corner and her face flickered in the half light, waxen and white.

Earlier in the afternoon, Sarah had fallen into a fitful sleep, her head on Bee's lap as the shock subsided and she was left spent. Bee had stroked her niece's hair as her own tears dropped onto the back of her hand, her rosary clenched between her fingers. She now had two people to care for, her son and her niece.

As the day wore on, Bee felt the need to see her son's face, to touch him and hold him close. 'I have to go and see Ciaran,' she said. Grief had robbed her of her vitality and left only weariness and despair. Her face was puffy and red from crying, her voice flat. 'I'll be back as soon as I can, in an hour or so.'

Tears continued to pour down Sarah's cheeks as the door clicked shut. For the first time, she and Michael were alone together, though they both knew that wouldn't be for long. The village women would be back again soon, to sit with Angela. In the face of adversity, the women of Tarabeg always supported each other. Regardless of past animosities or feuds, they stood in solidarity with each other in times of need, in death as in life. Angela McGuffey had benefited from this companionship in so many ways over the years, often finding parcels of food on her doorstep when Kevin McGuffey went missing for weeks at a time. They would not leave Angela to face her journey to her maker alone.

Michael wasted no time in telling Sarah the plan. It felt unseemly, but others had urged him to move swiftly. 'If you wait, you will lose,' Brendan had told him, and the words rang in his ears as he looked down into the face of his Sarah. A face that was different from the one he'd recalled when far from home. She was almost twenty-one. Her puppy fat had fallen away, her cheekbones were more defined and her eyes were larger, albeit haunted and bloodshot and full of pain. He had left a girl and returned to find a beautiful woman who'd been prepared to leave everything and everyone she knew to keep herself for him, not knowing if she would ever be able to come back, or, for that matter, if he would. He looked now deep into the eyes that were peering questioningly up at him.

'If we are to be married, we must do so after your mother's burial. Only Father Jerry will marry us so quickly, after everything. We will have to move fast' – he turned his head to the corpse lying between them, as though addressing her too – 'so we will, Angela. We have to, and I know you will forgive us.' He turned back to Sarah. 'Brendan O'Kelly is arranging the funeral and the requiem Mass.'

Sarah made a small sound, a stifled sob, and Michael held her into him as tightly as he could. He'd been wrong. This was a ridiculous idea. How could she marry when she was supposed to be in mourning for over a year before it could even be considered. He wanted to absorb her pain, take it and carry it for her, but the reality was he couldn't, she had to do it alone, and this would be the last thing she wanted. He would do anything to save her if he could.

'I'm sorry,' he said, getting to his feet, 'this is too much for you to deal with all at once. Your mother, this tragedy and getting married. It's not how it should be.'

Sarah rose with him, rubbing her hands down the front of her skirt until he held out his own for her to take. Someone had hung a width of black mourning cloth over the window, so the only light came from the candles, even though the sun was only just setting.

'Come here,' he whispered. 'Angela won't mind,' he said as he glanced down at the serene face in the coffin.

Sarah turned back and followed his gaze. 'Look at her,' she whispered. 'I've never seen her look so young or so peaceful.' She gulped down a sob. 'The torment he put her through... Bee always said to her, every time they had one of their sisters' tiffs, that he would kill her one day, and... and... he has.' She clamped her hand across her mouth to stem the fresh bout of tears and her shoulders heaved.

In seconds, Michael's arms were about her. Gently, as the wave of grief subsided, he led her towards the door and opened it out onto the view of the ocean. They stood in the doorway and Michael filled his lungs with the briny air as he pulled Sarah into his side. There were no words he could say to ease her tears. His instinct was to hold her and say nothing, to let her cry her grief out.

The sky blazed scarlet and orange as pillars of gold pierced the mirror-still surface of the green ocean. A lone fisherman bobbed, stationary, half a mile out, a black silhouette against the flaming sky. His curragh lurched from side to side as he hauled up a heather-twisted lobster pot he would have dropped before the storm, a pot Sarah had woven. Dolphins broke through the glassy calm and circled, ready to swim in his wake as he rowed to shore.

Sarah turned her tearstained face up to Michael. 'I want us to be married, Michael. Daddy, he is such a bad man. Aunt Bee thinks he's near mad. I haven't told you half of it – I can't, not yet. 'Tis the way it has to be – we have to be married, if you still want me.'

He heard the tears catch in her throat. She was beyond comfort for the loss of her mother, and yet it felt to Michael that with his return, even though her mother lay dead, a weight had fallen from her shoulders.

'Are you strong enough to do this?' he asked her as for the first time he kissed her salty lips. He needed to see her eyes, to reassure himself that this was still what she wanted and had been waiting for; that despite all of this, she was stable enough to make a decision. More than anything, he did not want it to be something she regretted later.

'I am.' She nodded vehemently. 'I can do anything, face anything, as long as I know you are never going to leave me again. Ever. If we can't be together, then I may as well follow Mammy to heaven and throw myself over the cliff. God knows, I've wanted to. I would rather do that than live without you and be hounded by Jay Maughan.' Her lip began to tremble and she began to shake again, just at the mention of Maughan's name.

Michael grabbed her into his arms and buried his face in her hair. It was thick and salty from her voyage across the bay and from Bee's tears.

'I am never leaving your side, Sarah. We will spend every day of our lives together – do you understand that? There is nowhere better than this to live and I know that now. I am yours, Sarah, and you are mine. You kept me safe. It was only the thought of you that brought me home. We will make Tarabeg our own piece of heaven, together, you and me.'

*

Back in the village, Teresa Gallagher buttered a hot oatcake and pushed it across the table to Rosie. 'I wonder what Brendan needs to speak to Father Jerry about so urgently. I can't imagine, with all that's going on. He only ever comes when there is trouble in the village.' She sighed. 'God, that poor girl, she must be distraught, losing her mammy, and her own daddy being the one to kill her like that, and him on the run.'

Teresa poured tea for her and Rosie, then sat on the chair closest to the fire to drink it. 'I never thought we would be laying out a body today, did you?' The steam rose from her feet and clothes and the oatcakes failed to overpower the smell of wet wool. 'I'll pop in when Brendan has left and ask Father is everything all right. With a bit of luck, he'll tell me what it was he wanted.'

Rosie swallowed the scalding tea as she washed down the oatcake. She hadn't eaten anything for hours and was grateful to Teresa for both her home cooking and her friendship. She placed her cup on the saucer with uncustomary care and, looking up, said, 'I know why he's here. He wants Father Jerry to marry Michael and Sarah as soon as the mammy is buried, and he wants that to happen tomorrow. I heard the men talking.'

'God in heaven, no! That cannot be – surely not,' said Teresa, her own cup only halfway to her mouth. 'How can he do that? People are always asking Father Jerry for the impossible. They think because he's a man of God, he can perform miracles.'

Rosie didn't reply. She had picked up the final piece of oatcake and was about to pop it into her mouth, when Teresa spoke again.

'Mind you, they would make a lovely couple, would they not? They are both obviously just mad for each other.' She immediately flushed, embarrassed.

The oatcake never reached Rosie's lips. As she smiled and replied, 'Oh, yes, grand,' it disintegrated between her clenched fingers into a thousand crumbs.

Chapter 10

As the women gathered at the house to begin their over-night prayer vigil, Bee urged Michael to return home. 'Go home to your mammy,' she said to him. 'She will be desperate to see you.' He was torn, afraid to leave Sarah. 'Go, this is for us now, the women. Leave Angela and Sarah to me. You do what you have to and there's plenty to keep you busy.' Sarah was sat at Angela's side, holding her hand. The wake, the ritual of death was in full flow and he knew he was out of place if he stayed for much longer. The cottage had filled almost in minutes with the women from the coastal cottages and the village, rotating their hours, in and out. Keening, whispering, praying. The cottage of candlelight and shadows was filled with the clicking of rosaries and the making of tea. There they would remain until the time came to carry Angela on a spiritual wave of love and companionship, all the way into the ground.

Nola rocked back and forth in her son's arms, crying and wailing from the depths of her own dismay. She had been proud of herself when he'd first arrived home, maintaining her composure, not wanting to embarrass either of them, but the news of the shooting and Angela's death had torn away her defences.

As Michael pulled her into his chest, she occasionally surfaced for air, her words garbled. 'Oh God, Michael, 'tis you. 'Tis. 'Tis you. I thought you'd never come back, and then... then... you were nearly shot in your own village.'

The tears flowed again and he crushed her into him with an urgency, almost hoping that he might suffocate her distress.

'I have prayed so much the entire time you've been away, my rosaries are worn to dust and me knees to the bone – I can barely walk,' she cried.

'Mammy, Mammy, shush, what's wrong with ye? I'm not dead, I'm here.'

Nola pulled back from him and cupped his face with both of her hands. 'Would you look at ye,' she said through her tears. 'Yer face has altered beyond all recognition, I hardly knew 'twas you when I first saw you.'

'Aye, 'tis usually a horny woman with big tittics gaspin' for her life that she finds here in me bed that surprises her,' shouted Daedio. He was keenly feeling the lack of attention being lavished on himself, and his stomach was crying out for his supper.

'Oh hush your mouth, you dirty, disgusting old man,' Nola retorted over her shoulder. Reaching down, she threw one of the cushions straight at Daedio's head.

Michael laughed. 'Your aim is just as good as it always was, Mammy.'

Nola smiled as she wiped her eyes. 'God, there were so many telegrams.' She gasped. 'And they were going all over the place. Jesus, you couldn't walk into Tarabeg without hearing the name of someone you had known having died in some foreign land. Boys who went from the farms just for a bit of money and the adventure, that was all they was after, and instead they died, Michael. I thought every day one would be coming here too. Every time I saw yer daddy coming around the bend in the cart being pulled by that mad horse, I was terrified to see his face in case it wasn't the horse but him rushing to bring me the bad news. Oh, Michael, never have I been so glad to see anyone in my life. Never, never.'

Seamus coughed. 'The boy hasn't had much of a welcome home. I'd say it's been all go, wouldn't you all agree? 'Tis a good rabbit stew he needs in his insides, and a pot in his hand, and then we can all have a talk about what will be happening, Nola.' He self-consciously touched his cap and scratched his head beneath it. He wasn't used to making decisions in his own home.

'Thanks, Daddy.'

Their eyes locked over Nola's head.

'Anyway, I'll be taking the pail down to Pete – don't you be worrying about that, Nola.' And with that, Seamus swung open the door and the fresh evening air filled the room.

Less than an hour later, they were all seated around the table. Michael felt his shoulders ease as the hot stew hit his belly and the porter ran in his veins. Seamus refilled their mugs.

'You know what the English say, don't ye?' said Daedio from his bed. 'That God invented the drink to stop the Irish from conquering the world. So don't be complaining, Nola – we are only doing God's work.'

Pete Shevlin was at the table for supper and slowly, after a number of questions from Daedio, Michael passed on snippets of information about the war. They were all aware that it would be disrespectful to talk about Angela and her death while they were eating; that would have to wait until the dishes had been cleared and the pipes lit.

'Did ye have sugar in France?' asked Daedio before he heaped three spoonfuls into his tea.

'They have none in England or north of the border, so they say. Mind, we shouldn't have this – it has been short, though not in scarce supply altogether, but we have the ways.' Seamus tapped the side of his nose with his finger.

'Shush, Daddy,' said Nola. And then, dropping her voice to a whisper as though there might be someone around to hear, 'There's been a fair bit of the smuggling going on, Michael. Around the coast, up and over the border. We did all right, so we did. Paddy got all kinds of things taken over for us. The price we got for the eggs, you wouldn't imagine. They must be starving over there.'

'They don't have much in Liverpool,' said Michael. 'They're on the ration books for every bit of sugar, butter and meat.'

Seamus gasped. 'The meat as well? Jesus, would you believe it?'

Michael didn't have time to answer before Daedio spoke again.

'Why is no one listening to me?'

They all turned around from the table, even Pete, to look at Daedio lying in the bed.

'What have you to be saying then?' said Seamus. 'We are all listening, Daedio. About to educate us all with your opinion on the war and the rations in Liverpool, are you?'

'Pipe down, Seamus, if you know what's good for you. I may not be able to run, but I'm a fast swing with this.' He picked up the stick that lay by the side of his bed and waved it in the air. 'I'll tell ye what I have to say. Michael, fetch me my cedar box, 'tis on top of the press.'

Michael had been brought up never to question his elders and did as he was asked. His grandfather owned a carved cedar box and in it, Michael knew, he kept papers and money. It was a chest that neither he nor any of his brothers had ever been allowed to touch.

He bent down, threw a couple more peat bricks onto the fire, then reached up for the box, carried it across to the bed and laid it on Daedio's knees.

'Open the lid, and on the bottom there's a layer of leather – it fools yer mammy. Slip yer hand down the side to feel it under the papers and pass it to me.'

Michael rooted down through the money. The letters he himself had sent during the war stared back out at him from the top, each carefully opened with a knife and placed in order in the box. It felt strange in the amber glow of the firelight to see his own writing. If I'd died, he thought, this would have been all they'd have had left of me. Shaking his head, he pushed the photographs and the Mass cards for relatives long gone to one side. Grandma Annie's rosary clinked beneath his fingers, and then he felt it, the change in texture from the wood and paper, and found the pouch he was looking for, flat on the bottom of the box.

'What is it?' he asked as he handed it over to Daedio.

'Wait and see. Sit ye down,' his granddaddy replied.

Nola and Seamus frowned, neither knowing what Daedio was up to.

He appeared relieved as he opened the toggle and a sheet of paper that looked as if it was parchment slipped onto the bedcover. 'Pick it up and read it,' he said to Michael. ''Tis yours.'

Michael's eyes opened wide. He no longer felt tired, and there was a strange tingling down his spine. He reached out, slowly picked up the parchment and held it in his hands, his eyes never leaving his grandfather's face.

'Go on, read it. Read it out to us,' Daedio said.

Michael carried the document towards the table and the light from the hurricane lamp in order that he could see it better. 'I will, but I'm not sure I understand it. It has my name on it and it says it's "a deed of right to the land belonging as drawn according to the boundaries as marked to the person as aforementioned". That's my name – is that me? What does it mean, Daedio?'

Daedio tutted. 'Bring it here.'

Michael looked to his parents for enlightenment, but both seemed as confused as him.

'It means the seven acres on the other side of the road from Paddy's, the land that leads down to the river, and the land across on the other bank too. See the Sacred Heart above the line at the top?' There was a square of land drawn from the boundary wall of the church; it stretched away to the foot of the bridge at the side and right across the Taramore river. The river ran directly across the land, half an acre from the road, although the river itself was excluded. 'See?' said Daedio again as he jabbed his finger impatiently at the drawing on the parchment. ''Tis yours, all seven acres, in the middle of Tarabeg, yours.'

Michael couldn't take in what his grandfather was saying. He shook his head. ''Tis mine? What for?'

Daedio, exhausted from the excitement, lay back against the

pillows. 'What for? Well, if I were sixty years younger, I would be building meself a shop, I would that. It's right opposite Paddy's and that's useful. As long as you don't want to open a butchers, that is. Michael, your father tells me what they are all saying down in the village. Now the war is over, there will be new things coming into the shops – feck knows, we've had nothing here in Ireland. De Valera, for all his big words about keeping the trade going, didn't manage that so well for us out here in the bog country. Thank God we grow most of what we eat.'

While Michael listened with rapt attention to Daedio's every word, Seamus and Nola were agog, having had not a clue about the land or his grand plans. Nola kept sipping at her porter in a rare moment of speechlessness and Seamus sat frozen, his pipe suspended in the air.

Daedio was making the most of it. 'Listen to me, will ye. Stop, think. The war is over and I don't think we can even guess how much things are going to change around here. The fishing will come back, for a start. Captain Carter still owns the Taramore river and he'll be selling licences to Englishmen – "tourists", he calls them – and more and more of them will be coming here for the salmon. Sure, why wouldn't they. The captain told me himself, we have the best salmon fishing in the whole world, right here in Tarabeg, and those same men, they have money and they will want to be spending it. And there's the new quarry up on the top. There will be more men coming to work, and their families will be following. Be the first, Michael! Go on, open a shop in Tarabeg and make your fortune, because, believe me, the gobshites, the mouthy bastards, the fat lazy maggots, the indolent cowards, those not wanting to take on the brave men like yourself who fought for the British, they will be the first with their hands out to take the money when it starts being spent over here. They are the ones you have to jump over, and that parchment in yer hands, that is how ye will do it. This, Michael, this is to be your wedding gift, from me. For you and Sarah.'

Daedio took a swig of his porter and slumped back against the pillow. If Michael didn't agree, he would be breaking his promise to Annie on her deathbed, the same promise he'd made to his own parents on theirs – that there would always be a Malone on Tarabeg Hill. Malone sweat had soaked the soil, and their blood had stained the crops during and following the famine. His plan was to keep Michael in Tarabeg, close by, and this was the best way to do it.

'When it's time for Seamus to meet his maker, God willing, you will have a son of your own to take over the farm here.'

Michael studied the parchment and read the words again.

Seamus spoke and his words were loaded with disappointment. 'Why didn't you ever tell us about this, Daedio? Me and Nola.'

'Annie didn't want anyone trying to influence me – I promised her.' He tapped the side of his nose. 'We can tell the whole fecking world now.'

Michael rose to his feet and paced up and down in front of the hearth. 'But, Daedio, I don't know anything about running a shop.' Even as he spoke, he felt the excitement rising in his belly. Not a word his grandfather had said was wrong. He could be his own man, run his own business and make his own fortune. He could dress Sarah in fine clothes and not the rags she wore now. 'When did you buy it?'

'Nearly sixty years ago, before your father was even born. The day after we bought it, we had the Maughans thrown off the land, and Shona, she's been carrying a curse for me ever since. Watch out for Jay and Shona – she's still alive and casting fecking curses on everyone she passes. Her father and grandmother, they thought it was their own land, until I bought it from Lord Carter, right out from under them. They have never forgotten. They are a no-good bunch of scavenging child thieves, and that Shona, she scares everyone half to death. But this way, it keeps them out of Tarabeg and roaming the coast. I did the village a favour, so I did – even if no one knows it was me.' He chuckled and rubbed his chin.

Michael folded the parchment and slipped it back inside the pouch. 'Daedio, is this true, is this real?'

'Aye, of course 'tis real. What do you think you're holding in yer hand, a pair of fairies' titties?'

Despite the sorrow and drama of the day, Michael snorted with laughter and almost spat out the porter he hadn't yet swallowed.

Nola tutted in disgust. 'Well, I think if I hear another thing, I'll be dropping down dead meself. Have you ever known a time like this, Pete?'

All eyes turned to him. The only sound in the room was of him eating, and he was aware of it. He looked nervously around before buttering another slice of bread, picking it up and leaping to his feet. 'I'm away to my bed,' he said. 'Big day tomorrow.' He winked at Michael, snatched up his mug and shuffled his jacket over his shoulder with his free hand. The door clicked shut and they heard the dogs in the old cottage barking their greeting as he approached.

Daedio was the first to break the silence.

'Feck 'em all, boy. You will make your own work, and you

will give others work and you will make that fortune you were always talking about.'

Michael slipped the leather pouch back into the box and lifted it onto the press. A plot of land and it was his! He could see it, was familiar with it, had roamed it and poached it, and knew exactly where his grandfather meant. He could walk the perimeter in his mind's eye. There were riverside pebbles in the form of a chair he had sat on and which were still where he had laid them. It was the one piece of wasteland in the village where you could reach the pebbly shore of the Taramore river without having to cross the bog or the bridge. He had gazed out over it when the mail van had brought him back home.

Nola stood and carried the dishes over to the sink. Both she and Seamus appeared stupefied.

'That land? How, in God's name? I don't understand,' said Seamus.

'Ah, now, I thought you might ask that, and all I have to say is where is your mother when I need her, eh? I told her before she went that I should tell ye all, but it was her doing not to. She said I had to wait until there was one left with a nature for the place, who didn't want to leave Tarabeg and shouldn't be driven abroad for work or money if they had heart for staying. She was adamant that there always has to be a Malone in Tarabeg, because there always has been.'

Nola sank slowly onto the bench that ran the length of the table; it had been carved from one of the trees on the hill by Daedio himself, long before she had arrived on the scene. 'What land is this? Not *that* land? No Malone ever had enough money to buy that. The land opposite Paddy's? That's not ours, 'tis Captain Carter's,' she said, looking as confused as Seamus.

'Ah, well, you're wrong there,' said Daedio. ''Tis land bought with the dollars Joe sent back to my daddy from America after the famine. I still have some of the dollars too.'

'How?' said Michael. 'How did your brother get the money?'

Daedio was known as the storyteller in the family and he never tired of repeating anecdotes about the Malones, but this one was new to them all.

'Well, this is a bit of news ye have here, Daedio,' said Seamus.

'How?' said Michael again.

Daedio looked uncomfortable. 'Now, Michael, don't be asking me that, would ye.'

Michael, Seamus and Nola looked at one another.

'Daedio, I have to know where the money came from,' said Michael.

'Well, don't be blaming *me* for not telling ye – I just did as Annie said. I was only following her orders. Nola, pour a whiskey – haven't I just given the lad the best wedding present anyone in Tarabeg ever received?'

Now was the time. Daedio knew there was no getting out of it. The secret he had hidden for so many years, from everyone except Bridget, was waiting to be told. Annie had been right, he did know instinctively that the moment had come.

'Look, me and her – Annie, everyone – feared waking up to another attack of the blight more than I have the words to tell you. Blight meant people starving, babies with swollen bellies. No one knows why it came – twice, remember – and we weren't even allowed to farm for two seasons after it went. Daddy's memories were strong and there wasn't a year went by that they didn't worry themselves sick. As soon as the money arrived, Daddy said it had to go to buy land and to keep it for the future, and so that was exactly what I did.'

'Where did the money come from, Daedio?' Nola's tone was one they all knew and feared. Her eyes locked on to Daedio's.

He had tried to avoid this bit, but to no avail, nothing escaped Nola. 'A robbery.'

Nola gasped and crossed herself. 'Holy Mother of God, are you serious? Michael, you can't have it.'

'Yes, he can. And shut up, woman. He can have it, because we couldn't, and no one is going to be coming after the money now. Jesus, 'twas some sixty years ago and no one has turned up here looking for it, have they?'

Seamus stood and walked over to the fireplace. He placed his arm on the mantelpiece and, towering over Daedio, who suddenly appeared very small and uncertain in his bed, asked, 'What did Joe rob?'

Daedio's voice trembled as the words rushed out. ''Twas a bank, in America. Not just any fecking bank, either – a big one.' In truth, he was relieved to be unburdening himself after so many years. Since Annie had died, keeping secrets all to himself had been hard.

'There, I've said it. My daddy didn't know what the hell to do, so I bought the land to hide some of the money, in case our Joe came back looking for it. Captain Carter asked no questions, he didn't care. But Joe, he never did come looking, we never heard from him again after the money arrived, and Mammy and Daddy wouldn't spend a single note on themselves. Kept it all for him. The stupid fecker sent it stuffed in that cedar box, and the note he sent with it is still in there. Mammy said 'twas the will of the Lord that the box hadn't been opened and had arrived here safely and who were we to challenge the wishes of the Almighty.'

'What happened to Joe? Does he have any family of his own?' asked Michael.

Daedio shook his head. 'The last I heard was he died in an American jail, and that was so long ago, I can't even remember who told me. I think there's a letter, in the box there.'

Michael looked up at the box, felt tempted to take it down, to find the letter, but he had one thought only – to tell Sarah.

Seamus, Nola and Michael all exhaled at once. Nola threw a dish cloth in the sink and slumped into the rocking chair.

'Well, don't be looking all pious with me,' Daedio almost snapped. 'What do you want us to do? Write to the police in America? Annie never did.'

Michael now shot to his feet. If the money was good enough for his grandmother, it was good enough for him. His thoughts were clear. 'No, Daedio, I do not. You're right, 'tis a long time ago. No one will be knocking on our door.'

On Annie's orders, the unused bundles of dollars had been kept. She'd hidden them behind a stone in the wall close to the fireplace. It had been something of a surprise to Daedio to discover how much money there was. The hundred-dollar notes were wound into tight cigar-like bundles, rolled and tied by Annie's own hand. The fifty-dollar notes had been pressed with the flat-iron into packs and wrapped in paper. Daedio had been about to tell them of the fortune hidden in the wall, but, deflated by their reaction to the provenance of Michael's inheritance, he decided against it. That could wait for another day.

'Why were the Maughans on the land in the first place, Daedio?' asked Michael. 'Why do they think it was theirs by rights and not the Carters', if that was who you bought it from?'

Daedio wriggled up the bed, fired up with the prospect of

telling a story he had never before been able to. 'Ah well, you see, the old Lord Carter, he fled back to England as soon as the famine came. He thought the land was jinxed because his first wife had visited and lost her baby. Very sick, she was, in childbed, but Shona Maughan's grandmother saved her. When the Carters left, the grandmother, she stopped the carriage on the road and asked could the Maughans remain on the land. The wife, she was in the carriage and she said yes, they could stay, because she was grateful for her life. The Maughans took that to mean for ever, but Lord Carter didn't agree with that at all. So when we approached the agent to buy and a deal was struck, the Maughans were moved on. The wife, she was dead by then, died giving birth to the second child. The only thing Lord Carter wouldn't sell was the river, and even though it runs through your land, Michael, it still belongs to the Carters, and their English ghillie, he is as smart as the Irish ever were.'

'What a day and a night. I need the pipe.' Seamus leant over to the hearth, picked up a dudeen and lit it from a straw wick he took from the bundle tied up with braided grass that he sat and made himself on dark winter evenings. The peat burnt and the room slowly filled with a blue-grey haze from his pipe. 'Tarabeg will grow, for sure it will,' he said.

'I need a drop more whiskey in me tea,' Nola said as she left the table and walked out to the scullery.

'That is the only sensible thing I have ever heard you say,' said Daedio as he held his mug up to Seamus. 'We could all do with a drop more in the tea to celebrate.'

Nola banged a bottle of Jameson down on the table and pulled the mugs into the centre. 'Seamus, pass me the pot,' she said as she unscrewed the bottle.

Daedio's eyes never left her hands as she poured first the

milk, then the tea, and then sloshed three helpings of whiskey into just three of the mugs. His jaw dropped. 'Oi!' he roared. 'Where's mine? Are you going to let her get away with that, Seamus?'

Seamus looked at Nola, who grinned back at him. 'Sure, I was only teasing,' she said, and laughter filled the room once more.

Seamus, a man of hard work and few words, was more than impressed with the enterprise of his father, who had kept all of this secret from his only remaining son. As was his way, he was waiting for the right words to come to him before he passed comment.

Daedio held up his mug. 'To the future.'

Nola, Seamus and Michael picked up their mugs and echoed his words. 'To the future.'

And they all felt it, the emotional charge in the air, the cool breeze that wafted across the room, the sudden dancing and flickering of the candle flames as if the door had been opened and a single rock of the chair. Michael swallowed down his whiskey, which now held only a dash of tea. His eyes widened as he looked at the others to see had they noticed. A shiver ran down his spine and he drained the last from his mug. He had. They had. No one spoke. Nola blessed herself and picking up the whiskey bottle smiled, but only Daedio knew for certain who and what it was.

Chapter 11

The news of Angela's death would not normally have caused a stir outside of Tarabeg, but the fact that she was murdered, and buried the very next day, and that her daughter upped and left the family home and married within hours, created a scandal that carried all the way across the Nephin Beg to Newport and beyond. It even reached the ears of those who owned telephones, as far away as Galway and Cork.

'God in heaven, the telex has never been so busy,' said Mrs Doyle, sounding very self-important as she bustled about the post office. 'It'll be wearing out at this rate, so it will.'

''Tis a shameful disgrace,' said one customer, who, disgrace or not, had barely left the post office for fear of missing out on the latest news.

'A sin,' ventured another, who was equally entrenched.

But Mrs Doyle, having received her instructions from Father Jerry, via Teresa, was having none of it. 'Oh hush now, will you. Father Jerry knew what they were doing and sure, so did Brendan O'Kelly. One a man of God, the other of the law. How is it you think your opinion is worth more than theirs put together now? It was their idea – both of them agreed to the wedding happening quick. Hadn't Michael and Sarah waited long enough to be wed? Besides, there was no big celebration, as ye well know. It was all done with the minimum of fuss.'

'Aye, but what if her father comes back and the guards don't catch him?' said Philomena O'Donnell as she held on to young Theady's hand. 'This one hasn't slept properly since he heard the stories running wild about the shooting. What if McGuffey comes back and wants to finish us all off in our beds when he hears the news that the marriage took place and not one of us stopped it or said a word to condemn it?' She placed her hands over the ears of her son, who squirmed himself free in objection.

'Oh, I wouldn't be worrying about him,' said Mrs Doyle. 'Kevin McGuffey won't be darkening this village with his shadow again. Well away, he'll be by now. Ye can sleep safe in yer bed, Theady. There are no bad men in Tarabeg now that he's gone. Keeva has been scared herself, haven't you Keeva? I told her the same thing.'

Keeva turned from the shelf, which she was filling with pads of airmail paper. The biggest selling commodity in Tarabeg. She squatted down next to Theady. 'What's bothering you then, Theady? You've been a right misery guts, so you have. Can't get a smile out of you for love nor money.' Her face was on a level with his and she smiled at his woeful expression. She noticed the pale blue bags under his eyes and the greyness of his skin. 'You poor boy. Yer mammy's going to be here for ages yet, do ye want to have a lie-down on the settle in the back?'

Just at that moment, the bell rang and Mr O'Dowd from the school walked in with a letter in his hand. Theady looked up at him and without a second's hesitation placed his hand into Keeva's, which was outstretched. Keeva noticed that his palms were clammy.

'You are an angel, you are, Keeva,' said Philomena. 'I can't be going home yet when there's so much going on here.'

'A letter do you have, Mr O'Dowd?' asked Mrs Doyle. 'Is it to your mother in Dublin again?'

Philomena's ears pricked up.

'My, I hope she knows what a lucky woman she is to have such a dutiful son. And how's Miss O'Hara? We haven't seen her in here yet this morning.'

'Good morning, ladies, and sure, isn't it a fine one too, with the salmon due any day now.' The day the salmon made their journey up the river always caused excitement in the village and was the busiest night of the year in Paddy's bar. 'Yes, I do have a letter, and yes, I do want it posted, otherwise what would be the point in my calling in here? Do you think I come just for the tea? Was that a cup you had on your tray for me there, Keeva?'

The ladies laughed as his eyes rested on Keeva and young Theady and he watched the curtain fall behind them as they slipped into the back.

Keeva led the boy to the settle and made him comfortable, laying a cushion under his head and a crocheted blanket over him. 'Are you comfortable, Theady?' she asked. 'You don't look at all well, so you don't.'

Theady's eyes had welled up with tears. He wasn't used to such kindness from anyone other than Miss O'Hara.

Keeva smiled down at him.

'I'm scared,' he said in what was almost a whisper.

She had noticed the tears but decided not to say anything.

'Go on, have a little sleep,' she said. 'Everything is hard when you are scared and have had no sleep. I know what it's like to be scared. We have a ghost at the farm and sure, sometimes it runs under my bed and I don't get a wink for the rest of the week, never mind the night. Your mammy will be in here for half the afternoon and you, you look dead on yer feet.' She tucked the blanket in around him. 'There's a big fire and there's no Kevin McGuffey coming around here.'

A moment later she was back around the curtain and in the shop, just as Mr O'Dowd turned around from the counter. The look he gave her as he walked to the door made a shiver run down her spine. Sure, you can get your tea elsewhere, she thought to herself as she continued to unpack the airmail paper. For all Mr O'Dowd's popularity in the village, Keeva had never warmed to him. The chatter about Kevin McGuffey and the secret wedding continued. It had been going on all week and wouldn't let up for several more weeks yet.

Mrs Doyle could not have been more wrong. Kevin McGuffey hadn't gone far at all. He had waited in the cave where the goods for smuggling were stored until Maughan eventually turned up. McGuffey had known he would because he had Maughan's share of the money from the last smuggling drop in a leather pouch attached to his belt. Maughan would follow him to the ends of the earth to find it and he would begin that journey there in the cave.

He kept himself hidden, slipping out during the night, taking water from a well and smashing open tinned meat stored in the cave for smuggling north of the border. He consumed several bottles of whiskey and frequently fell into deep sleeps, only to wake with a start when he thought he heard Angela calling his name. There had been times when he'd hit her so hard, he'd wondered would he one day kill her, so he'd long planned what he would do should that ever happen. He would not hang for it, no, by God, he wouldn't. He would escape. And now here he was, about to put his plan into action.

He heard the faintest sound of the muffled hooves of a horse and dared to venture out to the mouth of the cave even though it was daytime. Just as he'd suspected, Jay Maughan was walking down towards him. His caravan was parked under the escarpment, protected from the wind. He could see Shona's head peering around the canvas and he noted the rags tied around the shoes of the horse. It was Maughan's way of making sure no one heard them when they crept into villages and took a new child. There was no tent up and no fire lit, so it appeared they had no intention of staying.

'Have ye heard the news?' Jay shouted. He was only just inside the cave and McGuffey pulled him further in.

'Shut the feck up,' he hissed. 'The guards are outside the cottage.'

Maughan stepped back from him and defiantly thrust his hands deep into his jacket pockets as he retreated towards the cave wall, which was running with water from the cliff. 'Do you think I'm not aware of that?' he said.

McGuffey didn't like his tone. The hint of respect Maughan usually reserved for him was missing.

'You are a fecking wanted man and if they catch you, you will swing,' Maughan said. 'She's fucking dead.'

McGuffey threw his head back and laughed. 'Do you think I'm hiding out in the cave because I didn't know that?'

Maughan sneered. 'Yeah, well, I bet you haven't heard that

she's already fecking buried and that your precious Sarah and Michael Malone are now man and wife.'

This, McGuffey did not know. But apart from a slight rocking onto his back heels and a sudden draining of the colour from his weather-beaten face, he gave nothing away.

Maughan covered the ground between them and, stopping less than a yard away, stared into McGuffey's cold eyes. 'Did ye hear me? She's married. To feckin' Malone. That wasn't the plan. You said I could have her and then he would have fecked right off to Liverpool or America, like every other maggot from around here.'

McGuffey replayed Maughan's words in his head as though he was analysing each one individually. His eyes glittered with anger, but he said not a word.

Maughan jumped back. He had thought McGuffey might hit him, but now he sensed his confusion and continued to taunt him. 'Your wife wasn't cold in her grave before they were wed.' McGuffey continued pacing the cave. 'And where's my money from the load to the North? I want good money for that whiskey.'

This time, McGuffey did respond. Reaching into his jacket pocket, he pulled out the pouch and threw it to the ground. It landed on a wooden crate of porter. Turning on his heel, he carried on walking to the back of the cave, where he'd stashed his own money and his gun.

'Don't be throwing my money around,' Maughan shouted back. 'What do you think I am, a fecking animal?' Nonetheless, he ran over, grabbed the pouch, slipped it into his jacket pocket and marched after McGuffey.

The cave was dark, but McGuffey knew every undulation of the floor, every foothold, and felt some satisfaction at hearing Maughan stumble. He picked up his own pouch and his gun and, ignoring Maughan, pushed past him, strode out of the cave and into the daylight.

Maughan took a moment to steady himself and then, concerned for Shona and the horse, rushed out after him. Maintaining a safe distance, he checked his pouch. 'Only half the money we agreed!' he yelled in disgust. 'You're all fecking talk,' he shouted. 'You can deliver me fecking nothing. Not your daughter or the money, and now there's no fecking land because Malone is staying put. We would have got rid of him if you had kept your end of the bargain. You can't do fecking nothing right, can you? All fecking talk.' He spat violently in McGuffey's direction and watched with his mouth open in surprise as McGuffey stormed up the embankment to the cottage.

As McGuffey had suspected, the guards outside his cottage were nowhere to be seen. They had gone into the village to attend the wake and had never returned. As far as they were concerned, he was long gone.

He threw open the door and as it banged against the wall, he stood on the step and stared inside. It was empty. The shadows of lazy ghosts moved to the side and allowed the sunlight to stream in. Clean and empty. Once the burial was over, an army of women had turned up and given it a thorough once-over. There was no indication that Angela had lain there, cold and dead. All that remained were the echoes of her screams from the many beatings he'd given her. Angela had gone. Sarah had gone. McGuffey was standing in the emptiest cottage in Mayo, and he knew it.

He stepped inside and looked around. He heard the sound of ghosts shuffling as he marched through the room to Sarah's curtained-off area at the end. For the first time in his life, he felt confused. In this cottage, nothing happened without his say-so. How had this emptiness come to pass? The willow-wood rail and its curtain left the wall easily beneath his angry fist. He ripped them both down and flung them to the floor, grinding his heel into the pole, breaking it in a number of places.

Maughan appeared in the doorway and began to laugh. A shrill, hollow laugh.

McGuffey fingered the long barrel of his gun. He flicked off the catch with his thumb and lifted it to his shoulder.

Maughan's laugh quickly became a whimper as he retreated, running backwards and yelling, 'Put the feckin' gun down, you fecking madman.' He fell and smacked the back of his head on the ground. For a brief moment, there was nothing but blackness and silence. As he opened his eyes, he blinked at the brilliant whiteness of the clouds, and the gulls flying overhead. Light became dark as McGuffey's face blocked out the sun above him, his gun still in his hand.

McGuffey began to laugh. Nothing more than a guffaw, thrown out of his throat and down at Maughan. 'Get up,' he said.

Maughan blinked, his eyes adjusting.

'Get up.' This time there was no mistaking the menace in his voice. This was the McGuffey Angela and Sarah had lived with every day.

Maughan pressed his elbows into the stony ground and clumsily shuffled backwards, casting nervous glances over his shoulder. When he was sure he had enough space, he sprang to his feet, turned and ran back towards the escarpment.

McGuffey's laughter rang in his ears. It had moved up from his belly and become a roar. 'Run, you little maggot!' he shouted. 'Run!'

Minutes later, McGuffey was walking back down to the beach with his gun, and the few possessions he owned packed into a lobster net. Maughan was already saddling up his horse and Shona was keeping watch from the front board. McGuffey spotted her and his heart raced. He moved to the left to avoid her. She was like a black cat; no one walked across her path. She was doing something, casting a spell on him, cursing him, he was sure of it. He could do more harm right now than any spell, he thought, but his cocksure swagger was gone.

'Where are ye going now?' Maughan shouted over.

McGuffey turned and spat his tobacco onto the shale. 'To the North,' he replied.

Maughan laughed out loud. 'What, you're leaving Eire to live under the fecking English? You fecking hate them.'

McGuffey had already begun walking away, not interested in Maughan's reply. But now he stopped, impatient at having to explain himself, and fixed his eyes on Maughan. 'And that is why I'm going. There are plenty in the North feel like I do. I won't be back. No one in Eire will be after doing anything. They are all too busy running down to the post office to get their hands on the next parcel of hand-me-downs to arrive from America or the next envelope of dollars or pounds. Money has made them like mad old women.' He glanced towards Shona to see if she'd heard him. 'It's robbed them of their memories, their debt to our ancestors and our past. May they all rot in hell. Jesus feck, a parcel of wool arrives in the post and the famine is forgotten. A twenty-dollar bill and no one cares that we were sending ships loaded with grain to England whilst people here starved to death.'

'That was nearly a hundred years ago,' said Maughan incredulously.

'Aye, a hundred years ago my grandfather was made by the Board of Works to build a road that went nowhere, for a bowl of shite to eat at the end of it. He was so starving and broken, he couldn't manage to walk the seven miles back home with the piece of rotten bread they'd given him to take back for his kids. My family, who lived here, in that house, they died lying on the ground eating grass that stuck in their throats and swelled their bellies, every one of them. The British as good as murdered them. You and every other fecker who takes the Judas shilling may forget that, but I won't. Holy shite, I won't. I won't be happy until I've seen every one of the British blown sky high.'

Maughan had no answer. The hatred came off McGuffey in waves and it always had. He was consumed, obsessed by the need for vengeance. Jay and Shona stood and watched as he pushed his boat out into the bay.

McGuffey kept the boat close to shore, hugging the rocks so as not to be seen until he was far enough away. He'd barely rowed ten yards when he turned, took aim and fired one shot. It hit Maughan in the flesh of his leg. The gulls screeched, rose from the water and circled in surprise. Above Maughan's screams and the roar of the waves, all that could be heard was the sound of McGuffey laughing.

Chapter 12

Paddy and Tig Devlin were shaking fresh sawdust on the bar floor and Keeva was dallying in the butcher's shop. Josie had no idea why she was lingering so. 'If you don't get along with that ham on the bone,' she said, 'I'll have Mrs Doyle in here giving out to me.'

'Oh, I wasn't dawdling, Mrs Devlin.' Keeva bristled and looked put out as she left the shop.

Tig put his head through the dividing curtain just in time to catch Keeva's retreating back and the jangle of the bell. His heart sank and he let the curtain fall with a swish as he returned to the bar. Often when he heard her voice he managed to find some excuse or other to slip into the shop. Keeva made his pulse race and he could barely stop thinking about her. It had been that way for years now – ever since the night they'd walked home from the Long Hall of Romance with Michael and Rosie O'Hara and some of the others. When Michael had walked Rosie up the boreen that night, Tig would have given everything he owned to have accompanied Keeva home, but he'd been too embarrassed to ask. They lived in the same village and saw each other every day, so if she were to have the slightest notion of how he felt about her, he would be lost, with more to bear than simply a short leg and a bad chest. A broken heart, he thought, had to be the biggest disability of all.

Keeva had no idea how he felt about her, and Tig was adamant she never should. Josie and Paddy might have been blind to their son's impairments, but he was sure no young woman as beautiful as Keeva would want to look twice at a man who needed a stick to walk and at times could barely breathe.

Before Tig could settle his thoughts, he heard a horse pulling up outside, and then a shout. It was Michael. Tig had barely seen him in the weeks since he'd returned from the war; he missed their easy chats, the sharing of confidences and jokes. But Michael was all grown up now, with a wife to care for and a different sort of future ahead of him, and he rarely made it down to the bar. Tig was happy for him, but he would have been happier still if he'd had his own future mapped out.

Tig and Paddy went to the door and stood there smiling at the sight of Michael helping Sarah to slide down from the saddle. Both father and son were thinking the same thing, that even the bright sunlight could do nothing to warm the waif of a girl who looked as though she was almost being held up by Michael. She was thin, as grey as a January sky and looked as though there was barely any life left in her.

Michael had been sent down into the village with Sarah on Nola's instructions. 'Take her to the land, show her around, give her something to look forward to, to heal for. It might help, you never know. She needs to see that there is something up ahead, something to live for, to make her mother proud of her. I can't think of anything else that will help with the grief. You know what Bridget says, she has no potion to heal the pain of loss. Captain Bob and Bee are coming tonight and it might give her something to talk to them about.'

Sarah's grief was profound and alarming, and in the weeks since her mother's death it had not lessened. She had somehow held it together through the funeral and the wedding, but as soon as she'd walked through the Malones' front door, with Michael by her side and Captain Bob and Bee behind them, she had collapsed. Her knees gave way and Captain Bob caught her as she fell. Bee had almost envied her – she'd had Ciaran by her side, which gave her no choice but to stand and be stoic.

'Mother of God, take her through to the bed, would you, the poor child.' Nora fussed around Sarah as Captain Bob and Michael carried her into the bedroom.

Through the open door, Bee could see lady's-tresses in a vase on the wooden bedside table, and a fire glowing in the grate. There were rag rugs on the floor, and a hand-crocheted coverlet was laid over Sarah. A candle was burning inside the glass lamp and in the sconces and the room looked to Bee like a sanctuary that came with its very own Nola. Sarah would be safe and, not only that, she would be cared for. A tear came to Bee's eye.

As Captain Bob came back to her side, he squeezed her hand. 'She is going to be well looked after. We can worry about you now.'

Weeks had passed and at least Sarah was now eating, although, as Daedio commented, 'not enough to keep a worm wriggling'.

Michael waved at the Devlins as he tied up the horse. 'Tig, come here, me and Sarah have something to show you.'

'Sarah can see from here, thank you very much,' said Josie, who came bustling out from behind Paddy and Tig. Josie had also been given her instructions by Nola. 'Come on, Sarah, I have rashers for your second breakfast on the range. Bridget's coming to join us and I've no doubt the moment Keeva hears you're here, she'll be straight back down the road. I want us to try this Instant Coffee Philomena's son sent over from New York. She brought me half a jar, so she did, in exchange for her sausages, and we're to have it with hot water and milk, so she said.' Josie waved Tig and Michael away with the flick of a tea towel. 'Go! Go on, you two, off with you. Go.'

Sarah looked dazed but took the hand Josie held out for her without complaint and gave Michael a smile that made his heart flip. Her first spontaneous smile. She was healing.

'Follow me.' Michael beckoned Tig across to the other side of the road, spun around and gestured at the seven acres. 'You see this? This land?' he shouted.

A frown crossed Tig's face. 'Every fecking day, you eejit. I live there.' He pointed back over at the bar and the butcher's shop – his family home.

'I know that,' said Michael. 'I mean this, here, where we're standing. I mean all the way to the church there and down to the bridge here and then across on the other side of the river there, and the road is the end, here.' Michael whirled around and pointed at the four landmarks in turn.

A note of unease entered Tig's voice. 'Why would ye be asking me that? Have ye gone mad, Michael?'

Michael roared with laughter. 'No, I have not, only with the madness that has possessed me because 'tis all mine now, that's what.'

'Yours? How? How can it be?'

Michael laughed again. 'I can hardly believe it meself. Because Daedio bought it when God was a boy. That's how.'

'Daedio? Why?'

'Because he was keeping it for whichever one of us had a nature to stay and not go to America, and that was me.'

Tig let out a sudden breath. All he could say in response was, 'Feck.'

'Aye, feck it is.' Michael grinned.

'What are ye going to do with it?' Tig changed his grip on his walking stick, leant on it more heavily. 'Will ye build a house? Where will ye work, Michael? Ye would have to be back out of yer bed before ye got in it, if ye was to work up at the farm.'

Michael turned his back on Tig and looked up to the quarry. There were now more men up there than there had been even on the day he was married. 'See that? Those men that look like ants in the sky, up on the quarry? They are the future. I'm going to open a shop.' He turned back to Tig. 'Like yer daddy, I'll have the shop at the front and the living at the back. I'll sell all the things everyone has to travel to Ballina for. Pig feed, groceries, all the new things coming into the shops in Galway and Dublin, that kind of thing. Now the war's over, there'll be lots of new things to buy. Chocolate, pots and pans, flour and the like. I'll be selling it all – cigarettes too.'

When they were halfway across the land and Michael had listed all the things he wanted to sell, Tig asked, 'But what will ye do about the Maughans? People buy half of that stuff from the back of their caravan when they come into Tarabeg, and Jay buys plenty more, Michael – stuff he shouldn't, stuff the customs men don't know about, that he takes onto the boats and sells in the North.'

'Smuggling?'

'Aye, he's done mighty well on the back of it. And they mend the pots and the pans too. Jay welded this to the bottom of my stick.' Tig held up his metal-footed walking stick for Michael to inspect.

Michael was disappointed that Tig was throwing obstacles in his way. 'Is Jay Maughan your friend now then? He's no friend of mine, I can tell you that. Nor Sarah's.'

Tig shook his head. 'Of course not, but—'

'Jay Maughan can do what he likes, but a shop is the way. You should see them in Liverpool, Tig. They sell everything, all right. I was there before I was demobbed.'

Tig stopped to catch his breath and fell a few steps behind. 'Are you going to make Tarabeg like Liverpool, Michael?'

'Jesus, no, but I am going to make money and I am going to make Sarah happy. Now get on my back because I want to go and collect the missus and show it all to her.'

Tig's heart sank. The shop would undoubtedly cause trouble with the Maughans. But Michael was in no mood to listen to anyone who wasn't agreeing with every word he said. He was unstoppable. Michael wouldn't hear it and he couldn't see it, but Tig felt a cool wind blow on what was a hot day as his best friend ran with him on his back, just as he had done since they were boys, across the land he now owned.

Keeva slapped the brown-paper parcel containing the four slices of ham on the bone down on the counter and stormed into the back of the post office.

'Morning, Keeva,' said Ellen Carey as she marched past her. Keeva totally ignored her.

'What's got into her?' Ellen mouthed to Mrs Doyle.

'I wouldn't be having the faintest idea, but some days she is the Devil himself to be with. I only sent her out for a nice bit of ham for me tea. She was happy enough to go, all right, she always is – it's when she comes back it's the problem.'

Both women craned their necks to see if they could make out what the banging was that was coming from the back of the post office.

'What's she doing?' asked Ellen.

'I'm sure I have no clue whatsoever, but I'm not asking her in that mood.'

'I think you're very wise,' said Ellen, 'but one of us will have to soon. The tea's nearly out.'

Keeva was so mad with herself, she practically thrashed the wooden case containing the next load of air mail paper. As usual, her mood swerved between intense anger and extreme self-pity.

She sat on the crate with her chin in her hands and sighed. She just wasn't pretty enough for Tig to take notice. He'd never noticed her and he never would. This was it, her life. Making tea for everyone in the village who needed the post office. Cooing over every baby that was born. Marvelling at the romances and weddings of others. Even Sarah McGuffey, with a murderer for a father, was married. There was only one boy Keeva had ever been interested in and he didn't even know she existed. And it wasn't for the want of her trying – she called into the Devlins' at least once a day. She grimaced and looked round at the cases of bottled holy water still waiting to be unpacked.

'Are you free, please, Keeva?' shouted Mrs Doyle, more tentatively than was normal for her.

Keeva stood. Yes, this was it, her life. 'Coming,' she replied. Without being asked, she hauled up the tea tray and carried it into the shop just as the post office bell rang.

It was Philomena. 'Well, I'm sure, we all know why it had

to happen,' she said as she half closed the door and peeped down the road, 'but if it was my daughter-in-law, I'd be keeping her indoors for another year at least.'

'Who?' asked Mrs Doyle as she stamped a letter for Ellen.

'Sarah McGuffey, or Malone, as she is now.'

'Why, where is she?'

'Stood on the road opposite the Devlins' with Josie, Bridget, Michael and Tig.'

Mrs Doyle sprinted around the counter and they all pressed their noses against the glass to see.

'Why don't I go over and ask how she is?' said Keeva, her mood lightening in an instant at the prospect of having a reason to place herself in Tig's company once again.

'Yes, go on, Keeva, you go and be asking how she's feeling and see if there's any news.'

Keeva didn't need asking twice. Two minutes later, she walked up to Sarah and opened her arms as Sarah, nervous at first, smiled for the second time that day and allowed herself to be hugged.

Sarah now began to make steady progress. 'We can only wait for time to pass,' Nola said to Michael as he sat at the kitchen table. 'Thanks to the actions of her madman of a father, not a soul from here to kingdom come is condemning the marriage, and Father Jerry is even putting it about that he did what he did because he had to, to save her from her father's gun. And never was there a truer story. You've only to think of Jay Maughan and his leg, so you do. Shona had to throw all she had to save it, so they say in the post office. Mrs Doyle says there was nearly two murders in one week.'

She shot Michael a meaningful glance. 'Aye, he's a good shot all right, that McGuffey, and because of him, Jay Maughan will be limping worse than Tig forever more. Bridget said, the infection in his leg was that bad and if it hadn't been for Shona knowing how to stop the bleeding, he would have been dead in minutes, just feet away from where he killed Angela, imagine that, here in Tarabeg. I told Father Jerry, "That story will do nicely, Father. Keep it going." And he said to me, "Well, I don't have to. As many people are talking about the madman with the gun, and about Maughan's leg, as they are about Sarah."'

Nola looked out of the kitchen window. Sarah was sitting on the cart out in the field with Pete and Seamus, who were loading the peat stacks into sacks. The sun was high and hot and Nola thought that each time Sarah stepped out into the sunshine, it was as if she had been touched by a paintbrush. Her colour returned and a few more freckles appeared on her nose.

Michael had been down in the field with them, but being the fastest runner, he'd been sent back to fill up the stoneware flasks with tea.

'Run as fast as yer legs will go,' said Seamus. 'I'm as dry as a dead donkey's langer.'

'Me too,' said Sarah from the back of the cart, where she was stacking one sack on top of the other.

The three men stopped dead, held her in their gaze, and began to laugh in unison.

'Well, I had better run then,' said Michael.

He helped himself to a hot floury potato cake and wrapped three more into a cloth while Nola filled the flasks. 'Do you think her daddy will ever come back?' he asked her. They were never alone in the house together, mother and son, now that

Sarah had moved in. He gasped for air to cool the hot potato cake that sat in his mouth.

'Not likely, I would say. What would he be coming back for? Maughan won't want nothing to do with him now he's walking worse than Tig. And the smuggling has died away. There's not a fisherman among them who wouldn't run to the Garda as soon as look at him. No, there's only trouble and the prison barracks waiting for him if he dares show up here.'

'He's in Ulster,' Daedio piped up from the bed.

Nola and Michael both turned round to face him. 'How do ye know that?' asked Michael.

'Because Mrs Doyle knows, she told Father Jerry and he told me when he came up here to give me communion. There's a lot in here' – he tapped the brim of his cap with his finger – 'that you don't know about, and ye might be a lot more knowledgeable if ye had a mind to ask.'

Michael would have grinned at Daedio if they'd been talking about anyone but McGuffey. 'Do you think he'll come back, Daedio?'

Daedio shook his head. 'No, I don't. He's already caught up with those madmen and their bombs and guns. He must feel right at home.'

But Michael wasn't so sure they had seen the last of him.

'Right, here's yer tea. Run back with it now and don't think I didn't see ye taking the potato cakes – did ye think I wouldn't let ye have one?'

Michael grinned as he scooped up the two flasks.

'Go on now, and if yer back begins to break and ye feel like complaining, just thank the Lord that you aren't me, stuck in here with that miserable sod all day.'

'Right, I am out of the door,' shouted Michael before he

could hear Daedio's response. He ran back across the field to Sarah. Leaving her even for just a few moments made him feel unsettled and afraid for her safety. He had pledged to her that he would never leave her side again.

It was at night, under the cover of darkness, when Sarah shed her tears. No words of comfort would ease her pain, so Michael, fearful of saying the wrong thing, held her close and rocked her until she had cried herself out.

As she began to heal, not a soul mentioned Angela or her death. Whenever Sarah spoke of her mother, she met the equivalent of a blank wall, a change of subject. 'No one will speak of her, Michael,' she said to him one night, soon after they'd got into bed. 'If I mention her to Nola, she doesn't answer me. Why is that?'

'Ah, now, I will never understand the ways of women.' Michael pulled her closer. He wanted her to move on, past the sadness. He knew that Angela's death was viewed as a sin, not Angela's sin but nonetheless a sin that shouldn't be spoken of. 'But you can talk to me all you like. I'm here, aren't I? And tomorrow Bee is coming up with Captain Bob and Ciaran.'

Sarah could never tell Michael of the things her father had done, or that even though he was gone, she felt threatened by him still. Every morning she woke with the hope that today her thoughts might be free of his menacing presence, free to mourn and love in peace, but that hadn't happened yet.

Michael sensed her disquiet and responded as best he knew how. The tragic circumstances of their reunion had intensified their closeness and their love for each other. The two of them stood together, facing down the grief and fear of the past and looking ahead to an uncertain but exciting future of building their own home and business.

Despite her sadness, Michael had been pleasantly surprised at the intensity of their lovemaking. At first she had felt nothing but guilt. 'We can't! Mammy...' she had whispered to him the day after Angela had been buried, the night they were married.

'You can,' he'd said without any shadow of guilt or doubt. 'Because this will make you feel better, that's why.'

And he'd been right. For a short while, her mind had been relieved of the pain and her belly of the ache that had not left her since the moment she'd looked into her mother's vacant eyes.

Their lovemaking was life-affirming and the nights were when she and Michael were at their closest. Afterwards, Sarah always fell asleep with her head on his chest, and he kept his arm around her shoulders, holding her close.

None of this was lost on Daedio.

'They was at it again last night,' he'd said to Nola that morning when she came into the room. He said the same thing every morning.

'Oh, shut your filthy mouth, would you. They is man and wife in the eyes of God. They can do what they like and I don't want to know.'

'Oh well, suit yerself, but ye will when the head of that iron bed comes crashing though the wall and lands on you and Seamus. Tell you what, he's good, keeps going nearly as long as I did when I was first married.'

Nola stormed out of the kitchen in disgust and complained to Seamus, who was in the cowshed with Pete. 'Yer father is a disgusting pig of a man and I shouldn't have to listen to the filth that pours from his mouth.'

Seamus suppressed a grin. 'Well, I'm guessing that if you keep shouting at him and blowing up like you do, he'll keep at it, what with you giving him such great satisfaction with all your huffing and puffing.' He winked at Pete. 'I'll tell ye what though, Nola, with all that going on every night, there must be a babby on the way soon. I'd have managed it by now, eh, Pete?'

Nola's face turned puce. 'Jesus, the men in your family, your minds are all as bad as one another, along with yer dirty mouths. All ye say is fit for the midden, the lot of ye.'

She picked up the milk pail and marched back up to the house, bent over sideways as she heaved the bucket up the path, the roar of Pete and Seamus's laughter at her heels. But Nola was a happy woman. She loved having Michael and Sarah in her home and though she knew it would end once they had built their dream of a shop on the land Daedio had given them, she was determined to enjoy every minute until that day came.

A few days later, Bee came up to the farm to see Sarah, as she did every Sunday. Captain Bob was now a more frequent visitor to the village and she'd brought him and Ciaran with her. Nola was busy in the kitchen. She smiled at Sarah and Bee, then shooed them out the door. 'Go on out, the both of ye. Take the boy and show him the piglets. Feed them while you're there, would ye. Go on, ye have lots to talk about.' She inclined her head towards Captain Bob, who'd joined Seamus and Michael at the table. 'I can manage with this lot here. You get off now while I make them some tea.'

The moment they were out of sight of the house, Ciaran ran off, revelling in the change of scenery, the green mountain so different from the sea view he was used to. It was something Sarah was also still adjusting to.

Bee folded her arms around her niece. 'How are ye? Does Nola treat ye well? Some mothers-in-law can be right scolds.' She stood back and pushed Sarah's hair away from her face, searching for an honest answer.

The ferns on the boreen were shoulder high and dripping dew and Ciaran had leapt over the ditch to the field. 'Watch out for the bog holes,' Sarah shouted. 'There's a leprechaun lives in each one and they aren't friendly.'

Ciaran screamed and came running back, throwing his arms around Bee's legs.

'There, that'll teach ye,' said Bee.

'Keep to the boreen,' said Sarah, 'and just around the corner is the pig pen. Don't disturb the pig and I'll let you feed her.' As he ran off again, with greater care this time, she turned back to Bee. 'Nola couldn't be better. She's a dote of a woman. In some ways, I'm so lucky, and then in others…' Tears, never far from the surface, jumped to her eyes and began to slide down her cheeks. Bee pulled her into her arms and Sarah stiffened, looking her straight in the eye. 'I don't know what others are like, but I couldn't ask for better than Nola. The only thing that's wanting is that no one here really knew Mammy and no one will talk about her. Why is that, Bee? No matter what I say, I can't get them to talk about Mammy, and sometimes I want to, so much.'

'Well, I'm here now. Talk to me. When we're together, we will always talk about your mammy, because, Sarah, she lives in both of our hearts, she does, and when you and I are together, 'tis really the three of us, because she is right here with us.' Bee hooked her arm into Sarah's as they began to walk. ''Tis a funny thing, death. Those of great religion don't see the need to cry, because the person who has died has gone straight on to heaven and the Lord will have saved them a room of their own in his house. You know that waits for all of us, Sarah.'

She pulled Sarah into her side for a hug and looked about her at the greenery. The fresh air smelt and tasted so different there to how it did at their own house by the shore. 'I often think about Rory in that house that God had waiting for him, you know, in the room, like the priest tells us about from the pulpit, and I think, Jesus, Rory never lifted a finger in the entire time I was married to him, who the hell does he have cleaning the fecking room for him, because he won't do it! And you know what I think now?'

Sarah, smiling, shook her head and looked sideways at her aunt.

'I think he has Angela – she'll be cleaning it and looking after him and waiting for me to join them.'

Sarah took out her handkerchief and wiped her eyes. The thought that her Uncle Rory might be with her mammy made her feel better. 'But what about Captain Bob?'

'Oh, well, that's all good. You know, he wants me and the boy to leave Tarabeg and for him to leave his scold of a wife and for us all to be off to America. I've told him I'll think about it. Maybe one day.'

Sarah looked alarmed. 'Bee, no!'

'Now then,' said Bee, 'you are right. The answer is no, not for a very long time.'

'Do you not worry about what Uncle Rory might think? In his room like, in heaven.'

They were nearing the pig pen and Ciaran was standing on the wooden slats of the cage Seamus had made to keep the piglets in. He was peering over the top. The smell of the piglets hit Sarah and Bee long before they reached the pen.

'No, I don't worry about Rory. Yer mammy will have told him all about Captain Bob and he wouldn't want the boy to grow up without a daddy. Oh, sure, Rory is his daddy and I will never let him forget that, not for a moment, and nor will his grandparents. I will always talk to him about Rory and how his son was the world to him, but there comes a time, just as it will for you one day, when things get easier and you move on. And you know, Sarah, if ever anyone was being watched over, 'tis you. Angela is watching over you, that's for sure.'

'Mammy, look, the pigs!' Ciaran shouted.

'We're coming, Ciaran. And get down off that fence before it breaks and the pig thinks you're one of hers and won't let me have you back and we have to go home without you.'

Ciaran jumped down off the fence in shock and Sarah laughed out loud at the expression on his face. Bee looked at her and felt warmed.

'Does it help, the time you have alone with Bee?' Michael asked her later that night. They had retired to bed as soon as was polite and possible. Newly reunited, newly wed and surrounded by people all day, they never actually went to sleep until much later. Instead, making up for the time they'd lost while Michael was away at war, they talked for hours.

'Oh, God, it does,' said Sarah as she lay on her back. 'When Bee and I talk, it's like Mammy is back with us for that time. I can feel her, Michael. It's as if the more we talk about her, the more she joins us, and my heart feels lighter. Sort of how it used to be, the three of us at home in the kitchen...' She gulped down the lump that came to her throat. 'I will get better, Michael. I love it here, but life has changed so much for me. Everything is new. At least the cows are getting used to me now.'

Michael laughed. 'And the chickens chase you, I've seen them.'

Sarah laughed too. 'Oh God, the chickens. I'm going to give them names. Daedio thinks I'm mad.'

Michael snorted. 'Daedio thinks anyone who doesn't hold the same opinions he does is mad, but he's harmless.'

Sarah turned onto her side to face him. 'Do you know what I miss the most, apart from Mammy?' She began running her fingers up and down Michael's bare chest.

He shook his head, almost absentmindedly. Her hair had cascaded onto his chest and he picked up a long strand. It felt silky and soft and he wove it over and through his fingers.

'I miss the sound of the ocean and, you know, sometimes when I wake up, for just a minute I can hear it. And then it's gone. Just like that.'

Michael frowned. 'Sometimes I think I can hear shellfire,' he said in a low voice.

'Oh God, that must be awful.' She had raised herself up further and, alarmed, had stopped running her fingers through the dark hair on his chest.

'No, it's not that bad. 'Tis only for a few seconds, like, but it still happens.' He pulled her back down, missing the warmth of her body against his. 'It's our minds playing tricks. It will all stop soon because we have a life together now, and all that comes with it, and that's what we'll get used to. It will take time, but we will get there.'

As if on cue, the donkey that was in the habit of walking out of the shed at night and standing close to the house, next to their window, let out a bray. They both turned their heads towards it and Sarah grinned.

'Noises like that, that's what you'll get used to,' said Michael as he laughed. 'We're starting the building this week – the stone came down from the quarry today.'

'Why didn't you tell me?' Sarah shrieked, playfully beating his chest with her hands.

He grinned as he grabbed her hand in his and moved it down his body, onto his lower abdomen. Sarah, without encouragement, continued its journey. 'With a bit of luck, we will have a babby soon,' he said, his voice thick. 'A new home, a shop and a babby.'

Sarah's reply was smothered by his lips, which had suddenly and urgently covered hers as he pulled her down on top of him. She thrilled at his hands roaming her body, exploring and becoming familiar with each part of her, and she responded in kind. Her heart glowed at the idea of a new life growing inside her, little knowing it had already arrived.

Chapter 13

The front door to the shop was painted red and so was the door to the rear, the one that led into the yard housing the cowshed and the dairy. The yard had high whitewashed walls, beyond which you could see the mountains that rose behind the Taramore river and extended all the way to the coast. Half an acre from the rear door was the bridge that crossed the river from one side of Michael's land to the other. Directly across the wide and often muddy road from the shop's front door was the side entrance to Paddy's bar. Paddy could not have been more delighted. On a glorious autumn morning, just as the weak sun rose overhead, he stepped out of the bar with a spring in his stride, cleaning his hands on his butcher's apron, and made his way across the road.

'Michael, you are a genius, so ye are. You have blocked the view of the bar from Teresa Gallagher entirely. Who in God's name would have known that would happen when you started building,' he exclaimed. 'That'll mean more takings for me. We can open all the hours we want now.' He rubbed his hands in glee but failed to see Tig, who was sitting on a rafter and had taken aim with his half-filled bucket of water.

The water cascaded down, soaking Paddy, and was quickly followed by a burst of laughter that saw Tig almost dislodge himself and come hurtling down after it. Paddy took his cap off and shook the water from it. Looking up at the half-thatched roof, he shouted, 'Tig, you little bastard, I'll be skinning your arse when ye finally get down.'

'He's not coming down until he's finished. I've told him, I'll send a pillow up.' Michael laughed as he dropped a huge lump of quarry stone to the floor and, pushing back his cap, wiped the sweat from his brow. 'He insisted on being put up there, to get on with the thatch. I'm in no mind to lift him down until the job's finished.'

Sensing a further episode of satisfying horseplay to his benefit, Paddy winked at Michael. 'Aye, well, ye might want to pop over for a drink later, Michael, and ye might be having a convenient lapse of memory with regard to who's sat on yer roof when you leave.'

They both looked up towards Tig, legs dangling from the rafters and a worried frown on his brow as he strained, without success, to hear what they were saying. 'Oi, what are the both of ye talking about? I can tell it's about me. Shout so I can hear ye too.'

'Not bloody likely,' Paddy shouted back. He and Michael's men roared with laughter and Paddy turned to make his way back to his own shop. Halfway across the road, he stopped and retraced his steps, this time with concern etched on his face. 'Oh, Michael, I almost forgot why I came out to see you. Josie said the Maughans are camped not a mile out. John O'Donnell was in the shop this morning, said Philomena had walked out to where they are, to have her palm read by Shona. I'm telling Father Jerry meself, as soon as he comes in. We make our best efforts to keep the Maughans away and not to cross the old woman's hand with silver when she comes anywhere near. Thought you might want to know. And apparently Maughan has a woman now.'

'Well, that's good news then – he won't be after mine any more.' Michael took a puff on his pipe.

'Aye, God knows who he found to live that life. John said she's from Clew Bay and she's a widow.'

'They must be different people altogether over in Clew Bay,' said Michael. 'I feel sorry for her, whoever she is. She must think she's married into purgatory.' He bent his knees to retrieve the lump of stone destined for the stable block. With one heave, he leant slightly backwards and looked up towards the village crossroads. 'Why do they have to come here at all, Paddy? Will they ever just leave us alone?'

Paddy thought for a moment before he spoke. 'You see, Michael, it's like this. They were thrown off the land – by your granddaddy, we never knew why that happened, we thought that Captain Carter had paid Daedio to do it – and they never really went away. I might be wrong, but I reckon that Shona had a notion to take the land back one day. God in heaven knows how she thought she would do that, but now you've gone and built a place on it and... The Maughans have been trading in these parts for as long as I can remember and your shop, well, they're bound to be curious, are they not? Selling is their business, it's what they do. There's not so many calls coming across the border for goods any more, so I hear, and smuggling was half of how they earned their money. I'll be the first to admit' – Paddy leant forward and cupped his hand round the side of his mouth so that no one could hear him – 'but not to Josie, mind, I did very well from the smuggling business meself.'

Michael lifted one leg and rested the stone on it. 'I heard a farmer from Roscommon was arrested trying to walk over the border with three pigs,' he said. 'When the border men stopped him, he said he was lost, with three pigs in tow!'

Both men looked at each other for a second, then burst out laughing at the audacity of the man.

'What happened to him?' asked Paddy.

'He was put in a cell overnight and the pigs were confiscated.'

Paddy whistled. 'Holy feck, that's a harsh price. But there is a border and 'tis a sign of the times. I reckon the Maughans will be trying to sell more around here now the border trade has gone with the rations. They'll be having more in the North than we do here. Isn't that just a turnaround altogether?'

Michael looked up the road, distracted, still pondering Paddy's news. A shadow crossed the sun whenever someone mentioned Jay Maughan's name. 'Why would anyone want to buy from the Maughans?' he said. 'That wicked pair. Even Josie won't touch their money until she's washed it. I reckon it'll be a relief for people to shop at Malone's.'

'Aye, I reckon you're right, but that won't stop Jay trying to cause trouble. Just watch your back.'

They both heard Josie calling for Paddy, and he turned and made his way back across the road, raising his hand in a farewell salute.

Minutes later, Michael dropped the stone at the back of his new house and sat himself down in the cow byre Seamus and Pete had built. A wooden stall, carved by Daedio, had already been fixed to the wall with a ring and a chain. It stood ready and waiting, and Michael ran his hands over the smooth wood that had been worked with love.

So many friends and villagers had willingly donated their hard labour to help them out. With their bare hands they'd made a reality of the plan he and Sarah had drawn. Once the roof was finished, a priority to keep out the rain, the goods would start arriving and he and Sarah would leave the farm. Everything was perfect, except for the continuing presence of the Maughans.

He picked up the earthenware jug of cold tea as Tig, still up in the rafters, began banging wooden plugs into the joists. 'Come down for your tea, Tig,' he shouted up.

As he walked around to what was to be the kitchen of the new cottage, a heavy feeling settled in his gut. Jay Maughan might have found himself a wife, but with his wounded leg, he'd be finding it harder to get manual work, and he'd not thank Michael for becoming a rival trader. And Shona was no friend of the Malones, Daedio had made that very clear. The feeling of dread would not shift.

He came back to the shop area and looked up at the roof to see Tig kicking his legs in frustration.

'Where have you been, you feckin' useless lump?' Tig shouted down. 'You were so quiet, I thought you'd gone and left me here. Me mouth is full of the dust.'

'Sorry,' said Michael, grinning.

'You don't mean that,' Tig shot back. And then, more seriously, 'You know, I have the best view in the world up here. I can see the river, the hill and the coast, but best of all, I get to see Keeva bobbing in and out of the post office. I need a leg down now, Michael.'

Michael stood to give his friend the shoulder he needed to collapse onto before he hit the ground. 'Keeva is it then? How long has that little flame been burning?' Tig blushed and looking sheepish, kicked a stone with the toe of his boot. 'Oh, since we were about ten I think. Yeah, when we were in school. But, for God's sake, don't be telling her. She wouldn't be looking twice at the likes of me now.'

'Jesus, and this is the first I know of it? You are a dark horse, you are that Tig, and get away with you, she would be a lucky woman to have a man like yourself. I'll have to see what I can do about this.' And to a chorus of protest, he knocked Tig's cap off with the back of his hand.

The farm on Tarabeg Hill had been a hive of activity for weeks. Stools were being carved and a kitchen table had been hewn from a tree that had been felled when Daedio was still a boy; it had been stashed outside the cowshed for a special occasion, which this most certainly was.

Every morning, Daedio insisted on being carried by Pete and Seamus to the old cottage. He sat outside the front door and whittled and carved, all the while firing off instructions that tested Pete's good nature. Today was no different.

'You've carved one leg shorter than the other on that,' he said, nodding at the stool Pete had nearly finished.

Pete was used to this sort of commentary, but that didn't make it any easier. 'I have not,' was all he said in return.

'Yes, you have. Wait until you put it on the floor. Sarah will slide straight off and onto her arse if she sits on that.'

Pete took a deep breath, put down his tools and walked away, as he often did, to the big house and Nola.

Nola lifted her head, and within seconds a knowing smile had crossed her face. 'Oh, 'tis nice to see someone else realises what he can be like,' she said. Recognising Pete's frustration, she reached for the kettle. 'Stay here a bit. Take the old maggot a drink out, but wait a while. He would drive anyone to distraction – anyone except Sarah, that is. He thinks the sun shines out of Sarah, so he does.'

Pete pulled out a stool and rested at the table. 'He does that. 'Tis "Sarah this" and "Sarah that". You would think she was his own daughter.'

Nola poured the hot water into the pots. 'Ah, well, he was a father of sons… He told me once that if Sarah ever has a baby girl, he'll live for another twenty years. He must be the only one praying that she will!'

Their eyes met, neither spoke, and then both erupted into laughter as Pete said, 'Let's hope she has boys then.'

Wiping her eyes with her hankie, Nola handed Pete the mugs. 'God, we're wicked, we are. I'll have to go to confession now for that, God help me.'

'You didn't say a word,' said Pete as he made for the door.

'No, but I agreed with you and that's sin enough.'

'Ah, sure, he's not that bad, and we didn't mean it. Nothing is as awful as it seems, Nola, after one of your brews.'

Pete strode out of the house and back to the old cottage, his humour restored. 'Daedio, I'm bringing ye a brew. You're a great man for the tea. Get your gums around this and stop yer carping at me.'

Once all the carving of the stools and the table was finished, Michael and his father oiled them. Daedio had produced money from the cedar box and given it to Michael and Sarah to buy stock and the remainder of their furnishings, including some pretty floral fabric Sarah had found in Galway, and presses for the kitchen and the bedroom. Pots and dishes were collected from Newport, and Michael and Sarah had a whole week in Dublin, making contacts for trade and purchasing goods for their new home. An iron bedstead was chosen and ordered.

Mrs Doyle was in second heaven when the goods began to arrive at the post office awaiting collection. Of course, everything had to be shown off before it was removed.

'God in heaven, would you look at that. Feel it, would you,' she said as she almost demanded Sarah show her the latest bolt of curtain fabric to arrive. 'I have never in my life seen anything like it,' she exclaimed. 'Stay there, don't move, I'm away to tell Ellen Carey to lock up the shop so she can come and see for herself. Keeva, make Sarah more tea.'

Keeva liked Sarah, and her parcels were the light of Keeva's day. 'Oh God, Sarah, you can't go until Rosie finishes up at the school and takes a look herself,' she said.

No sooner were the words out of her mouth than Teresa walked in, with Rosie O'Hara right behind her. Rosie had been on an errand for Mr O'Dowd while he minded both classes and had been hurrying back to the school when Teresa had as good as kidnapped her. 'The post office has all manner of things arriving, I didn't want you to miss out,' Teresa said as she hurried on ahead. 'They know how to make furniture with style in Dublin – there is nothing quite like it. You will know what I am talking about any minute now.'

Once through the door, she grabbed Rosie by the sleeve of her coat and pulled her towards the women standing around the parcel, its brown-paper wrapping almost torn open. Rosie's reluctance was more than noticeable. 'Would you look at that, the palest lemon, and those sprigs of pink flowers, where are they from? What are they called?' Teresa demanded.

'Miss O'Hara is the teacher, she can tell us,' said Philomena O'Donnell. 'And she can tell me why Mr O'Dowd keeps Theady in detention so often when he's there every morning, up with the lark, collecting the kindling for the school fire.' Philomena pushed in front of the other women to address Rosie directly. 'He's making my Theady right miserable. I cannot get a peep out of him and the only way I can get him up to the school is to tell him that you need the fire lighting. I say to him, "Miss O'Hara will freeze half to death and die of the cold if you don't get along there, Theady."'

Rosie felt horribly self-conscious as the woman scrutinised her. She had never spoken to an audience of adults as she was now about to. Children were her audience; with children, her face didn't burn red and her hands didn't shake. She had only called in at the post office because Teresa had dragged her there. She had become comfortable in the company of Sarah and Keeva, but this was like the Spanish Inquisition. She wanted to melt into the walls as all eyes turned to her.

'I... I don't know, Mrs O'Donnell. I teach the girls' class,' she replied. She began to perspire and her skin prickled; she wanted to flee.

Philomena O'Donnell was not to be put off. 'Well, you find out, Miss O'Hara. Everyone around here has good things to say about you and I'm not saying it is anything to do with you, for sure, but my Theady, he's all I have left now that the others have gone, and by the way, that's a lovely bit of fabric you have there, Mrs Malone.'

Mrs Malone! Sarah's stomach still flipped when someone called her that. She met Rosie's eyes, felt sorry for her having been put on the spot.

Rosie felt weak with relief that the women's attention had

been directed away from her at last. 'I have to go,' she said quietly to Teresa as she headed for the door.

'Don't let that woman put you off,' Teresa hissed. 'Sarah's opening the bed linen now – take a look first. Mrs Doyle said they have ordered the finest.'

Bed linen. The words froze in Rosie's brain. Teresa had no idea that every night, in Rosie's thoughts, Michael lay on Rosie's bed linen. That she felt the heat from his warm flesh as she closed her eyes and filled her nostrils with the smell of him. That as she breathed, she heard his breathing next to her.

At Teresa's prompting, she now slowly turned her head and saw the scalloped, embroidered edge of a linen sheet that someone was holding and pressing against their face.

Sarah wanted to snatch the sheet away from the woman holding it. Having been raised on the coast and not in the village itself, she wasn't used to the ways of the village women. She sometimes mildly resented their interference and their probing into every aspect of her life with Michael. Rosie, though, wasn't like that. Sarah felt sorry for her and the way she'd been interrogated by Philomena. She wanted to make her feel better. 'Come up to the farm and we can see it properly, Rosie,' she said as Rosie brushed past her to reach the door. 'And when we move in, you can be the first to visit the new house.'

Rosie flushed with pleasure.

'Can I come too?' asked Keeva, who was collecting up used teacups and placing them onto a wooden tray.

Sarah laughed at something someone was saying to her and Rosie thought how her laughter sounded as sweet as she looked. She gave her a nervous smile. 'I will. I would like to.' She turned to the assembled women. 'I have to get back to the school. Goodbye.'

As the door closed behind her with an insistent jingle of the bell, the women stood around staring after her.

'Well, I hope she gets our Theady sorted,' said Philomena as the door reopened and the bell rang out again.

Two more women rushed in. 'Which shop did you get this bolster in? I could have made you one of those for half the price,' one of them said.

Sarah turned to answer and Keeva's heart sank. Sarah hadn't responded to her question. She had barely spoken to her, seeming to prefer Rosie. She sighed as she placed the last cup on the tray. She knew the reason; she wasn't good enough. She was just a shop girl who would never have the opportunity to flee to Liverpool or anywhere else. Her wages just about covered the food and helped her mother, who was now riddled with arthritis and incapable of working. Keeva's life was in Tarabeg. Even in such a small village, there was a social ladder, and Keeva sat on the bottom rung. No wonder Sarah didn't think to invite her to her new home. As far as it went in Tarabeg, Keeva was part of the furniture.

As Sarah and Michael arrived back at the farm in the horse and cart, Nola came to the door.

'You were all day collecting a few things from Mrs Doyle's. She'll have you moving in with her next.'

Sarah could tell that Nola was slightly aggrieved. Michael could tell that Sarah was a big hit and Nola was jealous. She liked the hours she spent with Sarah and resented sharing her with Mrs Doyle and half of the village. Not to mention that almost every woman in Tarabeg had seen Sarah's curtain fabric before she had.

'The things we are buying for the house are causing such a commotion, Mammy,' Michael explained. 'Mrs Doyle wouldn't let Sarah go until everyone had seen what she had bought.'

'The cheek of the woman,' said Nola as she wiped her hands on her apron and went back inside. 'She has no right to be telling everyone. I'll be going with ye next time and I'll be telling her to mind her business.'

Michael smiled down at Sarah and kissed her head. 'Go and show Mammy the material and make a fuss. She's upset that everyone else has given you their opinion before she even had the chance.'

'And tell me, Michael, how do you know that?' asked Sarah, smiling up at him.

He noted the confident and cheeky twinkle in her eye. She was like the ferns that lined the boreen, he thought. Tightly furled when she arrived, just like the ferns during the winter, and then the sun came, bringing warmth and a welcome relief from the storms. Under the care of the Malones, Sarah had slowly opened up, and now she smiled freely, of her own will and not just when she thought she should. He lifted his cap and for a brief moment let the autumn breeze cool his brow. 'Because I feel the same, sometimes,' he said. 'I get jealous too.'

Sarah pushed him playfully in the side. 'You! I'm your wife. You can talk to me and see me as much as you like.'

'Ah, I know that. But when I see how much of your attention Daedio gets, how much you talk to him and laugh with him, I feel a bit jealous too.' His confession had made him feel foolish and he put his arms around her shoulders and pulled her into him. 'Even Daddy notices how well you and Daedio get along. I think he might feel a bit jealous too. Sarah Malone, you have come from the coast into Tarabeg and you've stolen everyone's hearts with your long, golden-red hair and your big, generous smile. And the fact is, no one knows how. How did someone who grew up with an animal like your father turn out to be just like you?'

Michael could have bitten his tongue off as soon as he spoke. He felt Sarah's shoulders stiffen under his hand and he almost groaned out loud at his own stupidity.

'Because of Mammy. Mammy was nothing like Daddy. He was the dark and she was the light. He was bad and she was good. He was bad, Michael, and Mammy, she was an angel.'

'Come here,' he said and he threw both arms around her and hugged her to him so tight, she almost squealed with the pain of it.

'Are those two all right?' asked Daedio from inside the house. He was leaning forward on his bed and peering out of the door.

Nola knew full well it was Sarah's return he was waiting for, and he was growing impatient. 'They are well and good. Leave them be,' she said with a note of reprimand in her voice. 'Don't be going askin' when they come indoors. They are entitled to their privacy.'

'Don't even say such a thing, woman. Aren't I asking you so I don't have to ask them? Why would I be prying into their personal business. Hush your suspicious mouth now.'

Just at that moment, Michael and Sarah stepped into the cottage.

'Ah, here ye are,' said Daedio. 'What was all that talking about outside? We don't keep secrets in this house.'

A wet cloth came hurtling through the air and would have landed square on his ear if he hadn't shifted to the side.

'See that, Michael? She could have killed me with that. Your mother, she is worse than mad Mary from the mission, she is. She needs locking away in the asylum.'

Michael laughed, picked up the wet cloth from the bed and handed it back to his scowling mother.

'Come here, Sarah,' said Daedio. 'I have something to show ye. Michael, pass me the box.'

'What, again? What's in there this time, Daedio? Did you find this box under a rainbow?' He passed down the cedar box to Daedio and flopped into the rocking chair.

Sarah sat in what had become her usual place, on the end of Daedio's bed. 'I've a ton of stuff to be showing you, Daedio,' she said. 'We have everything for the house now and soon everything for the shop will begin to arrive.'

Daedio wasn't listening; he was too busy digging around in the box. 'Aha, got it. Here it is.' He held out a small folded linen cloth to Sarah. ''Tis yours, and it matches your beauty.' He looked pleased with himself as Sarah unfolded the cloth and pulled out a green emerald heart on a gold chain.

'I can't...' she stammered.

'Oh yes you can,' said Daedio. 'There's no one else around here young and pretty enough to give it to.' He shot a meaningful look at Nola, but he couldn't keep the grin from his face.

'Yes,' Nola replied, 'but there is someone old and ugly enough to give it to you, Sarah. It will look lovely on you. Here, let me fasten it.' She moved around the table.

'Ah, is it Christmas in here?' said Seamus as he too came in and, stamping his feet dry on the rush mat, saw what was happening.

'It will bring you luck,' said Daedio, ignoring Seamus.

Sarah turned to Michael, who smiled at the sight of the

gleaming emerald nestled into the milky white skin in the dip of her throat. 'You look like the prettiest girl in all of Ireland,' he replied, and they both knew he meant it.

'And here's the rest of it.' Daedio handed Sarah a leather pouch full of money.

Tears welled up in Sarah's eyes at the fact that he'd placed the pouch in her hands and not Michael's. She looked back anxiously, but Michael just smiled.

'Spend it with care,' said Daedio. 'I'm guessing 'twill be quickly used. Once it's gone, 'twill take hard work to put it back, but this is what it was for. Go on, make yourself the home you want, spend some on clothes to put a smile on your face and make sure you put some of it into the business so that you get it back over time. And don't any of ye tell her where it came from.'

He grinned as Sarah looked down at the money in her hand: notes rolled up tightly in a bundle resembling a large cigar.

'But I've never had money, I don't know how...'

'That's why you'll be good at it,' said Daedio. 'You'll be careful. You need things for the house, and Michael, as soon as the building is finished, you will have to go on your travels for more things to sell or you'll be sat in an empty shop.'

As Nola and Michael fussed over Sarah and the necklace, Seamus poured himself and Daedio a drink. Then he sat on the end of the wooden bed in the spot that Sarah had just vacated. He began to talk about the wild redcurrants he had collected and how Nola was putting them into a pie to have with cream that night, and the juice she was keeping in jars to have later.

But Daedio wasn't listening. He was staring at the wall by the fire and wondering, should he tell his son now? His eyes were fixed on the slight gap in the stonework. He hadn't managed to push it back fully when he'd taken the roll of notes out to place in the cedar box. Nola had been quicker than usual collecting the milk and he'd had to hurry as he stumbled on his sticks back to the bed. He'd given Sarah only one of the rolls and that had made her and Michael the richest couple in the village. There were at least another five hundred bigger rolls. Seamus and Nola thought that the money from the robbery had all been spent on the land, but the truth was, that was only a small part of it. Daedio's father had kept the rest untouched, thinking Joe might be coming back for it sometime. In all, Annie had told him, the money in the wall came to more than they could count. He didn't even know how much, but the cost of the land had been two hundred, so it had to be a lot of money, he assumed.

'Daedio, are you listening to me? 'Tis your favourite pie tonight.'

Daedio sipped on his porter. Was now the moment? Should he ask Seamus to push the stone back in a little further?

'Well, what's going on here? Are we celebrating something?' Pete was at the door. He removed his cap, as he always did – the only man in the house who bothered – and hung it on the gun nail in the wall.

'Michael, I think we should tell them now.' Sarah was standing with Nola, and Nola, who knew that apart from Michael she was the only one to know Sarah's secret, winked. The women in the village might have seen the curtain fabric, but this news was in the family.

Sarah looked at Nola. 'You tell them,' she said, and as she looked back to Michael, the love that shone from his eyes could have knocked her over in a flash.

Nola was pink with pride. 'I'll tell ye quick, before I embarrass meself,' she said. 'Sarah is having a babby.'

In all the excitement, the pouring of the best porter, the tears and the making of plans, Daedio forgot about the stone in the wall. 'Oh Holy Mary, I've known for weeks,' he said. And, swinging his legs around from the side of the bed, he stood up unaided, without even having to grab the side of the chair, for the first time in years.

Rosie flew back into the schoolyard just as Mr O'Dowd stepped out onto the path, ringing the brass hand bell. The noise of the children running and playing died away as one by one they hurried into line and stood dead still before him. He failed to see or acknowledge Rosie as she closed the gate behind her, but her attention was grabbed when she heard him say, 'Go on inside, Theady. Make my tea and then sit by my desk.'

Her eyes immediately sought out Theady, who looked downcast and almost tearful. His small voice whispered, 'Yes, Mr O'Dowd.' As he walked inside, ahead of the others, it was as though he was carrying the weight of the world on his shoulders.

Rosie tried to think of something to say, but there was nothing. The only words she could hear in her head were, 'Come and see us when we move in,' which drowned out everything else. Despite resolving not to go and see them, she knew that if it meant she might see Michael, be closer to him, maybe even speak to him, the forces of hell could not hold her back. She would become Sarah's friend and she would be there, in Michael's home.

Chapter 14

It was September and harvest time and Sarah felt something close to joy the morning she woke and saw villagers coming up the hill to the farm to help. She and Nola had been cooking and baking for two days solid and now it was time for the outdoor work to begin.

'You go and help in the fields,' Nola instructed. 'Josie and Bridget will help me here in the kitchen. They'll be coming up on the cart. Even Bridget's Porick turns out for harvest, fat and lazy though he is. Mind, 'tis only for the porter and the food, of course. Make sure he works, now.'

Michael had left already. He and Seamus and Pete had been out in the oat field since first light. There'd been a stiff breeze the previous day, which meant the crop would have dried, and conditions could not have been more perfect. There was no sign of rain, but with crops to be brought in on more than a dozen farms thereabouts, and a limited time to do it in, when the weather was right, every man, woman and child worked a fifteen-hour day. If the skies were clear around the time of the harvest moon, they carried on through the night, grabbing the odd hour of sleep on the edge of the field until the last of the oats had been threshed.

Over the last couple of weeks, Sarah and Michael had joined the other villagers at whichever farm the thresher was at. The dicing with the elements, the meeting of new people on the different farms, and the satisfaction of bringing in a good harvest had all helped ease the acuteness of Sarah's grief. With the joy of the life growing inside her, her heart felt lighter. She and Michael collapsed exhausted into bed each night.

'How will they get the thresher up our hill?' Sarah had asked on the cart home one night.

'The same way you're getting up here,' Pete had replied. 'Once it's done its job at the Deans' farm, six men will load it onto their cart and it'll be pulled up here the following morning. We have flat fields all right, you just have to get up the hill to reach them.'

Sarah felt a thrill of excitement: it was a challenge, to get all the crops in before the rain, and it was one she relished. For the first time, she felt like an integral part of the community, working in unity with the others to save and store a year's labour for the families of Tarabeg. She felt as though she belonged, and the importance of that welled up inside her and at times brought her to tears. It seemed that every person knew her name, and the children especially loved her sweet way with them. The whispers had stopped. She had proven herself by rolling up her sleeves and cutting and stacking along with the rest of them. Everyone knew and liked Sarah Malone from up on Tarabeg Hill.

'I can see the Deans' cart,' she shouted from the boreen in through the open door to Nola and Daedio.

'How many horses has he on it?' Daedio shouted back.

'Two, I think. Yes, two.' Sarah had her hand up to shield her eyes from the sun, which was low on the hill.

'He has the thresher and the old crones on the cart as well then,' said Daedio. 'And I bet I know what weighs the most.'

'He's stopping and getting down,' shouted Sarah.

'Aye, he's making the lazy buggers walk the last yards while he turns into the field with the thresher.'

His words were barely out before Sarah, jumping up and down, shouted again. 'Look, everyone's coming up the hill behind him – they're all here!' She could see the tops of heads bobbing up and down, some with their red, brunette or raven-black hair gleaming in the sun, others in scarves or caps. The shouts and whoops of children reached her ears as they all turned into the field behind the thresher to begin their day's work. Clasping her hand over her belly and her growing infant, Sarah grinned at the sight of them and realised that at that moment she felt truly happy.

Josie and Bridget, the old crones Daedio had been referring to, broke away from the villagers turning into the first field and made their way up to the house, carrying baskets in front of them, scarves tied neatly under their chins. They smiled and raised their hands and waved to Sarah.

'Lord in heaven, that hill gets steeper every time I visit,' puffed Josie from just outside the door.

'No, it doesn't, you just get fatter,' Daedio's voice boomed out from the bed.

They all heard a yelp of pain and a shout of abuse before they saw Nola emerge from the front door, tea towel in hand, grinning. 'Don't you be taking any notice of a word he says now, d'you hear me.'

'We wouldn't be here, Nola, if we ever had,' said Bridget.

'Can I go now, Nola?' asked Sarah, looking down into the field.

'Yes, go on, off you run, but be careful now. Michael will know when to bring everyone back for lunch.'

Sarah had already learnt the ways of telling the time up on the hill. Lunch was ready when the sun sat directly above the old cottage.

The three women watched her as she ran down the hill towards the field, her hair flying up behind her.

'Does she know yet,' asked Bridget, 'what it is that she's carrying?'

'No, you know I don't have the sight like you, and no one else has told her yet, though there's plenty of women in this village after your crown, Bridget. Do you know?'

Bridget smiled as she emptied the contents of her basket onto the scrubbed wooden table that was already heaving with the first bake of the day, ready to feed the harvesters.

'What is it, Bridget?' asked Josie as matter-of-factly as if she had been asking her the time of day. 'You must know.'

'I do indeed. Has been obvious to me since I knew she was carrying, and that was long before you knew, Nola. Do you want me to say?' Bridget took the last pie out of her basket and laid it on the table with the rest.

Nola thought for a moment. 'Aye, go on then, but don't be telling anyone else. We'll keep it to just the three of us. Let's put the kettle on first.'

Ten minutes later, sitting on the bench and enjoying the last sit-down any of them would have until the harvest was in and they hit their beds, Nola jumped up. 'Hang on, we need a drop in this.' She poured a generous measure of whiskey into each cup. 'Do you know, it's bliss when Daedio is taken off me hands.'

Daedio had been given a piggyback by Pete down to the field, to supervise the harvest from his favourite position in a chair made out of last year's bales.

'Go on, I'm ready,' said Nola. 'Tell us then, what is Sarah carrying?'

Josie tittered with excitement.

'She's only had one sip,' said Nola, winking at Bridget, 'and her, Paddy's wife. You would think she would be immune from the fumes on his breath alone, wouldn't you?'

Bridget snorted and almost choked. 'She swears she never touches a drop, don't you, Josie.'

Josie grinned, her short curls quivering and her apple cheeks glowing. As they laughed, she thought how lucky they were to be such close friends.

''Tis a girl.'

A gasp escaped from the other two.

'Well, well, well. A baby girl. A little helper for you, Nola, and her mammy. Isn't that grand,' said Josie.

''Tis a girl for Daedio – 'tis what he is praying for. I'll let the old maggot keep praying. I won't be telling him.'

'Shush,' said Bridget. 'Annie is here, she's listening to you.'

Both Josie and Nola felt the change in the air, the coolness that passed in front of them.

'Oh, I'm sorry, Annie.' Nola straightened her back and looked around the room. 'I do look after him, you know, just as you would like.'

'She knows that,' said Bridget, patting Nola on the hand. 'She's here all the time, watching you. Annie has never left. She says she has work to do and she can't leave until it's finished.

She also knows what he can be like, she's saying, and... I can't hear, Annie, what was that?' Bridget's expression remained unchanged. 'I can't hear her. Come and sit with us, Annie, try again in a minute.'

The three women shuffled up the bench to make room at the end and carried on with their drinks.

'Annie was just telling me I was right,' said Bridget. ''Tis a girl, and a blessed marriage all right, no one can doubt that now. If the good Lord thought they had been married in haste, there would be no child on the way.'

'What child, who?' Daedio shouted from the door as two young boys carried him past in a fireman's lift.

Nola sighed. 'See what I have to be putting up with,' she said.

'Might have known you would all be sat on your arses. These lads, they want a drink, and we need to get some more water drawn from the well. The sun, it's blazing in the sky, it is. A perfect day for the harvest. Could life get any better than this?'

Bridget looked at Nola and grinned.

'Is there any chance of his joining Annie before this babby arrives?' asked Nola.

'No, none at all,' said Bridget.

'Well, he can enjoy the surprise of being told it's a girl by Michael himself then.' Nola drained the last drops from her mug.

Minutes later, the three women were busy laying the wooden planks for the trestle table across its blocks outside the old cottage and scrubbing them, ready to receive the food that had been in preparation for two days. Bridget and Josie had both brought bread they had baked that morning and some of the children had run up to the house with parcels of butter and cheese from their own kitchens.

'Give me a hand with this, would you,' said Josie to Bridget, and the two women dragged out bales of hay from the cow-shed to use as benches for people to sit on. The table was laid with jugs and wooden platters, and the smell of gammon sizzling in the pan drifted out from the kitchen. Dishes of buttery mashed potatoes and greens stood in the hearth on skillets, keeping warm, and there were fruit pies and jugs of cream to follow. Sarah and Nola had made cakes and biscuits the night before, and the scones would be served with wild raspberry jam. Sarah, Bee and Ciaran had picked the raspberries the previous Sunday afternoon. Bee had taken almost as many back home to Rory's parents as they'd picked for the jam.

When the women were done and satisfied, ready well before midday, they sat on the bales with a second round of tea laced with whiskey and waited for the crowds to make their way up the hill.

'I've been doing harvest every day since I could walk,' said Bridget as she sipped her tea.

Nola flopped down beside her. 'May we always be doing it, God willing.'

'I'm not sure we will,' said Josie, turning away from look-ing down the hill and towards the other two.

A shot of fear ran through Nola. 'Why would that be, Josie? Why would anything change?'

'The war, that's why. Look at us. We live a life as close to heaven as anyone could want. Oh, I know, everyone loves all the fancy things that come in the post from America and England, but isn't this the best? Aren't the poorest among us the happiest? Don't those who have the least, laugh the most? Look at the McGintys – first out to help at every harvest, so they are.'

For a moment there was silence as they all looked towards the nearest field and sought out the carrot-haired McGinty children, working hard. Their thoughts were interrupted only by the excited barking of the dogs, the calls of children in the field and the thrumming of the thresher in the background.

'Every month, it seems, someone else leaves Tarabeg,' said Bridget. 'There is the worry, right there. If people keep leaving and deserting their houses and fields, the place will alter for sure. Who will be left? You are lucky Michael is staying, Nola, but in every house and on every farm the young ones are flocking to the boats and different shores. Everyone wants to up and away now the war is over.'

Nola wiped imaginary dust from the top of the table. 'Well, Michael and Sarah are staying and that's for sure.'

'Yes, but your others have all left,' said Josie without hesitation. 'The price we pay for living here is that our children leave us. Eire is a country awash with the tears of mothers. Is that a price worth paying? I'd rather change came so that the mothers who come after us can see their children grow old and know who their grandchildren are. So they can have a family not just for a few years only. If Michael wasn't staying, Nola, who would look after the farm when you and Seamus get older or when your time on this earth is done?'

Tears stung Nola's eyes. The hurt they all carried, every one of them, rushed to the surface when absent children were spoken about aloud.

'God forgive me, I shouldn't say this,' said Josie, 'but I'm thankful for Tig's impediments. At least I get to keep him.'

'Aye, we got to keep one each,' said Nola. 'God must be smiling down on us.'

Bridget had no children, but she sensed her friends' loss.

'I think things will change and mightily so,' she said. 'No loving God would want mothers to suffer like you two have. I think we're going to be the last to live through these harvests, the last to know this way of life. There will come a day, and it won't be long, Nola, when you are too old to plant and Michael is running his shop. Teresa Gallagher's sister is now a widow. When she dies, I asked Teresa, would she be taking over the farm, and she was quite adamant. "I will not," she said. So there's another farm that will stand empty. How it will happen, when it will happen, I do not know. But there will come an autumn when the boreens and the roads won't be full of people rushing out to bring in the crops, the thresher will lie still and there will be a different way of life here. When that happens, I for one will have a pain in my heart as mighty as any, and I hope to God I'm six feet under and I won't be here, but I fear it might be closer than we think and I won't be spared. The farms will be idle. The village will become a ghost town. The houses will stand unlived in, this I can see.'

'The only things idle around here are you lot,' shouted Daedio, coming back into view, this time being carried up from the fields by two different lads.

'Is your belly empty, is it, Daedio?' shouted Nola as she stood up.

All three women looked up to the sky above the old cottage. 'Right, the sun is almost there. It's nearly time, let's start carrying the rest of the food out,' said Josie. And they all bustled back into the house.

Chapter 15

The house and the shop were finally finished, six months later, on a warm spring day.

'Sure, would you look at the weather, isn't the good Lord smiling down on us?' Michael said to Sarah as he twirled her around in the kitchen.

Sarah was in no mood for dancing. She was busy forking steamed salmon. Tig and Michael had poached the salmon out of the Taramore river the summer before and it had been smoked and lying in Paddy's cold room ever since. 'I'm mashing it onto bread and butter and cutting it up onto the salver. Will it be enough, Michael?'

'Will it be enough?' Michael took in the wooden platters of sliced bread covered in moist fleshy red salmon. 'Sarah, that's a feast. Even Jesus didn't have the Guinness to go with the fish.'

'Is it true that the only man not to have an invite is the ghillie?' asked Sarah with a grin.

'Aye, it is. But he'll come anyway. I have to hope he can't tell the taste of his own fish.'

'I've saved him a pie. The salmon will be gone by the time

he hears the music and walks down the hill. He will think we've all been eating the pie.'

Michael hugged his beautiful young wife into his chest. 'Ah, you're learning the ways.' He laughed. He could barely contain his excitement as he spun her around. 'They'll be talking about this day and the opening of our shop all the way to Galway, Sarah, and they'll be doing that for a very long time.'

Michael Malone may have had the banter, but Sarah was one woman who would not be taken in by it, and never had been. 'And isn't that exactly what you'd be wanting, Michael? Isn't that just what all this is for?' She grinned up at the man who had not given her an easy life over the past months, with his mad ideas about his shop and his fortune.

Over his shoulder, Sarah watched through the back door as Nola came into view, a basket in one hand. She was helping Seamus lead a cow in. They'd brought it down from the farm into the shed at the back, a housewarming present from the two of them. As she placed the basket on the ground and let out three chickens, Seamus opened a sack and a cock flew out and strutted around the yard. He tied the cow to the ring in the byre and one of the chickens fluttered onto its back, where it remained, surveying the scene before it.

The new curtains lifted in the spring breeze and their weeks-old baby, Mary Kate, stirred in her basket on the table. Sarah bent over her to check and stroked her downy cheek adoringly. 'Would you look at all this,' she said, straightening up and gesturing expansively at their surroundings. 'We're here, we've done it now, Michael Malone.'

A row of wooden chairs had been laid out under the window on the cinder path, placed to keep mud from the goods that would be set outside the shop for sale, along with straw bales covered in blankets and cloths for people to sit on. While everyone gathered and watched, a wooden stepladder was erected by Tig, who stood on the bottom and held it. Mr O'Dowd handed him the nails as Michael climbed up and gave the shop the finishing touch, the sign that said 'Malone's General Store' over the front door.

'Right, let's crack open the drinks, Paddy. Malone's is open for business.'

'Let me help with the barrel, Paddy,' said Mr O'Dowd, who could roll a barrel with one hand and require no additional breath to do so.

Sarah, now with Mary Kate in her arms, beamed as neighbours, family and friends began to cheer. She thought her heart would burst with pride.

'That'll be yours one day,' said Ellen Carey, peering into the shawl in which Mary Kate lay sleeping.

'No, it won't,' said Michael. 'She'll do better than this, won't she, Sarah?'

Ellen looked put out. 'Oh, get you and your big ideas, Michael Malone. Is not owning the newest and biggest shop in the place enough for ye? I'll tell you what, I have spent my entire married life in ours and a better life I could not have had.'

'Yes, but your fingers are raw and you can hardly see from sewing all hours into the night, Ellen. God willing, I want more for her. I have big ideas for meself but even bigger for this one.' Michael laughed as he pulled back the shawl and smiled down at his daughter with her mop of bright copper-red hair. Sarah's milk was dribbling from the corners of her mouth. Her large blue eyes stared back up at him as though she understood every word that was being said. One arm pushed free of the shawl as she stretched and pursed her lips, her face contorting as if she was trying to speak and reply to Michael with her own opinion.

'She's been here before, that one,' said Ellen. 'I knew Michael's gran, Annie,' she said as she turned to Sarah. 'She was best friends with my big sister Julia, along with Mrs Doyle. Inseparable the three of them were, until Julia emigrated to America, and then they wrote to each other every week, until Annie died. That's her all right – Annie, all wrapped up in that shawl. Mary Kate, she's the image of her. She's back again, but then that's life here, isn't it? No one ever leaves, really.' She laughed. 'But I must! To help Nola and Josie with the food.'

Sarah smiled down at her baby and stroked the crown of her head, leaving one hand there protectively.

'Can I have a look?' a voice at her elbow asked. It was Keeva.

'Yes, here you go.' Sarah dipped the shawl down. 'She hasn't changed much since you held her yesterday.'

'Oh my giddy aunt, isn't she just gorgeous. You know who she looks like – Granny Annie. I remember her when I was little and we used to walk up the boreen to the Malone farm to buy butter.'

'You're the second person to say that today,' said Sarah.

'You are lucky,' said Keeva. 'I would love to have a babby one day, but I can't see it ever happening for me.'

'You don't know that! You might meet someone who takes your fancy soon. Lots of new fishermen coming to the village, they say.'

'Oh, I've met the boy who's taken my fancy. But there's no future there.' Keeva had averted her eyes and was stroking Mary Kate's cheek with her finger. It was the first time she had ever spoken her secret out loud. There was something about Sarah that made her feel she could. Her serenity, her warmth, her smile.

'Do I know him?' asked Sarah

Her words pulled Keeva's gaze back to her and secured her confidence. 'Oh, aye, you know him all right. It's Tig. He's the one my heart is for. But please don't be saying anything – he's not interested in me.'

'How do you know that? He might be mad about you.'

Keeva laughed and removed her hand from within the shawl, where Mary Kate had been clinging on to one of her fingers. 'Oh, God, no, he really isn't. I see him every day. He doesn't even notice me or know I'm here, I'm sure. Besides, he could find himself someone better than me, if he had a mind to.'

'Sarah!' Michael shouted over. 'Quick, here, would ye.'

'I have to go,' Sarah said apologetically.

Keeva was used to having short conversations. Even though people smiled at her and were quite pleasant, no one ever seemed to want to talk to her for long, always preferring to turn to Mrs Doyle or another customer. So Keeva smiled herself now, said, 'Oh that's fine, see you later,' and, turning on her heel, went in search of Mrs Doyle. She could at least stand next to her employer without feeling as though she was intruding.

The fiddler arrived and struck up a tune. Paddy, on his way to the back of the butcher's to fetch a barrel, grabbed Bridget by the arm and swung her around to the music.

'Oh, would ye get off me, Paddy. Grab your wife if you want to dance.'

'I can't, Bridget. She told me if I ever made her dance again, I'd never be able to father another child.'

'Oh God in heaven, you aren't still at it, are you, Paddy, not at your age?'

Paddy winked as he danced off. 'Now, I can't be embarrassing my poor wife, with all she has to put up with, but there is a very good reason, Bridget, why Josie starts every day with a smile on her face and a twinkle in her eye.'

Sarah, laughing at the exchange, placed her hand over her brow and squinted up the road to see if she could catch sight of Bee and Captain Bob, bringing Ciaran over from the coast. The sky was an azure blue, flecked with the white tails of scudding clouds, and the sun hovered over the mountains in the near distance. The river was high, and where they stood the roar of the water was almost as loud as the noise from the village street behind. Sarah had wondered, dared to hope, that some of her former neighbours from the shore might also come along. Bee had not sounded confident but had promised to let them know they would all be welcome.

Michael slipped his arm around Sarah's shoulders, his mug of porter in his other hand and a twinkle of happiness in his eye. His heart felt light and his head dizzy. 'Don't be worrying – they're coming. I told you, Captain Bob called into Josie's and left a message to tell us they'd be here.'

Sarah nodded and smiled. She missed Bee, and she missed her mother. It was the one sadness in her life, that her mother couldn't share in her good fortune, be a part of her new life.

Michael blinked and shook his head as he looked down at Sarah. She was his wife, the mother of his child. He had done it, achieved everything he had set out to do on the day he'd left for the war. As he sometimes found himself having to remind Sarah, the tragic consequence of their love for one another was not theirs to shoulder – it was not they who had murdered Angela. The birth of Mary Kate had seen their luck turn a corner, of that Michael was sure. 'I hope it lasts...' he said as he pushed Sarah's hair back over her shoulder.

Sarah tore her eyes from the road to the coast and looked up at him. 'The party? Paddy tells me it will be the morning before everyone leaves. We won't get to bed tonight.'

Michael laughed. 'Oh, I didn't mean the party! I meant this, today... our good fortune. Us! You, me and the babby. It feels too good to be true. Almost as though it couldn't possibly last because I don't know a single man in the whole world who has my happiness, and so how can it? How can it last?'

As sadness darkened her eyes, he could have bitten back his words. It had been all good for him and yet she had suffered, she still needed time. He'd been a fool. But before he could apologise, Mary Kate wriggled in her arms and the cloud that had crossed lifted.

Hugging the baby onto her chest, Sarah took a deep breath. 'I hope so. I want more of these little bundles.' She bent her head and nuzzled the ear of her baby.

A shout came from the road. 'Michael, help us get this on its end to give it time to settle.' It was Paddy, following Mr O'Dowd out of the back of the butcher's bar as he rolled the stout down onto the road. Josie was behind them, carrying a wooden tray of mugs for the ladies and for those men who'd forgotten to bring their own.

'No need,' said Mr O'Dowd, and he flipped the barrel on its end almost before Paddy had finished speaking.

'Tig, bring out the whiskey barrel that was delivered yesterday.'

Paddy was secretly grateful that Michael had chosen not to buy a slicer and sell bacon. It was the only argument they'd had since he'd returned from the war and he was thankful that Michael had backed down gracefully. The competition would have been difficult between friends.

John O'Donnell arrived with Philomena and Theady. Philomena walked straight over to Michael and Sarah and wished them well, whereas John O'Donnell avoided Michael's gaze, bent his head low and walked straight over to Paddy at the barrel. 'Ah, John, now, you are the last man I thought would be here today, drinking Michael's stout, eating his food and wishing him well, given how much you have to say about how he earnt the money that's paying for it.' O'Donnell scowled. 'Do I get a drink, or what?' he asked. Paddy tilted the tap on the barrel and fixed him with his gaze, 'Oh, aye, ye do. For no other reason than Michael is a man who would never bear a grudge against anyone who had cursed him with maggot-mouthed words. You see John, there are those that follow and there are those,' he tilted his head towards Michael, who was stood with his arm around Sarah who was showing off Mary Kate to Philomena, 'who get on and make a life for themselves with the toil of their own hands and ideas; those people don't have time to be bearing grudges.' He handed the pint over to John. The stout had overflowed as he spoke and was dribbling down the side. 'Oi, O'Donnell,' shouted Michael. ''Tis grand to see you, you are very welcome in exchange for a fair word and a good luck wish.' Michael laughed and O'Donnell swallowed hard. He had been taken in by McGuffey and his talk of revenge for those who had fought with the British, but now that McGuffey was gone, the war long over and Michael providing the drink, his sentiments were softer. 'May God be with you,' said O'Donnell and held up the pot Paddy had placed in his hand. Michael smiled. The last of the cynics had been won over.

Along with the rest of the village, Paddy appreciated Michael's generosity in paying for the stout for everyone in the village. Mrs Doyle had commented on this more than once already. 'Jesus, heaven save us. Your Joe would be turning in his grave if he could see the money that's been spent, his hard earnings being poured down the throats of the likes of this lot,' she said to Daedio, who had been placed in an armchair in the middle of the road, where he had been sitting all morning, grumbling to some, laughing with others.

Daedio swallowed hard, the only moment of the day when he felt uncomfortable. Joe's ill-gotten gains could not be called earnings by any stretch of the imagination. He made a note to tell Michael to be careful – people were noticing that the dollars were being cashed and spent. Dollars they thought Joe had sent home as a result of his success in the building of New York. Daedio had sent Michael to Galway to cash the bundle he'd given to Sarah. He had heard some of the women, too, passing comment on the necklace Sarah had not taken from her neck since he'd given it to her, and the dress she was wearing today had made some stand and stare. He would speak to Michael when the party was over.

Some of the old men from the village had pulled their chairs close to him and they sat around in a half circle, smoking pipes and drinking stout, talking about wakes and parties from the past. But mainly, as was their way, they recalled relatives who had long since died, people they'd all known, whose legacy was the wealth of stories about grudges and antics that kept their descendants entertained on days such as this. Each one a storyteller.

'I reckon we have just enough barrels to keep us going until the morning,' said Josie to Nola.

'They have to get through this one first.' Nola turned to watch as Paddy, bent double and with one hand on each end of the whiskey barrel, began rolling it across to the front of Malone's. Tig was on the other side, struggling to navigate it over the cinder path. As Nola handed out the mugs, Father Jerry came into sight with Teresa Gallagher and Rosie tagging along behind.

'Oh, here comes trouble,' said Josie. 'Teresa Gallagher is hot on Father Jerry's heels.'

'Trouble? She's no trouble. 'Tis me she's after.' Daedio removed his pipe and, leaning forward in his chair, followed Nola's gaze to the end of the street. 'Can't keep away from me, she can't. Why do you think I stay up on the hill? 'Tis to give me my distance.'

Nola grinned as, sure enough, Teresa made her way straight over to Daedio. She stood in front of him, the sun on her back, and her shadow loomed over him. The men groaned and hugged their pots closer, as if expecting Teresa to reach out and snatch them away.

Before Teresa could speak, Daedio got in there first. 'If ye be coming here to join our company, Teresa Gallagher, then you be leaving yer preaching up at the presbytery. Ye have nothing to say that will prevent me and my friends from enjoying this party on a day of celebration and good fortune. And what's more, we are wetting the babby's head and you and your tea-drinking ways won't be stopping us.'

'Is that porter in that mug?' Unsmiling, Teresa leant over to peer into the pot.

'It is not, 'tis stout, and what is more, Teresa, 'tis my stout, not yours. And before you start, you tell me, where in the Good Book does it say that no man should be drinking stout, or porter for that matter, on the day his youngest grandson opens his new shop and house by the fortune the good Lord bestowed upon me, to provide me with the ways and the means to gift the land upon him as a result of my own family's hard work and sacrifice on foreign soil. Tell me that – go on. Where in the Bible does it say that? Eh?' Daedio pulled on his pipe and threw a look of deep self-satisfaction towards his attentive and admiring neighbours.

Teresa made to speak, but Daedio cut in. 'See, you can't. She can't,' he repeated to his friends as he once again bent forward to ensure they had all heard. 'There is nowhere in the Bible it says that ye can't be enjoying a celebration of good news in Tarabeg. I have searched myself, from cover to cover. Now, if ye want to join us, Teresa, ye can, but first ye must have a drink to wet the head of Mary Kate, my bonny granddaughter who is the image herself of her grandmother Annie.'

Teresa folded her arms. ''Tis a sin to drink, Malone, and ye know that. 'Tis evil and the comfort of the Devil himself.'

'That's as maybe, Teresa, but not here. Not here in Tarabeg. As God is true, 'tis a little bit of heaven that we have just here. We can do what we like because all of these people, they are good people, Teresa, and everyone is out to enjoy a day to remember. Now sit down and hush. Nola, fill my pot, would you?'

Mrs Doyle, having spotted Teresa, pushed two chairs together. 'Come on, Teresa, sit down. Everyone here likes a little drink, and surely to God, did you ever know a happier village? Tell me, isn't that the truth?'

Teresa Gallagher could not argue. Good humour was the nature of the people in rural Eire. Money was scarce, but as long as everyone had enough to eat, they were happy in their disposition, despite the loss of their children and the fading shadow of the famine. True, there were the curses of Shona Maughan and the madness of Kevin McGuffey; and there were the fairies, who lived in the bog holes, robbed them of their pregnancies just a few months in, afflicted their children with the invisible touch of a wing, and, on occasion, sent a poor harvest. But despite all of this, they were still the happiest people. 'I find the degree of joviality in this village unreligious,' she said to Mrs Doyle as she grudgingly settled in a chair.

A few yards away, Brendan, Mr O'Dowd and Father Jerry were standing together, admiring the front door of the shop.

'Not a man alive doubts that he knows what he's doing,' said Brendan. 'You can smell it, the success. Sure, 'tis a fact, he's a lucky man and all. He'll double the money spent on this, and more, you mark my words.'

Father Jerry nodded. 'Aye, there's no doubt. You know, I have no notion what half of the things are he has in there. Every time he comes back from Galway or Dublin with more, it makes my eyes pop from out of my head. Stockings he has for ladies, next to the fishing tackle.'

'Stockings?' snorted Mr O'Dowd, who had emptied his first pot and was swinging it by the handle. 'What woman in this village doesn't knit her own stockings? I ask you. He'll be turning their heads. There's things the women of Dublin have time to do, because they don't have to be knitting stockings. It seems to me, if you want it in Tarabeg, Michael Malone has it. The provisions of Dublin are at our door and the ways of Dublin will be coming here too.'

They all turned to look as more people came down the road from the boreens and the farms to join them. Josie and Michael met them and handed the mugs around to Michael's would-be future customers. The children danced around excitedly and took the sweet oat biscuits Ellen Carey had carried over on a tray from the kitchen at the back of the tailor's shop.

Michael had left Sarah with Nola and was now making an exaggerated fuss of Mrs Doyle and Teresa Gallagher. He had persuaded Teresa to accept a small toast. 'Just a drop, go on, or ye'll be dying of the thirst. Water is only good for the fishes.'

Mrs Doyle squeezed his hand. 'Michael, what a joy this all is. What a change. You've brought life back into the village. Everyone is beside themselves with the excitement. I think you will be doing a roaring trade. I gave thanks this morning at Mass for all of it. A new shop in the village. Isn't it just wonderful, and a new wife and a babby. You are a lucky man, Michael Malone. A lucky man, you are.'

Michael had no reply. It was the truth. The expression on Mrs Doyle's face was soft and caring. She had been the friend of his grandma and he remembered her visits up to the farm when he was a boy. Michael Malone was rooted in Tarabeg, by memories and ancient ghosts and a deep affection for the village that no temptation from abroad could break.

With every full mug that was placed in a villager's hand, loyalty to shopping at Malone's was declared right there and then. By the time they had started the second mug, there was a lifelong pledge to abandon the tinkers and Castlebar market and to use only Malone's for all their future purchases. Michael was no stranger to work and observant of human nature. He knew exactly how to endear himself to the villagers, old and new.

The afternoon sun dipped lower in the sky and cast long shadows across the fast-flowing river, its peaty, tea-coloured water rushing over the stones through Michael's seven acres. Seamus and Pete had brought down from the farm extra straw bales; they bound the bales together with rope and made rows of benches that glowed a deep buttery yellow in the sunshine. Mr O'Dowd had even taken the donkeys up the boreens and transported down the infirm in basket chairs strapped across their backs. 'I could do this quicker if you just jumped on my back, Mrs Power,' he said to Keeva's mother and Mrs Murphy. 'All you had to do was wrap yer legs around my waist and hold on good and tight – you can remember how to do that, can't you?' They laughed so hard, Mrs Murphy's last tooth fell out on the way.

It didn't take long before the first neighbour began to doze, a smile on his face, a pot in his hand and feeling happy, thanks to Michael Malone.

As the villagers stood and admired the shop, inside and out, gasping over the new goods and chatting in the street, the fiddler, who attended every gathering in Tarabeg, small and large, was joined by one of the farmers from up in the hills on his own fiddle. Six men carried the piano down from the Murphys' house and set it on the side of the road. Someone began to play tunes they all knew and the tapping of feet began to play a tattoo on the dusty road. Paddy continued filling pots and mugs and Tig took his mouth organ from his trouser pocket. The blended sound of piano, fiddles and mouth organ filled the air and, with the fading sun on their faces and Guinness in their bellies, people began to relax. One or two jigged to the rhythm and the children formed a circle and danced their traditional dances in the middle of the street, sending up clouds of dried mud around their ankles. The only sounds louder than the music or the river were the howls of laughter as villagers danced and clapped their hands in time to the ever quickening rhythm.

Sarah could practically feel the beat coming up from the road and through her legs as it pounded into her heart as her own feet began to tap, her hips swayed and yet still Mary Kate slept in her arms, oblivious throughout.

'Come away and dance with me, will you,' said Michael as he ran up to his wife and circled her and his daughter in his arms.

'Are you mad? Get off, she will wake any minute if you don't stop.'

But Michael would not take no for an answer and, handing Mary Kate to his mother, he took his wife for a twirl. The crowd parted and everyone clapped as he spun his Sarah around.

'You see that?' said Daedio to the men sitting around him. 'That's what me and Annie danced like. Do you remember? When we had the fair and Seamus was a lad and we were dancing out here, long before Paddy built his shop.'

The men nodded and for a moment fell silent as they wondered where the years had flown and how it was that one minute they'd been young men dancing a jig and now they were the old men sitting on the side. 'That was me and Annie once,' repeated Daedio, almost to himself.

The space outside the shop was full and Father Jerry, having taken the Angelus Mass, now flopped onto a bale and looked settled in for the night. It was a Sunday and Michael had timed it right. The farmers and those in the remote dwellings, like his own Aunt Mary in the lodge up on the next hill, had travelled in for the Mass and now he would keep them there with the promise of food and drink and a seat to rest their weary legs.

Bridget and Porick McAndrew had arrived and joined in

the festivities. Bridget had set herself up inside the shop and was telling fortunes, a safe distance from Father Jerry. She was reading palms and supplying potion to those who found the trek to her farm too much. Sarah brought Mary Kate over to her, carrying her across her chest, tucked into her shawl, and Bridget stood on tiptoes to peek at her.

'She's special, that child, mark my words,' she said to Sarah. 'She could have the sight. There aren't many born that have that look about them. I'm thinking your Michael will be right. Her future isn't here in Tarabeg, I see her across the water, and…' Suddenly her face clouded over.

'What is it, Bridget?' asked Sarah, a note of alarm in her voice. 'What is it?'

Bridget recovered herself. 'Nothing. Nothing at all. I have a God-awful pain in my leg.' She bent down and rubbed her leg, averting her face from Sarah. 'I just told you, this one, she's special.'

Sarah smiled, relieved.

'As God is true, she will be worth a hundred times her father when her days are done, that I do know.'

'She is due for another feed soon,' Sarah said, feeling the now familiar tingling and swelling of her breasts and a desperate need to relieve the fullness.

The musicians and dancers had stopped to take a break and fill themselves with the best pork any of them had ever tasted, cooked over a pit on Michael's seven acres. The children ran back and forth with wooden platters of the steaming, succulent meat. Suddenly Sarah heard a voice call her name. It was a child's voice and one she knew; it was Ciaran shouting to her. Her heart had been aching and her happiness incomplete, but now he was here.

'Sarah! Sarah!' He ran to her, waving, and threw his arms around her legs.

Turning sharply, she saw two cartloads of new arrivals. Driving the first cart were her Uncle Rory's parents, waving to her, and the second was driven by Captain Bob. In those carts they brought to Sarah all of her past, all the way to Tarabeg, which was her future. People who had known her since she was a child. People who knew her mother and could tell her that as well as looking like Michael's relatives, Mary Kate looked just like one of her own. She thought her heart would burst as Bee waved and all of her former neighbours did the same and called her name excitedly.

Michael ran towards the first cart and guided the horse by the harness to the post to pull up outside Paddy's.

'There you go, it's your day now, too,' said Bridget as she squeezed Sarah's hand. 'They have all come for you, Sarah. Just for you.' As Sarah hurried over to greet her friends and neighbours, she missed the shadow of concern that crossed Bridget's face and nor did she see her kiss the rosary she took from her pocket. Bridget dabbled in many things she ought not to, and some she had every right to, but her last line of defence was always the rosary.

The sun set and the moon rose. The air was uncommonly warm for a spring evening and the glow of the meat-roasting pit took the edge off any chill. Children slept soundly on the tops of bales, tucked up into capes and shawls. Michael and Sarah had chosen a full moon night so that people could find their way home should they leave before dawn, and the village bathed in its magical silver light. Josie had fetched the candles and hurricane lamps, but there was barely any need.

As midnight approached, the merriment showed no sign of abating. Paddy and Josie made their way back into the bar to prepare the next round of refreshments.

'I don't think anyone will be leaving until we're drunk dry,' Paddy said as he wheeled out another barrel.

'Sure, was it ever any different?' Josie replied. 'The ocean lot won't be leaving until the sun is up, they know how to dance, and Sarah will want to keep them here as long as she can. I've put the pies in the oven and Sarah's is full too. Mrs Doyle has the bread in her kitchen and it's being carried down now. It'll be time to feed everyone again soon and there is still some of the pig left out in the pit.'

Josie was bent over the range, sliding out a tray full of hot meat and potato pies. The steam rose to greet them and Paddy's stomach groaned in response. Josie picked up the corner of her apron, lifted a hot pie and held it out to her husband.

'God, you are an angel,' he said as he took it, using the corner of his jacket against the heat. As he bit into the buttery pastry and hot salty gravy dribbled down his chin, Josie flicked the rest of the pies from the cast-iron tray onto a wooden platter.

'Will ye take a look out there,' said Paddy, sucking in the air to cool the last of the pie in his mouth.

Josie glanced over her shoulder.

'If I was a man with a pencil and paper and a gift for the drawing, I would want to paint that sight right now and keep it for ever. Sure, was there ever such a night?'

Josie placed her palms in the small of her back and straightened. Much to her surprise, a tear filled her eye. Out of the door was a vision of pure joy. Out there were the friends they had grown up and lived with every day of their lives, dancing, talking, singing and laughing. Some of the children, too excited to sleep, were running around on the periphery, slower than they had been earlier, their energy reserves depleted. Tig was sitting on a bale with Michael and Bee, and Captain Bob was showing him a trick with a coin. Tig threw his head back, laughing. The silvery light of the full moon cast an eerie but beautiful light over the scene.

Paddy slipped his arm around his wife's shoulders. 'What's up wit' ye?' he asked as he placed a kiss on her cheek.

Josie lifted the corner of her apron, which was still warm and floury from the pie, and wiped her eye. 'I wish I knew. I have this feeling, Paddy. Like we are the last. Like this is the last. That maybe there will never be another night like this. You know, with the new quarry, the things that people talk about, 'tis all changing, and I don't think Tarabeg or any of the villages around here will stay the same. Every person here tonight has known each other all of their lives – we're family, not neighbours, and, jeez, so many have married from one family to the other over the years, we really are. Can it stay the same, as good as this? It can't, can it?'

Paddy shook his head. He couldn't disagree with her. 'Maybe it will all be for the better after all. Maybe it gets as good as it will ever be and then it has to change. We are the lucky ones who get to be here, when that happens.'

'Aye, maybe.' Josie sniffed and wiped her hands on her apron. 'But I can't think how you could match this. If laughter and long living is the best ye can ask for, how can any change be for the better when we have the best already? 'Tis one thing for us to get the best, sure it is, but I want that for Tig, and Sarah's baby. We don't need the best, they do.'

'Aye, well, some things won't change, Josie. When was the last time anyone died before their ninetieth year? Look how many live to over a hundred. There's a reason they call Ireland God's own country, we are blessed by saints and the good Lord himself. Nothing can change that.'

Paddy opened his arms and his wife stepped into them. Over her shoulder, he saw Sarah and Tig in conversation alongside the latest arrivals to the party. His wife was right, he knew it, and a great sadness slipped into his heart.

'I haven't seen the babby properly for days now.' Tig had hobbled across to Sarah, his stick tapping on the hard-baked earth. 'What a grand man Captain Bob is, and all the way from Ballycroy.'

'He is. And Mary Kate hasn't changed much,' said Sarah.

'Does she still look like her daddy?'

'Everyone says she looks like Grandma Annie, but I wouldn't know.'

'Ah, well, doesn't matter who she looks like, she's yours and Michael's. You are mighty lucky to have a babby as bonny as she is.'

'You'll have one too one day,' said Sarah, who knew exactly what she was doing.

'Me? Who would want me? No, I'm just happy that you've asked me to stand for Mary Kate, though you'll have to put up with me being around all the time, keeping an eye on her. I'll be happy with that, being her godfather.'

'Well, I think it's time you stopped feeling sorry for yourself and realised that there is a very lovely young lady in this village who has eyes only for you. And when you do, I might be bothered listening to your protests.' Sarah turned and began to walk away.

'Sarah, stop, who?' Tig was trying to run and Sarah, worried that he might fall over, stopped and looked back, laughing.

'Oh, interested now, are you?' The moment she saw his face, she took pity on him. He was stricken, anxious. He didn't speak, just stared at her, and she saw a flicker of hope in his eyes. 'Tig, 'tis Keeva from the post office, she told me herself.'

'No! When? What did she say? Tell me her exact words.'

'Well, let me think… She said she was interested in you but you never even noticed her. She said she knew who her heart was for. Yes, that was it, her exact words.'

Tig collapsed onto a bale and Sarah laughed. 'Tig, it's not that big a deal that you need to fall about…'

'Oh yes it is.'

Sarah thought she had never seen a smile so broad on the face of any man other than her Michael.

They broke off the dancing and the card playing and the drinking when Nola and Josie shouted for everyone to help themselves to food. Seamus and Pete had laid long planks of wood across straw bales and this makeshift table was now heaving with hot pies and chicken and slabs of sliced meat, next to buttered bread and pots of salt.

'Stop, everyone!' The voice of Father Jerry rang out even as Teresa Gallagher was still whispering in his ear. 'We must give thanks to the good Lord for tonight, and a special blessing for Michael, Sarah and the babby. And, before we eat, also for the food. Have we all forgotten?'

Impatient muttering rose from those who had drunk well into their cups and could just about stand and those who could smell the chicken and the hot pies and were hungry.

'The father had forgotten to give thanks himself until Teresa Gallagher reminded him,' said Tig to Pete.

There was more murmuring as those who had already helped themselves to food from the table set it back down. Hands were clasped together, hats removed and heads bowed as Father Jerry began.

'Thank you, Lord, for the food we eat with friends, and know 'tis of your will and blessing. Michael and Sarah, may the Lord bless you and Mary Kate, and your new venture and your beautiful home. May joy and peace surround you all, may contentment latch your door, and may happiness be with you now and love be cherished evermore.'

There was a moment of silence, broken by a hungry cry from Mary Kate, swaddled in her shawl in Sarah's arms. The crowd slowly lifted their heads and, remembering the food, shuffled towards the table. But they were to be thwarted once more.

Michael was the first to hear them, alerted by the sound of horse's hooves in the distance. It was a moment before Sarah herself noticed that the chatter around the table had diminished and silence had fallen, so focused was she on the needs of Mary Kate. But then she registered the rise of an anxious murmur, which melted straight into silence. Or maybe it was the cloud that arrived from nowhere in the sky and covered the moon that made her look up and her heart beat faster. They had all heard it before, the clatter of hooves and the rumble of wheels as the dust cloud rolled along the Ballina road and into the village. No one spoke and plates and mugs were held still as Shona Maughan, driving her caravan and horses, came into view. Her wild hair hung down from her hat in escaping tendrils like the tails of white rats.

The crowd parted as Bridget stepped out into the street. 'She takes her strength from those horses,' she said to Josie, who stood next to her. 'She has no age, has always been here.'

Shona's teeth were as black as her skirt. As they all looked on, she spat her chewing baccy to the ground. About her shoulders she wore a brown and black Aran spun blanket; her skirts came down to her ankles, revealing her worn leather boots. She pulled the reins close to her chest and Sarah could see that the skin on her hands was as black as her uncut nails.

Shona leant over and whispered to her son. Sarah felt her eyes resting on the emerald around her neck. She lifted her left hand to cover it. The chatter of the children who were still awake and the whispering of the revellers fell away to absolute silence. The only sound was that of the running river in the distance.

'You be taking our trade with that shop,' said Jay Maughan from the seat next to Shona. He too spat a black wad of chewed baccy onto the ground at Michael's feet.

Michael knew it was no coincidence that the Maughans had arrived during the party for the shop opening – he'd been expecting them. They would have picked up the news in one of the coastal villages as they passed through.

In fact, the news had been delivered in the form of a taunt. Many locals hated the tinkers and feared that bad things happened when they turned up. A few days earlier, some villagers who'd taken a drink had let the alcohol loosen their lips, shouting, 'We won't be needin' you and your like soon, Maughan – we have the brave man himself, Michael Malone, to be buying whatever we be wanting.'

Jay Maughan had listened in silence. He rarely spoke to those who lived in the remote villages, or their children, who threw stones at his wheels when they left.

'Are they talking about the Malone shop?' Shona had asked him as she cracked the reins on the horse's back. 'I don't know, but we need to make it our business to find out. Seems to me that Malone is after making trouble. I will sort it with my fists, and if not, you will sort it with your words. We will put the fear of God into them, one way or another.'

Maughan was a man used to letting his fists and boots do the talking. Ordinarily he would have paid no regard to there being twenty Tarabeg men standing around him. He knew, they were more terrified of Shona and her reputation, than they were of their own wives. But for Maughan a far bigger fear was the officer from the Garda, who was sitting on one of the straw bales. He'd been chatting to Mrs Doyle, gathering nuggets of local information from the nosiest woman in the west, a woman who knew the ins and outs of the comings and goings of almost everyone in the village. Now, though, the guard had his eyes fixed on Maughan as he puffed on his pipe. He had a new car, from the government, his pride and joy and the source of all his self-importance, and a new stone cell to replace the barracks that had been in place since the days of the famine and the deportations but had been burnt down by the Black and Tans.

Maughan gave the guard a long hard look back. He knew only too well that he was mad keen to use both the car and the cell and he didn't fancy taking his chances again, having spent enough time in the old cell. Maughan was also only half as brave without McGuffey at his side and as he looked at Sarah with the baby in her arms, he spat again.

Michael had broken away and moved towards the caravan, which stood silhouetted against the moonlight. He shouted up to Maughan, 'Times move on, Maughan. There's no need to be taking it to heart – there's plenty of villages along the coast that will still need to buy from you. And Jesus, nothing reaches Belmullet, no one delivers there, they will be glad to see more of you.'

He reached his free hand to his cap and pushed it back in order to take a good look at Shona, on the driving board of the caravan. 'People are moving into the villages and hereabouts every week to work up at the new quarry. They say 'tis going to be huge and they will move the whole mountain in a generation. The men will be coming from all over Eire to work here. They're labourers, not farmers, and they need food every day. They have to know when they can get it, 'tis long hours up at the quarry. You don't always come when you're expected. And when you do, people don't know what you'll have for them. The women will have money in their purses, and they will need to buy the food.'

Maughan didn't answer at first, just leant over and whispered something in Shona's ear.

Sarah had moved to her husband's side. She placed one restraining hand on his arm and with the other she held on to Mary Kate. She was unaware that the eyes of the women of the village were all trained on her. The first person at her side was Bee. 'Don't go too close, Sarah,' she said as she tugged on her sleeve. Captain Bob had moved around to Michael's side, followed by Seamus and Pete and Brendan, who, a full head taller than Michael, fixed Jay Maughan with his stare as he puffed on his pipe.

Gradually the rest of the villagers moved up to stand alongside and support them, in number if not in voice. Sarah sensed movement behind her and, looking over her shoulder, saw Rosie and Keeva walking fearlessly towards her. The crowd parted and they came forward to stand one on each side of her.

Keeva wound her fingers into Mary Kate's shawl and stood so close to Sarah, she could feel the warmth from her body. Bee smiled down at her. 'Welcome, brave lady,' she whispered. Keeva, despite the tension of the moment, flushed with pleasure.

Rosie moved around the side of them both and stood next to Michael and Captain Bob.

The crowd began to murmur; they were shamed, two fearless young women had led the way, and they were feeling bold. Shona was losing her power as Bridget worked hers. Shona's eyes met Bridget's and they locked on, the two women in their own battle for dominance. Beads of perspiration stood out on Bridget's brow. Josie, who had hung back with her, slipped her hand into hers and squeezed it tight.

Shona never spoke. No one had ever heard her voice, except for Bridget. When she read palms, she wrote down her words and Jay translated. Her lips moved, but her words went unheard. Each time that happened, people feared it was a curse falling from her mouth. Rumour had it that in every village she bestowed upon one woman the ability to heed her warning. Some said that Bridget McAndrew not only heard her but knew where Shona's curses fell.

Shona was staring down at Sarah and Mary Kate. Leaning across the driving board, she again whispered into Jay's ear. There was a sharp intake of breath from the mothers in the crowd, followed by an instinctive sweeping up of sleeping children into arms, as though they feared that Shona had instructed Jay to jump down and steal them. A breeze ran down the road and cut through the warm night air. The women tightened their shawls about them as a cloud floated across the moon and darkness fell.

Jay, having appraised Sarah, turned his gaze back to Michael. He was not going to shift and his mood was now as black as night. 'We came often enough for you all before. How would Tarabeg have managed until now without the Maughans? I told you, you be taking our trade, Malone.'

Michael had fought in battles and held men in his arms as they died in agony; he was not afraid of Jay or Shona and he was determined to stand his ground. He pulled himself up to his full height, stepped right up to the running board and met Maughan's gaze. 'You have a horse and caravan, you can trade anywhere you like, just not here any more.' He had been waiting for this showdown since the day he decided to make his own way and he had his answers ready.

'You won't be lasting long,' Maughan hissed in his face.

Maughan was losing his temper, and his presumption that the village Michael was born and raised in should trade only with the tinkers and not one of their own was making Michael lose his own. 'Off ye go, little man, and take your old witch of a mother and yer stolen children with ye,' he said, taking a length of the reins in his hand and making to slap the horse on the rear. 'Or maybe the Garda should come and ask ye a few questions?'

Shona had cracked the whip before Michael slapped the horse, anticipating his action, and it reared up, sending clouds of dust swirling into the air. The dust settled in the eyes of those children who were still awake, making them cry and run for shelter behind their mothers' skirts.

Swinging the caravan around on two wheels, they rode off, but not before Shona had turned her head, looked Sarah straight in the eye and said something. No one heard the words, but everyone felt the menace flying through the air. She had a reputation from the east coast to the west and all the way down to Limerick. Death, failed crops, disease and even a three-legged goat were all blamed on Shona Maughan and her curses. Ellen and Bridget exchanged knowing looks. The menace carried to them on the wind and settled about Bridget's ears. Bridget kept her expression neutral, aware that all eyes had now fixed on her. The dust flew up from the back wheels and rendered the caravan invisible as it thundered down the road to Belmullet.

Sarah's knees had gone weak. 'Thank you,' she said, turning to Keeva.

Bee put her arms around her. 'Here, give me the babby. God in heaven, I wasn't going to leave you stood there with that child. Maybe that will be the last we see of them now.'

'Michael Malone, why did you have to go up to the horse, why couldn't you just leave it, say nothing? That's the way you deal with the Maughans – say nothing to them and they can say nothing back to you.' Nola was walking towards them with Teresa by her side.

'Rosie, come away,' Teresa shouted, belatedly.

'That was brave of you,' said Michael to Rosie. And then, 'Thank you, Captain Bob, I appreciate you doing that.'

'Not at all,' said Captain Bob.

Rosie, her heart beating so fast she could hear it, said, 'You're welcome,' and joined Keeva and Bee.

Michael moved closer to Sarah and Mary Kate. As he placed his arms around his wife's shoulders, he said, 'Don't be fretting now, she wasn't looking at ye.'

Sarah looked down at the baby, now safe in Bee's arms. 'She was looking at both of us,' she said to the wide open and knowing eyes of Mary Kate. 'What did she say?' she asked the crowd who had formed a protective circle around them both. She placed her hand protectively on her daughter's head.

'Nothing,' said Michael. 'She said nothing because she is nothing.'

Only Bridget had heard and she slipped her rosary from her pocket for the second time that day.

'There is only one family that will be anyone or anything around here and that's the Malones,' he shouted after the disappearing caravan. 'Oi, Paddy, more Guinness – are ye slacking or what? Am I not paying ye good money to give everyone a good time? Fiddler, your drink is on its way, play something for the children to dance to.'

Sarah knew there was no use asking her husband again, he would never tell her what he'd heard, if indeed he had heard anything, which she doubted.

Within minutes, the men were drinking and the mothers and children dancing. Tig sat on a bale and with drink in hand chatted to Keeva. Their heads moved closer and closer together and they remained that way, as the bright full moon, with its knowledge of all that had passed since the beginning of time and all that was to come, settled on the worn pebbled bottom of the Taramore river to watch.

Chapter 16

Six years later: 1952

With each year of Mary Kate's life, the shop grew and thrived thanks to its local customers as well as the fishermen, quarry workers and passing tourists, who were becoming more numerous. Michael spent a week a month travelling, bringing all manner of exciting products back from Galway and Dublin in his new flatbed van. Often he took with him lists of errands villagers requested, and he was more than happy to drive the extra mile. Those same villagers were his friends as well as his customers and as he was one of only half a dozen people in Tarabeg to have made the change from horse to car, it was seen as his duty.

Sarah minded the shop, and Mary Kate joined her when she returned from school, perching on the three-legged stool that had been carved by Pete, under the barked instructions of Daedio, with her name engraved around the rim of the seat. Although she was only six, Mary Kate already had homework, set by Miss O'Hara. This she did in the shop while eating the delicious brack and butter and drinking the dish of tea Sarah set ready for her.

Michael spent his days either out buying and delivering, or tending the acres he'd turned over to crops. By night he was often busy poaching wild Atlantic salmon. The previous week he'd been out in a torrential downpour until dawn.

'I'll be growing the gills of the salmon out in the river any day now. I'm wet more than I am dry, so I am,' he said as he slipped in through the back door at first light under a curtain of rain. Standing in front of the fire, bent over and with water dripping from the brim of his cap, the hessian sack with the night's catch weighing heavy on his shoulder, he shook his oilskin over a bleary-eyed Mary Kate. She screamed and ran away, as she always did.

Sarah scolded him for putting water all over the kitchen floor, as she too always did. 'Will you get the hell out of here with that thing,' she hissed, pointing at the catch, 'and take it over to Paddy's right now if ye want to eat today.'

Michael, who always half expected to be greeted as a valiant returning hunter, pulled a dejected face. 'Oh Jesus, woman, aren't I wet enough? Paddy said he'll be over here this morning to fetch it once I've put Mary Kate's bike out to let him know.' He gave his wife an exaggerated wink.

Sarah, the woman everyone described as having the patience of a saint to be putting up with the ever more fanciful notions of Michael Malone, was standing in her nightshirt, and Mary Kate was next to her, in her own night clothes, with her teddy hanging from one hand, a thumb in her mouth, her head tilted and a grin on her face. She almost giggled as her parents did mock battle yet again, standing in a puddle of river water that was slowly spreading across their kitchen floor.

On the nights her father was out fishing, Mary Kate slept next to her mother in her parents' big bed. Both being light sleepers, they woke together the moment they heard boots crunching on the stony ground at the back of the house. Michael never knew that when he was out poaching, Sarah barely slept for fear of his being caught by the ghillie and put before the magistrate. Or, far worse, his curragh sinking in the wilder reaches of the Taramore river and taking him with it. The memory of her Uncle Rory and his untimely demise cast a long shadow. Michael Malone could do many things, but swimming wasn't one of them.

Mary Kate was blissfully unaware of the significant role her bike played in the poaching activities of the village men. It was one of many tactics used to foil the ghillie and it had been devised by Michael on the Christmas Day Mary Kate had come down the stairs to find her first bike waiting for her. The way the bike faced, and which side of the door it was placed, sent a message to Paddy, Seamus, Pete, Father Jerry and anyone else who had the nerve and could be trusted to poach with them. 'I'm taking the bike, don't move it, Mary Kate,' was an order Mary Kate had learnt never to question. To the village side of the door, front wheel facing the church, meant 'poaching tonight'. Facing the coast was a message for Paddy, meaning 'fish to be collected'. If Mary Kate ever parked her bike at the front herself, she would be scolded by Sarah as she furtively scanned the street. 'What are you doing, child? Bring it round the back, now.'

In a village of just under a hundred people, every movement was seen and noted by someone, not least Mrs Doyle. Information was currency in Tarabeg. A nugget of gossip, however small, was reason to throw on a shawl and a headscarf and visit the post office or the shop. But it never appeared suspicious that even in the worst of weathers, after the heavens had opened and rinsed the dust off the village streets, the little bike still stood guard. Only occasionally would someone comment when in the post office, casting a distracted glance at the bike, 'Does nothing keep that Mary Kate off her bike? Out in all weathers, she must be.'

A wild Atlantic salmon could weigh as much as an eight-year-old child and the spoils went far. Paddy and Josie were the only people for miles to own a fridge big enough to store whatever Michael and Tig brought home from their fishing expeditions. Paddy did not poach, but he gutted, filleted and divided the spoils, taking a share for himself. He ignored any guilt he felt about this in the same way he ignored the indigestion he got every time he put too many rashers on his bread in the morning.

The rules were that there could be not a whisper about Father Jerry joining them. 'If Teresa knew the father poached, she would drop down dead on the spot,' Josie always said when the subject came up.

'She knows,' Tig always replied. 'His clothes and boots will be wet. Teresa Gallagher, she turns a blind eye to what suits her purpose, that being fresh salmon for tea.'

'If ye are caught, Tig, who will run the show here?' Paddy protested every time Tig and Michael tried to persuade him to join them. Even though the path to the back of Paddy's shop and the shed with the fridge was only twenty yards away, it could be a treacherous twenty yards for Michael and Tig to tread, with easily identifiable dripping sacks of salmon slung over their backs. It was unlikely the ghillie would be standing in the main street, but someone else would. John O'Donnell would happily earn a sixpence from the ghillie in exchange for a useful piece of information and then spend it in Paddy's bar. For some, farmhands who lived on what they grew, bartered for extras with eggs, and whose wives made what they wore, a sixpence was a luxury that could be saved towards a boat fare and escape.

Josie had told Paddy she would kill him with his own cleaver if he poached. 'I will not live with the shame,' she had screeched at him the first time he'd told her he was thinking of joining in. 'If the cold didn't kill ye, 'twould be me meself doing it with me bare hands. Either that or you would find yourself in the barracks. Blacken my name and I won't ever forgive you.'

Paddy knew his place. It was well and truly under the thumb of Josie.

A cold, clear night had arrived and the stars twinkled distantly as the poaching party approached their usual place. The only significant illumination came from the thinnest slice of orange moon. Away from the bridge, the rush of the river as it tripped over centuries-worn pebbles was tantalisingly close.

'Another minute and we'll be there,' said Tig, who always spoke too much when he was nervous.

The ground became soft and the icy water lapped over the toes of their galoshes. They had arrived. As the chill crept through to their bones, they stood to catch their breath.

Only half an hour earlier, Paddy had been helping Tig prepare and load up his bag. 'Make sure Michael puts the bike out as soon as ye are back,' he said. 'I'll move Murphy's pig over to make room in the fridge.'

Tig had been pulling up his waders and gathering up the

tackle from where it had been laid out ready. His light would be a candle lantern attached to his head. It stood on the table, waiting, unlit and covered in a cloth to prevent anyone from the bar seeing it. The bar was now empty, the last customer long home, and the night was dark. 'As soon as Sarah and Mary Kate are in bed, I'll be off.' He and Paddy moved to the window and gazed across the road, waiting for the light to come on upstairs above the shop.

'I wish ye could come with us, for the craic, Da.' Tig's eyes were alight with the excitement. Pete and Seamus were joining him and Michael tonight and would be hoping to take a fair catch back up the hill in the cart before the village awoke. Tig would have given anything for Paddy to have accompanied the four of them, but Josie was adamant and she'd been joined in her protest by Keeva, who was learning his mother's ways.

'Do you have to go, Tig?' she'd asked. 'Your mammy says breaking the law is the worst thing.'

'Oh take no notice of Mammy, Keeva, she has never been any different, and when have we ever had any problem?'

'Well, we have two sons to look after, so don't go getting yourself caught.'

'Never, not me. In a few years, those boys will be coming with me.'

Keeva had playfully slapped him on the back, knowing that no matter how much she attempted to emulate his mother, Tig wouldn't listen to either of them.

Across the road, Michael was wrapping up the sandwiches Sarah had made. He tucked them into the wicker basket that he tied across his back with a leather strap.

'It's him himself,' Paddy said, as Seamus and Pete came down the road, Pete leading the horse by the harness to make less noise, rags tied over its hooves to muffle the clip-clop. Pete led the horse and cart around the back of Michael's shop. 'It will be a good catch tonight,' said Paddy. 'He's a lucky fisherman is Seamus. I'll be watching for the bike.'

'Will ye not come with us?' asked Tig for the umpteenth time.

Paddy took off his cap and rubbed his head. 'Ah, no. How many times have I told ye, Tig, I'm an unlucky fisherman. Since I married your mother, I swear the fish see me coming and they're off. No, 'twould be a wasted night's effort for ye all if I came along too and that's for sure.' Before Tig could ask him another question, Paddy put his head out of the window and looked both left and right. Then he slipped his head back in and took the arm of his son. 'Go on, God be with ye. Don't worry about the boys and Keeva, all is good here. Have a good night.'

Without another word, Tig hopped across the road to Michael's.

An hour later, now safely on the banks of the river, the men were about to start.

'Sshh, listen,' said Tig as he stood with the lime sack in his hands. 'Can you hear, is it Father Jerry?'

They heard the familiar low whistle of their occasional companion. The call of Father Jerry, the man chastised by Brendan O'Kelly for breaking the law, asking to be guided to wherever on the banks Michael and Tig were.

'Joseph and Mary, why can't he just turn up at the house at the right time. He always comes along at an awkward moment,' said Seamus.

'Here, light me candle.' Tig bent his head to reveal the opening of the lantern.

'No, I'll strike a match, 'twill be enough,' said Michael, taking a box of matches out of his pocket. He struck the match, his heart beating wildly for fear of being seen. Bending down, he lit it within the cave of his cupped hands and turned his body in a semicircle so that its light could only be seen for a few seconds at a time. Anyone not looking for it would mistake the flickering orange glow for a faerie or a firebug. The village was steeped in faerie folklore. The light was enough. Minutes later, they heard the unmistakeable crunch of Father Jerry's feet hitting the stony ground, and soon after came the sound of him puffing for his breath by their side.

'Evening, Father,' the four men whispered.

'Evening. Shall I bless the water first?' whispered Father Jerry.

'Why should ye have to?' asked Tig. ''Tis fecking ridiculous that you can't fish from your own land, Michael. Sorry, Father.' Tig looked sheepish at having sworn. He was always nervous on these occasions, mindful of his mother's complaining and Keeva's words.

The five men placed their bags and nets on the ground and stood for a second, listening for the sound of any other footsteps. Their eyes searched for the flickering headlamp of the ghillie having been alerted by the match. They had unnerved a grouse or a fox, as something scuttled away through the coarse grass, off towards the edge of the field, which Michael had planted with oats. The gently beating wings of a large bird swooped by, unidentifiable as it blocked out the stars during its passage overhead, and then came the telltale call of an owl in dignified objection at having been disturbed from the thatch of a house.

Turning back, they scanned the village for signs of life. There was only one cottage still lit. In Maria Murphy's window the flame of a lone candle warned away the ancient ghosts. Maria, ninety-nine years old, was afraid of being alone in the dark. She lived her life, day and night, in the light, believing that the moment she found herself in darkness she would be called to her maker. Almost entirely deaf, and short-sighted, she was of no concern to Michael, knowing as he did that she spent more time asleep than awake. She would be dozing on the chair in front of her fire. The rest of Tarabeg enjoyed the sleep of the blessed and the innocent. All except one villager. Rosie O'Hara saw the light. Rosie knew what was occurring. She sat in her chair by the fire in the dark interior of her teacher's cottage and waited for the next glint of life out on the river.

The men turned back to the Taramore and bowed their heads as Father Jerry whispered his prayers. As soon as he'd finished, Seamus spoke. 'I have an even better idea, Father. Here, from Daedio.' He took a flat stoneware hip flask from his pocket and passed it round. 'He said he can't be here in body, but he can in spirit. Not the Holy Spirit, Father, but the one that keeps the blood running to our toes.'

The men suppressed their laughter as they each took a swig of whiskey from the flask.

'Tig is right,' said Pete once they'd each taken a second swig, ''tis feckin' mad that you can't fish from yer own land.'

Seamus slipped the flask back into his jacket pocket.

'No one knows that more than me, sure they don't.' Michael's brow furrowed with impatience, as it did every time the subject was raised. He was as frustrated as the rest that he couldn't legally claim the salmon that thrived in the Taramore's deep pools, which the English landowner, Captain Carter, charged British and German tourists huge amounts of money for the right to fish. Michael sometimes watched the boats on the river in the middle of his land, his irritation eased only by the pounds the visitors passed over his counter and into his till. 'At least they buy some of their tackle from me,' he said. 'Mary Kate nearly blew it for us the other day.' Seamus, who was fastening his net, looked up in surprise. 'Yes, your precious granddaughter, she who can do no wrong. One of the tourists was buying a new salmon fly. Complaining, he was, about not being able to land a catch. Mary Kate says to him, all innocent, "Why don't you use the lime, like Daddy. You just tip a bag in where you want to fish and it knocks the salmon out."'

'Feck,' Tig said, standing there with a bag of lime in his hands.

'Don't be worrying now,' said Michael. 'The fella packed up and headed home. He wasn't after anything I had. He wanted the fly to catch the fecking fish for him. He had neither the skill nor the patience to be a proper fisherman.'

'Shall I tip the lime?' Tig asked.

'Aye, I brought two lots,' said Michael. 'Should knock out half the salmon in the river. 'Twill be a good catch tonight.'

The five men looked at each other. It was almost pitch black and they could only see the whites of each other's eyes as they all erupted with laughter, the irony of Michael's condemnation of the poor fishing skills of the English tourist not lost on any of them as the lime fizzed and hissed in the water around them.

'I'll be holding the nets,' said Father Jerry. 'I have a harder time than you convincing Teresa Gallagher where the salmon come from. I'll be telling no lies when I say I don't know who caught it. I won't be watching now – you just say "Net!" as usual.' He turned his head away from the shore and stood with the biggest keep net firmly out to his side.

The others grinned as they moved out into the river. Not one would admit that the only time they could breathe freely was when their catch was bagged and they were safely home through their own back door.

'Net,' hissed Tig, and the light on his head guided the hands of Father Jerry to catch the biggest salmon the men had ever landed. It was all they needed, so they waded back to the shore.

'Sssh!' It was Father Jerry.

The men stopped dead in their tracks. Tig reached up and placed the palm of his hand over his light. They were once again plunged into darkness. No one dared speak. They knew the tone of voice, felt the fear slip into their bellies. All thoughts were of Tig. The worst nightmare had always been that if they had to run, how would they manage with Tig? Hearts beat wildly and they all stood rooted to the spot. Only Father Jerry moved as he let the sack containing the writhing salmon slip soundlessly to the ground. They all heard a whispered prayer as their hearts steadied to a rhythm that allowed them to think clearly.

'Look to the bridge,' whispered Seamus.

They all turned as they saw the familiar car of the ghillie pass slowly across the bridge. The sound of a car engine was something they were still unused to and they all squatted down as close to the ground as they could. The handbrake crunched on, the engine stopped and the car door creaked open. This all above the gurgle of the running river. A torch beam shone brightly and swung across to the river. It couldn't reach them, but it was a sure sign the ghillie had seen them.

'Feck, you all go,' hissed Tig. 'I can't move as fast as you. Go! Go on, all of you. I will say 'twas just me.'

'Not fecking likely,' said Pete. 'If we go, you go on my back or Michael's. We aren't leaving you behind.'

'Look, he's going down to the side of the bridge, he's going to walk over.'

'Trespassing,' said Michael.

'Not if he's the ghillie,' said Father Jerry.

And then something happened that amazed them all. They heard the faint squeal of a woman's voice and they watched as the ghillie looked towards the river, back to the road, once more to the river and then with reluctance in his step and a backwards glance moved back to the road.

'What the...?'

'It's Rosie O'Hara,' said Father Jerry. 'She walks down to the bridge when she can't sleep. She must have fallen or something.'

'Head for the church wall – slowly,' said Michael. 'But don't get up, and don't leave the salmon.'

Rosie O'Hara let out another wail, one that sounded more like a fox taking an unsuspecting nocturnal animal.

'Miss O'Hara!' the ghillie exclaimed. 'Goodness me, it's you. What would you be doing out at this time of night when the whole village is asleep? What on earth is wrong?'

Rosie gasped. 'I think I've hurt my ankle,' she said, grabbing it and rocking backwards and forwards.

'Shall I knock on the principal's door?' the ghillie asked, looking concerned.

'Oh no, not at all. If you could just help me back to the teacher's house, I'll be fine.'

He glanced down at Rosie's ankle and then, with a look of regret, over his shoulder. 'Of course, let me help you. Why in God's name are you here?'

'If I can't sleep, I often walk down to the bridge. The water, I find it soothing.'

'Can you bear any weight?'

'No, none at all.'

'Right, well, let's get you into my car and I will drive you up. You've cut yourself too – that will need tending to.'

The five men as good as belly-crawled across the land. In no time, they'd skirted the ripening oats, scaled the low church wall and hidden behind a row of gravestones. From this safe vantage point they watched as Rosie O'Hara was helped off the ground by the ghillie and escorted back to the teacher's house.

'Did ye pray for Rosie O'Hara to have a sleepless night tonight, Father?' asked Seamus from behind his gravestone.

'Did you pray for her to fall over?' asked Pete from behind his, which he recognised as being that of his own sister. 'Jesus, our Mary will be turning in this grave with my arse in her face.'

'Did you pray then for the ghillie to take her home?' asked Tig.

Father Jerry shook his head. 'I prayed for the fattest fish to ever swim in the river to come tonight.' His voice came from behind a particularly large gravestone, which hid him completely. 'And I'd be thinking my prayer was answered. I could barely lift the net.'

They all began to snort with laughter and relief as the hip flask was thrown from one hiding place to another. They watched the car park outside the teacher's house.

'Who would have told Nola if we'd been caught?' asked Seamus as he passed the flask to Pete.

'I would, Daddy,' said Michael. 'Would you have told Sarah?'

'Oh aye, of course I would,' Seamus replied.

'Who would have told Keeva and Mammy?' asked Tig, his voice catching at the prospect.

'Don't worry, Tig, that would have been me too,' said Michael.

'Aye, well, brave men, who would have told Teresa Gallagher?' asked Father Jerry.

There was a moment's silence before the men answered as one. 'No one, Father – you're on your own there.' And they were once again consumed by laughter.

Rosie thanked the ghillie profusely. 'I will be absolutely fine. I'll just put it up until the morning.'

'Well, Miss O'Hara, if you don't mind me saying, there isn't much of a moon tonight, so there's no light. Better to keep your walks for when there is at least some light.'

Rosie closed her cottage door. As she did so, she turned to face Teresa Gallagher, who was sitting in her chair by Rosie's fire with her finger over her lips, urging her to be quiet.

'Did they get away?' Teresa asked once they'd heard the car leave.

'Well, I gave them enough time,' said Rosie. 'Look! I actually had to fall, and I really cut my knee.'

'I'll bring you double salmon for that tomorrow,' said Teresa, tutting in sympathy as Rosie peeled the ripped stocking from her grazed and bleeding knee.

'Will you tell Father Jerry that I saw the ghillie's car on the Ballina road and came to your door?' asked Rosie.

'Holy Mother of God, do I look mad? No, I will not, Rosie. I'm a respectable woman. I don't want him thinking we watch his every move. If he knows I know he poaches, he might stop, and then where would we be, without the salmon?' Within minutes, she was gone. She didn't want to be caught herself by Father Jerry.

Rosie had formed a bond with Sarah, had become a regular

guest at her house. She never wanted that to end, had found huge comfort in the friendship, and her fondness for Mary Kate was something she struggled to contain. Mary Kate was often her reason to be at the Malones', to help where she could, and that was where she was at her happiest. To spend time near Michael was enough, albeit also with his adoring wife and child. It was enough to see his face, smell him, bathe in the warmth of his smile. It was all she needed. It was Michael Rosie had fallen to save, not Father Jerry.

Chapter 17

'I have a hunger in me belly to make more money,' Michael said to Sarah, as he did almost every night. 'To do better than we are.'

They were sitting as they always did at the end of the day, in front of the fire in the hearth Michael had built with his own hands, taking their nightly glass of porter, their reward once they'd cashed up. The two of them worked hard from morning to night; they knew no different way of life. They were at the service of Tarabeg and, in turn, Tarabeg filled the till. Sarah was up at five to bake the bread and milk the cow, and as she often told Michael, 'What I can't fit in before eight o'clock isn't worth doing.'

She clicked her tongue at him now. 'We should be content with what we have, Michael. All the effort that went into building this place!'

Michael rocked back and forth in the only possession he'd brought down from the old farm, his grandmother's rocking chair. Nola and Daedio had insisted he take it. 'I know that wherever that chair is, Annie will be there too,' Daedio had said. 'I don't need looking after, but you do. Take it.'

Breathing in deeply after lighting his pipe, Michael sat back and enjoyed the dying glow of the crumbling peat. 'Do you remember the night we decided we would do it?' he asked.

'How could I forget! There was no stopping you.' Sarah smiled as she wound the wool.

'Reading the letters that are coming back from America, I'm in no doubt we did the right thing. I wish the lot of them would come back home even if only for a visit, just to put a smile on Mammy's face. I'm going to suggest to Daedio that I pay him back some of the money he gave me and he sends it to the others to buy tickets home.'

'God, wouldn't that be lovely,' Sarah said wistfully. 'Can you imagine the party we would have if they did.'

'I can. But none would be as grand as the party we had the night we opened.'

A frown crossed Sarah's face. 'A curse was put on me the night we opened – everyone said Shona threw a cast over me that night.' She looked up, tried to catch Michael's eye. 'Sit still, will ye? How can I wind when you are rocking back and forth.'

It had come as no shock to Sarah that Bridget McAndrew had turned up on their doorstep the day after the party, carrying a basket of potions and herbs. Bunches of herbs were threaded into the thatch, and placed all over the house. A potion of Bridget's and a bucket of holy water was sprinkled over the stone walls of the cottage, inside and out, and Bridget herself burnt something in the cow byre and then in the dairy and then in the house itself. After that she moved on to Sarah and Michael themselves. They had to swallow potions and stuff their pockets with crushed herbs. 'Look, I don't trust Shona,' she'd said by way of explanation. 'No one does. She is as old as the hills and her powers are weak, but we need to put up a defence against any wickedness she might have been up to last night.'

Sarah remembered those words still, but Michael wasn't taking the bait. 'Aye, as God is true, wasn't that the best night this village has ever known?'

'It was that.' Sarah wound the last of the wool with a flourish. 'There hasn't been another like it, in more ways than one. You do remember, don't you, that Bridget thought Shona was up to something.'

Michael shook his head impatiently. 'Sarah, we've gone from strength to strength. Even the Maughans come here now to buy their baccy. Jay can't get his baccy any cheaper than he can here.'

'They shouldn't scare people so.'

'Aye, well, people only have to look at the success of Malone's to know that there is no power in a gypsy's curse any more. Not in this day and age.'

Sarah looked up at the ceiling, alerted by the sound of Mary Kate turning over restlessly in her bed upstairs. She wished she could be as unconcerned about the Maughans as her husband, but the fact was she'd guessed, she knew, what Shona's curse had been, and it had worked. There had been no other child since Mary Kate.

Mary Kate's room was right above them. Sarah glanced over at Michael and put her finger to her lips, then cocked her head, waiting for the stillness to return. At six, Mary Kate sometimes had bad dreams, crying out for Sarah to come and comfort her. She hoped tonight wouldn't be one of those nights.

Mary Kate turned onto her back and counted the stars in the black sky. She'd woken to the sound of her parents' voices, as she often did, their words filtering up through the floorboards. She liked hearing the gentle rhythmic creak of the rocking chair, but most of all she liked listening to her parents' conversations, especially their stories about people she knew in the village. They laughed about the antics of the customers who came into the shop. They discussed Mrs Doyle's bad leg, and Tig and Keeva and their two tearaway boys, her friends, Aedan and Iain, and Mary Kate's big cousin, Ciaran, who came home with her after school and had his tea in the back of the shop before he walked home to the shore. Sometimes they talked about the time before she was born and the day they met, and often they talked about their hopes for her future. It was when they talked about the night of the shop opening and the Maughans that she listened hardest. A gnawing feeling came over her when they were mentioned. She sensed from the change of tone in her mother's voice that something had happened on that night and that it still concerned her.

As she listened now, Mary Kate heard her father's rocking chair creak to a standstill. Then came his footsteps as he walked towards the press. 'Go on,' he said, with a smile in his voice, 'just another drop.' Mary Kate smiled too. Everything was fine and just as it should be. As she heard the reassuring pop of the straw stopper and the chink of the porter mugs, she pulled the covers up over her shoulders and snuggled into the pillow.

Downstairs, Sarah finally took her eyes off the ceiling. Her daughter had fallen quiet again and she could have a second mug of porter without worrying. She changed the subject quickly, hating any discussion about the Maughans in the house. ''Tis a full moon tomorrow night. Bee and Captain Bob are coming over with Ciaran. I'm roasting a quarter pig and they can take the rest back with them when they leave.'

*

"Tis one reason to look forward to a full moon,' said Michael. 'For the visitors from the shore. That and the fact that you are always warm and ready and as randy as a sow on heat.' He grinned as Sarah threw a ball of wool at him. The summer that year was warm and bountiful for the harvest and the wild fruit. Mary Kate and Sarah roamed the hills with Bee, Ciaran, Keeva, Aedan and Iain, collecting basketsful to take home and preserve to last them through the winter. As with the harvest, the women moved from one kitchen to another to help with the storing and preserving. Bee always came to Sarah's kitchen for the entire day, along with the Devlins and Nola.

With the doors open to let the draught through from the shop to the back and the sound of the river roaring in the background, the women worked away through the warm and dusty afternoon. Josie and Keeva were on wild elderberry syrup, which they were decanting into glass jars ready to be poured onto fruit pies in the winter. Sarah carried a large copper pan over from the stove, the overheated deep purple redcurrant liquid almost splashing over the side. Bee picked up the big wooden spoon and began stirring to prevent it from sticking.

'God, even that makes me feel sick. I think I might be caught again,' said Keeva as she slipped onto one of Sarah's stools.

'Again?' said Sarah, looking up, and they all noticed the dismay in her tone.

Bee caught her eye and raised an eyebrow.

'Well, don't be looking at me like that,' said Sarah defiantly as tears sprang from nowhere.

Bee said nothing but placed an arm around her niece's waist and pulled her handkerchief from the sleeve of her cardigan. 'Here, go on,' she said.

Sarah took it gratefully. 'God, I am so sorry, Keeva, it's just that every month I hope that will be me and it never is. It's Shona's fault, she cursed me the day this place opened, and that's it, there will be no more for me.'

Nola was already making the tea and searching for the emergency Powers whiskey in the press. 'Shona is so old,' she said, 'all she worries about is waking up every morning and wondering if she can keep breathing in and out all day. Here, take the tea and a drop of whiskey for your nerves.'

'You're joking, aren't you?' Sarah wiped her eyes. 'Only weeks ago they were here for the baccy and her flaming barley sugars – God, why do we have to sell to them? – and she's still driving the horses with the strength of a man.'

Josie took her tea from Nola, who continued. 'Well, whatever Shona said or did, it hasn't worked, has it? Look at ye, the house is lovely, and the shop is growing as fast as Macy's, or so I'm told every time I get a letter from New York. I tell them all about it and they write straight back and say, sure, we think Michael will be on his way here and taking over by the sounds of it. And look at what you have – everything you wish for. 'Tis all grand. Stop yer worrying, it will happen if God means it to.'

Bee had moved over to the oven and was removing the jars she'd placed inside to warm and lining them up on the table. Using a cloth, Keeva unscrewed the lids ready to receive the steaming fruit syrup; she was too afraid to say anything to Sarah.

Sarah, having had a sip of her strong tea, took over the

stirring. 'I'm grateful for the shop and how 'tis all going, so I am, but, Bee, there's been no other babby after our Mary Kate and 'tis not for the want of trying.'

At that moment, Keeva's two little boys came charging into the kitchen, then raced straight out again.

'Would you look at them!' said Bee. 'Surely to God they grow more in a hot summer, don't they? 'Tis not just the oats sprouting up at a grand rate.'

The sound of Ciaran, Aedan, Iain and Mary Kate playing out the back filled the kitchen.

'Oh, I'm so sorry, shall I take them home? They're such a noisy pair.' Keeva looked unsure of herself and her welcome.

'No, you won't, not at all. Stay here and help fill these jars,' said Sarah with a smile that hid the hurt she felt. Keeva could be like a timid mouse, always ready to run away if she felt unwanted, and Sarah resolved never again to let her even guess at the pain the news of someone's new pregnancy caused her. She would be ready next time.

The kitchen was warmed by the sun and the fire from the range and the women were covered in a film of perspiration. Sarah checked that the ties of her floral apron were fastened tight, then picked up a spoon, dipped it into the pan, raised it to her nose to smell it and began to slowly fill one of the jars.

Bee looked up at Sarah from under her lashes and held her own spoon mid air. 'If Shona Maughan is wilting and we don't think she's as powerful as she once was, what do you think Sarah needs to do, Keeva, to have another?'

'Well, that's not hard, is it?' said Keeva. 'If you've had one, you can have a dozen. Are ye, you know, doing it right, Sarah?'

Sarah flushed to the roots of her hair as both she and Bee gasped. Sarah might have expected a comment like that from

Bee, but not from the timid girl she still regarded as little Keeva, and not in front of her mother-in-law. 'Oh God, of course I am!' Sarah almost screeched. 'I got caught with our Mary Kate, didn't I?'

'Yes, I know, but sometimes, if you don't lift your hips up in a certain way, you know, you can't get caught, that's what Bridget McAndrew told me just before Tig and I got married. And here we are, two boys later. I had no trouble at all.'

Sarah gawped. 'Bridget told ye that?'

Bee finished filling another jar as Josie answered. 'Bridget knows everything, Sarah, even how to keep a smile on your husband's face. I've been doing it for years.'

'Doing what?' Bee and Sarah asked together, mouths wide open as they stared at Josie in disbelief.

'Aye, aye, I can't believe you don't know.' Keeva laughed. 'And Michael a man of the world, in and out of Dublin all the time.'

Sarah laughed nervously. She strongly suspected that there was something she was missing.

'If you ask me, it would be more useful if she could tell some women around here how not to get caught,' said Bee. 'Theady O'Donnell was Philomena's thirteenth child. I know that's not so unusual, but it's just unfortunate for the kids, with a woman like Philomena for a mother. Thank the Lord that poor boy's escaped and gone to the seminary now. One of them finally made the woman proud at last, studying to be a priest, so he is.' She gave Sarah an encouraging smile. 'But go on, go and see her, Sarah. It can't do any harm, can it. We need something to look forward to and wouldn't that be all. An end to all the speculation. Jesus, we'd all be queuing around Shona's caravan begging for her to put a curse on us. You've got rich, had a few years to get going, and then if you were to have another babby on the way... Thank you, Shona.'

The women picked up their teacups and laughed.

Draining hers, Sarah said, 'Aye, but the tipping of the hips... What, like this?' The whiskey had met an empty stomach and entered her bloodstream fast. She placed her hands on her waist, pushed her hips forward, looked down and began to laugh.

Keeva jumped up and stood next to her. 'Aye, like this. Press this bit of your back onto the mattress, right in until you feel the bedstead, and then push up and squeeze in. As God is my judge, you'll have Michael on top of you every five minutes. He'll be inside you faster than he can get his pants unbuttoned, mark my words, and there'll be a babby in that belly in no time.'

The laughter from the kitchen reached the cinder path at the front, where Michael was opening a fresh sack of potatoes. He heard it and smiled, straightened up, pushed back his cap and looked over the road. Rosie O'Hara was walking from the school to her house and she raised her hand in greeting. Michael lifted his own hand back to her and for a moment, just a fleeting moment, he remembered her kiss and felt guilty that she had never married. He knew without being told that it was his fault. She'd been at the house only yesterday and, as always, she'd done and said the right things. But there was something in her eye, an interest, a depth, a forbidden fruit, and when she fixed him with a look, locked her eyes onto his, when her hand brushed against him, he felt a quickening of his heart, a shortness in his breath and a stirring in his groin. He fought it, but the guilt swamped him and sent him running all the way to confession.

In the kitchen, the jars had been filled and packed into straw-lined wooden crates which were now stacked up on the table and the floor. Bee had made fresh tea and they all sat down at the scrubbed table.

'Sarah, was Rosie O'Hara here yesterday?' she asked.

'She was. She came back with Mary Kate for tea after school and helped her with her homework and her reading. Why?'

Bee was stirring an extra spoon of sugar into her tea. 'Could you ask her to keep an eye on Ciaran for me. He was doing so well in class, but Mr O'Dowd, he's kept him behind twice now, and when I asked the man why, he spoke to me as though he had a piece of gorse stuck up his arse.'

'Mr O'Dowd?' said Josie. 'Never. He's the nicest man in the village. You probably caught him on a bad day, Bee.'

Some of the children left the village school to board, but others, like Ciaran, who were children of widows or were needed to work the land, remained there until they were thirteen or just stopped attending altogether.

Sarah put her cup in her saucer. 'I remember Philomena O'Donnell had the same with Theady. You have never seen a boy as happy as he was the day he finished and went off to the seminary in Galway. Cried in Philomena's arms, she said.'

'Well, would you look at him now. Jesus, that woman has become unbearable and there's nothing can be said to her. Being the mother of a priest in training puts her closer to Father Jerry than Teresa, or so she says. I swear to God, Teresa will let loose one of these days, she's driving her mad, so she is.'

At just that moment, Ciaran came into the kitchen with Iain straddling his back and waving an imaginary whip in the air, as though Ciaran was his horse. Sarah noticed that his smile didn't quite reach his lips and there was a greyness around his eyes. 'Are you all right, Ciaran?' she asked him. Her heart folded with concern for the boy she loved as much as she would one of her own. 'How are you finding class with Mr O'Dowd?'

Ciaran didn't answer. He looked to his mother, who nodded, then he took a biscuit off the plate and ran outside.

Sarah recognised the look in Ciaran's eyes. It had once been in her own. It was fear and it had tainted her own childhood. 'I'll speak to Rosie tomorrow,' she said to Bee. 'She'll find out what's going on.'

Later that night, the house asleep, Sarah stood in the kitchen drinking a glass of water. She had taken Keeva's hip advice to heart and practised it to the letter. 'Holy Mother of God,' she whispered to herself as she sipped on the water. 'What was that?' She'd been swept away by the passion, the intensity of it, and her head had seemed to explode with pleasure. She'd been lost, unthinking of everything, and what was more, she could tell that Michael had enjoyed it as much as she had.

She heard his footsteps on the stairs and his frame filled the doorway. 'Sarah, get yourself back up these stairs now. You can do that again.'

Giggling, she ran up the stairs after him.

Chapter 18

It was a foul day. Fat raindrops battered the four-paned glass of the shop window with the force of small pebbles as Mary Kate sat on her wooden stool behind the counter and squinted at the bleak, muddy road outside. Pools of water were forming on the cinder path below the window and her bike, propped up against the limewashed wall, had been blown onto its side and was now half submerged in an oversized puddle, one pedal breaking the surface like the hand of a drowning man. The wind slipped in through the cracks in the door and howled as it ran around the shop as the candle flame dipped a curtsey and Mary Kate shivered as she checked over her shoulder for ghosts. She pulled the shawl her mother had wrapped around her even tighter.

The street was empty and the sky was heavy and almost as dark as night. Today was a Saturday and everyone Mary Kate knew would be huddled indoors right now, if they didn't have to be out working in the fields. The road towards the river was close to becoming a river itself. Fearing that she might not see a customer for the entire day, Mary Kate gave up trying to stare out at the street, picked up her school book, sat back and sighed, her eyes on the book, her ears listening for the tinkers.

Sarah had been trying to comb out her bright copper-red hair while she sat on the stool in front of the range. She had wriggled in protest.

'Mary Kate, will you keep still. How can I get the bird's nest out of the back of your hair if you keep moving like that,' Sarah had chided.

'Mammy, I don't want to sit still. I hate my hair.' Mary Kate kicked her legs against the stool and began to cry. Mornings and hair were a never-ending battle. 'I want your hair, not mine.' Sarah's hair was smooth and neatly gathered into a ribbon. Mary Kate's hung loose and wavy and was prone to tangles.

'Well, listen to me, will I be telling Granny Nola that you don't want your hair done when you know she's visiting with Granddaddy Seamus today? And you turning seven in a couple of months! Sure, that will make her cry when I tell her what a bold girl you've been, and won't you know it, her tears will run all the way down the hill. Doesn't she just love your hair when 'tis all tied up in nice ribbon?'

Guilt-stricken, Mary Kate stopped fussing straight away. She loved her Granny Nola and the thought of making her cry was enough to make her sit ramrod straight. She restricted her protest to clenching her teeth and squeezing her eyes together.

'We have worse things to worry about today.' Sarah tried a diversionary tactic. 'The tinkers are due. They were up on the coast at the weekend, so Aunty Bee said, so sure as God is true, they'll be here any hour now.'

Mary Kate's brow furrowed with concern. 'Mammy, you

won't tell Granny Nola, will you?' She opened her big blue eyes and turned to look straight at Sarah.

Sarah's heart constricted. She moved closer to her child and pulled her into her as she buried Mary Kate's face in her floury apron. 'God, no. Never. I was only kidding now because you kick up such a fuss.' For a long, luxurious moment she stood stroking her daughter's now silken hair, and Mary Kate, silent, absorbed the love she felt passing to her from her mother's hands.

Half an hour later, while they were waiting for the bread to rise, Mary Kate and her mother brushed the shop floor and Mary Kate wiped down the counters and shelves. Then she went out back to the kitchen to help her mother pack up the orders to be delivered to the farms. 'I'm going to be shopkeeper all day today,' she said.

'Well, you can, as I have so much to do back here, and the rabbit needs skinning for dinner, but watch out for the tinkers. The thieving kids took a skillet from the door last time they came through, when you were at school. Bought the baccy and then sent the lad back to take it when I was washing the money, so keep your eyes peeled.'

Mary Kate wasn't as bothered as she might have been on a sunny day. She wouldn't see the outdoors anyway.

'We won't be getting no customers in this weather,' said Sarah. ''Twill be a poor day for the takings and that won't be pleasing Daddy. You'll be fine.'

Washing the tinkers' money was a ritual when they came into the village. The Maughans had taken to stopping outside the shop and shouting down for baccy and barley sugars. If Jay could have lived without his baccy and Shona hadn't discovered a sweet tooth, they would never have stopped. They would pull up outside the shop and Michael would throw the baccy and barley sugars up to Shona. It was as if the earth stopped spinning when she called. The wind would drop, the birds ceased singing and Michael felt his chest tighten as though it was more difficult to breathe. Jay Maughan knew it, and he would grin as he threw the money down at the same time as Michael threw the baccy up, deliberately missing Michael's hand so that it landed at his feet and he had no choice but to grovel. Neither Mary Kate nor Sarah were allowed to touch the money, only Michael could do that. As soon as he got back inside the shop, it was thrown into the scullery sink and scrubbed, before it could be placed into the wooden till.

'Get your hands off. Don't you know it's cursed,' he'd once shouted at Mary Kate as she'd scrabbled around on the floor to pick up one of the blackened pennies. She'd wanted to save her father the indignity of bending down. 'Don't ever touch the tinkers' money, promise me?' Mary Kate had nodded in earnest, too young to understand the meaning of a curse and too obedient to ever disobey.

The weather was so bad, there were no skillets or pans hanging outside the shop today. 'If we open the shop door, everything will get soaked and blown off the shelves,' said Sarah. 'It will have to stay closed. Anyone fool enough to go out in this weather will know we're open – aren't we always.' Looking at the torrent of water cascading down the windows, Mary Kate was relieved to hear that.

What little floor space there was inside the crowded shop was stacked from floor to ceiling with zinc baths, animal feed, pots and pans, skeins of wool already wound by Sarah, and hessian sacks of potatoes. There were jars of sweets, baskets of vegetables, sacks of flour, tubs of bicarbonate of soda, and on the cold shelf always a slab of cheese and jars of whatever preserves Sarah had made. Baskets of already cut and dried peat blocks almost entirely filled the doorway, ready for the new tourists who rented the keeper's cottage out on the road to the coast. Michael had wanted a side of bacon on the cold slab to sell rashers as he was open longer hours than Paddy, but even he knew that making enemies was not the way to make money. Paddy would never have forgiven him and it would have as good as started a village war. There was also some 'exotic' produce, as Mrs O'Doyle described the tins of ham and the hair ribbons that sat on the shelf behind the till along with the baccy.

Most of the fresh produce came from local farms and the rest came from Michael's jaunts about the country. He could be gone for a full week at a time. It was his increasing variety of wares that angered the Maughans. He now stocked pots and pans, the very things they had traditionally sold from the back of their caravan. He was taking their trade. He even offered a knife-sharpening service, and the villagers were glad of it. They were glad of anything that gave them a reason to avoid Shona. The Maughans having no excuse to ride up the boreens to the farms was a relief to everyone who lived on them. 'We won't need your pans or any knives sharpening, I took them down to Malone's,' was a cry the tinkers were hearing more often as one door after another closed in their faces.

Nearly seven years on, Michael Malone wished he'd built a shop twice the size. He could have filled it with even more stock and then he might have been able to buy a bigger van and bring back an even greater variety and quantity of goods to Tarabeg. Right now, the shop could hold no more. 'I'll be having to move out of the house and back up to the farm with

Nola and Seamus if you keep bringing back more things to sell,' Sarah had complained.

'Aye, but I bring more back because I sell what we have and that's how we make the money,' Michael had replied. 'Have you seen how many men they're taking on up at the quarry? 'Tis getting huge, so it is.'

Something made Mary Kate look up from her book; she had no idea what. Her skin prickled and her eyes stung. She looked around the shop, but there was no one and nothing. The air was still and all she could hear was the faint sound of running water in the scullery and her mother singing, competing with the downpour outdoors. She looked back down at her book, tried to read a line, failed. Her concentration had evaporated. She looked at the wooden till drawer, as empty as it had been when the morning began.

If a customer came in the door, she was under strict instructions to run for Sarah. As an only child, she was allowed to do many things, but taking the money was not one of them. She decided that as there had been no customers, she would go back into the house, find her mother and sneak one of the hot oatcakes she could smell and dip it in some buttermilk. She had another look about, felt more settled, closed the book and was about to slide down from the stool when a sudden sharp thud on the window made her jump.

The face of Shona was pressed against the glass, her white hair splayed, blocking out the light. Mary Kate screamed. Her book slipped from her fingers to the floor and she almost fell off the stool. She charged into the kitchen and didn't stop even as she knocked over two chairs and sent the neatly stacked bags of oats flying.

'God in heaven, what is it?' shouted Sarah as she threw

down a half-skinned rabbit and ran with bloody hands to her daughter. 'What's wrong, are you hurt, what?' She furiously wiped her hands up and down her apron and reached out to grab Mary Kate as she came hurtling towards her. Sarah held her at arm's length. 'What is it? Who is it?'

But Mary Kate could not reply. Her face was as white as a sheet and it was clear to Sarah that something had scared her.

'Wait here,' she said. 'Watch the dog doesn't come in from the yard and take the rabbit.'

Sarah's heart beat wildly as she slowly and nervously made her way through to the shop at the front. Michael had gone up to see Daedio at the farm and was to bring Nola and Seamus back down for Mass. He was dropping off feed on his way up. He'd begun a new service of delivering feed to the more remote farms, leaving the bags at the bottom of the boreen. He saved the farmers a day's work having to collect it themselves and he could barely keep up with the demand. He was paid the cost of the feed, and some offering in kind was always left for him at the drop-off point for his trouble. Eggs, a homemade cake or pie, a quart of poteen, or if the farmer was in hard times, a bunch of wild flowers, picked and tied with braided grass, or a straw dolly for Mary Kate.

Sarah stopped breathing as she turned the corner from the kitchen into the shop. Looking up at the closed door, she realised that because it had been kept shut against the driving rain, she'd forgotten to drop the bolt at the top. The shadow of Jay Maughan hobbling past the window made Sarah want to scream herself. The man she had escaped being married to; and outside, in the caravan, the life that had very nearly been her own. She shivered as she moved towards the door. 'Be brave,' she whispered. 'Be brave, you're a married woman.'

She straightened her back and stood on tiptoes to drop the bolt. Her mouth was dry and she knew she was no less afraid than her daughter. Through the rain-smeared windows she could make out the shadowy outline of the horse and caravan. The sound of metal sliding against metal filled the silence as the bolt fell. The instant she dropped her fingers to the handle, the door flew open with the force of the wind, and standing directly before her was Jay Maughan.

Her hand instinctively flew to her throat. Despite wanting to appear brave, she let out a sharp gasp. He smiled, his anger at having had to step down from the caravan forgotten for a moment as he savoured her discomfort. His cap was so sodden that water streamed from its wilting peak, across his forehead and down his face. Sarah almost jumped as two drenched and half-dressed waifs ran to his side. He brought different children every time and the eyes of these two never left Sarah's face, one pair inquisitive, the other mocking.

Maughan wiped the water from his eyes with the back of his hand, his irritation having quickly returned. 'Why have you closed?' he demanded menacingly. He took a step forward, his fists clenched at his sides.

Sarah cautiously glanced across the road to the butcher's. She couldn't see the front door from where she stood but was hoping to catch sight of Paddy or Josie moving through to the bar. There was nothing; no one to be seen anywhere in such foul weather.

'We want baccy for me and the barleys for Shona, and be quick. Where's the girl?'

'What girl?' asked Sarah, wondering what she was going to do. She didn't want him to come into the shop, but she was afraid that if she closed the door and left him standing in the rain, he would break it down. She had no choice but to leave the door open as she stepped back inside.

Just as she'd feared, he followed her. 'You know what girl. Your girl.'

Right at that moment, Mary Kate appeared in the doorway.

'Mary Kate, stay back!' Sarah shouted louder than she meant to, betraying her fear.

'Yes, stay back, girl.' Maughan laughed. 'Nice hair. Shona had hair like yours. Do you want to come to the caravan and meet Granny Shona?'

Mary Kate stepped to her mother's side and grabbed her hand. Sarah found her voice. 'No, Maughan, she does not. You have your baccy and barley sugars, now go.'

Jay ignored her. 'Where's your man?' he asked as he wiped his nose with the back of his hand.

She cast her eyes out of the door. There was no sound. No sign of Michael or anyone else. She took a deep breath. 'I told you, Maughan, go. Your wife is waiting in the back of the caravan. Is there nothing you want for her?' Sarah didn't know where she'd found the words. She sounded a lot braver than she felt. Michael had stood between her and this man every time he'd passed through the village. This was the first time she and he had met face to face.

Maughan wasn't listening to Sarah, his eyes were fixed on Mary Kate. 'How old are you now, girl?' he asked her.

Sarah squeezed Mary Kate's hand. 'It doesn't matter to you, Maughan. Go.'

'She's not as old as this is, this present from your daddy.' Maughan pointed down to his wounded leg, where McGuffey had shot him.

Sarah had no words. She stared at him, waiting for his next salvo, frozen at the mere reference to her father. But she could sense danger and she would stand between whatever it was and her Mary Kate.

'She might be in need of a family soon, so you remember me, girl. I'm here. I'll be waiting. Your granddaddy promised me. I saw your daddy, Sarah. Came back, he did. Pays me money for news, he does. Said he was sorry about this, me leg. Told me he wants news of the girl. I can pass on the news now. Pretty little thing, isn't she?'

'What do you mean, she'll be in want of a family? She's in want of nothing. She has plenty of family.'

'Ah, but nothing stays the same, does it, Sarah? You know that. Your own mammy dead, yer daddy gone. You didn't know that was happening, did you? Things change. I can tell your daddy that I've seen the girl and what a pretty little colleen she is.'

A rage came over Sarah. A red rage. A mist fell across her eyes and she lunged at Jay with her nails. Almost screeching, she went for his face. 'Get out! Get out!' she howled at him.

The fear of her father and her repulsion for Maughan drove her hands as her fists rained down on his face. She heard screams from somewhere behind her. It was Mary Kate and she sounded terrified.

Maughan gripped both of Sarah's hands in his huge fists and held her by the wrists. He was much stronger than she'd expected. His eyes blazed and spittle ran down his chin as he pressed his face close to hers. 'Your daddy has a special message for you too. He will get you back, miss. But I told him, Shona will get you first. This house, this shop, 'tis on our land and we will take it back and you will suffer for it one day. You will pay.'

The noise of the van pulling up outside and the squeal of its brakes made Maughan drop her hands. Sarah staggered back towards Mary Kate and grabbed her, almost wrapped her skirts around her to protect her, as Michael hurtled through the front door. 'What the feck are you doing inside here!' he shouted. But before he could gather his wits, Maughan had stormed past him and out to the caravan, where Shona and the two urchins were waiting.

Michael followed him. 'Oi, I'm talking to you! What are you doing in my fecking shop?'

Seamus was helping Nola out of the van and he raced after his son. 'Don't cross him,' he said, all too aware of Shona's power. 'That's enough.' He pulled Michael back by the arm.

'What's he up to?' Michael demanded as he shook Seamus's hand away. He turned and ran back into the shop. 'What was he up to?' he screamed at Sarah. And then, seeing how distressed she looked, how both of his girls looked, he grabbed hold of them and pulled them to him.

Sarah was rubbing her reddened wrists. Her hair had fallen out of her ribbon and was tumbling over her shoulders, and she was struggling for her breath. The emerald heart, given to her by Daedio, felt hot against her skin as she pushed the chain to one side.

'What did he do, Sarah? Tell me.' Michael looked into her face. 'Did he touch you?'

Sarah lifted her wrists to show him. 'I tried to hit him, I did it first. Michael, he's in touch with Daddy and was asking about Mary Kate.'

The blood left Michael's face. There wasn't a single parent in the west who didn't live in fear of their pretty young daughter being stolen by gypsies, but this, this was his worst nightmare.

The words he didn't want to hear. 'Do you think he was after taking Mary Kate?'

'No, no, don't be talking like that,' said Seamus, who was now indoors, with Nola right behind him, panting. He looked over at Mary Kate and saw that she was listening to every word. She was a clever little thing – which Nola put down to her being an only child, a rarity in Tarabeg – and she was obviously terrified.

'What's going on?' Nola asked.

'He's talking crazy. He thinks Maughan is after taking Mary Kate,' whispered Seamus.

Michael was heading out the door again, but Nola grabbed his arm. 'Come back into the house,' she said. 'Please, Michael. You know how we deal with them – we don't speak. Don't rise to it. You know Bridget's instructions.'

Michael fell to his knees in front of Mary Kate. 'Tell me what happened. Tell Daddy. What did the man say?'

Mary Kate was as sharp as a whistle. Taking a deep breath, she straightened her shoulders and spoke to her daddy almost as an adult would. 'The old woman's face was pressed up against the shop window and she was staring at me, Daddy. I was a bit scared, wasn't I, Mammy, just a bit though, not a lot. I was very bold with her, really.' She looked up at her mammy, hoping she wouldn't betray her and tell her daddy that she'd screamed with fright. She wanted him to think she was grown up and brave.

'And what did the man say when he came in to the shop?'

'He told Mammy he wanted to see me.' The sudden rush of courage that had fortified Mary Kate left as quick as it had come and she began to cry.

Michael stood and scooped her up into his arms. 'Come on,

in the back, everyone. I should have killed him and finished off what McGuffey started.'

Nola was at the fire and put the kettle on the black iron trivet that stood over it. 'You would have been a fool to do so, then or now,' she said. 'The man can be dangerous. Bite your tongue and let him buy from you whatever he wants, whenever he wants it. And keep Mary Kate always in your sight. You can't cross these people. They're too powerful and dangerous.' And then, in a voice loaded with meaning, 'Michael, we need to have someone in this shop all the time, not just Sarah. You are making enough money now. She can't be looking after the house and the shop, 'tis too busy. There needs to be an extra pair of eyes kept on Mary Kate.' She lifted the teapot. 'For every problem there is an answer. Right, everyone, drink your tea. Sarah, where's the brack? The child is shaken and she's too young for the Powers.' She began pouring a large dollop of whiskey into each adult's mug.

Half an hour later, Bee had arrived. As she and Sarah calmed Mary Kate and Seamus talked to his son, Nola had an idea.

'Michael, Sarah, I think I know who you can take on for help.'

'Who?' asked Sarah.

'And when Michael goes away in future, one of us is going to be sleeping down here at the shop,' Nola continued.

Bee had been about to give them her own news, but in the light of events decided against it. When she heard Captain Bob arrive outside, she ran out to meet him. 'I haven't told them. There's been trouble here – the Maughans turned up.'

'What did they want?' asked Bob, his antenna up.

'Maughan's spoken to McGuffey and he was trying to scare Sarah.'

Bob placed a kiss on Bee's cheek. He knew exactly what she'd be thinking. 'If that's the case, you and I will have to put our plans on hold. It's not the time to tell them about America. I won't come in now, I'll away up to Brendan's house and then over to Paddy's bar and see what people have to say.'

Bee hugged the man she had grown to love and trust and marvelled at his understanding. They'd been about to tell Sarah that they were ready to try a new life and join Captain Bob's sister.

'It can wait,' he said as he kissed her and made off.

'I bet Rosie O'Hara would love the job,' said Keeva, who had heard the commotion and run over with Josie. 'She can hardly clothe herself. I'm guessing she would jump at a bit of extra money. The school is ten until three. I bet she would come before and after. What do you think, Michael?'

Michael didn't answer at first. He would have preferred it not to be Rosie O'Hara, but he couldn't put into words why. She was the best teacher to Mary Kate and a solid friend to Sarah.

Later that evening, Teresa Gallagher walked up the boreen to Rosie's house and was delighted to find her unwrapping an elderberry pie out of a tea towel. 'Where did you get that from?' she asked.

'I had visitors,' Rosie said, beaming with pleasure.

Teresa was instantly suspicious. She could read Rosie like a book.

'Nola Malone and Sarah came here to offer me a job at the shop and they brought it as a gift.'

Teresa took a plate out of her basket. 'A job? You already

have a job, and don't they just know that. Look, I've brought you some salmon.'

Rosie was wearing her hair tied into a tight bun at the nape of her neck. Her long, old-fashioned skirt had belonged to her late mother and Teresa noticed that the hem was frayed and in desperate need of repair. She had mended it half a dozen times and she had no idea how they could tidy it up again without removing another inch.

'I know, but wasn't that great of them to ask me.'

'Ask you? You can't give up the school. Have you taken the job?'

Rosie placed the pie onto a plate painted with shamrocks. 'I have. It's for before and after school. They offered me ten shillings a week. Can you imagine! How could I not? They wanted me full time, but I've said only during the school holidays. Otherwise it's eight until nine thirty in the mornings and then after school from three thirty to six.'

Teresa removed her coat and hung it on the nail by the door. The top of the stable door was open and she took in the view. The teacher's house was elevated and now that it had at last stopped raining she could see all the way down, across the churchyard, straight on to the Malone shop, where more lights than usual were burning, and across the river.

'When will you be starting? Go on then, put the pie in the oven to warm up and I'll have a slice. Just a little one.'

'From tomorrow. I will work all day Saturday and have Sundays off. Sarah Malone said she would give me a hot supper each day, so I won't have to be worrying about waiting to cook potatoes when I get home or you running over with supper for me, which is very kind of you and I'm grateful, but 'twas very nice of them to offer.'

Teresa removed her hat pin and replaced it in a firmer position. The hat never came off, even when Teresa ate. 'Don't be worrying about food,' she said. 'I can always drop a plate up during the day and put it on a pan on the embers for when you get home if needs be. It is a good thing, taking this job. Not just for the money too – you will get to talk to people.'

Rosie smiled and turned to put the kettle on the boil. No one left a Tarabeg home without having had tea. It wasn't the idea of working or talking to people every day that thrilled her. She, Rosie, would be in the home of Michael Malone and she would see him every single day. She would have worked Sundays too if Sarah had asked her, despite what Teresa and Father Jerry would have said.

Teresa watched Rosie closely as she slid the pie into the oven next to the fire. 'Will you enjoy the job?' she asked. 'Sarah Malone, she has a few fancy ways with her ribbons and things and she has a strange way with the dress and shoes. She's getting a bit big for her boots, if you ask me, but she's a good enough woman at heart and she never misses Mass.'

Rosie looked down and hid the flash in her eyes. 'Aye, I'll enjoy the job. I'll work hard. They won't be sorry they took me on.'

In their own kitchen that night, Seamus voiced his concerns to Nola. 'How much did you offer Rosie for the job?'

Nola looked up from the drink she was making for Daedio. 'She's having ten shillings a week and, sure, that will transform her life. She only has the fifty pounds a year from the school. She eats what she grows, with a bit of help from Teresa. She nearly bit my hand off, she did.'

'Aye, but, Nola, there's a reason why Rosie is the only unmarried girl in the village. She still burns a candle for Michael. Couldn't ye have opened a can of worms?'

Nola looked up at her husband. 'Seamus, that was thirteen years ago. Do not be ridiculous. Our Michael never walked out with her – it was more in your head than theirs. She will be so grateful for the work, and besides, she's a great one for the religion.'

Seamus smiled to himself as he remembered how much Nola had wanted Michael to marry the schoolteacher for nothing more than her badge of respectability.

'A close friend of Teresa's she would not be if she wasn't a good person. I'm just relieved Sarah has help now and protection.'

'She needs that all right,' said Seamus. 'Maughan is up to something. We can't take our eyes off that child.'

'Where's the Powers, Seamus? What a day, I need a drop in me tea.'

Seamus grinned. 'When don't you, Nola? I swear to God, you drink more of the whiskey than the tea. We all had a fair bit down at Michael and Sarah's.'

'Sure, I could drink more than you if I had a mind to,' Nola replied with a straight back, folded arms and an air of indignation. He poured some into her mug and walked to the fire to light his pipe.

He could stare into the fire and Nola could not see his thoughts. He had seen the way Rosie looked at Michael; he'd known all along. What he couldn't understand was how Nola, the woman who knew everything, hadn't seen it. He knew his son was as in love with his wife as any man could ever be. That thought did nothing to calm the unease running through him.

His eyes were drawn to the wall and as he placed his hand on the mantel shelf, he noticed that one of the stones was slightly proud of it. He lifted his hand and gently pushed it back into place. He'd been about to pull it the other way, to see what was behind it, but he heard a whisper, 'Push it back, Seamus,' in his ear. He turned to see had it been Daedio, but he was still snoring lightly, as was his wife, with her face flat down on the table.

Chapter 19

Sarah waited in line in the post office to be served by Mrs Doyle. It was a queue that defied convention and took ten times as long as any other ever known as each woman in it had her daily chat with Mrs Doyle, then with the other women, and then with Mrs Doyle again. Some were served tea as they waited by Keeva, who still worked there, during school hours, which also defied convention. For Keeva it was a simple choice: help in the post office or the butcher's. She hated blood.

Sarah had called in to top up her supply of holy water. She kept her statues of Our Lady fixed to the front door and the back, and at the base of each was a small well which each morning was wiped out by Rosie with a cloth and refilled with the precious holy water. Since the day Jay Maughan visited the shop, Sarah had added two more statues. One on the mantel shelf over the fire and the other in the bedroom on the night stand.

'Blessed by the Pope himself, this holy water is,' Mrs Doyle had told everyone when she returned from her visit to the Vatican with a suitcase full of bottles and virtually a shipping-container load on the way. With no evidence to the contrary, everyone believed her. Much to Michael's annoyance, she had secured an endless supply of it, direct from the Vatican apparently, and it had become the fastest-selling product in the west of Ireland, available only from the post office in Tarabeg. 'Sure, we need to keep Michael on his toes, do we not?' Mrs Doyle said to Sarah now.

'That we do.' Sarah winked as she took five bottles from the shelf. 'But don't let Michael be complaining, Mrs Doyle. He has enough variety to sell in our own shop.'

As the women stood behind her, holding fast to their baskets, they studied the shoes on Sarah's feet, the scarf around her neck and the coat on her back. Her emerald glinted around her neck as it rested against her creamy décolletage. The women were silent, appraising, condemning. Not until she left the shop would the full commentary begin. Her new cornflower-blue dress, a purchase Michael had made in Dublin, was known as an A-line dress and was a mind-boggling phenomenon to the women, especially Ellen Carey, who had almost taken it apart and put it back together again before Sarah had worn it a second time. Sarah was taking full advantage of Michael's buying trips and the new fashions hitting Dublin via Liverpool. Keeva and Rosie, who benefited from the cast-offs, could not have been more delighted. It was not a case of Sarah asking for new things but of Michael living his dream; he loved nothing more, once he had deposited his new wares in the front of the shop, than to show off what he had bought for his girls in the back.

'Oh don't be worrying about me now, Sarah,' said Mrs Doyle. 'I have my hands full catering to the tourists. I have the maps, the magazines and these.' She pointed to the never-ending row of pottery donkeys on the shelf with 'A Gift from

Eire' painted down their sides. 'I can't sell enough of them to the fishermen. I'll be wearing out me shoe leather the amount of times I have to run around the counter and fill up that shelf.'

Sarah smiled. 'Well, 'tis Mary Kate's birthday, so I'll take one myself.'

'Oh God, well don't be telling Michael where you got it from.' Mrs Doyle laughed as Sarah stepped back and took a painted donkey from the dark wooden shelf.

'I won't. If I tell him it's your biggest seller, he'll be after stocking it, knowing Michael. We have enough in the shop, we don't want painted donkeys as well.' Sarah placed it on the counter with a twinkle in her eye.

For all her joking, Sarah was immensely proud of her husband. Michael was the great entrepreneur of Tarabeg, the man people came to for advice on everything from a low-weight potato crop to a shortage of money. As the youngest son of seven, he should by rights have been poor and living on the charity of his father, only to watch his eldest brother inherit the farm and all of the livestock. But Michael Malone was a survivor and had made good of not joining the crowds heading to the ships bound for Liverpool or New York. He had shown every man, woman and child that exile was not the only future awaiting those who loved their homeland. And Sarah loved him for it.

'And a pad of airmail paper, please, Mrs Doyle. Michael wants to be writing to his brothers in America himself. He has a surprise for Nola and Seamus.'

'Do you think they will be home for a visit?'

'God willing, but it's a secret.' Sarah tapped the side of her nose.

Mrs Doyle recoiled, a look of total shock on her face. 'Oh now, with this job, don't I know and keep better than anyone all the secrets of this place.' Then she dropped her voice. 'How is Bee, is she still with Captain Bob?'

Sarah was taking the money out of her purse and had failed to notice the silence that had fallen on the post office, awaiting her reply. 'How much is that for the water and the donkey, Mrs Doyle?' She chose not to answer the question. The captain still had a wife in Ballycroy. He and Bee were living a life as man and wife and he as a father to her Ciaran, albeit on only two nights per week. There had been the odd resentful comment at sinful living happening in such close proximity to the village, but these had died down quickly because Captain Bob was liked by everyone, and Bee, the defender of her beaten sister and niece when so many had turned a blind eye, even more so.

Mrs Doyle took the hint and changed the subject. 'And how is Nola and Seamus, I haven't been seeing either of them this week?'

'Oh, they are fine. Away up to us tomorrow for Mary Kate's birthday tea.'

'Jesus, no, that child is never seven,' said Philomena O'Donnell, and the following minutes were spent discussing the height of Mary Kate, the length of her hair and the scratches that were always present on her knees.

As Sarah turned to leave, she spoke to the ladies on the way out. 'Bye, Mrs Doyle, bye ladies, and thanks for the tea, Keeva, nice to be seeing you.'

The bell on the door jangled, and after a minimal pause conversation erupted among the waiting women.

'Well, would you be getting her, Mrs Doyle. Do they have

no manners, be putting you out of business, they will be. Tell them you are the one to be selling the painted donkeys first, not Michael Malone.'

'Oh no, not Michael, he wouldn't be doing that,' said Mrs Doyle as she fussed about her counter, wiping it down with a cloth ready to receive the next purchases. 'He's always been very respectful of my business and he has all the trade around here he needs. There's room for us both.'

'You won't be saying that when he puts you under,' said Susan Murphy, Maria Murphy's daughter. 'And did you see those shoes? Where in God's name did you ever see a pair of shoes like that – blue and with at least an inch and a half on the heel if I'm not mistaken! Michael Malone is doing a lot better than you are and that's a fact. When did you ever get a new pair of shoes, tell me that.'

'He bought them in Dublin,' said Keeva, who was wearing Sarah's old shoes. 'Real leather, they are.'

'Well, seems to me like he's spending everything he earns.' Teresa Gallagher had remained silent until now. She placed three painted donkeys on the counter. 'I'm sending them to America, to my nephew Pat in Chicago,' she said by way of explanation. 'They love the place – wonderful, so it is, they say – and they are all clubbing together to send me out there for a holiday. Can you imagine! But as grand as Chicago is, they can't get enough of home and won't they just love these. The shoes are from Dublin, you say, Keeva? Well, there's no worse city of sin in my opinion.' She turned back to face Mrs Doyle. 'You wouldn't catch me setting foot in the place, and Michael Malone spends more time there since he got that van of his than he does in Tarabeg.'

'No, God in heaven, what does he do there?' asked Susan

Murphy, who was helping herself to a cup of tea from the wooden tray.

'I wouldn't be knowing. But he comes back with plenty of fancy stuff for Sarah – shoes, scarves and the like. What does that tell you? Where does he get it all from, and who is putting those fancy notions into his head, and since when did Michael Malone know what an A-line dress was, that's all I would like to know, because it isn't Sarah Malone. I knew her as a kid, scampering down the rocks and running on the beach at the head. She wouldn't know a velvet wrap from a crown of thorns and I'll tell you this, neither does he. Someone else is buying that stuff and it is not Seamus Malone's son. Anyway, I haven't the time to be standing here having waited for Lady Muck for so long. No wonder she needed so much holy water, living with a man who spends half of his life in Dublin.'

'Well, 'tis not that I'd be worrying about,' said Philomena, who had joined the queue. 'They have more problems than that to be dealing with.'

Everyone fell silent as all eyes rested on Philomena.

'You know they built that house on the fairy path? And we all know what that means.'

Mrs Doyle blessed herself.

'How do you know?' Teresa asked, who was no longer in such a hurry.

'The storyteller told me. He said the fairies used that path from the river to the village and the Malones have built right across it. They will have nothing but trouble.'

Mrs Doyle tutted as she tore off a piece of newspaper to wrap the first painted donkey. 'They had that problem at my sister's. Had to plant a hawthorn bush for the fairies to go under, they did. Put it at the side of the house and from the day they planted it, they didn't have another moment's bother.'

Keeva carried the tray out to the kitchen. She had wanted to say that as the Malones were doing so well, the fairies must be mighty pleased with the shop, but she would only have been scolded by Mrs Doyle for voicing an opinion. Keeva knew the best way to a happy life in Tarabeg was to have no opinion about anything. She had thought that one of the women would have commented about Rosie working at the shop. But as had been the case with Rosie for most of her life, hardly anyone had noticed.

Chapter 20

The following day was Sunday and Mary Kate's seventh birthday.

She had lain in bed the previous night too excited to sleep. She listened to her mammy and daddy counting the money from the shop. Even she could tell that cashing up after the day's work was taking longer than it used to. It wasn't talking she heard most often now, nor even her parents laughing, but the sound of the pennies being counted into the tin. Then would come the chink of the key in the lock and the dull clunks as the peat blocks were removed from the hole in the chimney and the tin box slipped in behind.

Mary Kate was proud of her daddy. Early in the mornings, when he was home, he had taken to putting her in the front of the van and they would drive up the hills and wait at the bottom of the boreens to collect the children who were walking down to school without shoes on their feet.

Today, on the morning of her birthday, her father had been up at the sound of the cock crowing. The only person to wake earlier than Michael Malone was Father Jerry, and today Michael was up and out before the father was off his knees after his first prayer. The Malones' donkey, Jacko, who was rarely put to work these days and spent most of his time grazing the land between the back of the shop and the stony banks of the river, was the only living soul to see him leave.

Today's route took Michael south along the narrow, lonely road that skirted the Atlantic. He carried goods from the shop to those cottages that wanted fresher than what was taken by the boat, and he dropped farm feed along the way. By the time he'd returned from his morning errands, the kitchen of the Malone house was preparing for a feast. As he entered the house, the sight of Sarah standing at the table covered in flour did what it always did and made his heart leap.

'What took ye so long?' Sarah almost shouted at him. Her face was covered in flour and her arms were elbow deep in a large mixing bowl.

'Jesus, woman, will ye let me in the door before you start giving out.' Michael was framed in the doorway with the low river at his back and the mountains rising beyond.

Sarah bent her head to look behind him and check the weather. 'We have all your family on the way down this afternoon for her birthday, I've been at it since six and there hasn't been a sight of ye all morning. It's Rosie's day off. Do you think a birthday feast appears by magic?'

Michael was kicking off his boots. Dipping his fingers in the holy water on the wall at the base of the statue of Our Lady, he blessed himself. 'I do, yes, but I know my mother doesn't and she's just getting out of the van.'

Sarah's face dropped and then broke into a smile. 'You collected Nola in the van?'

Michael moved around the table and, slipping his arms

around the waist of his wife from behind, buried his face in her neck and began kissing her.

'Get off! You said Nola was coming in – she'll catch ye.'

'She is, but she's tying up Jacko first. He was halfway to the village, making his way to Mrs Doyle's back yard. He was after making a protest about the painted donkeys and Mammy's bringing him back. Has a soft spot for him, she does so. Mary Kate ran up with her. By the time they've caught him and finished chatting to half a dozen people, they'll be at least half an hour.'

Sarah turned around and faced him. She didn't care that her hands were full of flour or that she was covering her husband's back with her telltale handprints. He smelt of all the things she loved – the shop, their home, the inside of his van, and himself. She kissed him hard and wriggled closer to him as he lifted her up onto the table and slipped his hands under her skirt and up the length of her bare legs.

'Have we time?' she whispered, always anxious, fearing being caught by Nola or, even worse, her daughter.

He wasn't waiting for a reply as he undid his belt and pulled her forward onto him. 'We still want another baby, don't we?' He'd been aroused by nothing more than the sight of her alone at the table, wiping the flour from her eyes with the back of her hand. He pulled the ruffled neck of her dress down and exposed her breasts. Sarah giggled, but her laughter became a gasp as he slid his hands up and along the inside of her thighs, inside her underclothes and with his probing fingers, explored her and gently pushed her legs apart with his hands. 'Come here,' he whispered into her neck as he slid his hands under her buttocks and sliding her forward, slipped her knickers down her legs and dropped them onto the floor.

A baby, there was nothing she would love more. Moving the mixing bowl to the side, she leant back against the table, her hands splayed flat on the floury pine to give her purchase. One foot found the stool and Michael held on to her thighs and wrapped them around him. As she tilted her hips, Michael could wait no longer and plunged into her harder than he had meant to, but aware that they could be caught at any moment and that time was of the essence.

'Oh my God in heaven,' Sarah gasped.

'What?' said Michael. 'What? Is something wrong?'

'Jesus, no, it is not. Don't stop.' She gasped a second time as the mixing bowl smashed onto the floor.

Michael grinned. He couldn't help himself – the look on her face as he moved in and out, teasing her, drove him wild.

Having one of the busiest kitchens in the village, they had never made love on the table before. Sarah was making the most of it and Michael was loving it. As she threw her head back and yelped, a cup jumped off the table, but she didn't even notice.

Rosie, however, did notice. No one had asked her to work, but she had been invited as a guest to the birthday tea. 'I can't just turn up and leave Sarah to do all the work,' she had said to Teresa when she left Mass. As the shop was closed, she'd walked around to the back door to be met by the sight of Michael's bare backside, Sarah with her legs around his waist and her skirts splayed out over the table, and smashed dishes scattered across the kitchen floor. They were both making a noise like none Rosie had heard before, Michael grunting and Sarah almost screaming.

Rosie's hand flew to her mouth, but she was rooted to the spot, she could not tear her eyes away. It wasn't until she heard Michael let out an animal-like groan and saw him collapse over Sarah, proclaiming how much he loved her, that the pain in her heart got the better of her. She tiptoed away and slipped into the cow byre.

Hours later, the very same table heaved again but this time with the weight of smoked salmon. It lay on a wooden platter and reached almost from one end of the table to the other. A side of pork lay on the press and there were two huge bowls of buttery mashed potatoes, dishes of vegetables and the tallest, most perfectly risen Victoria sandwich cake any of them had seen.

The Devlins were at the table, Tig in between Seamus and Paddy, and Keeva and Josie next to Nola and Bridget McAndrew. Mary Kate, replete with as much salmon as a child could eat, had fallen asleep on her straw sleeper, which was at Daedio's feet. Daedio was also replete, asleep, and slightly drunk.

As she dozed, Mary Kate clutched her painted donkey and her mother's emerald. She insisted on wearing this whenever she was allowed. The first time she wore it, Michael had just returned from a shopping trip to Dublin and held a present in his hands for her. He crouched down on his haunches to her height, and said, 'Did yer mammy give you that to wear for ever?' Mary Kate shook her head, wondering if she might be in trouble. 'I bought it for you, but she stole it from me, so she did.'

'I did not,' squealed Sarah. 'Don't be filling the girl's head with such nonsense now.' She was at the sink with her back to them, and Michael grinned and winked at Mary Kate.

'She did so. I remember the day I bought it as if it were only yesterday. I said to yer man that I wanted a colour to match my daughter's eyes, but your man in Dublin, he said to me, I have no colour as beautiful as the eyes in your daughter's head, Malone, you shall have to be making do with this.'

'Sure, the man was a genius,' said Sarah as she turned back from the sink and, drying her hands on her apron, walked over to them both. ''Twas before you were even born, Mary Kate. Fancy that, a man with the gift of vision selling your father an emerald the colour of your eyes! And your father didn't even buy it, it was a present from Daedio. That is an example of how much baloney your father talks.'

Mary Kate had grinned at her father, torn between throwing her arms around his neck in thanks for the way he made her feel with his beautiful words, and begging impatiently to see her present.

'Stop, will you, and just give it to her,' the always busy and often impatient Sarah had chastised as she walked over to the scrubbed pine table, began shaping the bread with her hands, and with her foot kicked open the range door ready to receive it at just the right temperature.

Pete Shevlin was on the settle with Michael next to the fire. Sarah and Nola had persuaded Rosie to stay. 'No, you aren't doing all this work and then going back to your empty house. We want you to stay, don't we, Nola?'

Despite her reluctance, Rosie had enjoyed the afternoon. She rose to gather the dirty plates and carried them out to the scullery.

'Would ye look at that,' said Michael, gazing down at the sleeping child. 'She loves the donkey from Mrs Doyle's. After all the things I bring her home from Dublin, that's the thing she's been holding on to all day.'

'When are you next to Dublin?' asked Seamus as he tried,

with little success, to place almost a whole slice of cake into his mouth.

'Tuesday.'

Sarah was placing a fresh jug of stout on the table. She leant over Michael's shoulder. 'You never told me that,' she said.

'I have to. I can't have Mrs Doyle catching up with me. Need more stock. I'm right out of keep nets. You can't catch salmon without one.'

'How long will ye be gone for this time?' asked Seamus.

Mary Kate shuffled and stretched in her sleep. With his foot, Michael shifted her wicker bed closer to the fire, away from the draught that was running under the kitchen door. The sun had long since given up trying and had given way to a fresh Atlantic breeze. The flames leapt up the chimney and Michael smiled down at his sleeping birthday girl, her cheeks flushed pink from the warmth. Sarah smiled and handed him Mary Kate's blanket to slip over her; as she did so, he squeezed her hand. Mary Kate, the most precious thing in all the world to both of them.

'I'll be gone for a full week,' he said.

'Again?' Sarah exclaimed. 'Seems like you've hardly been home.'

''Tis a terrible place,' said Seamus. 'You be careful. They say the women in Dublin are as good as wild and they have no religion. The priests in Dublin have a terrible life, so they do.'

Michael noted the look of concern on Sarah's face and, grabbing her hand, pulled her down onto his knee. 'Quiet, Daddy, you'll be having my Sarah worried sick. Won't he?' He rubbed the small of Sarah's back with one hand as he held her hand with the other.

She looked down at him and smiled, and in front of his

parents and his guests, he took her face in his hands. 'Don't you be taking no notice of any of them,' he said. 'The only woman on my mind when I am away is the most beautiful one in all of Ireland.' Sarah grinned and kissed him on the nose. 'And right now, she has no idea what I'm saying because she's asleep under a blanket.'

Sarah jumped off his knee in mock disgust as they all began to laugh, and Michael managed to playfully slap Sarah's backside before she moved out of range. The only person who wasn't laughing was Seamus and when everyone had stopped, he reiterated his warning. 'I'm just saying, be careful, that's all. Dublin is not Galway and sure, that place is bad enough that I only go when I have to.'

Michael was about to pick up his jug of beer and looked under his lashes to Seamus. 'Daddy, you have never been to Dublin, what could ye be worried about?'

'The sin, the temptation. That's what,' Seamus fired back. 'You think ye know everything, Michael, but you are a stubborn-headed country boy and ye don't know all the evils of the world that are out there waiting to trip up a man like yourself who is making a good business for himself.'

Nola looked from one man to the other. She was drying dishes and could sense the tension building, but she knew how to handle it. 'Well, I saw Teresa Gallagher in the post office the other day and she was saying what a fine business it is ye have here.'

'I'm trying my best,' said Michael. 'We both are, aren't we, Sarah? And we have Rosie to help. Don't ye be worrying, Daddy, I know what I'm doing all right.'

★

It was twilight when Rosie left the Malones and made her way home. Maughan was waiting for her halfway up the boreen. She had not felt frightened when he'd first approached her, asking for information about Mary Kate. She had simply listened to his questions without answering them. The Malones had made her feel like family, especially today, and she loved Mary Kate. She didn't know how to get rid of him and she was afraid to tell Michael. He was hot-headed and she feared that if she did tell him, he could end up in jail or even swinging from a noose for what he might do. Rosie had learnt one thing, that Michael Malone was a man of great passion who didn't always think first. Telling him would bring greater danger than Maughan waylaying her when she least expected him.

He had tried to scare her when she first came across him in the boreen. Told her he wanted her to take Mary Kate to the river when Michael was away on his buying trips as her grandfather wanted to talk to her. He had threatened her with curses and all manner of hell that would rain down on them if she didn't, but she had stood her ground.

'You can do nothing. The good Lord is my protector, he is all I need. Now go, before I call the Garda.'

She was surprised to see him there today, but maybe he'd known it was Mary Kate's birthday. 'I'm not bringing the child, I have nothing for you and I never will.' She was firm in her voice and appeared stronger than she felt. She took some pleasure in watching him deflate.

'You will regret this,' he said as he spat on the ground.

'No, I won't. Don't ever block my path again or I will turn around and go straight to the guard. You will not get away quicker than he will catch you in his car. Tell McGuffey the same applies to him. Go from Tarabeg and take your witch of a grandmother with you because I will be straight to the guard house right now and telling him all about you.'

As she watched his departing back disappearing into the ferns, she began to shake violently. She had no idea where the words or the courage had come from. That wasn't a Rosie she had ever been before. She looked up towards her house and then down at the church. Turning on her heel, she headed back to the church to pray. She needed help.

'Sure that was the best idea you ever had, asking Rosie to work for them. She's a good girl and a grand help to Sarah,' said Daedio. 'They've gone from strength to strength, and he makes more money than the farm does now. Did you see them fishermen, buying the lines Michael had made up for them with his own hands? And he gives them advice, about where is the best place to fish on the river. Didn't I say it, that the salmon would bring in the business. Didn't I say that the fishermen would be coming.'

'Yes, yes, you did,' said Nola.

She, Daedio and Seamus were sitting in their horse and trap, making their way back up to the farm. The village below them was getting ever smaller as they climbed the dusty boreen. They had stayed almost too long and as dusk fell and the moon rose, one familiar landmark after another faded from sight. Daedio's snores lifted into the air.

'He's asleep more than he's awake these days,' said Seamus.

'Aye, he is. Heaven, I'd say. He's right too, the business is going well...' She sighed. 'But 'tis a shame, Sarah would have loved another child – and when so many in this village can have ten or more.'

'Well, it isn't for the want of trying. I swear they were at it only minutes before I walked through the door. Rosie was right behind me. If she'd arrived a minute earlier, she would have caught them too. Not having any babbies, it hasn't stopped those two.' Seamus grinned. 'I fancy a bit of that myself tonight, do you?'

Nola looked sideways at her husband in the twilight and grinned back. Despite his age, he showed no sign of slowing down. He was the serious and sometimes grim one of the family. But, with her, when they were alone, he was always the same, her playful and loving Seamus.

'There's no chance of ye getting pregnant now, is there?' he asked with a hint of worry in his voice as he cracked the reins.

'God, no. Not a chance.' She stared up at the moon. 'Doesn't seem like forty years ago we had our first one, does it, eh? Forty! Our Sean had quite a party for his big birthday, did he not, or so he said in the letter. And the others all there too...' Her voice wobbled slightly. 'Wouldn't you think they would want to come home from America and at least see that miserable old git sleeping in the back one more time?'

Seamus looked over his shoulder at Daedio, who was under the influence of five pots of porter. 'I'll give you this,' he said, 'having only one child is a queer situation altogether. Mary Kate may be the only one, but she has the looks and the brains of half a dozen. God has his ways and I'd say this, what's the point in having them when they all bugger off and leave you? What will happen to the farm when we have gone, and the house? Who will take it on?'

Nola had no response. They truth was that none of them would, but that wasn't what Seamus wanted to hear.

'What we have been working to leave, they will sell between them, and this will all belong to someone else one day.'

'Shush, Seamus, you know that's not true.' And quickly, as was her way, she changed the subject, because she was her children's mother and no one knew them like she did. She didn't want to look to the future, to when she and Seamus were no longer there and the boots of strangers tramped over Malone land.

Three months later, Sarah ran from the sink in the scullery to the yard outside and vomited all over the chicken feed, to the indignation of the chickens, who scurried out of the gate squawking. Mary Kate ran after her, closely followed by Rosie.

'Mrs Malone, are ye all right?' Rosie looked concerned.

Sarah couldn't answer at first. The ground was spinning and beads of perspiration stood out on her top lip. She wiped them away with the corner of her apron. She put her hand out to Mary Kate as reassurance and looked up at Rosie through watery eyes. 'I am, thank you. I don't know what happened, 'twas so quick. Mary Kate, back inside.'

'What's everyone doing out here?' asked Michael as he came to the door with a mug in his hand.

'Go on in,' Sarah ushered Mary Kate. 'Take her in, would you, Rosie.'

Rosie took Mary Kate's hand as she led her indoors. As she passed Michael, the hair on her forearm prickled.

'Michael, come here,' Sarah called out to him. She had one hand on the roof of the chicken pen.

He walked over to her and offered his mug. 'Do you want some of this? Are you not feeling good?'

Sarah pulled a face and looked down to the ground.

'Holy Mother, was that you?' he asked.

Sarah nodded. 'Michael, I think this means one thing,' she said. 'I'll call up to Bridget today, to make sure, but I think I know what she'll say.'

'What?' asked Michael, alarmed. 'What will she say?'

'That, well, maybe we have a babby on the way.'

It was a good few seconds before Michael responded. 'A babby? But it's been seven years.'

Sarah nodded. 'It has, and we've been blessed again.' She began to laugh at the expression on Michael's face.

'Oh, God, is it true?' Michael had long given up hope of another child, all hope of a son, and as the shock left him and he recovered his equilibrium, he picked up his Sarah and swung her around in his arms. At that moment he thought that there couldn't possibly be another man alive as happy as he was.

Later that day he took Sarah up the hill in the van to tell Nola, Seamus and Daedio herself. They left Rosie in charge of the shop with Mary Kate.

As they arrived at the farm, Nola rushed out of the house in a panic, and Seamus and Pete emerged hurriedly from the old cottage.

'What in God's name is wrong?' Nola demanded. 'Is it Mary Kate?'

'No, Mammy, 'tis not. She's safe with Rosie, like a good girl.'

'You look a bit peaky, Sarah, how are ye?' Nola looked at Sarah with a puzzled expression. She and Michael weren't expected. They rarely left the shop together and they had very obviously come for a reason.

NADINE DORRIES

Sarah winked at Nola. 'I'm fine, but Michael, you know what he's like for the tea.'

'Has the most beautiful woman in all of Ireland just walked into this house?' Daedio was in his usual place, lying on his bed in front of the fire, his back to the door. 'And very obviously, I don't mean you, Nola, unless I've gone entirely mad.'

'Jesus, won't you ever leave.' Nola kicked the bed as she walked past to put the kettle on the fire.

Sarah sat herself on the side of Daedio's bed and Michael said, 'I'm going out to the old cottage, to tell Daddy and Peter.'

'Tell them what?' Nola shouted after him, but it was too late, he'd gone.

'He wants to tell them our news,' said Sarah. 'That's why we came.'

Daedio winked at her. 'I already know it,' he said.

Sarah sat bolt upright. 'You can't do. I only knew myself this morning and I've only just been to see Bridget.'

'You don't need Bridget,' Daedio said. 'You just need to come and see me to tell you that you have a little boy growing in yer belly.'

They both heard a crash from the table and looked round to see Nola white with shock. 'Is it true?' she asked.

Sarah nodded as tears jumped to her eyes.

'Well now, in any other house that happens once a year, but here 'tis a special occasion. Get the whiskey out, woman,' said Daedio, grinning his toothless grin. 'Not that she needs any excuse, mind.' He winked. 'I'm not drinking me tea without it. I may not live to see the little fella arrive, so I'll wet his head now. Seamus, Pete, come away in here. Seamus, yer wife has turned into a blitherin' wreck.'

In the commotion that followed, it never occurred to Sarah

318

to ask Daedio how he knew, and he was glad of that, because Annie had told him much in the night, and some of it made him want to leave this world sooner than he ever would have thought.

Chapter 21

Rosie was surprised to find Theady O'Donnell sitting on her step when she returned home from school one autumn afternoon. He was back on a visit from the seminary and each time she saw him he seemed to have grown another foot.

'Can I talk to you, Miss O'Hara?' Theady was scrambling to his feet. 'My priest at school tells me I mustn't, that I must not breathe a word to anyone and that what I told him was a lie, but, I have to and I can't think of anyone else who would know what to do.' He appeared distressed, his eyes were opened wide and his voice was laced with anxiety.

Rosie opened her cottage door. 'Come on, come inside, you look a state. Would you like me to take you to see Father Jerry?' she asked. 'If it's about your work at the seminary…'As she looked into his face, a shiver ran down her spine. The time Sarah had asked her to look out for Ciaran, because Bee had concerns about Mr O'Dowd, flew into her mind. The long-ago words of Theady's own mother, Philomena, likewise.

'If I do, they will throw me out of the seminary, I would like to talk to you first, tell you, someone has to know because I can't keep this in here any more.' He pointed to his head and his eyes filled with tears. Rosie felt her skin prickle and tighten. Theady was seventeen now, almost a man and yet, here he was stood before her crying like a baby.

'Come inside,' she said as she held the door open to let him through. As he passed, she laid her hand on his back. Looking over her shoulder to the presbytery, she saw Teresa, stood quite still, watching them both through the window.

Bridget McAndrew was one of the busiest women in Tarabeg and was the first person locals called on should there be an ailment, an injury or a baby to be delivered in the village. Her basket rattled with the lotions and potions she'd been using for the past forty years, prepared with knowledge that had been handed down to her by her great-grandmother, who in turn had had the recipes passed down to her through generations before.

She was out in the field, cutting the peat in the autumn sunshine to harvest and store indoors ready for the long, cold and invariably damp winter, when she was summoned by Michael. He was struggling to get his van up the boreen leading to her cottage. The van could barely take it and twice he almost got himself stuck.

Bridget and Porick lived in a stone house that they all but shared with their cow, the sod-and-thatch byre they'd built for it having long since blown away. The house was at the foot of the mountain, directly opposite a stream in which there stood a stone sink and from where the McAndrews took their water. The boreen that led to their cottage was reached via a dead-end road that served just two farmhouses. It was a famine road, built a hundred years earlier by desperate, half-starving men forced to labour in exchange for food that was barely enough to survive on. The bogs were crisscrossed with such roads that led nowhere, roads for which men had sweated blood as they starved and died where they fell for no other reason than to be seen to have worked hard for whatever famine relief they received.

The McAndrews lived hand to mouth – potato to pan, pig to skillet, oats to bread – and their main income was the money Bridget was paid to deliver babies, heal the sick and tell fortunes. 'A witch, you are,' Porick chided. But he didn't say it too often, as like all Irishmen and -women, he was scared to the point of terror of the spirits that roamed the land, their land. Like many others, the McAndrews' house had been built before the famine and Porick had never been comfortable with the sighs and whispers he heard in the dark shadows of the night as his wife snored next to him. As the storyteller told them often enough, ''Tis impossible for so many to lie down and die on this very soil and for their spirits to leave us forever in peace. The good Lord will always be busy here.'

Porick ran the local taxi, but as hardly anyone went anywhere, he spent most of his day idle, which suited him perfectly. If there was need of the cab, it would be booked through Mrs Doyle. Most of his trade came from fishermen arriving at Galway station. He kept the cab at the rear of the post office and once a week he would call down into the village to be given his bookings by Mrs Doyle before heading over to Paddy's bar.

'Bridget, 'tis Sarah!' Michael shouted through the open window of his van as he drove towards her up the side of the hill. Bridget, looking up, was surprised she hadn't heard the sound of his engine on the springy bog.

'She's been in labour for hours – she asked me to fetch you.'

Bridget placed the flat of her hand in the small of her back and, straightening up, placed a hand over her eyes to shield out the sun, rare this late in October. She squinted up at Michael, who was now almost upon her. 'How many hours would it be?' she asked.

Michael abandoned the van, jumped out, and came running over to her. 'I reckon it's at least six. I've had to close the shop.'

Porick harrumphed next to her as he drove his blade into the peat. ''Tis all he be worried about,' he muttered. 'Not the wife or the babby, 'tis shutting the shop and the money he's lost.'

'Shut your mouth,' snapped Bridget. 'He cares more about his wife than you ever did about me. If you'd had your way, I'd have been giving birth in the fields.'

'If I'd had my way, you would just have been giving birth.'

Porick's remark stung, but then he'd meant it to. Bridget not having borne him even one son meant his life was hard; the work was his own to do, alone and for evermore. He had sympathy for those complaining about the children who had upped and left them; his had never come.

'Do you want to come back with me in the van?' Michael shouted, ignoring Porick.

'No, I do not. Go back to Sarah. I'll make it to the house and fetch me bag and meet you there.'

Michael did not look happy with her reply. 'Are ye sure? There's no danger in the van. Will I wait down on the road for you? It will be the quickest way to get you to Sarah.'

Bridget had dropped her shovel on the ground for Porick to carry and had already begun making her way back. She stopped in her tracks and placed her hands on her hips. 'If I wanted to come with you and get in that monster of a machine, I would have said yes. Did ye not hear me, Michael Malone?

And watch the tyres in the ruts. If you catch one, a broken van you'll have and I've no cure for that. You go back to your Sarah. Who is with her now?'

'Mary Kate is. Paddy's taken a message up to the farm for my mother to come down. She could be there by now.'

'Aye, well, Nola might be having to look after Daedio. I took a draught over there yesterday, he's not so good himself, so she might not be able to get away. He's worrying, Michael. Tells me he's seeing a lot of Annie. I think his time is near.'

'I was up there this morning,' Michael shouted down. 'He's fretting about something, but Mammy thinks it will pass when the baby arrives. He's worried about Sarah and so am I. Come on, Bridget, in the van.'

'Your bedroom window faces south, does it not?'

'It does.'

'Well, face the foot of the bed to the south, not to the fire. There was never an easy delivery in a north-facing bed, and to the west and east 'tis unlucky. Take the van back down, if you can, and meet me on the road in ten minutes. I'll be chancing it, but mind you don't drive fast.'

Michael ran back to his van, which had half of the boreen sticking out of the exhaust pipe. He shook his head, but, glad to have something useful to occupy his mind and his hands, he cleared the earth from his exhaust and started the engine. With no room to turn, he painstakingly reversed the van down the hill and waited for Bridget to fetch her basket.

Bridget's house was sparse, containing not much more than a hard mud floor, a table and two chairs by the fire. She kept her wicker basket ready by the side of the straw mattress on her truckle bed. Carrying it to the table, she checked inside. Her bottle of blue motherwort solution was almost full, as were her supplies of echinacea and nettle tea. She'd recently replenished some of own special concoctions, too, made from herbs and seeds she gathered before the sun came up over the horizon; nothing collected after sun up was of any use. The salix willow potion she'd brewed that morning was still warm, standing on the kitchen table.

She took four potatoes out of the basket under the table, threw some fresh peat onto the fire, and dropped the potatoes into the dry cast-iron cauldron hanging from the chimney, to bake ready for their supper when she returned.

As she made for the door, she popped the salix solution into her bag. She moved at her own pace, the pace of a woman feeling her age and accustomed to a life of hard work. She was fired on by the confidence that she had never lost either a baby or a mother in a village half populated by those she had delivered. Standing in the doorway, she looked out on the fields and Tarabeg below, and at the sun glinting off the river as it wound its way through, a sight that never failed to gladden her heart. Then she slammed the door shut behind her.

Nola almost flew up the stairs and into the bedroom to Sarah. 'Oh thank God, I got here in time. You are early, aren't you? Isn't it another month to go?'

Sarah was lying on the bed red-faced and with her hair soaked with sweat and tied back. The ticking mattress was overstuffed and bulged under the linen sheet. The window was open and the pretty floral curtains – made from the pale lemon and pink fabric that had caused such a commotion the day it arrived – lifted and dropped in the breeze. On the scrubbed pine side table under the window stood a tall china jug and a basin for washing. The fire was lit, filling the room with the distinctive smell of peat.

'Yes,' rasped Sarah. 'This one is early and troublesome, has been all along.'

Nola shot her a look of sympathy. 'You've been saying 'twill be a boy since the day Daedio told you. I wish to God he was wrong. That would give me so much pleasure telling him that, but you've been going along with him. I've never heard a mother so sure of what she was carrying.'

She turned to her granddaughter, who was sitting ramrod straight with nerves on the chair beside Sarah's bed. 'Come on, Mary Kate, I have a job to do before I look after your mother. Help me get the pots in the kitchen filled with water and onto the fire.'

Mary Kate was so relieved that her Granny Nola had arrived. She'd been sitting there ever since she got home from school and was faint with worry and hunger. Grasping at her granny's hand, she was only too happy to rush down the stairs away from the groans of pain she knew her mother was trying to suppress for her sake.

As they reached the bottom of the stairs, Michael burst in through the back door. 'Mammy, thank God! How is she?'

Nola shrugged. 'She's like every woman in labour, Michael – in agony, I'd be thinking. Is Bridget here?'

'She is, she's talking to Josie. Shall I go up to Sarah – is Rosie in the shop yet?' Michael was nervous. This was the first time he'd closed the shop since the day it had opened. He'd sent for Rosie, but a message had been returned by Teresa that she was busy with Father Jerry. At that moment, though, the shop bell rang and he heard Rosie calling Sarah's name.

Michael needed no further encouragement to remove himself from the simultaneous agonies of listening to his wife in childbirth and contemplating the money lost from not being able to deliver the pig feed. 'Right you are, I'm away in the shop to collect the deliveries.' Then he remembered himself. 'Oh no, I'm not, I can't, not yet. Bridget told me I have to turn the bed to face south.' And without further comment he took the stairs two at a time, shouting, 'Sarah, hold on, we have to turn the bed around.'

The sun had given way to the moon and it was now dark outside. Rosie had left for home and Michael finally closed the shop. No one came after dark, unless it was a full moon and the way was lit. For what seemed like hours, he and Mary Kate had kept themselves occupied making endless cups of tea for Bridget, Nola and Sarah upstairs.

'Nola, would you come here,' Bridget shouted down the stairs to Nola, who'd slipped out to fetch more water and provide Michael and Mary Kate with a progress report.

It seemed to Mary Kate as though her Granny Nola had been running upstairs with jugs of clean water and down again with bowls of dirty water all day long.

'It's nearly over, Mary Kate, and very soon you're going to have a brand-new baby brother or sister.' Nola picked up the biggest pot of boiling water and tipped it into a large china bowl. 'Michael, we need to fetch Father Jerry, and you will be coming to Mass with me in the morning, if everything goes well, God willing.' She blessed herself.

Just then the cry came down the stairs, 'Nola, fetch me the boiling water.'

Michael sat on the rocking chair by the fire and pulled

Mary Kate down onto his knee. He picked up her hand, kissed her fingers and smiled at her. She beamed back. They were both high on anticipation. Both knew that the softening of the muffled yelps and shouts coming from up the stairs had a significant meaning.

'I'm thinking Daedio is maybe right?' he said as he grinned, almost unable to contain his trembling nerves.

Mary Kate shuddered with excitement. 'I think Daedio is right too, Daddy. Mammy told me that if the babby was like me, we would hear it crying before we saw it. She said they heard me crying in Castlebar on market day. I don't believe her, you know. 'Tis not true.' A frown had crossed her face and Michael roared with laughter.

'Sure, it was. I was out with the pigs with Granddaddy Seamus and they were screaming for the hell of it, and Granddaddy said to me, "Shush now, I think that's your Mary Kate arriving I just heard. We had better be getting home."'

Mary Kate leapt off his knee in indignation. 'No!' she almost shouted. 'Daddy, I never cry. Crying is for babbies.'

'Aye, but you were a babby then, Mary Kate, sure you were, the noisiest babby in Tarabeg.'

She put her hands on her hips, about to protest, but Michael pulled her back down onto his knee. His smile made her warm inside. He was her hero and she was the proudest daughter in all Mayo.

Michael settled back into the armchair and his gaze fell into the fire. Mary Kate nestled her head against his chest. All the demons of worry scattered as he lifted her fingers and, kissing the back of her hand said, 'Mary Kate, when you wear that emerald, you are the most beautiful girl in all of Ireland, do ye know that?'

Mary Kate couldn't help herself. She put her free hand up to the emerald and, looking back at her father, nodded in earnest.

To her surprise, he guffawed loudly and hugged her tightly. As he did, she heard him whisper a silent prayer into her hair. 'Dear God, keep my family well and secure, and deliver Sarah safely through this ordeal.'

Mary Kate felt very grown up as she kissed his forehead and whispered back, ''Tis all right, Daddy, don't fret so.' And together they swayed to and fro, each lost in their own thoughts on his wooden rocking chair.

First came the hungry screams and then the thundering footsteps of Nola as she raced down the wooden stairs shouting, 'Michael, Mary Kate, would you come here, both of you.'

Michael jumped up so fast that Mary Kate fell from his knee to the floor with a bump. He reached down and grabbed her by the hand and almost pulled her to the stairs, where they collided into Nola, who, with tears in her eyes, said, 'Come on, you two, you can come up now.'

Michael scooped Mary Kate up in his arms and he ran up the stairs with her as though she was no weight at all. 'What's the betting you have the little brother you've been asking for at last, eh?' And then he shouted, 'Sarah, we are coming. SARAH!' he roared as they burst in through the bedroom door. He'd been gripped by a sudden vison, a manifestation of his worst terror, one that he had held at bay all this time. Now that he knew all was well and his defences were down, it came racing to the surface and caught him unawares. It was a sudden rush of disbelief, as though Nola had been deceiving him, hiding something from him. He pictured the curtains billowing in the moonlight, the gurgling of the river nearby, a tidy room, the fire lit, a wooden chair with the tapestry cushion Sarah had made when they were first married, and an empty bed, facing north.

As he crashed through the door, it banged against the wall so hard it brought away flakes of lime wash. Sarah looked up from the pillows, alarmed. Mary Kate glanced down and saw the pile of blood-soaked sheets and rags on the floor. She froze in Michael's arms, but all seemed well as her mother struggled to sit up in the bed and reassure them, her curtain of golden-red hair combed and hanging down over her shoulders.

Nola laid the hungry baby on Sarah's bare left breast, the one closest to her heart, and it seemed to Mary Kate as though her mother was lit from within.

'Oh God, Sarah, is it a boy?' asked Michael.

'It is that,' she said above the howls of hunger coming from the squirming red and wrinkly scrap of life in her arms. 'Come here, both of ye, while I tell ye,' she said with a hint of distraction. She tried to move the baby's head around with her hand to help him latch on to her nipple. 'Oh God, would ye look at him,' she pleaded to Nola, who leant over her.

'Come, Sarah,' said Bridget, and with the deftness of a woman who had had much practice, she cupped the back of the baby's head with one hand, took Sarah's nipple between her thumb and forefinger and connected the two.

'It's been such a long time.' Sarah grinned at Bridget.

'Aye, I had to do it with that one too.' Bridget inclined her head towards Michael. 'He was an awkward feeder.'

Sarah held her free arm out to her daughter and Michael, who were still hovering in the doorway. 'Come and see,' she said.

'Is it a boy?' Mary Kate couldn't help herself. She gasped and clasped her hand over her mouth at the sight of the now snuffling and silent bare baby boy, swaddled only in a towelling nappy.

Michael walked almost in slow motion to the bed.

Bridget was piling her potions back into her basket, minding not to interrupt the moment of introduction. She set great store by what happened in the first hour, in more ways than one.

Sarah grasped Michael's hand and as she did so, the tears fell out of her eyes and onto her cheeks. 'It is,' she answered, and then again, 'Look, see.'

With one hand on the carved wooden headboard, Michael leant over and kissed away the tears from his wife's face and the top of his son's downy head. It seemed to Mary Kate, as her parents spoke to each other in hushed and intimate tones, that she no longer existed. It was the three of them – they had forgotten her. Granny Nola was down on her haunches, busy scooping up the bloody sheets into the wicker basket, her long skirt and apron trailing on the floor. Bridget was standing at the pine table under the open window, silhouetted in the moonlight shining through the curtains, which were now still and flat against the wall. She was rinsing out one of her dark green bottles with water from a jug.

Mary Kate was standing in the doorway of a room filled with activity and yet she felt suddenly invisible. She looked at the carved wooden post at the foot of the bed and then down at her scuffed boots. She was used to her parents kissing. They were the most tactile of couples and she had grown up with all of that; she was often a part of it as they hugged together, she high up in her father's arms. But right now they were laughing and crying all at the same time, which was new and made her feel uncomfortable, not least because she had never once seen her father cry.

As if she could sense her strange loneliness, Bridget turned to look at her and smiled. 'You got to stay up late, Mary Kate,' she said as she forced the straw stopper back into the bottle. 'Life is going to alter for you after today.' And then without Mary Kate knowing why, Bridget stared at her and seemed to freeze.

Nola stood up, the basket firmly tucked under one arm and resting on her hip, and placed her free arm around Mary Kate's shoulders. 'I'll light a lantern for you to return, Bridget. Tig is waiting to walk with you and see you and Porick safe back. I'm not sure Porick can drive tonight. He's been in the bar waiting for ye. He can just about walk, let alone drive the cab.' And then she told Bridget the most welcome news. 'Josie has sent over some stew. She's sent a pot for us and one for ye both, to take back for you and Porick.'

Bridget smiled. Josie never let a bit of meat go off. If it was on the cusp, she would throw it into a pot and donate it to some poor family in need. She usually headed out to the sod houses on the Mulranny road, where children lived too close to the earth for a long life and parents laboured on their own smallholdings or on the farms of those that had enough work to feed them. 'Thank her for me and tell her I'll return the pot tomorrow before she goes to Mass.'

'Go on, sit on the bed,' said Nola as she bent her head and placed the almost reluctant Mary Kate next to Sarah. Once she had sat herself down, Mary Kate looked up at Nola and Nola was relieved to see a nervous smile cross her face.

Bridget then lowered her voice and, looking over to Sarah,

whispered to Nola, 'It took every drop of the motherwort I had to get that little fella out. Will you be around for the night?'

'I can be,' said Nola. 'Why? Are you worried?'

'Not at all. She's fine, sure enough, it's just with so much of the motherwort, I think it would be best, in case she bleeds. I'm not happy with how much blood she's lost already. But, sure, she was fine with Mary Kate and so she should be again now.' Bridget placed her hand on Nola's arm to stem the look of alarm in her eyes. 'She will be fine, I'm telling ye. Sure, would I be leaving if she wasn't?'

Michael and Sarah had dried their eyes and silence fell as they both watched their baby take his first snuffling feed. It was as if they were witnessing one of the wonders of the world.

Bridget moved towards the bed, close to where Mary Kate was sitting, which was as near to her mother as she could get. 'Would you look at the size of you, Mary Kate,' she said. 'My, you've grown a foot since I last saw you, I swear. Let's hope he grows as fast.'

'You haven't seen Mary Kate for months,' said Michael. 'You need to get to Mass more often, Bridget.'

'Mass!' Bridget snorted. 'Father Jerry has banned me. Said I had to stop using my potions on people and leave them to the power of prayer. I told him, not fecking likely. I'll go tomorrow to say thanks for this little fella's safe arrival though.'

'What in God's name did you do that made him so unhappy?' Nola asked.

'Sure, nothing at all. I put the dead hand of Annie, JP's mammy, on the McAffy girl when she was sick, and Jesus, he near hit the roof. I didn't know he was outside the cottage talking to the son. Annie had only been dead for not an hour and a half, her hand was only just cold, she hadn't yet passed over and the McAffy girl, she had the malaise so badly. It worked, though. I placed Annie's dead hand on her head and held it there for just the five minutes or so and she hasn't stopped running around since. Whenever I see her, she makes me stand and watch her do a jig, just to prove she's better. But you see that's what he doesn't like, that it works so well, and his prayers don't always, you know. And besides, I do go to Mass, he never turns me away. I go to the Angelus though, when it's quiet and no one can hear him giving out to me in the confessional. I said to him, "Are you going to pay for our keep then? Me and my fecking lazy bastard, we'd starve if I didn't make my potions." Right, I'll be off now then. Nola will be staying the night, Sarah. Michael, you know where I am if you should need me, don't you?'

Michael shifted on the edge of the bed and slipped Mary Kate across to her mother as he stood up to help Bridget with her basket. 'Look,' he whispered to Mary Kate, 'isn't he the grandest little fella you ever saw?'

Mary Kate looked down at her brother's red face and all the anxiety she had felt for the entire day slipped away. It was as though her heart had stopped. She gazed up into her mother's face, which swam before the river of tears in her eyes. Her mother looked concerned, a worried frown crossed her brow. 'Mammy,' said Mary Kate and held out both of her arms. She had no idea why, but she was about to cry.

'Here, come here, would ye.' Sarah laid the exhausted baby on the bed next to her with one arm then extended her other arm and cradled Mary Kate into her. She cuddled her into her chest and against the bare breast the baby had so hastily but uncomplainingly been plucked from. She rubbed her hands over her hair and kissed her head and face and wiped her tears away.

'My first job is to always keep you safe, you know that, don't you? You were our firstborn and that makes you special. You were so special, isn't it a fact, I couldn't bear to share you, and so I waited so long to have this little fella.' Mary Kate let her sobs go as Sarah wiped her face with the corner of the sheet. 'There now, stop, nothing has changed. We just have a new member in the family. Finnbar, we are going to call him, isn't that right?' Sarah looked up to Michael, who nodded.

'Aye, Finnbar Malone,' he said, as though practising how the name sounded out loud.

Mary Kate, for once void of protests as her mother covered her in kisses, thought to herself that in her young life this was the first time her mother had ever lied to her. How could she say nothing was going to change? It was a lie. Even at her young age, she knew that from this moment on, nothing would ever be the same again. They were no longer just three.

Bridget picked up her shawl, threw it around her shoulders and nosily descended the wooden stairs with Nola behind. Within seconds, Mary Kate could hear Nola banging around in the kitchen. The tantalising smell of stew floated up the stairs and made her mouth water. She was starving. Someone had come in through the back door and Mary Kate could hear the voice of Tig Devlin, ready to lead Bridget and Porick home. 'Keeva is desperate to come over,' he said.

'Right, Nola, if Sarah can have the luxury of you here for a few days, leave her in bed. Her milk will come in better that way because isn't it a fact, the minute she puts her feet on the floor, it will dry up.'

Michael went over to his tin, took out a pound and gave it to Bridget.

'If you need me, send Tig,' she said. 'Get her churched as soon as she gets out of bed – I don't need Father Jerry on me back no more. Make it there as soon as you can and then you can have the christening and the party. I'll be thanking you for this, Michael.' Bridget placed the pound into the pocket of her apron. 'Goodbye, Sarah. Come on, Tig, keep the lamp high and in front, we don't want to be tripping over any sleeping goblins on the way back, now do we. They won't be expecting us at this hour.'

Tig had sat Porick down by the fire in the McAndrews' cottage before he left. Bridget occupied herself refilling her bottles before she came to join him.

'Ye took your time with that one. Losing yer touch, are ye?' Porick was hail-fellow-well-met to strangers, a surly man to his wife.

Bridget would have loved to have brought the pan of stew down on his head, even though she'd carried it carefully up the hill, over trench and rut, and past the curious eyes of unseen animals, not to mention more than a dozen goblins, roused by their footsteps and the lamp.

Porick had busied himself around the fire while she was sorting out her basket. 'I hope those four potatoes was for me, because I've ate the lot.'

'Since when have you had four? 'Twas two each. If we had four each, we'd be out of potatoes weeks before the next harvest, as well ye know.' Each potato was counted and layered in straw on the shelf above the cow. The cow was munching and settled and Bridget looked down and saw that the metal pail was full and the cow had been milked; she wondered which of her neighbours had called in to help.

She thought she heard Porick snort with laughter. 'We have the stew,' he said.

Bridget lifted the pot out of her basket and placed it on the wooden table. She cleared away the straw that Josie had packed around it to keep it warm and untied the cloth. Laying the muslin cloth out, she picked up her spoon from her clean tin bowl, which sat next to his, and began to eat. 'If you want any, you can fetch it yourself. But I suppose you are too full of the stout and potatoes now.'

Porick looked sideways at her. The tantalising aroma had reached him, but he didn't speak; he didn't dare. With Porick and Bridget there were no big fights or rows, it was a war of attrition, each aiming to have inflicted the greater number of wounds by words at the end of the day.

After a few spoons, Bridget found she could no longer eat. 'Come, take your fill,' she said as she stood and wearily made her way over to her bed. 'There's no better stew than that made by Josie, but it won't last till tomorrow. She doesn't use the best meat for what she gives away for free. Eat.'

Porick didn't need to be asked twice. With a scraping of his chair and a grudging, muffled thanks, he sat at her place and ate noisily.

'Ye have the grace of Murphy's pig,' she said as she lay down on her side of the straw mattress and stared up at the thatched roof. She mulled over the delivery of Finnbar in her mind. 'I won't be sleeping the night,' she said to Porick.

The only reply was his slurping on the stew. She shut her eyes, but the demons would not leave her. She was being warned and she had no idea by who or about what. In that damp and almost pitch-black room, she felt the premonition. She had seen it in the dazzling eyes of Mary Kate as the little girl had looked up at her, and it lay heavy on her heart.

Father Jerry waited until Teresa had retired for the night before he unlocked the chest at the foot of his bed. She had tried to find the keys to it, this he knew, but they lived around his waist, day and night, and had never been removed since the chain-link had been fastened on to him by the bishop on the day he'd arrived. It had been the same for every priest of the Sacred Heart since who knew when. He had received his instructions in a tone both grave and clear. 'This is your responsibility alone. Should you die, instructions are in Galway as to what will happen in that eventuality. Do not speak of your responsibility. The knowledge must die with you. The Pope himself and a small number of people at the Vatican are the only people aware outside of Ireland. Do you understand?' He did understand. It meant that the responsibility being placed on his shoulders was immense, and he would receive a special place in heaven. He understood that he had been chosen. But now he was in danger. He had a job to do.

He lit a lamp and placed it on the wooden table next to the chest, then fell to his knees and said his first prayer of penance. He was wearing a white calico nightshirt and nothing else. Taking a deep breath, he lifted the lid, removed the heavy leather and brown-paper covering and gasped as emotion gripped his throat and tears filled his eyes. He had the same reaction every time. He pulled his nightshirt over his head, naked before his penance and God. He knew there had been attempts by the warrior monks during the Crusades to have the chest and its contents removed and sold to Rome, but Tarabeg had been saved by the words of St Patrick himself, written on the scroll he now lifted from the top of the chest and held in his hands: 'A message from Patricius to the people of Tarabeg.'

The scroll declared Tarabeg to be a place where no man would be touched by evil, a place that would be saved as heaven on earth by the protection of the word of St Patrick, who, in the writing on the scroll, said that he had found the people of Tarabeg to be the happiest, the kindest, the most godly and loving that he had met after landing on the shores of the west. That among the druids and heathens he had encountered in other lands, the people of Tarabeg had been the most welcoming of the deeper knowledge of Christ. The scroll was adorned with shamrocks, inked in St Patrick's own hand. It described Tarabeg as a place where the Holy Ghost was present in every home, residing in its people and lifting them up to a spiritual plane enjoyed by no other community in the land. It finished with the instruction that the scroll must never leave Tarabeg. If it did, the Holy Ghost would leave with it. It must reside within the church built by the people who had converted to Christ and had erected his house near the river. The scroll concluded with a flourish: 'All this upon the order of St Patricius.'

'Where have I gone wrong? What have I done wrong?' Father Jerry moved the scroll for fear his tears of penitence would stain it. Laying it down, he lifted out the cilice, a full-length hair shirt spiked with sprigs of dried heather and gorse that his predecessor told him had been threaded through the fabric by St Patrick himself. The heather and gorse sprigs turned mainly to dust and so, once a year, Father Jerry painstakingly replaced them.

He slipped the shirt over his head and flinched as the sharp sprigs pierced his skin. The shirt was open at the back. Bending, he lifted the leather whip and began his act of corporal mortification. Evil was running through the boreens of Tarabeg. He had been vigilant, he'd thought, but eight years ago there had been a murder, and now this, the revelation and confession of Theady O'Donnell. His heart had broken when Theady told him of the things Mr O'Dowd had done, and the things Mr O'Dowd had made Theady do to him. A man he had trusted, believed, called his friend, and all along he'd been practising his own form of evil, right under Father Jerry's nose, using him. The Devil had been laughing at him, had taken him for the fool he truly had been. Tomorrow he had work to do, and he would need the help of every villager, but throughout this night he had his penance to pay.

Chapter 22

Michael woke in the early hours, sat bolt upright and thought he had died and gone to heaven at the sight of Sarah and Finnbar in the bed. It had been the dream that had woken him, as it often did. Someone was shouting at him, warning him, trying to wake him. 'Michael! Michael!' the voice implored. He was sure it was his Grandma Annie. His heart pounded with the adrenaline of fear. The curse cast on Sarah by Shona played heavy on his mind, but as he looked over at her and his son, his heartbeat slowed and he chastised himself for being ridiculous. The candle in the lantern on the press was only halfway down. Together with the last of the embers in the hearth, it threw a warm glow across the room and chased away his demons.

It had been near midnight before he and Sarah had fallen into a deep and contented sleep, both aware that it was one of the most special nights of their lives. They were high on the miracle of new life and neither could stop staring in wonder at their son, who lay in the bed between them.

'He has your nose,' said Sarah.

'God help him,' Michael exclaimed. 'But thanks be, he has

your eyes. Does he not look just like Mary Kate did the minute she was born? 'Tis impossible to tell them apart.'

Nola had brought into the room the carved crib that every Malone baby had lain in since Seamus was born. A mattress of fresh straw lined the bottom and sides, and tucked around it was brand-new linen, testament to the growing prosperity of the Malone family. But Sarah had refused to part with her son. 'I've only just laid me eyes on him and I've waited so long, I'm keeping him with me.'

'I expected you to say that, Sarah. I did,' said Nola. 'I said to Seamus, "I wouldn't be worried about carrying it down from the farm today, she will do it her way, will Sarah."' She smiled, satisfied that she'd done all she could for her daughter-in-law, and took herself and Mary Kate off to bed.

It was a sin for Michael to sleep in the bed with Sarah until she'd been churched. For the next week he would sleep on a truckle bed next to the fire in the kitchen. But Sarah pleaded with him not to leave them. 'Don't go to the kitchen,' she said. 'Stay here with us for tonight.'

Eventually they decided to bank the fire downstairs, and Michael lay down on top of the bedcovers, fully dressed, his cap in one hand, Sarah's hand in the other. Together they listened to their son's contented breathing, to the river outside and to the gentle crackling of the fire that filled the bedroom with a warm orange glow.

'I wish this night could last for ever,' Sarah whispered before sleep claimed her.

'Sure, it will in our hearts. Don't be worrying, we won't be forgetting tonight in a hurry.' Michael squeezed her hand.

'We are lucky, Michael. Look at us. They were all wrong, they were. We are lucky.'

His fingers wound through hers as the exhaustion of her efforts carried her to sleep.

Now, in the wee small hours, his anxious fear and racing heart finally settled, Michael lay propped up on one elbow, wondering should he stay or go down to the kitchen bed for fear of disturbing mother and baby. Sarah opened her eyes and smiled up at him.

'I only woke to take a look at you both,' he lied, as Sarah gazed down at her son, who was rousing himself, his rosebud lips puckering and twitching ready for a feed. Michael's nightmares had always been his own and he had wanted to never worry Sarah and tell her about them. But every time he woke, he knew he had failed to do whatever it was Grandma Annie was urging him, seemingly ever more desperate for him to understand.

Their son calmed at Sarah's touch, and for what must have been the hundredth time, she feasted her eyes on him and then ran her finger along his cheek before she flopped back, exhausted. She was grateful for Nola and her last act of the night, which had been to ease beneath her head the new, plump, feather pillows and to put her into a clean nightshirt. She smiled up at Michael as he lay on top of the bed, his cap still in his hand, staring at the love of his life and his baby son. 'Would you look at you,' she said. 'You can't take the smile off your face.' And then she winced with pain. 'Michael, would you fetch me some tea?'

He sprang to his feet. 'I will. Right away. Don't be moving now.'

'And I need the pot on the chair so that I can go before the tea, I think.'

'Right, I have it. Here, let me help you.'

Five minutes later he left the room with the pot in his hand to empty downstairs. Nola had seen to all of Sarah's needs until now, and she would usher Michael out of the bedroom once morning came, but there was no shame or secrets between him and his wife. 'Should there be this much blood in it?' he asked, alarmed, as he looked at the pot and helped her back into bed. He saw her flinch. 'Is everything all right?'

She flopped onto the pillow and, as if objecting, their son let out an almighty wail. Sarah laughed. 'He's wanting feeding now. Everything is fine, Michael. I've just given birth to your son and he's the size of the marrow you put in for the show. Bridget said he was sucking so strong, I would have a pit of pain in the womb and some bleeding too. 'Tis all fine. Would you just be getting me the tea?'

Reassured, Michael left the room. He'd barely put his foot in the corridor before he turned and came straight back in through the door. Sarah was stroking the soft, dark hair on the baby's head as he lay in her arms, already firmly attached to her breast. She looked up in surprise.

'Sarah...' Michael had his cap in one hand – the bedroom was the only room in the house in which he never wore it – and the pot in the other.

'What, Michael?' she said, concerned at the look on his face, which was one she wasn't used to. She knew her husband better than he knew himself and he was as close to tears as he had been on the night Mary Kate was born.

'I want to be thanking ye,' he said as he looked down at the floor, embarrassed.

Sarah didn't speak; the moment was too precious. She was enveloped by the warm smell of new life. Her room was full of things heralding the new arrival, not least the crib and the linen crib sheets Michael had brought back from Galway. She had boldly embroidered them with a row of blue teddy bears across the top, just like ones she'd seen in a magazine sent from New York by Seamus and Nola's daughter-in-law. She'd even embroidered her own crisp Irish linen pillows with patterns of lady's-tresses. Looking at them made her heart glow. They didn't live in a sod house like so many they knew. They weren't dependent on the weather and a good crop. They had more than a little, just enough, and what they did have gave them security. Her life was so full of happiness. She felt comforted by the thought that her mother-in-law, whom she loved as much as she would any sister, was with Mary Kate, sleeping with her and looking after her as if she was her own daughter. She loved this family, the Malones. She never knew a father could be like Michael, not after the beatings she'd taken from her own father. Daily, she gave thanks on her knees at the altar of the holy sacrament in the village church for the love of family she had been taught through Michael and her own aunt Bee. Daily, she thought that she must be the most blessed woman in the world, despite the awful past. It was all well and truly behind her now.

'Ye don't have to be thanking me,' she said. ''Tis your work too. Is something wrong, Michael?'

As he raised his head, she saw his troubled thoughts racing through his mind. For the briefest moment, she felt a cold breeze cross her hot cheeks and her heart beat a little faster. The window was open, the stars twinkling outside in the deep navy of the pre-dawn sky. It had been left open on Bridget's instructions, to keep her cool.

'No, not now,' he said. 'Not with this little fella safely here and you asking me for the tea, just like you always do. What could be better, eh? Nothing more normal than you chasing me for the tea.' A grin crossed his face. 'Shall I poke up the fire and make ye a bit of toast?'

'Oh, I'd love that, would ye manage with the tea and all?'

'Jesus, woman, I can manage a bit of tea and toast. Is there anything else I can be doing, anything at all?'

Sarah looked longingly towards the window. 'Could you turn the bed back around now? I want to face the window. I don't like the room like this, I like the fire to be on the side.'

'Aye – your side!' Michael placed the pot on the floor, still concerned at the amount of blood in it, regardless of what Sarah had said, and stepped towards the bed. 'Bridget knows what she's doing though. I wasn't going to argue with her. No man with an ounce of sense argues with Bridget.'

'That says much for Porick, who never stops. I definitely need the fire on my side to keep the baby warm now, so stop your complaining, Michael Malone,' she protested. It was a standing joke between them that Sarah had the bed so close to the fire on her side that Michael was scared the mattress would go up in flames.

'Do you still feel hot yourself?' he asked her, his voice loaded with concern.

'Aye, I do. But Nola said that's nothing to worry about. I remember it from Mary Kate. 'Tis normal.'

Michael nodded. 'Bridget told me that might happen when I saw her to the door. She said we should see in the morning how you were. And Mammy told me she remembered how that felt. Happened after every one of us lot, she said.' He'd been relieved to hear it. The nearest doctor was in Castlebar, which was why everyone used Bridget as a midwife. There was no obligation to pay Bridget, but the doctor charged a handsome sum and spent most of his weekends residing in the tennis club in Galway and no one was convinced he was of any use in the labour room.

Michael stood at the iron bedstead and in two swift moves almost spun the foot of the bed round to face the window.

'That's better,' Sarah said. 'I can feel the breeze now and the babby has the heat.' She pulled the bedcover up and almost covered Finnbar as he lay across her lap, feeding.

Michael picked up half a dozen blocks of peat and threw them on the fire. As the loose dust hit the flames, it glimmered around Sarah like a cloud of bright glow-worms. The room took on a marmalade hue, illuminating his wife, reflecting from her long golden-red hair splayed out against the white embroidered lined pillow case and his longed-for, prayed-for son. He felt as though his own heart was on fire. 'I'll be back in five minutes, with tea and toast.' He bent and kissed Sarah on the cheek and then their son on the top of his head.

Sarah laid her free hand on top of his. 'When you've milked in the morning, be away straight to Mass and give thanks,' she said with an urgency in her voice.

He knew exactly what she meant and had no need to question her. He bounced down the corridor, almost forgetting that in the other room Nola and Mary Kate were sleeping.

Nola knew her daughter-in-law so well, she could anticipate her every need. Sarah's tea drinking was legendary, so Nola had left the tray ready on the kitchen table for the morning. As Michael leant against the press while he waited for the water on the fire to boil and the griddle to heat for the toast, he thought about what he would have to pray for when he got to Mass. The curse of Shona had bothered him throughout the pregnancy, but there had been no need to worry. He knew in his heart that Sarah had worried about it too, ever since she found out she was pregnant. But here she was, safely delivered of their baby son. All he had to do when he got to Mass was thank the holy Lord for bringing them through a time that was treacherous for so many women.

'Oh, holy Jesus, MY SON!' he shouted into the cap that was still clenched in his hand. 'Fecking hell, I HAVE A SON!' Tears ran down his cheeks and he felt as though his heart would burst through his chest wall, it raced so fast. He dashed the cap at his face to wipe the tears away, afraid that Nola would come into the kitchen and find him.

He had been scared for years that there would be no child after Mary Kate. More than anything, he wanted someone to be there for her, a brother to look after her, should she ever have the need of him. He'd been afraid that the curse had been that Sarah would be barren, and she had been. 'Seven years,' he whispered. That was what he had wanted to say to his wife as he'd turned back into the room, but the sight of her with his son in her arms had taken the thought right out of his head. But that must have been it. The curse Nola had insisted was there and was never off her knees praying against, it must have been for seven years. But now it was over. Done. And Sarah had borne him a beautiful son.

They had never spoken of it together. Never said out loud what others in the village had talked about. Afraid that if they voiced its name, it would manifest itself, bringing something damaging and unwanted. Sarah had never blamed him for riling Jay Maughan. She hadn't needed to ask him to go to Mass at all. He would be there.

★

At the sound of the church clock striking the hour and as the kettle boiled in the Malone kitchen, Father Jerry left the presbytery and cut across the shadowy graveyard to the church. He let himself in through the always open door and, seeing the candle lit in the Malones' kitchen, blessed himself. Mrs Doyle had told Teresa that it had been a safe delivery, and for that, given that Bridget McAndrew had been in attendance, he would give thanks.

The water boiled and Michael poured it into the teapot. Carrying the milk jug, he ran into the dairy and filled it from the pail. The cow spoke to him with the gentlest of snorts. She had been in since he'd miked her last night to the muted sound of Sarah's cries. He put his hand over the wall that separated them. ''Tis a boy,' he whispered. The cow snorted back and, grinning, Michael said, 'I'll be back when the sun is up, as it surely will be soon – there's not a cloud in the sky. And I'll tell ye all about it. I might even bring him in so ye can take a look yerself.'

Back in the kitchen, he sniffed the milk, poured it into the teapot with the tea, heaped in some sugar and gave everything a stir. He flicked the hot toasted bread off the griddle and covered it in butter, then carried the tray, more quietly this time, up to Sarah.

Halfway down the corridor, he heard the first cries of his son. It was a sound he had never heard before and for the briefest moment he stopped and listened as the child tested the capacity of his lungs. The tears sprang to Michael's eyes as he thought how much Finnbar sounded like Mary Kate had when she was a newborn. She too had arrived all-knowing and noisy, appraising her surroundings first before she fully opened her lungs, after which she barely stopped.

The cries from Finnbar made Michael hasten his steps. 'Her milk won't be in for days,' Bridget had told him, 'and he's a big fella. He'll be giving out for the lack of a good feed before the morning is out. The harder he tries, the quicker the milk will come in. A pound of rashers won't satisfy this fella for a while to come.'

'Jesus, have we days of listening to this?' he said out loud now, half smiling. As he entered the bedroom, he felt slightly disorientated. He'd almost forgotten he'd turned the bed back round to face the window. But it wasn't that – something was different, not quite right. Sarah hadn't answered him back.

'Jesus, Holy Mary!' he said as he banged the teapot and cup and saucer on the night stand and ran round to Sarah's side of the bed. He could not see his child, he could only hear him, coming from where Sarah lay.

As he staggered past the fire to her side of the bed, there was no mistaking what his eyes refused to let him see. Tears welled up and began running down his face. His son was screaming now, almost buried under the covers. He had fallen from Sarah's breast and was lying across the top of her thighs in a puddle of blood. Sarah's arm had flopped down by her side, her palms facing upwards. Her face was white and tinged with grey, and beads of perspiration stood proud on her face as she struggled to open her eyes.

Michael fell to his knees at the side of her bed and roared with such pain that he woke both Nola and Mary Kate. The two of them jerked upright in bed, and in that instant Mary Kate understood what it was that Bridget had meant. A sound resembling that of an animal in agony, the outpouring of her father's pain, marked the moment her life would never be the same again.

Across the road, Paddy and Josie had also been asleep. 'Paddy, did ye hear that?' said Josie as she dug her elbow into her husband's back.

'What the feck…?' mumbled Paddy, who was in the middle of a dream, buying the biggest bullock any man had ever seen at the Mayo county show, confident he had more than enough money in his pocket to do so.

'There it is again!' Josie sat up in her bed, shivering, chilled to her bones by the anguish carried on the air. She crossed herself. 'Jesus, Paddy, as God is my witness, this will be the worst day. There's something wrong over at the Malones'.'

Father Jerry had smoothed the linen cloth on the altar and lain down on the floor in supplication to the cross. He had much to pray against in this wild and rural corner of the west of Ireland. The winds of change had blown through their village, carrying evil with them. He was one man and he had been told in the night, at the height of his pain and penitence, that he had a battle to fight. He had begged God to forgive him his sin of complacency, for not having seen or recognised the evil that walked in their midst. The Holy Ghost had told him they were under attack and that he would need the villagers to work with him. He must commence an all-day and -night prayer vigil, as much progress had been made, under his very nose.

His first job today, once Mass was over, would be to eject

Mr O'Dowd from the school. He would walk over after Mass, challenge him with what Theady O'Donnell had said, and ask him to deny it was true. If he did deny it, Rosie had given him other names to use in his mission to expel him from the village as effectively as St Patrick had the snakes from Ireland.

Rosie would run both classrooms. 'We will ask some of the parents to help,' she'd said as she, Father Jerry and Theady had discussed the awful facts. 'Your mother will be happy to assist, Theady, I'm sure.' She had been resolute and then distraught, blaming herself for not having heeded the words of others.

'Let us pray together,' Father Jerry had said before the three parted. They had knelt and prayed for strength and courage and mostly for forgiveness.

Now, Father Jerry's arms were stretched out by his side, his robes splayed, his nose pressed against the wooden floor as he chanted his prayers of offering to the Son of God. The waning moon threw the last of its beams through the stained-glass window above as suddenly the church doors flew open with supreme force against the plaster walls. There was no wind; the night had brought a mild breeze at best. His chanting came to a halt, and the candles flickered and went out in the sudden chill that blew through the church. His head shot up and his mouth opened as if to shout. He knew what was happening and he was frozen to the spot.

An evil spirit was in God's house and had run across his back. It was exuberant and victorious. He scrambled to his knees and lunged for the cross from the altar to ward it off, but he knew already that he was too late.

Chapter 23

Josie had rolled Paddy out of bed and sent him across the road in his nightshirt to find out what was happening. By the time he'd returned, she was dressed in her mourning weeds and ready to do the work she already knew she would have to. Her heart felt so heavy, she could barely move. 'Oh God, Paddy,' she cried as he came in through the back door, white-faced and shaking his head.

'You'd better go over,' he said. 'They need you. It's Sarah. She had the babby and 'tis desperate, so it is.' Paddy blessed himself as he spoke.

At the Malones' she hurried around the house, carrying out the first important rituals. Bridget McAndrew brought life into the village; as the butcher's wife, Josie saw it back out again. 'Open the windows, quickly,' she said, 'and get the curtains closed.'

The lemon and pink curtains were fastened together, not a glimmer of daylight allowed into the room. A black cloth was draped over the pole as it was deemed by Nola that the pattern of the fabric was too frivolous for a room in which a woman lay waiting for the cool peaceful darkness of the grave. Candles were lit at the foot and head of the bed to ward off bad spirits, should they try and get near. The kitchen table had been cleared, ready for the coffin that was already being made.

Josie raced off to fetch Father Jerry and was not entirely surprised to find the church doors flung open, light spilling out into the graveyard and all the candles lit. Father Jerry was standing in front of the altar and appeared to be waiting for her. His black cloak was already fastened across his surplice.

'Who is it?' he shouted to her, his voice booming and echoing off the ancient church walls. His face was grey, his manner agitated.

'Father, 'tis Sarah Malone.'

'Has she gone yet?' he barked, already moving swiftly through the door.

'No, not yet, but nearly, Father.'

He pulled his cloak more tightly across his chest, almost in an act of protection. 'We have to save her.' He flew out of the church and down the Tarabeg road to the Malones', with Josie trying to keep up, gasping, ''Tis too late to save her, Father, she's lost too much blood. I've seen it before...'

Father Jerry had no time to explain. It was not Sarah's life he was hoping to save – that had been claimed already. It was her soul; that was his job and nothing else mattered. He had to win. He had no words of comfort to offer, not yet, not until his work for God was done.

Rosie was making her way to the schoolhouse when she stopped at the sight of Father Jerry running and Josie in his wake.

''Tis Sarah, she's going,' explained Josie.

'Going? Going where?' Rosie could not take in the meaning

of Josie's words; she felt almost disorientated. The village of smiles felt suddenly empty and cold.

'She's nearly dead, Rosie. 'Tis why I've been for Father Jerry.'

'Dead?' was all that Rosie could manage in response. She wanted to follow Josie but had to go to the school and her feet felt weighted to the ground. 'We are a frontier in the battle,' had been Father Jerry's words last night. 'It is nothing new, he – we will not speak his name – will never give up. We have been fighting the same battles, and losing many, since the death of Christ. You have an important job to do, Rosie. The children depend on you.'

Rosie was torn. With Father Jerry's words ringing in her ears, she turned and reluctantly headed to the schoolhouse.

Ten minutes later, Father Jerry came downstairs to join Josie in the Malone kitchen.

'Has she taken the sacrament?' were Josie's first words to him.

'Aye, she did and the good Lord will receive her, of that there is no doubt. She is safe. She was still alive when I arrived, her heart was beating and she took a breath after the sacrament, but, she has gone now. She was without sin, she is saved, thanks be to God.' He laid his hand on Josie's shoulder. 'May God bless you in the work you have to do. I'll be back later. I have to go across to the schoolhouse after I've taken Mass, but I will be back later today.'

With that he turned on his heel and was off up the path and back through the doors of the church, never once stopping to flinch from the searing pain down his back and legs. The pain was his constant reminder of why he was there and what he had to do. He had failed, but it would never happen again.

★

Teresa was in the presbytery kitchen when she looked through the window and saw Father Jerry leaving the Malones' and heading back up to the church. Laying her apron on the table, she moved along the wood-panelled corridor and opened the door to his room. The metallic smell of blood hit her nostrils, but the room was spotless. Her eyes lowered to the area in front of the chest and the dark, damp stain on the floor.

Closing the door, she made her way back to the kitchen. All was not well. The only other time this had happened was the morning after he'd buried Angela McGuffey. She would have his breakfast ready for him and help prepare him to face whatever it was. As yet she was unaware that it would be the most tragic day anyone could remember in Tarabeg since the time of the famine.

''Tis a bad business,' said Ellen as she and Brendan O'Kelly near collided at the Malones' door. Her eyes were red, she was in shock.

'Mass will be full today,' she said to Josie inside.

'Aye, everyone will know in a few minutes, and then after Mass they'll be heading straight here.'

The two women stood and looked at each other over clenched hands. Their eyes tried to make sense of what they were in the midst of.

'Let's just do what we have to,' said Ellen. 'There is nothing else we can do.'

The curtains throughout the house remained closed. Herbs had been hung on the wall in bunches, and the windows were closed after exactly two hours. They'd been opened to let

Sarah's soul escape to heaven, and then they were shut in case she tried to slip back in again.

Father Jerry returned just as soon as he had fulfilled his duties and Josie had finished the rituals steeped in superstition and the laying out. He prayed and led the mourners, and the house felt to Mary Kate as if, even though it was full of people, it was in fact empty. She slipped between bodies and legs and under callused hands that stroked her hair. She was kissed by toothless women with leathery skin draped in black shawls smelling of other kitchens. Money was pushed into her hand by men wearing frayed hats, cumbersome boots with no laces and raggedy trousers.

Throughout that day and the following night, Josie sat at Sarah's head, at first keening and then chanting the prayers of the rosary. Sarah was never left alone. The kitchen filled with women. They stood in twos and threes around the foot of the table, huddled against the kitchen wall, talking in mournful whispers while the candles threw their long and looming shadows up the walls and across the ceiling, over where Sarah lay.

Mary Kate blinked up at the undulating shadows and mistook them for angels. The hand of Ellen Carey slipped across her shoulders. 'I'm taking the babby over to my house, would you like to come with us?' she asked kindly.

Mary Kate shook her head. She could not speak for the lump in her throat and she could not cry for the painful weight in her diaphragm. Her Grandma Nola was lost to her, neither seeing nor hearing her. The only people who noticed she was there were Rosie and Keeva, who had not stopped crying since the moment they'd arrived. They had to look after the mourners, but they always made sure that one of them was holding her hand, and they didn't leave go.

With Sarah's death came the rain. 'Angel tears.' Mary Kate heard the words floating away from one of the huddled conversations. 'Angel tears,' Mary Kate whispered back, but no one heard her and no one asked where were Mary Kate's tears. The men crowded into the yard and stood outside in the street, the weight of their boots trampling the cinder path to dust as the mud began to seep through.

Teresa oversaw the scullery and the kitchen, with occasional help from old Mrs Doyle. A wake involved huge amounts of tea and stout and sandwiches. Some people had travelled miles to pay their respects, spending a whole day to get there on a bike or a donkey, and they were fed on arrival. A death was news and everyone in the west was desperate for news. 'Sorry for your troubles,' was the chant from everyone as they approached Michael, who seemed not to recognise the visitors or hear their words. Paddy and Seamus plied him with whiskey and the rest drank stout, the men bringing their own pewter mugs with them for fear of missing a pull from the barrel should there not be enough.

Mary Kate peeped out of the shop window, which had been draped with a cloth, and watched as Paddy rolled another barrel across the muddy road. She had spent most of her time in the empty shop, where no one gathered. 'Daddy...' She tried to talk to him, but as he lifted his head she could see he was far away, somewhere else, caught between drink and despair.

P. J. Barrett, the man sitting next to him and almost holding him upright, slipped a penny into her hand. 'Go and find Nola, colleen,' he said. 'Leave yer daddy to us.'

And Mary Kate, dejected, turned away. Clutching the penny, she took it into the shop and placed it in the till. Although she couldn't cry, she could feel the pain of her heart breaking.

The trill of the bell of a bike as it rested against the wall didn't arouse interest as it would have once done; instead it brought a feeling of dread because it meant yet another stranger would walk with head bowed and hat clenched to her mother's side and into the candlelit room, able to do the one thing Mary Kate was not allowed to do, touch her mother. She hated them all. People she knew her mother had no time for peered over her coffin, and yet the daughter she loved was kept at the door. She knew if Sarah could feel her pain, she would be crying out for her.

Nola barely left the wooden chair next to Sarah's head on the opposite side to Josie. 'Look after your daddy,' she had said as Mary Kate hovered at the door, wringing the bottom of her blouse round and round between her fingers and thumbs.

'God, only twenty-nine,' she heard one woman say. 'And the boy never knowing who his mammy was.' And then, in the lowest voice, 'They say 'twas the Maughans' curse. Seven years...'

'No, stop. 'Twas not. Was it? Seven years?' And on and on it went.

There was a point when Mary Kate slipped onto the settle, next to Nola and rather than telling her to go back, Nola put her arm around her shoulders and hugged her to her. 'You're too young,' she whispered into her hair. 'Too young for this.' And the tears fell down Nola's cheeks and soaked into Mary Kate's hair and wet her forehead as they seemed to have been doing for days.

Mary Kate tried to force the tears to her eyes. She thought that if she did, if she could cry too, the pain she was carrying around under her ribcage might ease. It was becoming so heavy, so hard to carry. It kept weighing her down, dragging her to the chair, and when there was no chair free, to the floor. It had pulled her down next to Nola and she wasn't sure she could stand back up again.

She placed her arms around her grandma's rotund and comforting belly and buried her head into her side. Her nostrils filled with the scent of mothballs and earth and there they both sat, Mary Kate afraid to talk in case Grandma Nola asked her to leave. But it seemed that Nola was worn down into the chair too, as the hours passed and night fell.

The candles at the head of the coffin gasped and coughed to the end as the wicks drowned in the molten wax. She watched the extinguished tendrils of cloudy grey smoke as they wound their way up to the thatch. They were like the bedraggled wisps of Shona's wild hair floating in the air and they scared Mary Kate.

''Tisn't Bridget's fault.' A woman she didn't know stood before them and spoke to Nola as Josie changed the candles.

'Has Bridget been? I haven't seen her,' Nola replied.

'No, not yet. She wasn't sure of her welcome. I came to ask.'

Nola wiped at her eyes before she spoke. She unfastened Mary Kate's hands from around her side, dropped a kiss onto the crown of her head and sat her upright. 'Tell Bridget her job was to deliver the babby and that she did. Sarah was sat up in the bed when I left her, long after Bridget had gone home. The happiest woman in all of Tarabeg, Sarah was, and Bridget knew that. She was feeding the boy and loving it. She was smiling, telling me to be away to me bed. Tell Bridget that if she doesn't come, there will be talk. It's for her own sake and she is as welcome here as always.'

Nola had said the same thing over and over to every visitor who came into the house.

'Tut, tut, tut,' came the response, followed by prayers to Our Lady and all the saints in heaven. Mary Kate became used to the sudden gasping intake of breath, the silence when the listener made the sign of the cross and the 'God love us, no,' that invariably followed.

Josie sat under the closed window, guarding it with her life and looking through, dreading the sight of Sarah's soul tapping on the pane, demanding to be let back in.

'Why are you doing that?' asked Mary Kate. 'Why can't the window be open?'

Josie looked at her sideways, as if reluctant to take her gaze off the window, suspicious that Mary Kate had been sent to distract her. There was something in the air in Tarabeg and those that needed to be were on their guard. She slipped her arm around her. 'Because surely the soul of any mother would try to reach her little girl, 'twould be something Sarah would try to do, to want to come back to you, Mary Kate. Jesus, child, what mother would want to leave you and your daddy and that fine babby.'

And that was one of the moments when Mary Kate felt that she might fall down. When the room spun and shadows fell.

She stopped herself by concentrating on the chanting of the rosaries by Josie. 'Forgive our sins, oh Lord. Grant her eternal rest that she may lie in peace. Save her from the fires of hell.' And on Josie went, chanting, praying, hour after hour, occasionally relieved by one of the other women. Nola had let her stay on the chair, as if she sensed that standing was the hardest thing for Mary Kate to do. And there she passed her hours, eating when told, drinking when a cup was put in her hand, by whom, she had no idea. Her mother, just out of her reach, the darkness always there, and the women chanting, chanting.

At one point Nola laid Finnbar on her knee and then forgot she had left him there until he alerted her with his now familiar wail of hunger. 'Oh, God, Mary Kate,' she said, 'we have to take him to Julia. Her own is only four months and she has enough milk for two. Have you seen your daddy?'

Mary Kate hadn't. Not really. Not the daddy she knew. Not since the moment she'd heard him crying, 'She's dead! She's dead!' as he staggered around in the street, barely able to breathe or speak until Paddy got enough whiskey down him to stupefy his grief.

'Granddaddy Seamus will be back again soon,' said Nola as she hugged Mary Kate into her. 'He's organising everything up at the farm. Father Jerry is coming back and he's mad about Bridget, so he is. He's away up to the house to see her.'

'Where is Bee?' Keeva asked from the sink.

'She's on her way. She and Captain Bob and Ciaran were in Galway,' said Nola.

'Galway? What for?'

'I'm sure we will find out soon enough.'

Mary Kate stood at the back door as she watched Ellen handing Finnbar over to Julia, who lived on one of the neighbouring farms. 'I'm happy to come down each day,' she said. 'Once I get the flow going, it spouts by itself and I can fill a jug to feed him.'

Mary Kate looked at her breasts, which hung all the way down to her belly. This was a common enough practice among the women who helped each other out.

'I did the very same thing when Keeva was bleeding with the split nipples. Gave Bridget time to heal her properly.'

Ellen nodded. 'That would be best, but if you could keep him for a few days, until after the committal? Here, take some food.' And Nola filled a basket from the shelves in the shop for her to take back home with her.

As Finnbar left, strapped into the shawl across Julia's back, Mary Kate came her closest to tears. She wanted to run after the little brother she had held and already loved, but then she heard her mammy shout her name. 'Mary Kate.' Her mammy had come back!

Her heart flipped. 'Mammy,' she whispered, turning on her heel to look behind her and follow the sound of her mother's voice. 'Mammy's here,' she said, looking up to Ellen, whose hand she was still holding.

'Mary Kate!' The shout came again, and Mary Kate pulled Ellen out of the door.

'Mammy! Mammy! Mammy!' she shouted, then stopped dead in her tracks. It was not her mammy, it was Bee.

'Mary Kate!' Bee sobbed, running towards her, her arms open, tears streaming down her face.

That was the moment Mary Kate broke. When she knew she was connected to her mother's kin. As she fell into Bee's arms, the invisible thread that bound Angela, Sarah, Bee and now Mary Kate wrapped around them and for the first time, her tears fell.

It wasn't until they were on their way to the graveside that she felt the pain of finality. Then the farewell to her mother hit her with the force of the thresher. Her head clouded as she watched them lift the coffin out of the room, the brass handles aflame in the candlelight, the dark oak burnished red by the sunlight that streamed in through a part in the curtains. Her father, her Granddaddy Seamus, Pete, Paddy, Tig, Captain Bob and

Brendan moved haltingly backwards, negotiating the coffin around the door jamb. Her father staggered slightly and was steadied by Granddaddy Seamus, who put his arm out and grabbed him. 'Steady, man, steady. Don't drop her,' he said.

They were followed by the other men of the village as the road outside the shop thronged with people dressed in their mourning clothes and black shawls. They stood, some alone and praying, many huddled in groups and talking in whispers as the moment approached for Sarah to leave her house for the very last time.

The procession began moving towards the graveyard that faced the mountain St Patrick had lived on, with the river close by. And that was when Mary Kate realised that her mother was leaving the house and would never, ever return. She would never again comb out her hair and laugh with her. There would be no more kisses dropped on her brow while Mary Kate pretended to be asleep, her mother holding the candle aloft as she made her way to her own bed, whispering, 'Sweet dreams, my beautiful girl.'

There was a tightness in her chest that she could feel moving upwards, about to erupt. She screamed for her mother, to wake her. Held out her arms to reach her, to tear the wooden coffin away from her flesh and bones, to feel and touch and smell her. She tried to leave Bee's side and run to her mother, but her feet were rooted to the ground. She heard a gasp from the crowd, felt the hands of Captain Bob lift her as her blessed release from the pain she had carried in her heart for days eased. Darkness came and the wave of misery that had threatened to drown her finally took her down.

Chapter 24

Six months later

'Try and finish the food Josie's cooked for you.' Captain Bob pushed Bee's plate back towards her, still half full of the breakfast Josie had insisted they eat with them before they left.

The bar had slowly filled with people who'd come to say their goodbyes; others had gathered in groups on the street outside. Paddy and Josie had hosted a send-off for every villager who'd left Tarabeg and headed to distant shores since the day they married. Daedio had been brought down from the farm with his chair on the cart and was sitting next to Bee. He'd been determined to go. 'Get me down that feckin' hill, Seamus, or I swear to God I'll make Nola's life a misery.'

'What's new there,' Nola had whispered under her breath, but, as always, Daedio got his way.

The day was cold, still and lifeless, quite unlike the turmoil raging in Bee's heart. The women who were standing in the street pulled their shawls closer about their heads and shoulders to keep out the chill and gazed in at her through the window, the expression in their eyes a mix of pity and wonder. They had done this before, so many times. 'Take a tray of glasses out to them, Keeva,' Paddy said. 'We don't want no one catching their death.' As soon as he'd said the words, he wanted to snatch them back.

Bee, Captain Bob and Ciaran were leaving, sailing the following morning to Liverpool, and they were being taken to Dublin by Michael, in his van.

'I can't, Josie,' said Bee as she pushed the plate away. 'I feel sick to my stomach.'

Josie threw her a sympathetic glance. It was always the same. No one left with a spring in their step. Despite all the big talk and preparations, the saving of fares and the booking of tickets, when the day came, the village was awash with tears. The sound of voices thick with dreams as yet unrealised and the sight of hearts breaking became memories that lived for ever in the hearts of the exiled.

'Can I have it?' Ciaran looked hopefully from one to the other.

Bee forced a smile and pushed her plate towards her son, the boy with seemingly hollow legs who appeared to be little affected by the fact that all he owned was in a wooden trunk on the back of Michael's van, ready to be unpacked in a city he had only heard of, in a house he could only imagine.

Regardless of how nervous Bee felt, watching her boy eat never failed to bring a smile to her face. 'He's looking forward to it as much as I'm dreading it,' she said to Nola and Seamus, who were sitting opposite her. She looked around the bar at the other guests. Her words were met with wide-eyed silence.

'Come on now,' said Ellen. ''Tis not as if you can't come back if you don't like it. You still have your house here.'

The image of her cottage by the shore flew into Bee's mind, but instead of the immaculate thatch and white-painted home she'd spent yesterday packing up, she saw four bare and roofless walls, a front door in splintered fragments on the ground and the interior inhabited by the elements. She shuddered as Ciaran ate noisily, wiped his plate with a generous slice of fried bread and, gulping the last of his tea, asked, 'Can I go over to the shop to Michael?'

'Aye, but don't go down to the river, Ciaran, Michael will be wanting to leave shortly. The bags are loaded, 'tis just ourselves we have to get into the van now.'

'Right, everyone, time for a whiskey to set these good people on their way.' Paddy's voice rang out in the bar.

'I'll give you a hand.' Nola rose and followed him to the back.

'Everyone's outside,' said Keeva as she came back in through the door. 'God in heaven, you chose a day, Bee, 'tis freezing out there.'

Captain Bob laid his hand on top of Bee's. 'Are you having second thoughts?'

Bee's eyes filled with tears. She extracted a handkerchief from the handbag Captain Bob had bought for her in Dublin when they'd gone there with Michael to buy the tickets. 'You can't even begin to imagine the thoughts that are racing through my head,' she said as she wiped at her eyes. 'You know, there was a day when if you'd asked me, "Where will you be ten years from now?" I would have laughed at you for asking the question because the answer was obvious, I'd have seen myself being exactly where I was. But that was before… before everything. Thank you,' she muttered as she blew her nose.

'Ah, don't be thanking me,' said Captain Bob. 'This is all

my own selfish intention. And besides, we can't stay here, Bee. There are too many memories and… only so much we can expect people to turn a blind eye to. There sometimes comes a point in life when you simply have to brush yourself down and start over again, and for us that day has come. A new place to live, a new house and a new life. The future looks good, Bee.'

Bridget gave Bee a heartfelt smile. She'd seen it many a time, going back over fifty years – those who were sick to their heart at the prospect of leaving. 'Don't you be worrying,' she said, her voice bright and false as she took a glass of whiskey from the tray Keeva offered her. 'If it was so great here, wouldn't they all be coming back as fast as they'd left?'

Bee stared at her, at first uncomprehending.

'All I'm saying is, no one comes back. Who do you know from Tarabeg who has ever come back? God, if anyone does visit, 'tis like the poor person has visited the whole village. Everyone wants to see them and talk to them. Remember when Philomena's sister came two years ago and Ellen could not for the life of her understand why she didn't know the Barretts who had moved to New York?' She sighed. 'Dublin is never busy with people getting off the boat, is it? It's all one-way.'

Bee reached up to take the glass of whiskey Paddy was holding out to her. 'I'll be back,' she said, but in her mind she was asking herself when.

Captain Bob had secured a job as a captain, meeting the cargo ships and piloting them down the Mersey into the port of Liverpool, from where they had waited, out on the bar. He had already travelled to Liverpool and found them a house close to the docks. 'It has a kitchen,' he'd said to Bee. 'The range is still there, but it was damaged in the war, and there's a new gas cooker fitted next to it.'

Bee's mouth had dropped. 'A gas cooker? I have no idea how to use one of those. I'll be sticking to the fire.'

Bob had just smiled at her indulgently. He understood why the traffic from Dublin was one-way. Bee would soon discover how quickly women who left the west coast of Ireland adapted from the life their ancestors had lived for hundreds of years to all the mod cons England and America had to offer.

'Mammy!' Ciaran shouted from the door.

Bob and Bee swivelled round in their chairs as Ciaran came in, followed by Michael, who was carrying Finnbar in his arms and had Mary Kate at his side, holding his hand.

'God love you, come here,' said Bee to Mary Kate, who ran over to her and allowed her to pull her up onto her knee. 'I've been waiting for you.'

Captain Bob and Michael exchanged looks and locked hands. Bee thought she saw a tear in Michael's eyes as Nola rose and took Finnbar from him.

Nola carried Finnbar to the chair and laid him on Daedio's knee. 'Here he is,' she whispered as the old man looked inside the shawl. 'The future.'

But her heart folded as he looked up at her and said, 'I want Sarah back.'

'Shush,' she said before anyone heard him.

Seamus nodded to her as though to say, 'Don't worry, I have him,' as he sat down in the chair next to Daedio and Finnbar.

Bee had heard Daedio and she reached out one of her hands, plump, warm and soft, and pressed it down on top of one of his own, cold, bony and arthritic with age. She turned away from the men and looked into Mary Kate's eyes, on a level with her own. 'Don't you cry now. I've told you, your daddy will be putting you on the boat when the school holidays come and I will be waiting on the other side for you and you can stay with us in Liverpool, won't that be grand?'

'It will,' whispered Mary Kate, who had lost all her vitality the day her mother had died. It seemed to Bee that she had almost lost her voice too.

'You know we gave up America so that you could visit us in Liverpool – you know that, don't you? That's the only reason we're going there, so that you know there's another home ye have, just a boat ride away.'

'We've come to wave you off,' said Mary Kate so softly, Bee had to bend her head to hear her reply. 'Can Rosie come too?'

Bee stiffened and wound her arms tighter around Mary Kate's back, without answering. She shot Michael a look and she knew what the question was that was flickering in his eyes: 'Rosie is stood outside, can I bring her in?' He hadn't dared at first. Rosie had continued with the arrangement of teaching during school hours and minding the shop beforehand and afterwards, and that was working well. But Bee had been far from happy.

'Now that Sarah has gone, I can see something will happen,' she'd said to Bob. ''Tis in her eyes and everything she says. And Sarah not yet cold in her grave, and Michael and the child in mourning.'

Captain Bob had taken Bee into his arms. 'Aren't we the ones who don't judge? Isn't it you and me who know that we should take everyone and everything for what they are? Rosie is working at the shop, that's all. There isn't anything between them, and whatever else, we surely don't want Michael to be struggling with two children all alone, do we?'

That was the problem with Captain Bob – Bee never had an answer to refute what he said. He was her opposite. When she was mad, he was calm; he brought her down from the highs of indignation and made her think through her resentment and anger. He had the patience, she had none of it. He saved her, over and over and that was the reason she was abandoning all and everyone she knew to make a life with him where no one would know their past, no one would judge them. Captain Bob, he had saved her and she owed him that.

'If Nola has no objection to Rosie, if she can see what is the best for Mary Kate and Finnbar, surely you can too, my little Bee?'

'Yes, but Sarah was not Nola's daughter. She was not her blood kin, only I am, me and Mary Kate and as God is my judge Mary Kate, she will not like it.' Even as the words left her mouth, she knew how unfair they were. Nola had aged ten years in the week of Sarah's death and that was when Bee knew she had to get away. She could not grieve in front of these people, Sarah's new family. They mourned for Michael and his pain and for Mary Kate and the loss of her mother, but Bee, she mourned for Sarah and the past.

''Tis time,' said Captain Bob, who could not keep the flicker of a smile from his face. A man looking forward to his new life. He had sailed from Ballycroy without a backwards glance and he knew he would never return. He had left his wife and family well provided for and his heart skipped at the thought of his life with Bee. Captain Bob had plans of his own. ''Twill make all the difference, you all being here to wave us off,' he said to the people in the room as he stood.

'We wouldn't miss it for the world,' said Brendan as he raised his glass. 'Ah, here's Father Jerry and Teresa. They won't let you leave without a prayer under your wings.'

Minutes later, they were all standing in the street, glasses lifted, prayers said. Bee hugged everyone she knew, with Mary Kate never letting go of her hand. 'Marry as soon as you can,' were the only words Father Jerry said as his farewell. He was not happy.

'You will be needed,' Teresa whispered to Rosie as she sniffed the contents of her glass. 'That little girl will feel this as a second loss.'

'I'll do my best.' Rosie was nervous, convinced she'd be the one person Bee would not say goodbye to.

Bee finished her exchanges, storing in her mind the messages she had to pass on to the myriad of people she might bump into once she reached Liverpool and stuffing into her bag the letters she'd been asked to deliver. Finally she turned to Rosie.

'Right, everyone. Come on, Bee, time to leave,' said Captain Bob. He and Ciaran jumped into the van next to Michael.

Michael turned the key in the engine and the crowd fell silent. The moment of parting was the hardest. The van horn beeped. 'Bee, come on!' shouted Michael.

Bee looked into Rosie's eyes. She was lost for words.

Rosie scrunched up the front of her skirt and, looking past Bee's shoulder, saw people staring at them both, waiting for Bee, wondering would she change her mind at the very last moment. Nola stood with Finnbar in her arms, swaying from side to side. Seamus had his arm around her shoulders, wondering the same. It had never happened, but everyone always hoped it would. That the pull of love and place would be greater than the pull of opportunity.

Brendan was standing next to Father Jerry and both men had lit their pipes. ''Tis a big change when they leave,' Brendan said. 'Paddy will miss her in the bar.'

'Michael will miss her more,' said Father Jerry as he pulled on his pipe.

'How are we doing, Father?' Brendan glanced sideways at him. 'Are we going to be all right?'

Father Jerry stared down at the ground. He had never spoken a word about Mr O'Dowd and his sudden departure. If anyone asked him, he replied, 'He upped and left and isn't ever coming back,' and that was the end of it. 'We are, Brendan. We are all going to be just fine, even Michael.'

Both men looked back at the van and raised their hands to Captain Bob, who was grinning from ear to ear and waving furiously. Keeva approached the van and Ciaran, who was pushed against the window next to Captain Bob, cheekily removed a glass of whiskey from the tray she was carrying and knocked it back in one. The crowd roared with laughter, aware that the only person not to have seen him was Bee.

'Look after the kids well, will you?' said Bee to Rosie. She fought back her resentment, her suspicion and her jealousy at the amount of time Rosie would be spending with Mary Kate and Finnbar. 'I know Nola will be down to stay with them at night, but she's getting older, and you, you will be spending plenty of time with them. Discipline her only with love, both of them, do you hear? They have lost their mammy.' Bee's voice broke and she swallowed hard.

Michael wound down the window of the van to shout, 'Bee, come on, we will miss the boat tomorrow if you don't hurry yerself.'

Bee gave Rosie a stiff hug and turned away. She had publicly endorsed Rosie, given her her blessing. What choice did she have? Halfway to the van, she stopped suddenly, remembering what it was she'd really wanted to say, and turned back to Rosie. 'Don't forget that Michael is a man in mourning. 'Tis not a wife he's after just now, 'tis help with the practical things, the children, it's the children who need you.'

Rosie, grateful for the public acknowledgement and the hug, nodded and smiled. 'I will love them as though they are my own, Bee. Don't worry about any of them. 'Tis not just a job to me. I care for both Mary Kate and Finnbar, and as you say, they have Nola and family.'

Bee scrutinised Rosie's face. There was something behind the words, but she could not detect what it was. She walked towards the van and Rosie moved to join the crowd and wave away the van until the cloud of dust turned the corner. The wintry sun was low on the horizon and it wasn't long before the sound of the van engine was drowned out by the noise of the river crashing over the rocks.

Rosie, her arm aching from waving, let it drop to her side as she whispered to the parting image of Bee smiling through the rear window, 'But you must remember, Bee, I loved him first.'

Glossary of Irish terms

boreen	narrow country lane
boxty	bread made with grated potato and flour
colleen	girl or young woman
curragh	small wickerwork boat or coracle
dudeen	short-stemmed clay tobacco pipe
Garda	the Irish police force
hooker	single-masted boat, larger than a curragh, used by ocean fishermen on the west coast
poteen	illegal home-brewed alcohol, made from potatoes
whin	gorse